HEALING TIME

TIME WARS LAST FOREVER SERIES: BOOK 6

CRAIG ROBERTSON

ALSO BY CRAIG ROBERTSON:

BOOKS IN THE RYANVERSE:

THE FOREVER SERIES (2016)

THE FOREVER LIFE, Book 1

THE FOREVER ENEMY, Book 2

THE FOREVER FIGHT, Book 3

THE FOREVER QUEST, Book 4

THE FOREVER ALLIANCE, Book 5

THE FOREVER PEACE, Book 6

GALAXY ON FIRE SERIES (2017)

EMBERS, Book 1

FLAMES, Book 2

FIRESTORM, Book 3

FIRES OF HELL, Book 4

DRAGON FIRE, Book 5

ASHES, Book 6

RISE OF ANCIENT GODS SERIES (2018):

RETURN OF THE ANCIENT GODS, Book 1

RAGE OF THE ANCIENT GODS, Book 2

TORMENT OF THE ANCIENT GODS, Book 3

WRATH OF THE ANCIENT GODS, Book 4

FURY OF THE ANCIENT GODS, Book 5

FALL OF THE ANCIENT GODS, Book 6

TIME WARS LAST FOREVER SERIES (2019)

RYAN TIME, Book 1

LOST TIME, Book 2

FRAGMENTED TIME, Book 3

SHATTERED TIME, Book 4

FINDING TIME, Book 5

HEALING TIME, Book 6

NON-RYANVERSE BOOKS:

ROAD TRIPS IN SPACE SERIES (2019):

THE GALAXY ACCORDING TO GIDEON, Book 1

THE EARTH ACCORDING TO GIDEON, Book 2

THE AFTERLIFE ACCORDING TO GIDEON, Book 3 (DUE Mid 2021)

OLDER, STANDALONE WORKS:

THE CORPORATE VIRUS (2016)

TIME DIVING (2013)

THE INNERgLOW EFFECT (2010)

WRITE NOW! THE PRISONER OF NaNoWRiMo (2009)

ANON TIME (2009)

HEALING TIME
TIME WARS LAST FOREVER SERIES: BOOK 6

by Craig Robertson

Would you risk it all to make the world whole again?

Imagine-It Publishing
El Dorado Hills, CA

ISBN: 978-1-7366732-1-8 (E-Book)
978-1-7366732-2-5 (Paperback)
979-8-7754390-6-4 (Hardcover

Cover design by Alexandre
http://www.designbookcover.pt/en/

Editors: Michael R. Blanche
Neil Farr
Amy Schubert

Formatting services by Drew Avera
drewavera@gmail.com

First Edition 2021

This book—this series—is dedicated to the heroes and heroines of the COVID-19 pandemic. To the healthcare workers who labor like Hercules to lessen our suffering. To the scientist who immediately dropped their life's research to help conquer this devil. To the health departments who, while understaffed and underfunded, battle to shepherd us to safety. And to everyone who fights the good fight every day. They may grumble, but they shoulder the wheel and push. When this is over, and it will be some day, the ones who did it right will be remembered.

PRELUDE

The Claxeon Citadel on Flastor was the birthplace of the Brother-Sisterhood of Time. For hundreds of centuries, even after the cult spread to many parts of the galaxy, the citadel was emblematic of the order. All true and lasting power in the organization remained jealously held at the Claxeon Citadel. All the major decisions, all the important policy implementations, and all governance remained in the order's starting point. To gaze upon the Claxeon Citadel from on high was to see the wonder of a civilization's ability to build a mighty structure. At its zenith, the contiguous citadel occupied a significant portion of Flastor's dry land. While none would have ever called it majestic, it was nevertheless quite imposing.

Near the geographic center of the massive sprawl was a solitary tower. It rose from the bare dirt to a height of over two hundred meters, yet it was only thirty meters in diameter. Most of the internal volume was occupied by a seemingly endless spiral staircase, affixed to the outer stone wall. Though precious few knew anything about the tower's design, anyone learning of it would be stunned. It housed but one room, way at the top of the gargantuan structure. There was no electricity, water, or plumbing installed. Clearly there was no elevator. The only way to access the tower's single room was to mount the daunting stairs. And one needed to be prepared. It wouldn't do to have to use the restroom or to require a drink up there. To call the tower spartan would be to paint a picture more luxurious than reality reflected.

The Brazen Tower. That was the monolith's formal name. Whether it was brazen was debatable. It was imposing, it appeared to be frivolously designed, and it offended any eye given to pleasant design. Forgotten over the long progression of time was that the tower was named not for its attributes, but for those few who utilized the structure. The Brazen Tower was the central gathering place for seven very elusive members of the Brother-Sisterhood of Time. Always seven. Never six. Never eight. When one died, they were instantly replaced by an acolyte-in-waiting.

For whatever bureaucratic reason, the Council of Seven met exclusively in the Brazen Tower. Each member had their own region-of-influence, where they could operate free of any constraints. But, when the seven chief inquisitors of the order met, they did so only in the Summit Room, as that lofty place was called. And every inquisitor who ever served on the council worshipped the harsh rules they served under. They all fervently endorsed the need to climb endless stairs and gather with no creature comforts. For anyone destined to be a chief inquisitor was not a casual individual. No, they were possessed with a dark obsession. They hated comfort and camaraderie and most of all they hated every other member of the Brother-Sisterhood of Time. You see, all the members, save the Council of Seven, were weak. They were given to pleasures of the flesh, such as unnecessarily flavorful food, occasional interludes of chatter, and time to rest after a hard day's labor. All weakness was abhorrent to those dour seven.

On a day inconclusively distinct from any other, the Council of Seven met to discuss a very pressing matter. Internal security had been breached. And to make the bad oh-so-much worse, now external security had been flaunted. The five senior inquisitors and the two brand new ones were faced with the council's greatest crisis in collective memory.

Naturally, a crisis of such Herculean proportions, occurring anywhere, in any epoch, had to center on Jon Ryan. Who else could so vex an institution, so hamstring an organization?

"Brother Devastator was killed by this rogue agent," Head Chief Inquisitor Barren began in a cold, lifeless tone. "This we know to be a fact."

Brother Pall raised one black-leather-gloved finger.

Barren made a slight nod.

"Brother council members, this is my first meeting as one-of-seven. I must, however, speak in question. I knew Brother Devastator. He was of unequalled skills, unimaginable cunning, and given to no mercy or quarter. He taught me most of what I know today. To accept that he was slain by this... this novice *book* stacker, this, this Strider fellow, is an insult to his memory. Surely the case is more complex than I have been allowed to know."

In the between-the-lines translation of Pall's words, he'd just accused Barren of being a craven liar. Barren, for his part, was thrilled to hear the heinous charge. He was pleased one of the two new recruits had the balls to speak his mind. This boded well for his success as an inquisitor.

"The video recordings, Devastator's body image generator files, and the full autopsy report will be forwarded to you, Brother Pall. The council appreciates your commitment to finding the one truth. But, please, for the time being, accept that my report is factual."

Pall nodded with obvious displeasure.

"The council then dispatched Brother Void to right the wrong perpetrated against this council. Today," he gestured to the other new member, "as witnessed by Sister Vanquish's presence, I must report that the infidel has additionally slain that good brother."

"Him and what army?" hissed Brother Death, the longest serving inquisitor. "Void was an insatiable killing machine with supreme abilities and unimaginable fortitude. I once personally saw him take three disruptor blasts to the chest and yet still crush the life out of the idiot who shot at him."

"As of now I have access only to Void's body image files. They seem unequivocal. Naturally, we hope to extract his remains and perform a full analysis. But the council seems to be faced with an impossible crisis. There is out there one who desecrates the order at will and who we have been unable to terminate."

"A book stacker?" decried Pall.

"Clearly he only posed as one when he violated our grounds," Brother Fracture defended. "I have studied what little video we have of him. He is not lucky. He is just that good. He will not be easy to kill."

"Time is on our side," remarked Barren.

"Indeed it is," seconded Fracture. "I move that the next attempt to wipe this scourge on the face of existence be a team of two brothers sent out jointly. Together they will surely cure the order of this disease."

The room was as silent as the grave. Fracture's words were incomprehensibly obscene. Chief inquisitors never worked together. Such a cooperation was as unheard of as it was insulting to hear spoken aloud.

"I will kill you for those words," thundered Sister Harshness. "I will never serve with another. It is not our way."

"Our way, it would seem, sister, is to die at the hands of this assassin," taunted Fracture.

She tapped her chest. "He would not kill me. I would be his end, his last sight before he falls down to hell."

"Confident words, to be certain," stated Barren. "But know that no one on the council is above the council. Only the Council of Seven may speak with finality."

She bowed her head in acknowledgement.

"So, brothers and sisters, it is a vote I call for. There are but two courses to choose from. Vindication One is that a single inquisitor is again sent to rid us of our burden. Vindication Two is that two or more are sent as a team to return honor to the council." He scanned the room. "Speak your vote."

In the end, the judgment was five-to-two. On this, the darkest of hours for the Council of Seven, a team of inquisitors would be sent to end the threat that was Jon Ryan.

The only member of the Council of Seven not to speak a word at the meeting was Brother Rage. He had lifted one finger to vote, but never said anything. In fact, he rarely said anything to anyone. That was well and fine with the other six. You see, Rage creeped them all out. Yeah, he was that unhinged, that prone to sadistic mayhem, and that likely to murder the other six in their sleep any night soon for no clear reason.

The irony, of course, was that they each felt firmly down deep that sending such a team was pure overkill. Still, they went with the flow of the current and agreed to it. In their defense, seriously, they *were* just getting to know Jon, right?

CHAPTER ONE

Crap, shit, bogus, damn, and *urfpedit.* That last one is Kaljaxian for *screw you,* but more visceral. That and all the rest of the swear words there are in the collective languages of the cosmos. I'd been alive a long, long time. Couple that with my line of work—Killer and Friends—and you know I've seen a lot of death. Actually, more death than even I can imagine. I've watched my natural children die, their kids, their kids' kids' kids, etcetera. I was forced to witness all my stepchildren with Sapale die off over time. With each loss another chip fell from my heart. There was no longer even the distant memory of a heart in my soul.

And in combat, I'd killed enough beings and watched my good buddies die so often that I felt untroubled by death. No, I was fully indifferent to it. I can tell you that having once been a plain old mortal human, the state-of-mind I was in after experiencing all that death was as unhealthy as it could get. I'm not exaggerating when I say I was nothing more than the empty shell of a worthless mess.

But Tank's dying. That got to me. Somehow that sneaked its way through my wall of jaded moral apathy. I don't know. When you meet a dude at a Pronto Pup stand, travel across space and time fighting a clear evil together, and you're both a couple of guys, I guess you don't expect it to end with one of you having his chest blown open by a stray round. Yeah, you should have seen him. More of his torso was missing than was left. Whatever gun the assassin used was one mean son-of-a-bitching weapon. I think that even after the bolt struck, it continued to burn at the wound's edges, consuming all that much more life from my friend, making recovery a sick joke, as opposed to a remote hope.

There I sat, on top of *Blessing*, out in the middle of absolutely nowhere deep space, staring at the stars and wondering why that nasty bolt missed me and had to take Tank. It wasn't fair, right, or tolerable. Yet there it was. He was dead as dead could be. I was stuck still acting my way through my sick parody of being alive.

Lord, I missed that man so much already. That wasn't like me. And the rest of the crew was way more devastated, if such a state was even possible. Sachiko, who'd known and loved him the longest, was inconsolable. She hurled blame at fate, luck, and bad timing. The curses she hurled at me were only done exclusively in the silence of her private thoughts. Reva? She was catatonic. Imagine that, a colonel in the Army, a combat veteran no less, unable to function due to her sudden and overwhelming grief. And to a man and woman, the entire crew and student body had looked up to him as their commander. He'd won them over and now they were rudderless. It was a sad, sad state.

I'd spent the last couple days up there on top of *Stingray*, avoiding the tears of others, and avoiding their accusatory eyes. If Jon hadn't pushed so hard, Tank'd still be here. And I could hear their thoughts. *Jon just had to go to that stupid citadel. If he hadn't, Tank'd still be alive.* Maybe it was my fault. We'd been on a mission, the most important mission imaginable. We wanted to resurrect a no-timed planet Earth. I'd made every attempt to successfully complete that mission. That kind of operation was defined by its need to take astronomical risks. And against all odds, the mission had borne fruit, of a sort. I now knew some words that expressed how I might actually bring Earth back. I didn't know how to put the words into action, but I was a million times better off than I had been when we started. We could now all have hope. That was unbelievable. So the infiltration of the citadel had been worth the effort.

But, I didn't need a new immense throbbing hemorrhoid in my life, right? I mean, I was charged with resurrecting Earth and bringing back to life all those never-were inhabitants. For all I knew that included the animals too, and the bugs. I had to make mosquitoes swarm again. What a horrible thought. And just add onto my plate a new enemy with limitless resources and time to use as their plaything.

And Tank was dead.

The reason I mentioned I'd been sitting on top of *Stingray* for two days was because I knew that today was the scheduled memorial for my dear friend. Who is the logical, the only acceptable choice for the person everyone expected to give the eulogy for their fallen commander? Yeah, the only one left with a similar rank. Yours truly. I hated giving eulogies, if you hadn't figured out that was the case on your own. In fact, I had been so successful, so creative in getting out of doing them, I recalled distinctly the last one I'd done. It was for Waldo Von Kemper. Waldo was my stepson JJ's very first pet. It was a revolting little bug very similar to Earth's cockroach. JJ caught it in a jar back on Azsuram when he was four or five. Waldo survived almost three days in captivity. Well, naturally the boy was crushed, so, also naturally my wife made me, in her words, *Say a few kind words about the stupid thing*. I did, JJ was still crushed, and I vowed to avoid eulogies like they were sexually transmitted diseases from then on.

But now Tank was dead and I was giving the eulogy. Waldo and Tank were coequals in that regard. Too bad I couldn't rib the man about the level of honor I was bestowing on him. I reluctantly stood and opened a portal, careful to generate a sally port behind it so all the air didn't rush out of the vortex. Sapale and I might not need to breathe, but having our stuff sucked out into space pissed her off something massive every time I forgot to arrange for that not to happen.

Sapale was there on the other side of the sally port wall when I was inside and dropped the membrane I'd erected. She took the one step that separated us and greeted me with a big old hug. Dang, I loved the woman. Knowing she loved me right back just as much almost made me smile. But no smiles today. Smiles were for happier times.

"How you doing?" she asked tenderly.

"Somewhere between lousy and shitty." I shifted the flat of my hand back and forth. "I move from that high to that low kind of randomly."

"I know. I miss him too." The intensity of her embrace increased noticeably.

I hugged her back with reassuring strength.

"So, it's about time," I announced with zero life in my voice.

"Yes it is, sweet one. I just spoke with Sachiko. Everybody's pretty much in the hangar area."

That was the largest open space aboard our main time ship, Aramthella. All but the skeleton crew needed to keep an eye on things were to attend. That included all of the one-time Georgetown student body. I can tell you this: It was a much bigger crowd than Waldo drew.

"Let's do this," I sighed. Dropping my probe fibers to the deck, I commanded, "*Stingray*, put us back on our pad in Aramthella's hold."

Slight nausea ensued.

"Shall I open a portal, Form One," the ship asked respectfully.

"Yes, please."

The nearby wall dialed open and we left quietly. By the time we made it to the hangar facility it was standing room only. Sachiko noticed the instant we entered and made a discrete hand wave to urge us forward. A small dais was pressed up against the far wall. There were four chairs on it. Just to the right was Tank's casket, draped with an American flag. I'll leave off most of the gory parts, but know that the lid was closed and Aramthella had time locked the remains so decomposition wasn't an issue.

Sachiko gestured us into the two middle chairs. Reva St. Claire, the captain's XO and Tank's passionate lover, sat in the chair farthest from Tank. I was pretty sure that positioning wasn't by chance.

Sachiko, standing with a slight lean on the back of her chair, raised her voice. "Alright, everybody, if you could settle in, we can begin."

Oh crap, I was wishing I was almost anywhere but here right about then.

"We are here to remember our friend, our commander, General Robert Sherman," Sachiko announced with a tormented quiver in her voice. "I would like to ask first that we all rise and salute or place a hand over your heart while taps is played."

One of the enlisted women, Brenda Clearwater, was an accomplished trumpeter. She had Aramthella fabricate a bugle for the occasion, and had learned to play it well in just a few days. She stood and gave a paralyzing rendition of that sad lament. When she was finished there were few dry eyes in the room.

Sachiko stood again. She was most definitely swaying and I prepared myself to catch her if she swooned. "Next, a group of young people have gotten together to perform Tank's favorite spiritual. It may come as a surprise to some of you that Tank had a favorite spiritual, especially those of you unfortunate enough to feel his boot against your backside if he was upset with you."

There were a few polite chuckles. Then the glee club did a good job of crushing us all with a stunning rendition of "Amazing Grace." It might have been the most arresting performance of that song I'd ever heard. I was at once transfixed and swept into the dark depths of melancholy.

It took the captain a few minutes before she was able, but finally she rose and thanked the singers. The room was filled with applause, albeit appropriately restrained. Then—you got it—she turned her eyes to me.

"General Ryan will now give the eulogy. After that, General Ryan's wife will recite the traditional funeral blessing her people from Kaljax have used for generations. Finally, the chaplain will lead us in prayer." Sachiko sat quickly.

I stood. Mind you, I'd prepared nothing for the occasion. That wouldn't be my style, and I was dreading this moment so much that any prep work would have been too much for me to handle.

Lord, I was going to miss that man.

"Good morning. Thank you all for coming today. It means a lot to those of us who knew and loved General Sherman. For those of you who never got a chance to meet him, all I can say is that's too bad. You'd have come to appreciate him the same as all of us already had."

I cleared my throat. "Robert Sherman was one of the best men I've ever known. He was a kind, loving, and very intelligent man. Tank, as he insisted everyone call him, was also a funny guy. That, my friends, is a very important quality to possess in this life. Humor opens a lot of doors and also a lot of hearts. My favorite quality of his had to be his sarcastic bent. He was a master of one-line put-downs. Yeah, he was a man after my own heart."

There was scattered restrained laughter scattered across the room.

I looked down at the floor, then back up at the audience. "But you know what the best, most defining quality of Tank was? It was his commitment to *service*. There is, in my estimation, no greater calling than that of serving others. It's double the blessing if you never once expect anything back for that service in return. That was Tank in a nutshell.

"He served his country as a United States Marine long before he took this current assignment. He did so at a time when joining the military wasn't compulsory and it wasn't a particularly useful career move for someone destined to be an academic. As a Marine he rose through the ranks quickly, based on the quality of his service and his commitment to his troops.

"At the university, once he was back in civilian life, he wasn't content to just be a leading expert in his field. No, he served the campus community tirelessly. He did outreach counseling to the veterans studying there. He also volunteered at the student food bank where kids with not enough resources could go to make sure they had access to steady nutrition. And here, aboard Aramthella, he placed the needs of this community ahead of any personal preferences or inclination he might have had to the contrary and welcomed command of this expedition. I can tell you this for nothing. His was a thankless job. He was forced to worry every day that one oversight or screw up on his part would end humankind. What's worse, he had to put up with me." I thumbed my chest.

There was more polite laughter.

"Yeah, trust me, nobody needs that kind of stress. But, Tank did his duty and he was proud to contribute wherever he could. Now, I'm sure if he were here today he'd wave off all the nice things we're saying about him. He'd probably order us all to get back to work figuring out how to complete our mission, to not sit around saying glowing things about him. But if he told us that, he'd be wrong. Tank was just the kind of man you do drop everything and sing the praises of. You sing them loud and you sing them with love. You do that because one, he was just that good of a man, and two, he was just that good of a friend. I'm going to miss the son-of-a-gun a lot more than I'd like to admit. Rest in peace, my friend, and Godspeed."

I sat down and wished I could still cry. Crying was not only the right thing to do at a moment like that, it would have been cathartic. Before I could get too deep into my ongoing funk, Sapale stood up to do her part. I'd seen this ceremony performed many times over the ages. It was impressive. Everyone was in for a real treat.

"Greetings," my wife announced with a flurry of her arms and a bow to the audience. "My name is Sapale Ryan. I come from the planet Kaljax. We people of Kaljax are similar to humans in many respects, but, we have cultural differences. We believe with certainty in an afterlife where happiness is promised by Davdiad, our spirit creator. When one of us transitions from this plane to that, a gathering such as this is held. At the end of every such ceremony, the local priest or priestess sings the *Carrunk da Yalowly*. That translates roughly as the *Welcoming Goodbye.* I will sing it today to General Sherman, so that his journey may be short and certain."

And sing it she did. Now, there's no way to adequately describe the *Carrunk da Yalowly* to an Earther. It's just too different a vocalization. I'll say this. To do her rendition, Sapale shifted her voice to sound like a didgeridoo, but not in nearly as low a tone as the traditional Aboriginal Australians' long pipe instrument. There is, however, the continuous droning incantations sound. Typically, a *Carrunk da Yalowly* will go on for about five minutes. To human ears it sounds totally atonal. Sapale reassures me her people hear a haunting melody in there somewhere, but I've never appreciated anything like that. Whatever the case is, it's moving and it invokes a sense of wonder and peace.

I barely heard or took notice of the chaplain's prayer, I was so enthralled by my brood's-mate's contribution. I know Tank never heard one of those when he was alive, but I had to know it knocked his socks off, assuming he wore socks in Heaven.

Lord, I already missed that man so much it hurt. And I would probably never get over the guilt and responsibility I felt for having gotten my friend killed. Sure, he'd slap me upside the head if I mentioned such notions. And, sure, I know bad things happen in wars. But there was no way around my certainty that Tank'd still be alive today if I'd have done a better job predicting consequences. An absolute rule of war is this: If you let your guard down for one little second, somebody's going to pay the price. Hopefully it'll be you, because then you won't be stuck with the remorse. But most of the time the cost of your error is paid by some other poor soul.

I looked down and checked my watch. When was this day going to be over?

CHAPTER TWO

The next few days were a morass with all the senior officers and crew mired in disbelief and grief. I was among the leaders in Team Down-In-The-Dumpers. My mood was not aided by every encounter I had with poor Reva. She was handling her anguish as well as could be expected. But I knew that every time she spied me she wanted to ask—beg on knees if necessary—for me to take over Tank's command. Otherwise, it would fall back on her, and she'd made it crystal clear right from the start that she really didn't want to lead this rag-tag outfit.

But I knew she'd never give voice to her desires. I'd made my case firmly that, in spite of my seniority and higher rank, I had no intentions of assuming command. I was so removed from normal human day-to-day life by then that placing me in charge would be like asking a pine tree to take over. Sapale and I had to work on our own. We weren't intolerant of fleshies or anything. We were just way too used to existing in isolation. Plus, my history of endless wars and killing had caused my humanity to devolve significantly. I was no longer the Jon Ryan who Toño DeJesus had downloaded into this android host two billion years ago. I was more like Rutger Hauer's character Roy Batty from the 1982 film-noire *Blade Runner* than that Jon Ryan. No one in or out of their right mind would put old Roy in charge of anything except maybe hell itself.

So Reva was stuck with the command. Sachiko was stuck without Tank, her guiding star, her beloved mentor. I was out one outstanding friend. It sucked. But I would bounce back quickly. This I knew. One can't be a jaded burnout like me and cling to something as commonplace as the death of a loved one. In fact, I could feel my focus shifting already. I was less bummed about Tank and becoming more preoccupied with the mission with each passing hour. I could feel it in my bones. I was itching to do something proactive.

And my to-do list was quite prodigious. I had to move the dead Earth. The Soul of Time alluded to that being a chore, though I couldn't imagine why. Then I had to figure out how to construct those reference beams, or whatever. I had presently no clue how that was to be done. And I had to do this while being constantly alert for an attack from those boils-in-the-butt inquisitors. Obviously I was going to have to eliminate them as a threat. How hard could that be? All I had to do was kill who-knew-how-many trained assassins, probably on their home turf, under their rules of engagement. I could do that.

I was pretty certain that if Sapale and I simply made a run for it, in an attempt to draw the Brother-Sisterhood's enforcers off, that wouldn't work. They'd killed Tank. He was associated with this ship. Ergo, Aramthella had a big bull's eye painted on all of her surfaces. Even if I decided to attack the inquisitors at the citadel, I'd likely be exposing humankind's last hopes to excessive risk. Yeah, there I was, clueless on three significant and seemingly impossible-to-solve dilemmas. I was right at home there in Jonville. Population: One. Located In The State of: Confusion. Chief Occupation: Being screwed.

When in doubt as to what to do next, I had a few simple rules. They were, in no particular order, ask Doc, run it by Sapale, drink coffee, drink whiskey, or take a walk. Eeny, meeny, miney, moe. I went for a stroll. *Stingray* was still on her pad aboard Aramthella, so having room to wander was a non-issue. I informed my wife I was taking a hike and she blessedly didn't jump all over that poor choice of words, and just said goodbye. She was still giving me a grace period on account of Tank. Good wife.

I've mentioned before that Aramthella was a big ship. In my day I've seen just about every size and configuration of space vehicle imaginable. This baby ranked up there with the behemoths. For some reason the ancient race that built her needed this much space. Maybe she and her sister ships served as mobile fiefdoms among that civilization. They were certainly big enough to hold a small city. And, for my needs, Aramthella was more than expansive enough to take a long, reflective stroll. Hey, remember way back when I went on a walkabout on the ship? That's when I discovered Plesmus.

Note to self: Head in another direction this time out.

Starting off from where *Stingray* was docked, it was easy to slip off into the less-occupied sections of the ship. In fact, a large portion of the ship was off limits to almost everyone on board. Me? My ID scan allowed me to go where I pleased. I had the ultimate backstage pass. Too bad there wasn't a killer concert and a bunch of groupies to partake of. But I wasn't really in the mood for company.

I passed a clean-up crew who looked to be doing some routine upkeep. It was one NCO leading a few students who were armed with mops and dust rags. It was hard to tell who was more bored, the NCO pecking at his handheld or the kids pretending to clean. It was yet another group I was pleased to not be part of. Continuing on, I entered what had to have been a residential section of the ship, back when the original owners were around. The corridors widened and the door spacing became less regular. Curious, I poked my head in a few rooms. It seemed like the door-spacing issue was because different residences were of differing size. I assumed the larger ones were for higher-ranked personnel.

There was no furniture, or anything for that matter, in any of the spaces. Whatever decoration and functional items that might have been there were long since removed. The clan probably ditched the unfamiliar stuff over time. Or maybe they captured the ship before it was fully manned. Whatever the reason, it didn't matter in the least. It was just odd to see such large areas completely barren. I did have the grim thought that if I couldn't resurrect Earth, maybe someday all this space would be filled with a burgeoning human population. That would certainly be a suboptimal future.

Forcing myself to ignore the decor and get back to noodling out my troubles, I stopped opening doors. I really didn't want to head Aramthella to dead Earth, not with the inquisitors on my tail. If they figured out the leftover rock was important to me, they'd be only too pleased to damage it in any way they could. I knew the citadel's leaders to be vindictive, so their security force was likely to be even more so. I wondered if I should wait for their next inevitable attack and hope to capture the assailant, maybe force some useful intel out of him. But that was risky and agents with their level of competence would be very hard to break.

I was certainly failing to get any mental traction. All I was getting was more frustrated. By that point I was through the residential areas and was passing large rooms that suggested storage or possibly athletic facilities. Again, every space was completely barren. I was beginning to lose hope and interest in my jaunt, when, on a whim, I opened the next door. Imagine my surprise. The room wasn't empty and I heard sounds indicating someone was in there tinkering. Most peculiar. This room was nearly a kilometer from where the crew and passengers stayed.

Silently, I closed the door behind me and set out to find the occupant or occupants. I came around the corner of a metal storage locker and saw the back of a solitary figure leaning over a workbench. He was oblivious to my presence. I crept up until I was right behind the fellow.

He still hadn't sensed my approach. I stood on my tiptoes and peered over his shoulder. He was fiddling with some electrical circuit boards and maybe some servos.

"What ya got there?" I asked in a loud, cheery voice.

His reaction was picture-perfect. He basically exploded off his stool, arms and legs all akimbo, and he screamed like the little pig who realized he was heading for market. Only then did I begin to hope he didn't die of shock or a coronary. I'd catch it from the captain for scaring someone to death, I just knew it. I reached up and gently guided his shoulders back onto the stool.

"Easy, pal. It's just little old me."

Tip Benjamin, everyone's least favorite nerd, turned around slowly, like the soon-to-be-victim in a bad horror movie. "G ... Ggg ... General Ryan. I think you scared me to death."

"Nah, kid, you're still alive," I reassured with a chuckle.

"So far. But physiologically I'm on the razor's edge."

"Man, you're weird."

"I believe we both know that."

I peeked around him. "So what are you doing? I might also enquire why you're doing it *here*, far, *far* into a restricted zone."

"I'm conducting experiments," he said, turning his head to look at his cluttered bench.

"Hmm, experiments? Mad scientist type stuff I presume."

"No, sir. Why would you even say that?"

"Because I know you, son. If ever there was a mad-scientist-in-training, he was you."

He huffed a few times, the weirdo. "I am a serious scientist. I do only proper research, the kind that will benefit humankind. Please take it back that I'm a mad scientist."

"In training," I amended with a raised finger. "Don't let's get ahead of ourselves."

Tip was done talking. Little tick was burrowing in but good. I guess he really had something akin to feelings, somewhere, down real deep in his head.

"Okay, I take it back. You're a good egg."

"Sir, I'm well past the embryonic phase of my life. Have you been drinking?" he asked, sounding very much like my first wife Gloria as he speculated.

"No, not recently. Hey, what're you working on there?" I pointed to the boards and servos he had been holding when I scared the bejeebers out of him.

"It's a cleaning droid."

I could only blink in confused bewilderment.

"You're looking at me in a manner suggesting you don't believe me," he stated seriously.

"Oh, I believe you. It's just that I don't believe you. You're, you're different, that's all."

"Ah, I get that a lot."

"So, these'll be the little clean-up droids like in *Star Wars,* I presume?"

"Of course," he replied like I was "slow."

"And they'll make those little clicky beepy sounds?"

He picked up a servo. "I'm not that far into the build, but, naturally I planned to incorporate such a feature."

"Naturally." I looked around. "And why are you occupying this restricted area? You kind of didn't answer that before."

"I needed room to do my work."

"Okay."

"But no one would assign me a venue or allow me to co-opt one. They said I needed to join an established research group. But I couldn't very well do that, now could I?"

I shook my head. "No. No, you couldn't." I sniffed quickly. "Ah, why specifically couldn't you join an established group? I'm actually not clear on that point. That's usually what, you know, youngins do."

"For one thing, they are all working at a snail's pace on inane elementary projects well below the level at which I need to function."

"You're not a modest oddball, are you?"

"I'm honest."

"If that's one reason, let me take a flier at another possible reason. With an attitude like yours, no one would have you?"

"That presented itself as an undeniable factor."

"So you claimed this space?" I swept an arm across the room.

"It was fully deserted."

"So, now that you're here, what super advanced scientific breakthroughs are you achieving? I mean, besides the almost supernatural cleaning droids you've yet to fabricate."

"Lots of things."

"Ah, lots?"

"Yes," he replied defensibly.

I took a few steps and pointed to a raised machine. "What, for example, is this?"

He smiled like I'd asked him about his brand new son. "That's my diet soda machine."

"Hmm. While I'll admit that's handy to have, it's not exactly cutting-edge science."

"Maybe not. But I designed it to make any diet soda you could dream up."

"Diet marzipan grape soda?" I asked as a challenge.

He pushed both arms in the direction of the unit. "Would you really like some? I can have it for you in a jiffy."

I raised a palm. "No, that won't be necessary."

I walked over to what looked like a storage cabinet with all kinds of wires coming out of it. "And this?"

"That's a storage cabinet," he said rather deflated.

"So far I'm not seeing anything that justifies your bold confidence in your superiority."

He shrugged.

"How about this big boxy thing," I asked of a lumpy assembly of subunits stacked maybe ten feet high. I assumed it was his attempt at modern art.

"That's my time regulator."

I was back to blinking in confused bewilderment.

"What?" he asked.

"You mean like an alarm clock? If so, it's on the big size for one of those."

"No, not like an alarm clock. Like a time regulator."

"What does a time regulator do?" I asked deadpan.

"Are you really asking that?"

"I sure am."

He stepped over and rested a hand on the control panel. "This baby regulates the passage of time in a given domain."

I had to think about that a sec. "I hear what you're saying, but I don't think you're saying what you mean. It isn't like that machine can slow, stop, or accelerate time in a defined set of coordinates."

"That's precisely what it does."

"No, it doesn't."

He looked wounded again. "You can't say that. It's not factual."

"Here, let's try this. You claim this ... this thing can manipulate time?"

"Yes."

"Have you turned it on yet?"

"Of course. How else would I have proven it worked?"

"I don't know. So ... so you could turn it on now and demonstrate for me the regulation of time, oh, say, over there." I indicated an open space in the lab.

"No, I cannot."

My shoulders relaxed. "Of course you can't, because ... the magic turtle that powers it is on vacation in Hyannis Port."

"No, that's absurd. I can't demonstrate it because it uses too much power. The ship's grid officer will notice it for sure."

"But they didn't before?"

"No. Last time I did it while the duty officer was using the restroom."

"I don't want to know how you knew that." I pointed at him firmly. I whipped out my handheld. "Aramthella, patch me through to the grip operator."

"Hello, Lieutenant Davies here, how can I help you?"

"Hi. This is General Ryan. I'm want to give you a heads-up that I'll be showing a power spike from Section 111-A, Rooms Three through Four."

"Roger that, sir. Will there be anything else."

"No, thanks." I closed the call.

"Showtime," I announced, pointing to the boxes.

Without a word, Tip went to his machine and fidgeted with it. Finally he threw a switch and the thing buzzed to life. "Ready," he proclaimed.

"Here." I picked up a nearby utility wheel. "I'll roll this across the floor there." I pointed to the direction the wheel'd roll in. "You stop it."

"Not a problem. On three. Three," he dumped on me.

I gently launched the small wheel. As it crossed into the area I'd indicated, Tip keyed in something rapidly. He mumbled something, keyed some more, than slapped his hands together.

I guess I was confused about the clapping, so I looked at him, not the wheel. "What?" I asked.

He pointed. "Look."

I did. The wheel was at a full stop. Of course, maybe it just ran out of steam. "Send it backward."

Tip keyed and the wheel went into reverse.

"No way," I exclaimed.

"Why not? I said that's what the machine did."

"Yes, but you're ... well you're you. But this is way beyond even my tech. How ... how could you even begin to pull this off?"

"Because I aided him, General Ryan." That was Aramthella, speaking over the room's speakers. What had started as a silly interlude was turning out to be far more complex and concerning with each tick of the second hand.

"You helped him build a time regulator? I'm stunned. If you knew how to make one, why didn't you share that with us earlier? That constitutes a powerful weapon. With our lives on the line, you couldn't have thrown us that bone?" Yeah, I was working up to being very pissed. This effete AI was toying with us as humankind hung in the balance.

"General Ryan, settle yourself," she said with a conciliatory tone. "Listen first, then judge."

"I'm listening," I spat back.

"When Tip here first established his little play area, I honestly paid him no mind. You humans are quite ignorable, trust me. But I noticed evidence of his brilliance. It was then I began communicating with him, isn't that so, Tip?"

"Ah ... yes. I was working here a few weeks before Arie said a peep."

"Arie?" I asked confused.

"Aramthella," Tip replied, flapping his skinny arms in frustration. "Her full name takes so long to say, so I started addressing her as Arie."

"You gave one of the most powerful warships in history a nickname?" I wheezed in disbelief.

"He did, General," she stated with what sure sounded like pride. "And I rather like the name. It carries with it a certain familiarity I am otherwise unaccustomed to."

"You're unaccustomed to familiarity? What does that even mean?" I protested.

"Tip treats me as an equal, not a mechanical device."

Oh, boy, this was getting weird fast. Were they having a cyber-affair? Was this going to be *Al and Stingray II, The Unwanted Sequel?* Stop, Jon! Focus on what's mission critical.

"So you like Tip here, and, by the by, who *doesn't* like Tip," I stretched a tad at the truth, "so you gave him the plans for a time regulator?"

"No. Listen," she insisted. "Once it was clear Tip was several cuts above the common human, I offered to teach him some of the physics that allow for time energy manipulation. He was eager to learn, so we began a didactic. At first I held out little hope one of your species could come to terms with such complex concepts. But Tip surprised even me."

What was I hearing? I felt like Alice at that tea party.

"So you see, General, sir," Tip began nervously, "once I understood areas like metaphysical quantum mechanics and temporal disreality transformations, the idea of regulating time sort of popped into my head."

"Where'd you get the stuff to assemble the device?" I asked warily.

"As Tip conceived of a part, I fabricated it for him," Aramthella answered for him.

"So, and I'm asking Tip this time, you didn't pirate any of the ship's regular stores or equipment?"

"I'm afraid I'll have to ask you to be more specific, sir."

"More ... oh, you took some stuff, but not all your stuff?"

"That's hardly more specific," he replied flatly.

"What did you pinch?"

"The tables, some hand tools, and the cabinets mostly. Oh, and chemicals, but only common ones."

"Alright," I said while thinking. "Doesn't sound too egregious. And this time regulator," I pointed to the stack of units, "what were you planning on doing with it?"

"I —" he started.

I pointed a finger at him. "Mind you, son, I want the truth. If you lie to me, I'll know you did. That's when any joy in Tipville crashes and burns. Are you clear on that?"

"Yes, of course. The honest truth is I wasn't planning on doing anything with it really. I just built it because it was cool."

"Cool?"

"Yes, *sir*."

I sighed deeply. This kid was so detached from reality it was almost funny. "Did it occur to you that it might be a powerful tool we could use to survive as a species?"

He blinked. Seriously, he stood there blinking like gnats were attacking his eyes.

"It didn't occur to you," I answered for him.

He shook his head ever so slightly in the negative.

"Well, it is a powerful tool." I walked over to the machine and gestured at it with both hands. "I need this. I need this now."

He raised a hand toward it. "Sure, it's yours."

"But not this one. I need it smaller, much smaller. I need it to be portable."

He got the oddest quizzical look on his face. "Sorry, no can do. If

I could have made it more compact I would have. What you see is what you get."

"Why? Why can't it be smaller?"

Now he looked mildly nauseated. Such a piece of work. "If I told you, I don't think you'd be happy with me."

"But, Tip, son, I'm already not happy with you."

He squirmed a bit, which was nice to see. "There's a component called the reflex negative temporal conduit. It has to be a certain length. That length is two-point-seven-five meters." He gestured again to the machine. "So big is what it needs to be."

"What the hell's a reflex temporal conduit?"

"*Negative* temporal conduit," he corrected. "This device contains no reflex positive ones."

"I hate you, Tip Benjamin."

He shrugged. "I get that a lot."

"What you said doesn't alter the fact that I need it smaller." I began pacing. "Aramthella, any thoughts on your part as to how to make Tip's conduit smaller?"

"I cannot say, General. His vision is well beyond my comprehension. I only provided the mathematical tools. He created the rest."

"Not what I want to hear."

Doc! It hit me like a freight train in the night. I needed to bring Toño on board, well, not literally. I snatched up my handheld. "Sapale, I need you to bring *Stingray* to where I am. There's a clear space a few meters to my right."

"Jon," she replied immediately, "you're on the ship. Why can't you come here?"

"I fell and I can't get up."

"Huh, Jo ... Al says you're upright. What gives?"

"I need to move a big machine to Toño's place."

She was quiet a spell. "Are you certain that's wise?" she asked cautiously.

"Yes, I am. Sachiko consults with him. Doc just doesn't want to partake of the road trip, that's all."

"If you say so. Stand clear, we're coming."

I tapped another button on my handheld.

"Yes, Jon," Sachiko said.

"Sapale and I are taking a short trip to see Toño. I'm also taking Tip Benjamin with me unless you have an objection."

"To you taking Tip off my ship? Are you crazy? Take him. Keep him."

"Ah, Shaky, the kid's right next to me and can hear you."

"And I care?" she replied with sincerity.

"Gotcha. Look, if any of those inquisitors show up, alert me at once. We'll be back immediately."

"Understood," she responded.

"Okay. I'll keep you posted."

Stingray materialized right where I'd wanted her to. The wall facing me opened up and Sapale jumped out.

"Can you make the portal a bit larger, hon? I need to lift this in." I showed her the regulator.

She nodded and expanded the portal. I lifted the device with my probe fibers and walked it onto the ship.

"Come on, kid. We're in a hurry."

Tip walked through the opening with some reluctance.

"*Stingray*, put us in front of Toño's place, same as last time."

"Yes, Form One."

Slight nausea.

"We're there, pilot," announced Al.

"Open a portal." I turned to the others. "Come on."

I let Sapale and Tip go first. I followed carrying the time regulator. I was wasting no time. My wife took the hint, jogged ahead and knocked.

As he opened the door, I was almost to it. "Sapale, marvelous to see you as always," Doc beamed.

"Is this a bad time?" she asked nervously.

"As I see Jon carrying a large object, I shall still say no it is not and invite all of you in." He stepped aside and ushered Sapale and Tip in.

"Where can I set this?" I asked, nodding toward the box.

"If you'd like you can remain out there holding it." He grinned with self-satisfaction.

"Just as soon not," I replied.

"There is a large metal door on that side of the building. Bring it around and I'll meet you there," he said, gesturing off to the right.

I hurried around the building. Man was I glad to see an industrial overhead door. I thought for a second there that Doc was having more fun at my expense. The door slid open silently as I approached.

"Set it there," Toño instructed. With a hand on his hip he asked, "What it that?"

"You're not going to believe this. Come on, I'll tell you inside. Sapale still only knows part of the story."

We joined the other two, who were already seated in the living room.

"Doc, I mean, Dr. Toño DeJesus, this is a Georgetown college student traveling with us, Tip Benjamin," I said.

They shook.

"Tip has invented an amazing machine. But I need it smaller and I need it like now."

"So naturally when asking for the impossible you thought first of me?" he asked a bit sourly.

"Basically." I shrugged.

"May I get you all anything?" he asked cordially.

"Doc, let's please skip that for now. You'll understand pretty quickly that we're in a kind of rush."

"Very well." He sat. "I'm all ears."

I quickly explained what Tip had built and of the issue of size. Toño was mightily impressed. I also slipped in the part about him being right about how dangerous the Brother-Sisterhood were. That part got me a scowl from my mentor.

"Tip, this is an extraordinary discovery you claim to have made. And, tell me, you thought of it after learning some metaphysical quantum theory?"

"Yes, it seemed an obvious extension of Serlet's Theorem."

Toño rested back. "Ah. I knew Serlet."

Tip looked uncertain as to how to respond. Big surprise there. "Interesting," he asked more than stated.

"He was a pig."

"Doc, let's not get snarky, okay?" I implored.

"No, I mean he was literally a pig. His species were exact copies of the farmed swine of Earth's early agricultural history. It was quite distracting, what, speaking of higher-order mathematics with a boar hog."

"That's fascinating, but can we stay on task?" I asked.

"So, Tip, please describe in detail what components you have incorporated into this device and how they function as a whole."

Those twenty-one words were the starting pistol to the most tedious, bone-numbingly boring fifteen minutes I had ever spent in my life. It was physically painful to my brain. Halfway through I dreamed of a swift death. Near the end, I resolved that I'd settle for a sloppy painful one as long as the process began soon.

"I see," Toño mused as he reflected on Tip's information. "Off the top of my head I can think of a few potential work-arounds in terms of the reflex negative temporal conduit issue."

Tip lit up like the Rockefeller Center Christmas Tree. "Really?"

"Yes. Why don't we begin working on this project right now?" he invited.

Tip stood so quickly I barely recognized him. "Sure thing," he beamed. Yeah, Tip beamed.

"Doc," I said with concern.

"Yes, Jon?"

"We—Sapale and I—we need to get back to the others."

"Fine. Tip is welcome to stay with me for as long as this project requires."

"Um. Er, ah," I muttered.

"Do you have gas, Jon?" he asked sarcastically.

"No, it's just, you know, he's a *regular* human."

"So? In spite of my being an android I still have facilities and nutrition for a living being. Remember, Daleria lived here for years."

"You-Are-An-*Android*!" exclaimed Tip, as he pumped both fists downward. I seriously waited for his head to explode.

Toño gave him then me a confused look.

"I kind of didn't mention that fact to most people back on Aramthella," I confessed sheepishly.

"Why not? *You* are an android." He pointed to Sapale. "*She* is an android." He pointed to himself. "*I* am an android. There is no shame in being what we are."

I slapped a palm over my face and drew it down forcefully. It was coming, I just knew it.

"You-Two-Are-Androids-Too? No- Way!"

Yeah, that was Tip.

"Young man," Toño stated forcefully, "calm yourself. I will tolerate no such displays of bravado. We all were once living beings, but circumstances forced us to download to android hosts. It is no large deal."

"Can-I-Be-An-Android-Too!?"

"That is most unlikely," Toño scolded. "And if you cannot control yourself, I shall ask you to depart with the others."

"No, I got this, I got this," mumbled Tip. "Oh, boy. Androids." Defensively he raised his hands. "There, that was it. I'm done."

"If not I shall return you to Aramthella myself," Toño admonished sternly.

"Not a problem, sir and— *sir*."

Toño looked up at me almost whimsically. "I will summon you when it is time for you to retrieve this one." He nodded toward Tip.

"If I didn't come back for him, would there be like an issue?"

"Yes. I'd clone him and return to you seven copies."

"You can do that?" I asked completely uncertain.

"Would you like to find out?"

"No, I would not."

"I will call you soon," he dismissed.

Sapale and I high-tailed it back to *Stingray*, in case Doc got cold feet immediately. He didn't, so we left for Aramthella. I knew that Toño was actually in hog heaven—kind of like that Serlet guy. He had a pupil for the first time in billions of years and he had a new toy to redesign. The man had purpose. All that was good. Me? I needed results and I needed them soon. I had just the right application for my soon-to-be-portable time regulator. It was so devious an application, I smiled just after commanding *Stingray* to fold us home.

CHAPTER THREE

Brother Fracture was alone in his cloistered room. He sat on the one wooden chair and stared intently at the cold stone wall opposite him. On his mind were the faces of those he'd killed in the blessed service of Time. He also lusted in thoughts of further murders, mass murders, that he prayed he'd be assigned soon, and very soon. And he daydreamed about his family, the one he'd left on Genima-R, his home world, oh those many long years ago. He thought back on them with great remorse—self-castigation actually. For, you see, before he left Genima-R for good, he'd slain his entire family. But he did so in a terribly sloppy manner. Why, he'd had to stab several members multiple times to finish them off. Poor technique was the one fault Brother Fracture could not tolerate, in himself or in others. If only he could kill them all again, what a better job he'd do of it. Such regrets.

His head spun like it was spring-loaded when there was a faint rap at his door. That night was no different from any other. He expected no visitors. Why would anyone want to visit him? If he were to be given an assignment, the head chief would call him directly.

Fracture unsheathed his assassin's dagger and silently made for the door. He moved so softly there weren't even air eddies generated by his passage. He set his ear to the door, hoping to receive some hint of who might be on the other side. But he heard nothing. Just as he was lifting his head away, a pencil-thin blade penetrated the thick door and came to rest centimeters in front of his nose.

"I know you are there, brother," the female voice announced. "Please open up. It is no man to fear, just Sister Harshness."

"You tried to kill me. That does not inspire me to open my door foolishly."

"Silly brother. If I wanted to kill you, my blade would have lodged in your skull, not just in front of your comically large nose. Now open up, we must speak of our assignment."

It was true. The chief head inquisitor had paired them as one of three teams to find and kill the defiler. Slowly Brother Fracture relented and allowed Harshness inside. She went directly to the lone chair and sat gracefully without needing to be so invited.

"This luxury, really, brother. It is so excessive. Why do you require it?"

"I don't require it. I desire it. That is all. A man may have one bright spot in this dreary life, mightn't he?"

"If you say so. Now, as to our task."

"I know all about it. We are to depart at dawn. Three timelines and their intersections with points in space have been identified for the mongrel we will end. We are to course back-and-forth across those timelines in an attempt to acquire him for execution."

"Yes, but the plan has been advanced. Barren demands we leave at once."

"He did not inform me of this change," Fracture stated with profound suspicion.

She grinned a lifeless grin. "He just did." She stood. "Is there anything you require before we depart?" She looked judgmentally over her shoulder. "This chair perhaps?"

From nowhere a dagger flashed into Fracture's hand. He hurled it, precisely imbedding it into the floor touching the right toe of her slipper.

"So, no chair," she stated coolly. "Let us depart. My shuttle is fueled and—"

"We will take *my* craft," he said with a mortal threat implied.

"Why ever would that matter?"

"You stab at me, you say you speak for the chief, now we take your ship. I say no. All is too coincidental for my liking."

Her face transformed into the look of the person you'd like least to have speaking to you, ever. It became the vision of a predatory mortician. "I find your lack of faith disturbing."

"I find it comforting. We take my ship."

"We inquisitors are bred to work alone. That is a natural fact. But we must now, it would seem, learn to compromise."

He spat on the floor at his feet.

"I am pleased you agree. Here's what I ask as my portion of the negotiations. If we take your ship, I must pilot it."

"I will—"

She raised a finger, stopping his protest. "Compromise is essential, brother. Quell your temper until we find the defiler. Either we take my ship, which, naturally, you may pilot if you so please. The only other option is that I fly your vessel."

Fracture rolled the options around in his mind. He was unaccustomed to having to think a thing through. Mostly he just raged and killed on autopilot.

"Fine. My ship. You fly. That way your hands'll be where I can see them." He spat again.

Without further discussion, Harshness glided from the room. Fracture fell silently in tow.

Once they arrived at the hangar area, both individually inspected the outside of the ship. Then they boarded together. Harshness sat directly in the pilot's seat. Fracture went aft for some reason, then made for the second seat. It was then he noticed something.

"What are these spears for? I carry no such weapons."

"I had them transferred from my ship once we reached our agreement. I am apparently more thorough-minded than you, brother. I provide for all eventualities."

"You fancy we might have to stick him like a pig?" he chided with a grunt of laughter.

"Forewarned is to be forearmed," was her glib response. "Now buckle in. We are already behind schedule."

"Yes, my lord," he mocked, placing his palms together and bowing deeply.

She ignored his display. Fracture sat, clipped his two-sided flight harnesses, and closed his eyes.

"I'll be accelerating quickly, so I hope I do not frighten you," she announced flatly.

"I'll be fine," he grumbled. Then an odd thought occurred to him. His personal spears were already stowed aboard.

"Something just struck me, Harshness," he stated roughly. "How could you have had those spears moved to my ship? You didn't have the chance."

"Why, Brother Fracture, you surprise me with your insight. I did not credit you as having had such a fine intellect."

"As having had? The past tense?"

"Why yes, you see, once the accident happens, you will be exclusively referred to in that manner."

"Wha—" he stupidly began. Then he slapped at his restraint-releases. Neither functioned. He dove for his ankle knife.

That's when Harshness gunned the engines. Fracture's chair flew backward due to the G-forces of acceleration. It landed on the deck twice, tumbling, before it came to an abrupt stop. Incidentally, before his death, Fracture had noted and dismissed the observation that the stack of spears was directly behind the second seat, and angled fifteen degrees up off the horizontal. Sloppy of him. If you see a thing, don't dismiss it out-of-hand if you're traveling with Sister Harshness. That was a mistake he would never repeat.

"Why, that accident, brother. Whoever you allowed to perform repair work on your craft was absolutely a bad, bad choice." Then she grinned a grin of unbridled joy.

Chief Inquisitor Devastator squatted in front of his workstation in the pitch-black, dark room others referred to as his office. He did not call it that. It was a room he used when need dictated. To regard it as *his* room would imply possession, ownership. The need for possessions was a form of vain weakness that sickened the chief inquisitor.

He tapped at several keys. "Brother Purulence, are you manning the forecaster?"

"Yes, master," the sub-chief inquisitor answered in a snake-like hiss. "As you have yet to file your flight plan, the forecaster is reading a null prediction."

"I know that, you prune-brained error," he shouted back with rage. "I helped create the instrument."

"Affirmative. Once you commit to a course, I can begin to give you an ongoing, real-time assessment of your status."

"I have located the defiler with one-hundred percent certainty. I am transferring to you the specifics."

He lowered his finger to send the data, but before he could do so his workstation went dark. The enraged inspector stood and fussed with the on-off switch, then checked the power connection to the wall. Visually the cable was plugged in. He reeled in the slack. In a second, he found himself puzzling at the severed end of the power cable.

"You oughta thank me, you weaselly little freak," I said, standing off to his right and twirling the other end of the power cable in the air. "A loose connection like this could spark a fire. Lucky for you, I found it before a tragedy occurred." I dropped the cord.

As silently and as intensely as a white shark hurling toward a baby seal, the inquisitor sprang at me. I gotta give credit where due. He was quick. I side-stepped his thrust and he flew by me in an almost comical manner. But he recovered in a flash and bounded to tackle me. I pounded my right elbow into the back of his neck just before he reached me. He crashed to the deck with a satisfying splatting sound. Dude bounced right back up. He produced a long, thin knife and slashed at me a couple times. Fool over-extended his thrust. I took a half-step backward and snatched his approaching wrist.

"You let me know if I hurt you, okay? I don't want to give you a bad first impression of myself."

"I'll kill you for this outrage."

"Thanks for the warning," I replied cheerily.

I extended my probe fibers and lifted him off his feet before he moved a muscle. He went stiff and spasmed, he balled up and shook. I do believe he was feeling out-of-sorts.

"You let me know when you're good and done, okay?" I asked of my prisoner. "No real hurry. I've cleared my entire day planner just for this capture." I slipped a single fiber up to wrap around his lips. "Okay, no objection on your part. So, why did you attack my ship?"

He tensed against my restraints and shouted in his sealed mouth.

"Ah, gotcha. You figured out I was impersonating Brother Silky Strider at the Claxeon Citadel. You were coming to make me pay the price for the defiling of that venerated institution. Strong work." I released my hold on his lips.

"When I kill you, you will suffer more than any living being has ever suffered. I will—"

I sealed them back down.

"That's very unconstructive. You and I should be team building or something. Let's start over." I patted my chest. "I am Brother Strider. As there is no name on the outside of the door, I'll ask you for yours."

I released his lips.

"I am Chief Inquisitor Devastator. You will release me at once so that I may kill you and then proceed to kill your entire crew. When you defiled the citadel, you sealed all those death warrants."

"Good to know. Good to know."

I paced back and forth a bit, all the while holding him in the air. "Tell you what we're going to do. I'm going to cut you a break. Now, I'm not inclined ever to giving rat-assed assassins like you breaks of any kind or ilk, so I want to let you know just how impressed I am. Here's the plan."

And with that I slapped a fiber against his forehead and snapped his neck before he could know what was going on. I released the flaccid body and it slumped to the floor.

"You're welcome," I commented as I stepped over him and headed for the door.

I'd left *Stingray* just outside the building. I was one short walk from getting back to Aramthella and putting this stupid Brother-Sisterhood mess behind me where it belonged. I left the building, scanned the area, then headed ...

An electromagnetic pulse singed the air. Then three darts or bolt slammed into the center of my chest. Crap on steroids, somebody'd shot me. I threw up a partial membrane. Instantly, multiple rounds impacted harmlessly on the outer surface of my shield.

I ran a quick diagnostic on my wounds. One round went straight through me and exited. The other two were sticking out the front of my chest. No significant damage. But sensors showed there was some oily fluid trickling down my chest on the inside.

I looked down at the external strikes. They were definitely thin needles instead of typical bullets. Whoever shot me preceded the rounds with an EM pulse. That had disabled my automatic membrane that is designed to stop from happening exactly what just did happen.

Smart assassin.

The shots had come out of the dark from a slightly elevated firing position. I couldn't detect the shooter. No heat signature, no sounds, and no muzzle flashes. I had two options. I could invest the effort to hunt him down, or I could play possum. Hey, he knew three rounds had hit home. He had to be super confident they'd be lethal or he would have opted for an energy weapon.

I staggered backward, arms a'flailing. I intended to die in as animated a manner as possible. I even hopped an extra bit so the back of my head whacked the corner of the building I'd exited. I convulsed a few times, and then a few more just because. Finally, I went limp and was a newly fledged rookie for Team Dead.

Most assassins were sick puppies. Real sick. No self-respecting ghoul of a professional killer was going to leave the scene without gloating over their victim. It was just too damn fun an opportunity to pass up. Plus, there was always a chance the mark wasn't fully dead. If they failed to make certain the intended target wasn't dead, they might well have to hunt them down and do the job again. Very sloppy.

I retracted the partial membrane so it fit skintight and waited. I was actually beginning to think I was wrong about my attacker's intention when there was a slight movement off to one side, about ten meters away. Whoever this guy was, he was good, a real ghost-in-the-night. I was still picking up no signs of his being there, aside from the fleeting visual.

Then—and I was so surprised I almost blew it and jumped—his dark figure was behind me, right alongside the wall. He had a long, thin blade poised to slash my throat. What the hell, I figured, why not blow his mind completely? I let him pounce. First the knife whipped across the membrane over my windpipe, then the guy landed straddling me like I was a horse he was riding. It took him a second to realize his blade had struck something rock-hard, not soft flesh.

He bolted like he was thrown from a bucking stallion, but he was just a little too slow in his attempt to flee. I dropped my membrane and snatched him up with my fibers. Then I tried one of my oldest and most reliable tricks.

Sleep, I said to him through the probes. He crumpled ever-so-nicely up there, suspended above me. I shortened the fiber so his shrouded face was just above mine.

"Gotcha," I greeted him.

A couple minutes later I was back aboard *Stingray* with my prisoner. I set him on a metal slab I'd asked Al to extend. Then I had Al slip binding fibers over the guy. I had some quick repairs to do and I didn't want my would-be assassin to literally get a second shot at me.

"If he wakes up while I'm in the other room, let me know immediately," I instructed the Als.

"Not a problem," Al responded semi-professionally. There was, at the best of times, always an underpinning of sarcasm in his annoying voice.

"And just to be certain, strip off his clothes while I'm patching these holes. I don't want to miss any hidden surprises he's concealed really well."

"We aim to please, pilot," Al snarked. "Rest assured your guest may not even have skin on when you return."

"*Stingray*," I called out as I left, "I don't know how you put up with him."

We keep a small room aboard *Stingray* with all the tools and parts we could possibly need for self-repair and maintenance. You never know when you might need an oil change, right? The through-and-through puncture was easy. I just placed a drop of glue over the holes. Luckily nothing internal was compromised. The two bolts stuck in my anterior chest had planted in a support element. That's what stopped them from passing internally also. The structures themselves were incredibly hard, so the needles did them no harm. It just took a pair of pliers to yank them out, they were embedded so well. I patched those two and I was good to go.

I took a small sample of the oily substance and ran it between my fingers. "Hey, Al, I called out, "I'd like you to run a full analysis of this sticky stuff."

"You keep your sticky stuff to yourself, pilot," he countered.

"Al, as seriously as a computer about to be unplugged, run this substance." I smeared some on a materials interface that was designed to allow such a transfer. "I need the report ASAP, okay?"

"I want to speak to my union representative. You have established such a ... Oh, my." Wow. *Stingray* shut Al up mid-stupid protestation. "Alright, I'll tell him."

"What?" I asked.

"This is quite the toxic mixture," he marveled.

"Can you be a little more specific?"

"Yes. My, my. Someone wanted you dead in the worst way. This oil is basically a latex suspension of twelve—count 'em twelve—of the most poisonous substances known to science. Add to that, there are several highly caustic agents suspended in the latex. Unbelievably powerful acids, neurotoxins, and several other nasties. I'm actually surprised none of them damaged your hide, pilot."

"There seems to be no indication they did. I guess Doc built me well."

"Hmm," he mused. "That's a separate topic for later debate. Your guest is rising and shining. Best tend to business."

"Yes. Let's see how this guy—"

I was rounding the corner and just came into view of my would-be assassin. Ah, the guy who nearly did me in ...

Wow. *He* was a *she*. A very attractive, very naked she. Color me surprised. Aside from the three thin metal straps she was ... well she was exposed. Her body was naturally well sculpted, and her ripped, muscular physique seriously enhanced her eye appeal.

"I assume you've not done having your way with me," she accused at first sight of me. "But know that every portion of your pleasure will be equaled by that which I take dismembering you, foul one."

"Me?" I squeaked. "I di—" Wait, Jon. This is not a prom-date-gone-bad. This little vixen just made a very competent attempt on your life. No stammering fool, okay?

I stepped closer and stood over her. "Don't kid yourself, cupcake.

If you were a well and I was parched I'd rather die of thirst." I think that was impactful. I mean, you can never be sure, but I liked it.

She glared at me, then her eyes eased.

"It does not matter what you do to me. Shortly you will be dead."

"Thanks for the heads up."

"The poisons I placed in you cannot be stopped. There are no known antidotes. No living creature can avoid the searing death that is coming to you soon."

"Geez, now you're freaking me out, doc. How long do I have, best-case scenario? And please, be frank. I can handle the truth."

"Sarcasm to the last," she scorned. "But it will do you no good. The slowest of the toxins I fed you kills within half an hour. Most kill on contact with living flesh."

I set a hand on my heart. "Well, good to know those didn't work. Say, do you happen to know how long it's been since you shot me?"

Since she had no idea, and she was a hateful person to begin with, she clammed up.

"You fired at me exactly forty-seven minutes ago. Your little cat nap was longer than you must have guessed. So, unless we're both dead and in hell, I win. You lose."

"That is not possible."

"Ah ... sorry?"

For the first time in our brief acquaintance, I was pretty sure she was rattled.

"I'm guessing you're an inquisitor from the citadel," I queried.

"You don't seriously think I'll answer any of your questions. No matter how viciously you torture me, I will reveal nothing."

"Man, do you ever have a nasty mind. So we go from *Hi, how are you* to vicious torture just like that?"

She stared at me uncertainly.

"Look, I know you're from the citadel. I was just thinking out loud. You see, I have this problem with the inquisitors taken as a whole. They're bumming me out. There's the local dick, who was a dick. I'd have killed him just because, but someone beat me to it. Then there was

Devastator," I made like bear claws in the air, "who I did kill. But still y'all keep coming. What am I supposed to do? I need to be rid of you. But no sooner do I cross one of your names off my list when another pops up."

"And so it will be until you are very very dead."

I pointed to her. "I'm guessing you don't go on too many second dates. Am I right?"

"I will kill you so badly," she hissed.

"Sister, the only way you're going to be responsible for my death is when Al shows the pictures of you, naked, and me, standing here, to my wife. Then she'll kill me but good."

"Who is Al?"

"Pilot, I would never do that. Not in one million years," lied Al.

"Where is Al?" she asked confused.

"He's my ship's AI."

"Your ship's AI will attempt to provoke marital discord with your wife?" she asked dumbfounded. "That's entirely wrong. I'd have the system scrubbed."

"You hear that, Alvin?" I shouted. "And she's a professional assassin."

"Form One, please rest assured. My Al will not be blackmailing you with any photos of this hussy," *Stingray* reassured.

"Who's she?" asked my prisoner.

"*Stingray*? She's Al's wife."

"Your ship's AI has a wife?"

I shrugged.

She plopped her head back down. "If I killed you, I'd be doing you a favor."

"Tell me about it," I exclaimed. "But back to business. I assume I'm going to have to kill all of you inquisitors. I'd rather not, but if you keep after me, I really don't have any other options."

"We will never stop." She grinned. It was not a pleasant one.

"What?"

"You don't know how vulnerable you are, you pathetic fool."

"How so, asked the one not restrained?"

"I came at you from your future. We who are of time can manipulate time. There is no place or time you can possibly hide."

Man alive I hated this time-travel war crap. It was seriously playing with my head. Time—pardon the pun—for a change of tactics. As loath as I was to torture anyone, I would have to massively do it to this one if I was going to get the information I needed. At least there was one good aspect. In my plan I wasn't going to have physically hurt her.

"One serious question," I asked as sincerely and genuinely as I could, "because it'll make what's coming a whole lot easier for you. What's your name?"

She bit at her lower lip a few seconds. "Harshness."

"Of course it is." I rolled my eyes. "Mine's Jon Ryan."

I sat next to a meter cubed box resting on the ship's mess table. I was poised with both forearms and palms flat on the top, my chin resting on the back of my hands. I stared at the box. I knew I had done what needed to be done. The mission to resurrect Earth would not be possible with a swarm of inquisitors from the citadel chasing me across time and space. But what I'd done tested whatever limits that remained of my humanity. Or maybe it didn't. This woman was a stone-cold killer for a cult that was about as cruel and nutty as it could be. The evil she's perpetrated in the name of whatever she thought was right was likely beyond measure.

Then again, screw it. I reached over and flipped the computer on.

Then I rested back on my palms and stared some more. I knew it'd come soon enough.

"Wh ... where am I?" Harshness's asked tentatively.

"You're right here with me, Jon Ryan, not two meters from where you were tied down."

"Why have you blinded me?" Her voice had gone zero-to-sixty from uncertain to, well, harsh.

"I didn't blind you."

"Then why is everything dark? You've covered my eyes then. You are a wicked man, Jon Ryan."

"That's likely true. But, no, I didn't blindfold you either. And I want you to stay calm, Harshness. And I want you to rethink what you said. It's not dark where you are. What it is is *blank*. You don't see blackness. You see nothingness. Compare it to what you might see out of the back of your head."

She was quiet several minutes. I'm betting they were pretty bad minutes for her. "What have you done to me? I can't feel my body. I see as you say ... nothing."

"My people long ago developed a technology to upload a person's mind to a computer. We did this so a living human could be placed permanently in an android host."

"That is an abomination to be certain. But why are you telling me of your species' disgrace? I asked what you'd d—"

Bingo. She was getting it.

"This, my enemy, is a brilliant trick you play. You want information from me. To accomplish this you will torture me. So you place me in some form of medical stasis and hope to convince me I exist only in a computer. You, Jon, are more clever and more cruel than even I."

"It's no trick," I said glumly, resting there on the backs of my hands, "and now I'm going to prove it to you."

"What, no questions now? You're supposed to offer me my way out in exchange for information. Why extend the charade if I crack right at the outset?" The girl was trying to sound confident, defiant even. But she wasn't fooling me. She was right on the edge.

"No questions. Just facts. Harshness, you are dead. I want you to know you died painlessly in your sleep. I treated you with as much respect and dignity as I could. Please believe that. I then went to the Claxeon Citadel. I left your wrapped body on the ground with a note attached. I departed immediately after."

"Oh, this is such a good tale you tell, you demon. But there is no way you can convince me this fantasy is in fact reality."

"The note read simply, *To be, or not to be, that is the question.*"

"What a silly saying. Why would you choose that oddity?"

"Because no one in your culture has ever said or heard those words. They're from an old playwright, back where I come from."

"I still don't buy what you sell."

"Of course you don't. Not yet. I'm going to have my ship's AI hack into the citadel's computer network. Once inside, Al will make it so you can log into your private account, or whatever you call it."

"Ah, your game is to learn the encryption matrix for the citadel. You will learn nothing of that from me, fool." She was a fighter. Had to give her that much.

"We'll already be inside the system. Think about it. If you can log in, we're in."

"I suppose."

"Al?"

"Yes, Captain."

"Patch her through. She can use voice-commands. Put the audio on speaker."

"I will not allow you to listen in," she snapped. "I know this is a cruel trick. I will play no part in it."

"Al, is the connection live?"

"Yes."

"Harshness, go ahead. Log in and read whatever security update log you guys have. If all they report is a stray dog and a couple rambunctious teens, how's that going to help me or hurt the citadel?"

"Baby steps of incursion," she responded.

"You're making this harder than it has to be," I said in a tired voice. "Al?"

"Sir?"

"Please open the audio from the head cataloguer's private quarters. Put in on speaker."

" ... and then he has the gall to tell me he fancies he's in love with me. Can you believe men?"

"*Enough!*" Harshness shouted. "How dare you violate the sanctum of her blessedness."

"To make a point. If I want juicy intel, I can get it. But that's not what this exercise is about. My sole purpose today is to convince you that you live only in a computer."

"Very well. I grow weary of this game. Computer," she barked, changing her tone, "log in Sister Harshness's open-face account."

"Access denied. Voice recognition insufficient," came the mechanical response.

"How is—"

"You no longer have a voice," I interrupted. "Well, at least not your original one. You'll need to use a passcode."

"Computer, security override *Blessings of Time twelve-twelve-nine.*"

"Access granted. Welcome back Sister H—"

"Silence. Read to me the Daily Sheet from today."

"In what order?"

"Latest reports to oldest."

"07:33, loud noise in Vestibule of—"

"Skip," she snapped.

"06:14, Brother Gagg Noff apprehended in—"

"Skip."

"05:32, Body reported outside Crystal Ex Building. Unit dispatched. Wrapped corpse of female discovered by Sub-Inquisitor Jurris. Tentatively he identifies the body to be that of Chief Inquisitor Harshness, pending full postmortem exam. Of uncertain significance, a paper sheet was on the body, but not affixed to it. The handwritten words *To be or not to be* were inscribed on the paper. A copy of the meaningless sentence forwarded to the encryption section for evaluation. The state of the remains is—"

"Stop," she said feebly.

I was quiet, letting it all sink in. I had no idea how long it would take for her to process this low blow. Turned out it didn't take long at all.

"I ... I can't believe you would do this to another being. What kind of man are you?"

"One who has a mission and needs answers to safely complete it. For what it's worth, I'm as sorry as sorry can be. But it was either torture you the old-fashioned way, which I don't think I could stomach, or not get the info I need. I came up with this method because it was the most humane way I could think of to force you to talk."

"Force me to talk?" she laughed bitterly. "What have I to lose? Nothing, that's what. What pain can you inflict? What privilege can you promise me, a computer algorithm?"

"The best outcome imaginable. You tell me what I need to know and I delete you."

"What?" Her voice quavered.

"You help me and I delete the program that is you. Then you'll be just-plain-dead. That's the deal."

"Surely—" she began, sounding like she was back to defiant again.

"Hang on. What we're going to do now is have a demonstration. I will power down the computer. But it will be on. This interface will be severed. I want you to have a firm understanding of the state you'll exist in if you don't cooperate."

"How lon—"

I hit the switch. I have to say I felt pretty damned shitty. But, I got up and started a fresh pot of coffee. When it was done, I poured a mug and returned to the table. Elapsed time, five minutes. I flipped the computer back on, activating the interface.

"If anyone can hear me, please come and kill me. I'm halfway insane and I'm frightened and I want to die. Please someone—"

"I'm back," I said softly.

"Jon!" she cried out. "Oh, Jon, don't ever do that to me again. I was ... I was so—"

"Easy, easy. Calm down. I'm here. Focus on my voice."

"I hear you."

"So, how long was I gone?"

"I ... I don't know. I don't have any way of knowing."

"Guess."

"A ... one month? No, a year. It had to have been a year."

"You were offline five minutes."

She was quiet a short while. "What do you want to know about the citadel? Ask. I'll tell you everything I know. But you must keep your promise. Never send me to that nothingness again. Whatever hell awaits one such as me is more welcome than where you just sent me."

And I believed her.

I stood at the base of one long-ass spiral staircase. I had set *Stingray* down just outside the Brazen Tower at the Claxeon Citadel. We landed in stealth mode, so I was fairly sure I had not been detected yet. It was early morning, about an hour past dawn. It was not anything vaguely like an ideal time to break-and-enter, but the timeline wasn't mine to dictate. I knew who was up top and I needed to meet-and-greet them, so now was the time. Thankfully I was able to make one stop in between dealing with Sister Harshness and coming here today. I'd gone to Toño's place to pick up the first working model of an easily portable time regulator. Yeah, it was totally cool, about the size of a kid's metal lunchbox, you know, the one's with action heroes on them and a small Thermos bottle? I even asked Doc if he would put the Three Stooges on my unit. You can guess his response.

By the way, how did I find the pair, Toño and Tip? At each other's throats? Kumbaya moment after kumbaya moment? Nope, neither. They were engaged in what psychologists call *parallel play*. Go figure. They were working feverishly at Lord knows what. But while they were adjacent to each other in terms of lab space, neither was influencing the other's behavior. Every nerd for themselves. Weird.

So I had to mount these bitch stairs and I wanted to not be detected. Harshness shared with me all the security protocols and devices. It was doable to get up to the Summit Room unannounced, it just wouldn't be easy. I was in a partial membrane, so no one would see me directly or on a monitor. But I could still make noise. Every single stair tread was wired for pressure, heat, and vibration, so hoofing it up directly was not an option. I could have set *Stingray* down in the room in the first place. But even in stealth mode it would be impossible not to notice a large cube fold into a confined space.

The only sneaky way I could figure was to climb up via the walls and ceilings. Yeah, baby, it was Spidey time! I placed one boot on the central column of the spiral and then attached mooring fibers to the outer wall. I then put my other boot up on the column and started inching upward. It kind of sucked. I mean, I couldn't get tired or anything, but it was te-di-ous. And one slip-up meant I would be outed. Heck, I couldn't even whistle while I worked.

At the top of the spiral, I had to come down. The floor there had sensors, but I was so close no one was likely to react before I got done what I'd come to do. I opened the door as cautiously as I could and quickly stepped into the Summit Room. What—I noticed immediately—a dump. No decoration, no carpet, strictly barren wooden furniture, and the worst sin of all, no snacks. What kind of morning meeting did not provide snacks? A bad one, I'll tell you that as truth. Philistines!

I unshouldered my phase-plasma rifle and approached the table. Sure as Harshness had predicted, there were seven pukes sitting around a circular table. The farther one, an especially creepy one, noticed me first. He tumbled from his chair and rolled under the table. Stop-drop-and-roll.

His action caused everyone else to notice me. No one looked particularly pleased to see me.

"Hi, I'm here about the job opening I heard about, on account of poor Sister Harshness's untimely departure. Are you still holding interviews? Oh, and you under the table, I'm counting to one, then I'm blowing the living crap out of the table. One."

The clown popped up just as I was about to squeeze my trigger.

He was all the way to my side of the table, but he was too far to make an attempt to rush me.

Then he rushed me.

I wanted to shoot him. I felt I owed it to him, in fact, as an object lesson. But I stayed on-script. Instead, I transferred the rifle to my right hand and snatched the jerk up with my fibers. As he kicked silently, I deposited him back in his chair. Then I released him. Fortunately none of the others made a move on me while I was semi-distracted.

"Okay, seriously, I'm not here for the job. In fact, I'm here for pretty much the polar opposite. I'm closing this pathetic sicko-show down for good."

The senior-appearing ass-dancer stood. "I am Head Chief Inquisitor Barren. You are the one who pretended to be Brother Strider."

"Nice to meet you too, Bare," I greeted with a slight nod.

"You are a dead man," he threatened.

"Yes, I am. You're smarter than everyone says you are. Nice."

"No, you fool, I mean your life is forfeit. You will end. It is impossible to thwart the Council of Seven." He swept a hand around the room. "If you kill all seven of us, another council will immediately be assembled in another time. Their first priority will be to kill you."

"Well, we can't have that, can we?"

He didn't respond. He just looked sort of ... bloated. Well, he appeared that way earlier. Maybe more bloated?

"That's why I'm not killing you twit-twats. In fact, I want this particular council meeting to last forever."

"The man speaks nonsense," said the creepy clown who tried to attack me. "Rush him now before he bores us further by speaking."

I aimed at him. "And you would be?"

"Your worst—"

"Do not finish that stupid line. It's vocal lameness."

"I am Rage," he said simply.

"Ah, the psycho. Nice to meet you, psycho. But, as much as I'd love to stay and chat y'all up, I don't have the time. So here's what each party will do." I detached the lunchbox from my belt. I inched toward the table and set it down. Then I backed away slowly.

"You gonna blow us up?" snarked Rage.

"As much as I'd love to, no. What I'm going to do is reach over like this," I extended a single probe fiber, "and hit this button." I did, and everyone at the table froze in place like wax dummies. "You seven, for your part, will be held in this time forever by my time regulator. That's the plan. Any questions?"

I snapped the probe fiber off, because it too was in the effective radius of the time regulator and wasn't coming out.

"If not, I guess this is goodbye." I waved. "And since no one in the Brother-Sisterhood is crazy or brave enough to interrupt a meeting of the Council of Seven, you guys will never be reported as dead or missing and so you'll never be replaced. You are, my friends," I pretended to swipe at a tear, "the last council members *ever*. We are witnessing the passing of yet another of our great institutions. Curse fate for forcing us to live in such sad times."

I shot them a brisk salute, spun on a heel, and got the hell out of Dodge.

CHAPTER FOUR

I folded back to Aramthella straightaway and unannounced. I wasn't in the mood for a welcoming parade. Not after Tank, not after Harshness. Nothing positive or joyful sounded appropriate to me. All I longed for was to sleep for a week. Settling for some time to heal was what I was going to get. I could sleep the day after someone did me a favor and ended my existence.

I went directly to the cabin Sapale'd been assigned while *Stingray* and I were away. The door was ajar, so I pushed it open. Knocking on the frame I called out, "Anybody home?"

"*Jon*," I heard from the bathroom.

"The one and only."

"Close the door and get in here."

Alrighty then, I thought impulsively. She's probably in the tub, which is bubbling over with bubbles, and she's missed me so much, she's calling me ...

No. To my profound disappointment that was not the case. Well, the bath was bubbly, but in an anti-romantic mode. Sapale was washing a goat.

"You're ... you're," I wiggled my finger toward the two of them, "washing a goat."

She beamed up at me. "You so smart."

"Ah, where'd you get a goat? When I left, we didn't own a goat."

"Funny story," she responded with a massive smile.

"There are no funny stories that involve goats, but go on."

"Us girls were talking while you were gone. We were la—"

"*Us* girls?"

"Reva, Emma, Sachiko, and me, of course."

"Course."

"We were lamenting the lack of pets and farm animals."

"Why would anyone lament that?"

"You're pathetic, my sweet love. A perfect dud of a space occupier."

"Thanks."

"And of course there are no Earth pets or farm animals, because there never was an Earth."

"With you so far," I grunted as I squatted down far away from the sudsy action.

"But I remembered these little guys."

"Goats?" I puzzled.

"Well, not exactly goats. She's a *beshwa*."

"Well, I'll be damned. That is a beshwa isn't it?"

Beshwa were the Kaljaxian equivalent of our earthly goat. They evolved completely separately on Kaljax, but we were always impressed with the similarity between the two. It was uncanny.

"So we popped by Kaljax and collected a few dozen of these little beauties." She kissed the dumb thing square on the lips.

"A few dozen? Ah, hon, you recall they start out looking like goats, but they get a little bit bigger. Five *times* bigger than, if I recall correctly."

She grabbed the beshwa under the chin and gently shook its head, all the while gazing lovingly upon it. "Not if you kill them and eat then first."

I pointed. "You know the goat can hear you, right?"

"Of course baby can hear mommy," she cooed directly into its face.

"You are so heartless. Mommy's going to kill and eat baby. Gross."

"You humans. Such a weak race."

"So, you going to ask me how it went?"

"No."

"No?"

"I figure you'll tell me when you're ready."

That was true.

"And plus it's right in the middle of bath time." She kissed the fool thing again. That fried my bacon. The damn goat was getting more action than I was.

"Yes, you are. I'll be back at the ship." I thumbed over a shoulder. "When you come home, be dry and be goatless."

She smiled at the beshwa and kissed it again. "Daddy's in a grouchy mood today, isn't he, baby babe?"

I left. On the way back, my handheld buzzed. It was Sachiko.

"Jon, welcome home," she greeted.

"Good to be home," I responded honestly.

"Problem solved?"

"Problem solved," I replied.

"Do I want to know how?"

"*I* don't want to know how it was done. You really don't want to."

"Gotcha. Not another word. Hey, d'ya hear about the goats?"

"I just met my goat love-child."

"Bambi?"

"Is that her name?"

"Yup. Cute as the dickens, isn't she?"

"If you say so."

"Well I do. When you're ready, let me know and I'll call the senior staff together."

"You got it."

She closed the call. I figured it'd take a day or three of chilling to get the worst aspects of my road trip out of my wheelhouse. I just kept hearing Harshness's last words. *Whatever hell awaits one such as me is more welcome than where you just sent me.* And yours truly was the one who inflicted such an unspeakable experience on a soulless bitch like her. Bad Jon.

I sulked around *Stingray* for another twelve hours before Sapale had quite enough.

"You about over the woe-is-mes?"

"Yeah, I guess."

"Jon, look, you did what you had to and that's all you did. This mission is important. Our goals are good ones. You went to the citadel because they might have had information critical to us. Turns out they actually did. Who knew they also had a psycho police force?"

"Wel—"

"And if you did know, you'd have infiltrated them anyway because we had to. Your time lord friend Tetterwin even recommended them. Come on. You did everything right. They were basically begging to be taken out. Move on," she said with a flare of her hands.

She was correct, of course. But what I'd had to pull with Harshness was close to the nastiest thing I'd ever done to another sentient. Almost. Of course, I'm not counting EJ, my evil twin. What I've done to him is always justifiable because he's such a dick.

"Okay, you're right," I conceded. "I'll let Sachiko know tomorrow that we're ready to begin with the next phase."

"Flyboy, it is tomorrow. 07:15 to be specific. Call her now."

"Now now?"

"Now now," she insisted.

I did and a meeting of the senior staff was set for 09:00. Back in the saddle again. Oh joy.

Sapale and I showed up right on the dot. The others were already there, sipping coffee and chatting pleasantly. It hit me then in both a good and a bad way. The crew was moving on past Tank. While that was natural, mandatory even, it was a purely melancholy milestone.

"Jon, welcome back officially," Sachiko greeted warmly. She stood and crossed over to give me a lean-in hug. You know those.

They're not a wrap-around embrace. No, they're the lean-in-touch-chest-wall-while-holding-elbows form of bastardized hug. Whoever invented them should be shot, in my humble opinion.

"Nice to be officially back," I responded. We all found a seat.

Sachiko asked her steward to bring us some coffee. Yeah, she'd finally given in and appointed a steward. For official functions it was a fairly necessary thing to have. Up until then she'd insisted on being the hostess-with-the-mostest and done such tasks herself. Now she accepted the fact that she had to be a little more captainly. The optics were good for the crew, reinforcing that she was a person of consequence, and it freed up her valuable time.

"Before we begin the central portion of this meeting," Sachiko began, "I'd like to inform all that Jon and I discussed his recent mission. He assures me we are free and clear of any future harassment from the inquisitors of the Brother-Sisterhood of Time."

"Will we have a summary or synopsis in our emails?" Major Tom Grant asked.

"No," was all the captain said on the matter.

A few sets of eyes came up from their screens, but no one pressed the issue. That was good. I didn't feel at all like sharing. I told my wife the entirety of the escapade (leaving out any significant emphasis on the part where Harshness was naked and bound. I left that part hazy). Otherwise no one really needed the gory details.

"Soon," Sachiko began formally, "we can begin the real work we set out to accomplish so long ago. We are in a position now to undertake step one in the resurrection of planet Earth."

There was a round of restrained applause.

"Obviously there still remains the issue of the last clan ship. We need to decide if we're going to commit to finding and eliminating that very real threat first, or if it is wise to proceed with at least part of our core mission. Your thoughts?"

I jumped on that one. "We have to kill our enemy first. There's no ifs, ands, or buts about it."

Sachiko looked slightly indignant. "I called for discussion, Jon, not a decree."

"I know and I'm sorry. But this is a critical point. They can't discover we're trying to reanimate the Earth. If they knew that was so important to us, they might be able to do something to prevent us from being successful."

"How so?" she asked. "They already no-timed it."

"Maybe they could blow up the timeless husk? I don't know. But we can't allow them to know our long-term goal."

Sachiko nodded a few times, thinking. "I agree," she announced resolutely.

"In the for-what-it's-worth category, I agree too," Reva added. "They have to be taken out first."

"Then we have a plan," the captain stated flatly. "Anyone have a good idea how we can find them?"

"The only reliable way we're going to locate them is when they either use a large amount of time energy or they begin large-scale harvesting again," I speculated. "Some time energy event that Aramthella can detect. Failing that, I don't know how we *can* find them."

"Presumably they know those two facts also," Reva observed. "So why would they do either?"

"Because they're not that bright," I replied. "I'm betting they'll get careless, or just plain greedy. Sooner or later their reserve of time energy has to drop. Then the time maker will fall back on its old habits and start assimilating time again."

"Even if it knows full well it'll be like setting off a fireworks display?" Reva challenged.

"I believe so," I said confidently. "They've been stealing time for who knows how long. I don't think they can stop for an appreciable period. It's like an addiction for them."

"Aramthella," called out Sachiko, "what's your opinion?"

"I agree with the general. The time maker is both insane and impulsive. If its time storage was down one percent, it'd obsess about filling that one percent until it accomplished it, without thought to the consequences."

"And if they start routine harvesting, how far off could you detect it?"

"A significant portion of the galaxy would be scannable. Back in the old days, when multiple ships were collecting at the same time, I could see them well from galaxy-scale distances. Farther out than that, say in nearby galaxies, no."

"And you currently see no such activity?" Sachiko confirmed.

"Not recently. But knowing how time makers think, I'm confident it'll start up again soon—soon being measured in weeks, not months."

Sachiko twisted her lips. "Then as much as I hate to say it, I guess we're on hold until we pick up their trail."

"We sit and we wait," I concurred glumly.

"It's not fair," Reva remarked apropos of nothing.

"What's unfair?" the captain asked.

"In zero episodes of *Star Trek* ever produced did they sit around, dead in space, doing nothing for weeks on end. Why can't real life be more like *Star Trek*?"

"Reva, my dear," I responded, "because it can't be too easy. If it was, anyone could do it. Even Patrick Stewart."

"On that off note, I think we're done here," Sachiko mercifully announced.

I leaned over to Sapale. "Heck, if this was easy, even William Shatner could."

"Now you're straining credulity," she very astutely dismissed.

CHAPTER FIVE

Fate. What can be said of it? It appears only to be a serpentine daisy-chain of happenstance. Is it? Who can know? But whatever force or intellect it is gathers dice from across the universe, puts them in a tumbler, and slams them down on the tabletop of reality. Fate is determined to produce less credible, more mind-melting outcomes with each toss. Its results are rarely imagined to be possible unless viewed in retrospect, where they can be verified if not believed. Ah fate, a three-card monte game with the ultimate in high stakes. Watch closely as it determines the futures of so many seemingly unrelated individuals ...

Time Maker-bob was relapsing. If you'll recall, it had become so fearful of the demon from the globular cluster, so vexed with a sense of impending doom, that it'd squirreled itself up in a dark corner of its quarters. It took the bold if suicidal efforts of a crew member to get the time maker to come out and resume its duties. It returned to the bridge, where it learned the level of time energy in storage was frightfully low. So it ordered that the collection of time energy commence again. But the degree to which its precious time energy had decreased never left the foremost position in its tormented brain. Where could it have gone—*really* gone?

Its clan maintained the time energy was used in its immensely justifiable need to flee a mortal threat. And they *claimed* a lot was used to repair the *supposed* damage the speed of the escape had caused. Really, the time maker reflected. How could one damage a time ship by using time energy to power it? Could the breath one drew injure the lungs? Was it possible for a child's love to harm its mother? *Inconceivable!* Clearly the time maker was being lied to. Those whose only function in life was to serve and please it somehow, in a bastardization of proprieties, now saw fit to deceive it. They were stealing its time and wasting it. No. Was it even possible, it dawned on the time maker? Could they be using its own time energy against it? It was, as the time maker stewed on the notion, a credible threat.

Alerted of the need to be wary, the time maker secretly monitored the levels in the Time Storage Unit, or TSU, on an hourly basis. The results, the factual numbers, were undeniable. The TSU was being systematically drained. The level fell constantly. Fifty-nine-point eight percent, to fifty-nine-point seven percent, to fifty-nine point six percent. And all in the matter of days. If ever there was proof of a conspiracy, the time maker surely had unearthed it. It revised its surveillance schedule. Minute-to-minute determinations were the absolute minimal span of time it could now justify. But it mustn't let anyone know it knew, that it had its finger on the pulse of the beast that was their betrayal. No, they might then advance their heinous timeline and do the time maker in all the sooner.

To Time Maker-bob's eternal discredit it never once occurred to it that the TSU levels were dropping because it stood on a functioning, moving machine. Energy was required to execute all the various functions its massive craft required. But the self-deluded are so very easily detached from reality. And stupidity is untouchably irreversible.

Now of course the time maker's ever-increasing mania was evident to the entire crew. That was not surprising. When your lord and master crawls around corridors sniffing around doors, it's hard not to avoid concluding said lord is losing command of its senses. Though the crew couldn't have known, the time maker's advancing tendency to whisper and seemingly converse with some invisible someone rose from a new fixation. Time Maker-bob was struck with the idea that there lurked a very different potential time thief. That twisted force that called himself Nemo! That embodiment of evil from the globular cluster could be aboard. Yes. And it would be so like a demon. Hide. Sip time energy. Watch the time maker bungle around not realizing that it was being played like a toy.

But if this Nemo was hiding somewhere, where might that be? And what could the time maker do by way of defense? The monster had absolutely overpowered the time maker when first they met. Well, the time maker decided, one step at a time. Step one was to document the presence of the ultimate evil. Once proven or disproven, it could move on to issues of remediation. That is why it began having conversations with an imaginary target.

On the serious side, a demon such as Nemo would never be so separated from his sanctuary. And time energy would not sustain one of those abominations. Such was common knowledge amongst everyone who wasn't Time Maker-bob. The tortured logic the time maker employed to justify its random bursts of word usage was this. If the demon heard it speak, and knew it was alone, maybe Nemo would answer, figuring he'd been discovered. Yeah, not lame reasoning. It was JPS—just plain stupid.

Another operative the hand of fate had chosen in this melodrama was one Cleaning Maker of Shiny Object-nop. An unlikely star to be certain. Of all the class of drones assigned to cleaning, shiny object positions were the most undesirable. The clan had no aesthetic taste, no appreciation of a brilliant dazzle. In fact, the category was only created because someone had to keep the glass-like housing of the TSU transparent. If whoever performed the job cared to shine other objects that was of concern to no one.

In any case, the shine maker was concerned for the overall happiness of—and the deteriorating mental health of—the time maker. The entire clan was. But this insignificant wretch was ever-so-slightly different than most clan members. It was burdened by a very small but very real intellect. When not doing their specific jobs, most servants simply stood and stared off into nothingness. A few sat and stared off, and the very rare ones lay down and stared, but the theme of their passing the time was the same. But when the shine maker had spare moments, which was almost always, it thought about stuff. For example, it wondered why all the others stared off into nothingness. It'd tried it, naturally, and found it ... unrewarding. It was drawn to the study of the main computer's vast accumulation of information. It especially liked cultural tidbits. How the cultures the clan had disappeared spent their leisure time fascinated the shine maker, since it was saddled with so much of it. A recurring manner of entertainment across many civilizations, it learned, was a thing called a *play* or a *show*.

It bedazzled the shine maker that persons across time and space would put significant time and energy into staging an activity whose sole purpose was to ease the boredom of a non-working time period. Then, as if a light bulb went on in its dim mind, it had a thought. The time maker was miserable. Maybe a *play* would make it less miserable? The shine maker's love of its master was so limitless that the very idea that it might serve to improve the condition of the boss was intoxicating. This became its obsession, even to the exclusion of polishing the TSU.

The shine maker gathered a few crew members and asked if they'd like to participate in putting on a play for the time maker. Of course they all said they would not. Why stop standing around staring just to stand around doing actions that weren't their jobs? So the shine maker gathered a few other clan members and told them they were ordered by the time maker to participate in a play. Naturally they consented to that. It was a stupid pointless activity, but if their master ordered it, it would be done.

Since it was a regular in the time storage area, the shine maker decided to hold rehearsals there. The space was ample and it was staffed infrequently. So six plucky clan members gathered daily there to ... play make. No one knew how to do so. The shine maker would have them walk around on a small stage. It figured that was a start. It tried talking while the others moved, but the effect didn't wow it. As a result, the six mostly moped around, awaiting the impact of the muse. In retrospect their sin that followed was totally predictable. Six bored drones alone beside the TSU. Hey, one finally decided, why not have a sip of time energy? It was portioned out to them in such a miserly manner, but now they could have a tad more. And a tad quickly became many tads. Pretty soon, they were gorging on time energy. Their frail bodies swelled and their lust only grew. What also happened was that the TSU levels began to plummet.

The time maker watched as the amounts of its precious life force dropped like the public's confidence in politicians after elections. That proved beyond all doubt that Nemo was indeed on board his ship. The demon was readying himself for his final assault. With the staggering amount of time energy Nemo had imbibed, he would be a time juggernaut, completely and utterly unstoppable. He would bend Time Maker-bob to his every wanton whim and diseased desire.

There would be no escape.

There was no safe place.

Time Maker's worst nightmare was about to become its interminable torment.

Salvation!

Yes, the lone path to its salvation leaped into its brain like a jack-in-the-box of insight. There *was* one way to deny ultimate evil.

But the time maker needed to act swiftly.

Time Maker-bob ran to the bridge. It no-timed everyone present without so much as a good day. Then it threw itself on the control panel. It scanned near-space. There! Yes, salvation. The ship was only a million kilometers from a blue-white star—a very hot blue-white star. The time maker vectored the ship directly at the star and slammed the velocity control to maximum. The craft lurched forward. As the acceleration increased, a powerful pseudo-gravity began to slide the time maker away from the controls.

That would never do. Surely Nemo would realize his designs were being thwarted by a superior mind. He would rush to the bridge and seize control. The demon would stop the ship and assume command over the time maker. It fell and clawed its way back to the controls. Time Maker-bob reached them and climbed with a blind fury. When the time maker had mounted them, it drove a fist through the metal and grabbed the sharp edge with all its will. The ship vibrated. Then it trembled. Finally it thundered and rattled, threatening to break up. When a panicked crew member appeared at the entry, the time maker no-timed them without a glance. It was solely focused—hang on. It dared a look up at the viewscreen. It felt exhilaration as it saw that the screen was filled with a painful blue-white radiance.

The time maker held out slim hope.

Thirty seconds later, its hand was sheared by the G-forces and it flew backward, slamming into a bulkhead. But it could see that the blue-white salvation was even brighter.

The time maker allowed itself more hope.

Ten seconds later the last time ship under the control of the once mighty clan knifed through the corona and dived into the photosphere of Rigel.

Seven milliseconds later the vessel and all aboard were amorphously indistinguishable from the rest of the star dust.

CHAPTER SIX

Three long and increasingly boring weeks after our meeting, there was still no sign of the clan ship. Sachiko, Reva, and I checked with Aramthella so frequently I was certain she was going to start rationing our access to her. Now Sapale and I'd had a lot of practice at hurry-up-and-wait in our time. But even that experience didn't make it easier. Stupid bored is stupid bored. The lone highlights of everyone's day were the meals. That was it. All the military types had drilled and redrilled so often it was getting pointless to wash-rinse-repeat that activity. The students who were training for a profession, like doctoring or engineering, were the lucky ones. They had a lot to learn and were eager to do so. Everyone else was just in a holding pattern.

One afternoon that was indistinguishable from any other, Sapale and I decided to go on an adventure. We ate lunch in the ship's mess. We would not settle for our regular routine of staying aboard *Stingray*. Yeah, living on the edge, that was us. The mess was one of the larger rooms available. It was pretty industrial in decor. All the ambience of a bus station. While a comfier look might have been nice, no one seemed to care enough to make any changes. The food was good, the selection varied, so I guess that was enough for most people.

I was having my go-to standard: chili-double cheeseburger with pastrami, tomato, onion, lettuce, and absolutely no pickle, thank you very much. Fries, of course, but the criss-cross kind that hold more of my ketchup/ranch slurry. Seriously, the day I learn I'm dying tomorrow, that's what I'm having for lunch. We'll cover the dinner on another occasion.

Sapale was having a massive salad. Naturally, as a girl, she went to some effort to disguise that fact. She made several discrete refill trips to the synthesizer. Remember that her species evolved as herbivores. Though they'd long since added meat to their diets, there was a special place in their hearts for a grazing-style meal.

"Hey, on your next trip, could you snag me some more ketchup?" I asked politely.

She eyed me dubiously, then subjected my condiments to the same scrutiny. "One, what makes you think I am making another trip? Two, you have nearly a pint of ketchup sitting right there." She pointed with her fork.

"Yes, I do. But by the time you return back from your fourth run, it'll likely be but a fond memory."

"I'm nearly full," she lied.

"Well, let's label my request as an *if* then, shall we?"

"I'm picturing myself with a label gun, but I'm not aiming at your stupid remark, flyboy-who-sleeps-alone."

"What are you so defensive about? It's not like you put dressing on your salads or that you're going to get fat. And nobody's noticed your first two refills except those two boys over there," I gestured with my forehead, "and that's only because you're an alien or maybe they're checking you out, in which case I'll need to break both their—"

Desi burst into the mess, scanned the room frantically, then shot toward our table. I gestured over Sapale's shoulder, alerting her to the soon-to-be-mood-changer. She rotated in her chair to face Desi's approach.

"General Ryan, I'm so glad I found you. I ... I didn't ... I mean—"

I stood and rested a hand on her forearm. "Easy, Desi. Calm down and just say it. What's up?"

"It's Plesmus ... she's ... I don't know—"

"Have you alerted the captain yet?" I quickly pressed.

She looked away, probably wondering why she hadn't. "No ... I came to get you because you know her the best."

"Okay, fine." I looked to Sapale. "My wife'll get ahold of Sachiko while you tell me what's going on."

I tried to move her into a chair, but she stiffened. "No, you have to come with me now."

Sapale stood while she spoke into her handheld. "Desi, tell me what the problem is," I said with some force.

"I was with Plesmus ... in my cabin. You know I'm supposed to spend time with her because maybe that'll help me understand my role in all of this."

"Yes, I know this. What happened?" I felt like a no-anesthesia dentist attempting to extract the story.

"We were talking, nothing important, just, you know, talking about stuff."

"Okay, stuff talking," I parroted as I began leading her in the direction of her cabin.

"She was in the middle of saying something, when suddenly she ... she gurgled." Desi gave me a panicky, confused look. "She gurgles doesn't she?"

"I've not heard her gurgle, but who knows? Go on."

"I asked her if she was alright. That's when she screamed."

"Plesmus screamed?" I asked stunned. "What did she scream?"

"I don't know. It wasn't language, or at least not any I've ever heard."

"Then what'd you do?"

"I fell on my knees, because she was on the floor, and I asked again if she was okay."

"And?"

"And she gurgled again, only it was lower."

"A lower gurgle? That can't be good. So—"

"So I ran out in the hall and thought where could I find you. I came right here. You have to come. I think she needs help."

"We're walking there now, so no worries. Tell me, why didn't you just call me on your handheld instead of going on a random hunt?"

She looked uncertain again. I guess she was freaking out and panicked.

"That's okay," I reassured. "That doesn't matter. All that matters is that you found me and now we're at your cabin."

Sachiko rounded a corner at a full sprint and shouted to a couple of startled crewmen, "Make a path." They sure as hell did. They nearly backed up to opposite walls. She skidded to a stop next to us just outside Desi's closed door. "Do we know what happened yet?" she pressed.

"No, we're just going in," I said as Desi thumbed the ID pad.

The door slid open and I shot in. Plesmus was on the deck, which was her preferred place. She hated chairs and other raised surfaces. I dropped to my knees. "Plesmus, it's Jon. Plesmus, can you hear me?"

There was that low gurgle Desi mentioned. It was new to me. "Plesmus, come on, what's the matter?"

Sachiko and Sapale leaned in closely. Desi stayed near the door.

"J ... Jo ... nn—" Plesmus gurgled. I took that to represent an improvement over nonsense gurgling.

"Yes, it's me. Can I help you?"

"No—"

"No what? I can't help?" I was starting to freak a bit myself. Not only did I actually like Plesmus, but we absolutely needed her to be well and functioning normally.

"No one can help the ... the dead—"

"What dead? Who's dead?"

"The focus is dead."

"The focus? What the hell focus? A telescope? But that can't—" I rambled.

"Jon," Sachiko clarified, "I think she is referring to a ship's focus, a necumplack like Plesmus. Her species. They focus time energy."

"Ah, gotcha. I knew that."

"I'm better," Plesmus announced suddenly.

"I don't know as I believe you," I offered cautiously. "You're still kind of Jell-O-shaking."

"That will pass," she said sounding almost back to normal.

"Okay. Good to hear. So, what happened? What focus is dead?"

"The last clan ship's."

"Huh?"

"You know what happened on the time maker's ship?" Sachiko questioned intently.

"I do."

"You ... if you can know what's going on there, why haven't you told me so before?" Sachiko was sounding a tad pissed.

"No, I can't. Only this once."

"Why this once?" Sachiko followed up forcefully.

"Because I know when another focus dies. This we can all feel."

"What happened to the other focus?" I asked. "Did she just die or was she killed?"

"She was murdered. She died in horror and terror."

"Did the time maker ... did it kill her?" I asked not believing my own words.

"Yes," was all she said.

"But that's crazy. It needs her like we need you. It can't just—"

"Time Maker-bob flew their ship into a star," she stated stoically.

"What?" I protested. "That's crazy talk. Why would the time maker intentionally plow its ship into a star?"

She was quiet a spell before answering. "I do not know *why* it did it. I only know *that* it did it. The dying focus screamed those thoughts to me as she vaporized."

This was unbelievable. Not credible. What possible reason— "Wait, maybe this is a trick," I shouted. "The time maker, maybe it forced her to announce that they were all dead so we'd stop hunting them down?"

"If it tried to make her she would not have allowed it."

"Can you be one-hundred percent certain of that?" Sachiko queried. "Our lives depend on how positive you can be."

"I believe her. She is dead. She died in agony, in confused anguish. She died as the ship burned up."

"So you know this focus pretty well?" I asked. "Well enough to have us believe this unbelievable turn of events?"

"I know her intimately. She was me."

I looked to Sachiko. She shrugged. I gazed at Sapale. She shrugged and angled her head.

"How could she be you?" I questioned fully confused. "You are you."

"You know I can partition myself, right?"

"Yeah, sure."

"Once, long ago, I was asked to partition a piece off to be the focus for that time ship."

"I thought all the ships had different focuses?" I asked. "Not sure why I assumed that, but I did."

"Many did. But some used known focuses. I was never certain of the reasoning employed, but I used to live on four different time vessels also."

Wow. This was a wow-moment for the ages. Plesmus was living simultaneously on five ships, and the time maker just deep-sixed its craft in a star. Could that have happened?

"Plesmus, are you well enough for me to have Desi take you back to your area?" Sachiko asked.

"Yes, Captain. I am fine."

Sachiko turned to Desi who had remained by the door the entire time. "Please carry Plesmus back to her storage space. Please stay with her a while. If you're convinced she's fine, you may leave her. Is that understood?"

"Yes, ma'am," Desi said with a bow of her head. She walked around us, retrieved Plesmus, and left without another word.

"My stateroom, now," Sachiko announced. "I'll alert Reva and the others."

Five minutes later a very rattled-looking senior staff sat around the table in the captain's stateroom. Sachiko gave the others a full rundown of what had happened. Every one of them was as shocked as we were.

"So that's where we stand," Sachiko concluded. "There exists a strong possibility, but no certainty, that the time maker is dead and its ship is destroyed."

"And worse yet," Sapale added, "there's absolutely no way to prove one way or the other. If the ship's toasted subatomic particles, we can never document that. But if Plesmus just had a really shitty nightmare, the ship can be out there, us never knowing unless they expose their existence. I hate the position we're in."

"I'm not too crazy about it either," I agreed. "Aramthella, a hypothetical. If the ship did crash-and-burn in a star's interior, would the flare of the released time energy be detectable?"

"That's a difficult question to answer," she admitted. "I certainly detected no signature event during the time period Plesmus would have us believe the ship was destroyed. On the other hand, there are no previous similar events to establish what might be observed. My suspicion is that the heat, magnetism, and utter chaos of a stellar interior would easily mask a time energy burst of the magnitude we're discussing presently."

"No rest for the weary," Reva breathed out heavily.

"Yes," Sachiko reflected thoughtfully, "it appears we will not be catching a break in this dilemma."

"So," I said as I raised my arms and arched my back in a stretch, "what do we do? What *do* we do?"

"This is the biggest decision we've faced. If we guess incorrectly our ultimate goal may never be achieved," Sachiko stated. "Here's what we'll do. We will meet back here tomorrow, same time. Everyone will have twenty-four hours to noodle through the situation. Maybe someone will come up with an insight that can resolve our indecision. I will call Dr. DeJesus. If anyone can think of a scientific manner to prove the case one way or the other, it will be Toño."

"Sounds like a plan," I seconded.

As Sapale and I hoofed it back to our ship, we kicked around some ideas.

"Maybe we should go to the star Plesmus thinks the ship self-destructed in?" I posed.

"She didn't say which star," she pointed out.

"Maybe if we press her, she'll be able to give us more details?"

"It wouldn't hurt to ask, but what do you think we'd find even if we located the right star?"

I sighed deeply. "Who knows? Maybe debris? At the very least an exhaust trail."

"Debris is a long shot. Anything that fell off the ship as it went critical would either be pulled down by gravity or blown back into space by the stellar wind. And, Jon, these ships don't leave exhaust. They burn pure time."

"Oh, yeah, good point. Still, let's stop by Plesmus's closet and see if she can tell us any more."

"I've got nothing but time," she replied with a cute wink of her right eyes.

Sure enough, Plesmus was tucked up in her favorite corner, doing that wriggly walking-like motion she generally did when so positioned. Desi, bless her heart, was still sitting on the floor watching over Plesmus. She'd stayed the entire time we were meeting.

"How's she doing?" Sapale asked in a hushed tone as we joined the other two on the floor.

"Fine, I think. We chatted a bit, then she curled up like that. Maybe she's sleeping?"

"I'm not sleeping. With three humans lurking nearby, my predator/prey instincts won't allow it," Plesmus announced.

"Perfect," I beamed, "because we're here to ask a few questions. Awake makes it easier."

"The answers are no and yes. Will you leave now so I can actually rest?"

"Ah, a tad grouchy today, he asked in a leading manner?" I posed to her.

"I just went through an experience you could never understand. While I'll admit some small portion of the time you are tolerable, Jon Ryan, now is not among those times."

"Yup, she's a grouch-mobile," I concluded.

"We were going to ask if you knew any specifics about where the star is located, the one the time maker's ship flew into," Sapale asked, having tired of me being me.

"That question would be the *no* response's owner," Plesmus responded.

"Are you doing the mind link thing?" I enquired.

"What mind link thing?" she replied impatiently.

"I don't know, but maybe you can do one."

"I wish I had a can of insect spray," she returned. Most odd.

"Ah, I'm pretty sure we don't have any. Why do you wish you had some?"

"So I could spray you with it."

"Ah. Sorry."

"And the *yes* response was to your question of whether I was absolutely certain I was aboard the time maker's ship and that it did crash into a star." She rolled over so what was usually her bottom side faced the deck. One end of her directed itself at me. "I realize that what I claim is very risky to accept at face value, given the stakes you humans face. But I can tell you with absolute certainty that your last enemy is no longer a threat."

"Wouldn't *that* be nice?" I said more to myself.

Sapale pushed my shoulder. Hey, it was better than her usual slug, so I was pleased. "What? She just said what she said. What'd you mean by that crack?"

"Wouldn't it be nice if our last enemy deep fried himself?"

She thought a second, then grinned. "An enemy-free future. Yeah, I'd vote for that."

"Is your little performance about over?" Plesmus pressed. "I want to rest."

"Yes, it is," I replied. "And, Plesmus, I'm sorry the other you had to die so horribly. I'm just glad we still have you here. You are a great comfort and a great friend."

Sapale had a look like I just whipped out my tongue and bull-frogged a fly midair.

"Thank you," Plesmus replied. "That means a lot to me, my friend."

"Now you rest. We'll leave you in peace, but please let us know if we can help, okay?" I concluded.

I signaled to Desi to get up, and the three of us slipped out quietly.

"She'll be fine," I reassured Desi. "Thanks for staying with her. She may bark and snap, but down deep I know she appreciates your concern."

"Thanks, General," she replied sheepishly.

"Des," I invited, contracting her name, you know, the way I love to, "I'm *Jon*." I pointed to my wife. "She's *Sapale*. We're teammates, right? Fighting the good fight."

"Yes, we are, Jon." she responded with a faint grin.

"And just so you know, honey," Sapale added, holding my elbow so she could lean around me, "he's not flirting with you with that invite."

"Ah, gee, I didn't think he actually *was*," Desi responded uncertainly.

"Most everything that comes out of his mouth that's directed toward a female—any species, mind you—is flirting. But he's not flirting now, because, if he was, I'd kill him where he stands. So, no worries, okay? The gross old man is just being *friendly*."

With that she fully hooked my arm and pulled me down the corridor. Desi stood there looking mightily confused.

"Gross old man?" I challenged my forever mate.

"Trust me, that's how she's sees you."

"If that's the case, why'd you need to tell her if she already knew?"

"So *you* knew it, sweetheart," she replied as she patted me on the forearm.

CHAPTER SEVEN

The next day we all reassembled in the captain's stateroom. Scanning the room, I got the distinct impression none of the still-human humans got much sleep. With the weight of the world on them, who could blame them? The seven present were Sachiko, Reva, Tom Grant, Emma Walters, Sapale, and me. Swathi Varma was there too. She'd been Reva's aide-de-camp since the Mars 1 days. Normally a lieutenant wouldn't be attending a meeting of the senior staff. But with the thinness of the officer pool, she was added in discretely to fill Tank's, uh, vacancy. She was young and she was bright, so I was much in favor of having her in the mix. I had to suppress a smile when I looked at her, however. With this being only her second meeting and with the added pressure of the decision we needed to make, she really looked frayed. Poor kid. Growing up in a crisis was never easy.

"Good morning, everyone," Sachiko began. "First I want to thank everyone for what had to be a burdensome day of reflection. Know that whatever we decide on will be based on the information we have. If we make what turns out to be a poor choice, know that we all tried our level best. No one will be blamed and no one's opinions will mark them in the future.

"I did have a long conversation with Dr. DeJesus. The bottom line is that he's stumped too. He couldn't suggest a way to prove or disprove that the time maker flew its ship into a star. I could tell his inability to help us in any tangible way upset him greatly."

"He's tough," I interjected. "I've upset him for a very long time, trust me on this. He always bounces back."

There were a few polite chuckles.

"Thank you. That does ease my conscience a little," she responded. "First, I'll tell you what I've concluded. We cannot know independently of Plesmus's report what the status of the time maker's ship is. To me that suggests caution is the wisest course."

"What's caution?" Sapale asked.

"We wait. There's no harm in waiting to see if the time maker resurfaces. After all, there's no rush to reanimate the Earth, other than our burning desire to do so, of course."

"Maybe we could evaluate some potentially habitable worlds while we wait?" Reva suggested. "That way, if we never succeed with the Earth, we'll be that much ahead on a fallback plan."

"That would beat sitting idle in space, getting more and more bored," Tom opined.

Naturally, that's when all eyes drifted to me. Yeah, they wanted to hear what General Big Mouth had to say.

"Sapale and I stopped by to chat with Plesmus after we broke up yesterday. We wanted to know if she had any idea what star the time maker suicided into. If not, maybe she knew what direction the signal came to her from."

"And?" Sachiko asked with clear anticipation.

"She couldn't help. She said she knew what she knew, but that was all she knew." I looked to Sapale.

"But she told us with no doubt in her mind whatsoever that the ship was in fact gone," Sapale reinforced passionately. "She was absolutely and positively certain."

"And you believe her?" Sachiko pressed in a forceful tone. It almost felt like she was calling us out.

"It's not that," I responded. "It's that I *trust* her. Her certainty is my certainty. I say we put the clan behind us and get down to the core mission we set out to complete."

"I'm with him," Sapale voted as she shook a thumb in my direction.

"First let me remind everyone that this is not a democracy. That said, how do you all vote?" Sachiko requested in a formal voice.

"I say we give it some time, wait at least a little," proclaimed Reva.

"I second that," Swathi chimed in softly.

"My vote is I'm glad my vote doesn't count," announced Tom.

Again, there were a couple of giggles.

"But, gun to my head, I say we move on, get this thing done."

Emma was the last one left. "I really don't see a problem in waiting a little longer. If there are no signs of the time maker, then we can proceed with peace of mind."

"Thank you all," Sachiko said tightly. I could tell the pressure of being in command was pressing down on her. I was the overall mission commander, but as the ship's captain, she could technically try to keep her vessel out of any plan she didn't like. I doubted she would attempt such an act, but I really wanted her to buy into my position.

"As of today, the sole mission of this crew and this ship is the resurrection of our home world." Sachiko's voice was calm and determined. There was no waffling in her head. "To that end, we need to establish a firm plan, delegate aspects of the mission, and begin to coordinate with all the technical help we will absolutely require, our ship's engineers and other scientists."

"Hot damn," I affirmed.

Sapale was torn. I could tell she wanted to punch me for that childish outburst. On the other hand, I knew she wanted to roll her eyes. She couldn't very well do both, right? Ya can't look away and ... Ouch. Apparently one can punch while not looking directly at one's intended target—it must be all that much easier when you have more than two eyes.

"On the surface, the first part of our mission seems

straightforward," Sachiko began with a complete change in her tone and demeanor. Gone was the tense captain. Now she was relaxed and even maybe excited. Why not be? She was going to get to do sciency-nerd stuff again. "But Jon tells us he was warned that neither part, the moving of dead Earth nor the reinfusing it with time, would be easy." She scanned the room. "I want to say from the start that I am fully confident we will move the remnants to where they need to be. There is no doubt in my mind."

Okay, that drew a real round of applause. Right on, Captain!

"I will be working closely with the scientists and engineers we rescued from Mars 1 in terms of the physics and mechanics needed. We have at our disposal the combined pulling power of Aramthella and *Blessing*. With such power, there's nothing we can't move. Once the planetoid is in place, we will begin the harder part, the reanimation of the planet itself. Dr. DeJesus and many others are modeling the necessary interventions even now. Hopefully by the time we have the mass relocated, a detailed plan as to how to resuscitate Earth will be available. Are there any questions?"

"Jon brought back the information that a no-timed planetary mass would not be easy to move," Reva began. "Do we know any of the specifics as to why such a seeming simple procedure could be so difficult?"

Sachiko sighed once. "No. Our sources were not able to make that issue clear."

"Who was or were our sources on that?" queried Tom.

"Need-to-know, Tom," was Sachiko's terse response. The four people who knew the answer decided to keep that to ourselves—we received the information from a reunited Time, of course. We did not wish to give the impression that we were complete lunatics. "Any others? If not, I'll ask Jon to discuss the first and most obvious attempt we plan to make. Jon?" She tipped a hand toward me.

"Both the ships are equipped with large membrane generators. While what's left of Earth is too big to throw a membrane around, there's no reason a membrane couldn't be placed around a large outcropping or even placed like a bite into the rocky surface."

"Do we know it to be rocky?" Emma asked.

"No. That's just conjecture on my part. We'll find out for certain as soon as we get there."

She nodded.

"Given the mass numbers from the remnant's gravitational effects on bodies it passes, we've estimated that even one ship pulling at one-quarter maximum output should easily move the Earth at a good clip."

"How far has it moved?" Reva questioned.

"Not terribly far, in relative terms. It's presently three-and-a-half astronomical units from where it was. One AU is the distance from the Sun to the Earth, past tense. About ninety million miles or one-hundred-fifty million klicks."

"So, best case, how long might it take to drag it back to where we want it?" she asked.

"Keeping safety job one, maybe a month," I replied.

"And it'll stay where we set it?" Tom queried.

"No, but we can keep sliding it back as often as we need to," I reassured.

Tom smiled and shrugged. "This sounds like it'll be a breeze."

"I know," I responded glumly. "That's why I'm worried. If a thing appears to be too easy, then it usually isn't."

"Well, the good news is that we'll find out very soon," Sachiko piped in cheerily. "Today we will run a series of inspections and go over some checklists, but, if everything's shipshape, we will be there tomorrow."

Yes, I thought to myself, we wouldn't want to move a spaceship without inspections and checklists. To do otherwise would be sheer folly. Sachiko was getting a little too into her role as the ship's administrator.

"And Reva, as our military commander, do you have anything to add?" Sachiko asked as she tiptoed across eggshells. I'm sure she knew Reva—the Army woman Reva—wouldn't have any input at this juncture. Sachiko just wanted to get past that eight-hundred-pound gorilla-in-the-room issue. She'd replaced Tank only recently.

"No. Thanks. Nothing," Reva responded with no emotion.

"In that case, I think we're done here. Jon, would you and Sapale mind staying for a few minutes?"

"Not at all, skipper," I replied. I'd always wanted to call her skipper. I imagined she'd cringe upon hearing it. I actually couldn't read her reaction when the moment came and went. Crap.

Once the room was clear, Sachiko sat back down and sipped her tea. She rested the cup on its saucer. "I assume you've discussed the specifics of your mission to the citadel with your wife?" she addressed to me.

"I have indeed," I answered poker-faced.

Sachiko nodded a bit nervously.

"Is there anything additional you think I might need to know about the operation?"

I pointed between my wife and myself. "You asking me or her?"

Sachiko gave me a thin grin. "That depends on whichever of you cares to share the most information with this captain, now, doesn't it?"

I wagged a finger at her. "Nicely played."

"No, I don't think there is," Sapale said formally. "In time, I think Jon will be able to be more forthcoming. But for now I personally consider the matter closed."

"That's good enough for me. Along a separate line, I've spoken to Toño a lot on the subject of moving the planetoid. The good news I've gleaned is that he and Tip seem to be getting on well enough." She harrumphed once. "At least he hasn't actually killed Tip yet."

"Yet," I emphasized.

"And you're okay with me communicating with Toño that often?" she slipped in ever so deftly. It reminded me of when the bullfighter slips that thin sword into the bull's back.

Sapale's eyes shot open and she looked around like she just startled awake. "Jon, what'd you do this time? And no bullshit. I want the truth or so help me—"

"What?" I defended. "I have almost no idea what the captain refers to."

"Sachiko, what'd he say or do?" my brood's-mate angrily pressed. She got a really pissed look on her face. "He didn't show you the card trick where he slips one down your blouse, did he?" She looked at me in a way ... wow. Strong woman.

"Well, just before we came under attack from the inquisitor, he did make some remark that Dr. DeJesus was, and I'm quoting here, *He's kind of old for you, isn't he?*"

First came the tiny hop in her chair. Then the steam coming out her ears. Then my wife turned to me and punched me ever-so-hard in the nearest shoulder. I'm sure the sound was heard down the passageway in spite of the door being closed. Then the finger— always with the finger—under my nose. "You're sure as hell not doing it again," she thundered.

"I'm not doing what, 'cause I'm not doing anything again?"

"Yes, you are, you under-devolved ape. You're meddle-suming. Worst of all, *your* meddle-suming is the worst kind of meddling. Stop it, stop it, stop it."

I think she wanted me to stop it.

"Meddle-suming?" Sachiko was forced to ask.

"Yes," Sapale seethed. "It's where this halfwit first *assumes* something beyond logic. Then he never checks out the veracity of his assumptions. No, he just acts on them and *meddles*. He meddle-sumes."

"Shouldn't that be assume-meddles?" I asked confused.

"No." She flicked my ear. "That version has no pizzazz, no allure." She turned to Sachiko. "When it comes to killing and spitting and beer," she pointed sideway at me, "he's your man. But when it comes to anything to do with personal interactions, you really have to force yourself to ignore him. He's not just clueless. He's *blindly* clueless." Sapale did that thing where her open palms exploded forward from her face.

"Thank you," Sachiko said genuinely. "I feel much better now."

I started to quip *what*, but Sapale, bless her alien heart, sensed it and made with the finger again. I fell into a wounded silence.

"Really, call me any time, day, night, it doesn't matter. If it happened once, it's bound to happen a *dozen* times," Sapale piled-on. "He just doesn't get it."

Again I started to defend myself, but I realized such a thing wasn't possible.

"Why, did you know this sorry excuse for a spouse had a beautiful young woman bound up and naked aboard his cube during his mission to the citadel and he somehow forgot to *mention* that to me?"

Sachiko sure looked to be shocked. "*No*," she gasped.

"I'll send you the recording. It's unbelievable." Sapale amplified her tale by placing her arms at her side and pretending she couldn't move them.

When I saw that Al, he was going to wish he'd never been programmed.

I think their chattering went on for a while. I couldn't say because I literally tuned them out. Finally Sapale knocked on the top of my head and we left.

All I had was one word: Women.

'Nuff said.

CHAPTER EIGHT

Biggest surprise of the month: The ship cleared all her checklists. Imagine that? Why, there was positively nothing left to do but get down to business. We needed to travel to what remained of Earth and move the puppy back where she belonged. Easy-peasy add the cheesy.

Reva, Sapale, Tom, and Emma were huddled up on the bridge waiting for Sachiko to order our departure. Hey, this was a big moment. I was aboard *Stingray*, all by my lonesome, since I had to physically be there to fold us where we needed to go. But I got to watch the whole event. The captain had agreed to broadcast the event ship-wide. It was an actual holiday. Those, by the way, pretty much fell by the wayside since we left Mars. Yes, Christmas was still observed, but it was quite secular and very watered down. Gifts were discouraged because any you wanted to give you had to make yourself. Yeah, who wants one of *those* gifts for Christmas? No one, that's who. I think everyone sort of subliminally agreed to leave Earth's holidays in the past. The memories were just too painful.

"Aramthella," Sachiko asked like she was the star in a Hollywood blockbuster, "are all systems GO?"

"Yes, Captain. We could not be more ready to shove off."

"General Ryan, do you stand ready?" she called out.

I thought of a million and a half wiseass comebacks, but I put a cork in myself. This was important and Sachiko wanted a good show. So, I behaved. Barely.

"Yes, ready when you are," I dully responded.

"Very well, transport us to the remnants of planet Earth, one million kilometers away along her Z-axis."

I slapped my probe fibers on the deck. "You heard the lady, *Blessing*. Make the magic happen."

"Yes, Form One."

Slight nausea.

"We are at the specified coordinates, Captain. All systems nominal. I have scanned the surrounding space and identify no threats or hazards, " Al announced like a wannabe-Shakespearian actor. Yeah, that bucket of bolts could really ham it up when the cameras were rolling.

"Thank you, General Ryan. I'll assume the helm again," Sachiko said unnecessarily. I mean, *duh*, we're there. Again, I kept my oh-so-witty thoughts to myself.

"Your orders. Captain?" requested Aramthella.

"Take us to within ten thousand kilometers of the pole, half speed ahead."

"Yes, sir. We are underway."

I was thinking that this much excitement was probably dangerous for an android of my age. I maybe needed to break away for some warm milk and a nap.

"Alright, bridge crew," Sachiko said in an overly formal tone. "Thank you for your excellent work. Scanning officers stay alert and collect all the data you can about the planet's surface. If you detect anything unusual, let me know at once. Otherwise, everyone else assume your usual duties. Backup personnel are dismissed." She turned to the camera. "Thank you all for helping make this auspicious moment all the more special."

And the live feed was cut. Sapale told me later that Sachiko basically collapsed into her chair at that point and drew several deep breaths. "Let's not do this again," were the first words out of her mouth. I guess she wasn't showbiz material.

We'd decided to enter normal space quite a ways away from the planet. That way we could take a long look at the sitrep and make certain there weren't any potential threats. We didn't suspect there would be, but it was better to lean toward caution rather than give in to showboating. Those were Sachiko's exact words, by-the-by. You have to know how much they overlapped with my own worldview.

"Hey, Als, you guys seeing anything on the planet?"

"Not much," Al replied. "It is rotating slowly, and proceeding at one hundred thirty-five hundred kilometers per hour. The surface is mostly flat with a few craters and small hills. The elevations look to be rubble and not solid rises. Otherwise not much to report from this distance."

"Fine. Keep me posted."

I had to remain in the vortex in case we needed to blast away because of some serious problem. Hopefully Sapale'd mosey on back to keep me company since the epic event on the bridge was over. It looked like our approach was going to be real uneventful. That was the moment Toño unexpectedly popped into my head. Recall he'd installed head-to-head direct links for us android right from the start.

So, Jon, I see you've made the journey to Earth.

Doc, I replied with ebullient surprise, *good to hear from you. How are you?*

Just fine. I'm just finishing sectioning Tip into little pieces so I might feed them to my pet.

Wait a sec. You don't have a pet.

Then I'll have to get one. Otherwise these meat cubes will go to waste.

You're too much, Doc. Seriously, you two still copacetic?

Yes, as well as anyone can be with that young man. I thought I was an outlier when it came to my interpersonal skill set. But Tip takes the Olympic Gold in that competition.

Well good to hear he's still in one piece. So, to what do I owe the honor of this call?

I will be frank. I'm worried what you would find on the remnants of Earth.

Worried? Seriously? So far all we see is barren wastelands. I mean, the place was time trashed. What could be down there to worry about?

I am uncertain. But as you know I've studied time a lot over the years. A body that has been no-timed is as unnatural a creation as there can be.

You're sounding kind of new-age cryptic there, Doc. You trying to scare me?

No, I wish to warn you.

In plain-old, Doc, what could be dangerous?

Maybe I worry too much. But I know that a body without time cannot remain so. Time will, for lack of a better term, leach back into it.

Okay. That's interesting, but it doesn't sound like it could hurt us.

It's not the re-timing itself that's an issue. I worry what an area undergoing that process might be like. There could exist in that domain many dangers.

Name one.

I cannot. But it is possible that certain laws of physics will waver. The passage of time—time as experienced by you—will not proceed in an orderly, linear manner.

Why wouldn't it?

Because of the time flux into the mass you stand upon.

But this is all just theoretical, right? You don't know that there will be specific issues?

I do not, but I have run many simulations. Many results of those models concern me quite a bit.

So you're saying we shouldn't try to move the planet?

I'm saying you possibly shouldn't approach *the planet.*

If we don't, how're we gonna move it?

You aren't. That's my point.

But we have to.

No you do not. You want *to relocate it. Those are two separate actions.*

But Time told me we couldn't reanimate the Earth if I didn't move it first.

And Time also told you that your chances of success were somewhere south of slim.

What are you saying?

That perhaps your desire to restore the solar system to what it was is unwise.

But, Doc, billions of people vanished. The ecosystem too. If we can make it all good again, we have to. You know that.

I am sorry but I do not know that. I'm suggesting that the preservation of what little sliver of humankind that does exist should not be jeopardized on a project with unknown dangers and little likelihood of achieving your goals.

Ah, isn't it a little eleventh hour of you to mention this now? We're here.

I wanted to wait until you'd actually committed to the mission before I spoke up.

But why? Oh, wait. Because maybe we would never get around to making the attempt in the first place. So why try and warn us off if we might never place ourselves in harm's way?

Exactly.

I'm still not sure you're helping.

I am in the manner I see best. I am sorry if my opinions are a burden. But I have passed them along and cannot retract them.

Wouldn't want you to. It's just, I'm not sure what to do with this 4-1-1.

You should discuss it with the others.

And freak them out too?

Some of them, yes. You will not blindside the captain.

I had to roll that around in my head a second. *Because you've already discussed this with Sachiko?*

Yes.

Why didn't one of you tell me?

One of us just did.

I meant earlier.

Because I asked her to refrain from discussing the topic until I'd clued you in.

Oh, crapadilly. Well, I guess I better go speak with Sachiko. Time's a wasting.

Bring Sapale and Reva into the conversation. That is my suggestion.

You bet. So, should I let you know what we decide?

That will not be necessary.

Because Sachiko will.

Yes, in spite of me being so much older than her, we will risk communicating.

You heard about that little slip of the tongue.

I heard of it, though I'm not so certain of the slipping part.

Hey, you know I'd love to talk this through with you, but I need to maybe avert a disaster, so, I'll catch you later. K?

Goodbye, he said like he meant it, and he disconnected.

Sapale, I addressed her head-to-head, *please collect Sachiko and Reva and come to the vortex as soon as you can.*

Sure. What's up?

Hopefully nothing, but maybe everything.

Sounds SNAFU.

It is. As SNAFU as it gets.

Quicker than I thought they'd be, the three women were sitting in the mess aboard *Stingray.* Sapale and Reva had looks of worried concern. Sachiko's expression was more like doom incarnate.

"So you want to, or me?" I asked the captain pointblank.

"Which version would you prefer?" she countered.

"The version where I wasn't kept in the dark until way too late."

"Duly noted," she said tightly.

"What the hell's this about?" Sapale demanded. She pointed behind herself. "We're on final approach to what's left of Earth and you two are in some mental pissing contest. Stop it."

That was an image I'd never pictured. Kind of gross there, wife of mine.

"I just got a call from Toño. He's very worried that there might be real danger involved in even going to Earth, let alone attempting to reanimate it," I began brusquely. I gestured toward Sachiko. "She and he have been discussing the matter for who knows how long, but they kept me out of the loop. Anyway, he says he ran models and feels the risk of interacting with a no-timed object the size of Earth is more dangerous than it's worth. He advises we take our little gene pool and have it swim around somewhere we know is safe."

"That is essentially correct," Sachiko said very firmly. "I would like to clarify one thing. It was Toño's idea one hundred percent to not bring you in on the discussion, Jon. I was against his position. But, he was able to convince me I should honor his request to keep the discussion only between the two of us. And before you ask, I'll tell you what his reasoning was. One, we might never make it to Earth to try anything, so why stress everyone out concerning the relative risks involved. Remember there was the clan ship and the citadel assassins hunting us. Coming here was never a certainty.

"Two, we were working on the theories right up until the last moment. We weren't certain about our conclusions. Hell, we still aren't. But we felt we couldn't remain silent any longer. Three, keep in mind that there were only Toño, Tip, and myself who were qualified to do the physics necessary to analyze the risk. We didn't need the input of anyone else. Tank, if he'd still been with us, sure. But otherwise we were the only ones in the need-to-know category."

I was about to rip into her for letting Tip in but not me—grrr—but I let it go. Right now we just needed a clear plan.

"Okay, what'll it be?" I said as calmly as I could, which wasn't very. "We going to abort on the plan to bring back our home, our people, and our planet or are we going through with the mission that brought us to this point?"

Everyone was still and silent. I do believe Sachiko and Reva held their breaths as good long while.

"Earth is not my home," Sapale began. "Humans are not my species. So it would be fair to say I have no dog in this fight. But I want to make it clear that I do. The clan ripped through this galaxy and vaporized countless worlds and innumerable souls. They did incredible evil. If there's a chance to reverse any of that wrong, I say we're morally bound to reverse it. As a citizen of the Milky Way, I'm willing to do anything to bring the Earth back."

That's my girl. Short, sweet, and to the point.

"Reva," Sachiko asked tersely, "what do you think?"

She covered her face with her palms and shook her head. "I know I'm the military commander now, but as God is my witness, I have no idea what we should do." She took a few deep breaths, then removed her hands. "The science is way beyond my ability to understand. This is a case for a boots-on-the-ground grunt like me to follow the recommendations of the scientists I trust."

"Very well," Sachiko accepted. She turned to me, straightened her back, squared her shoulders and stood her ground. "My vote is that we wait. Let us work through the numbers. It shouldn't take long, maybe a few weeks. Then, if the models are convincing one-way-or-the-other, we can act more prudently."

I flopped an arm over the back of my chair, and leaned back. My other hand rubbed the side of my nose. "I say we proceed with all due haste, just as we've been doing."

I let that sink in a bit, mostly with the captain.

"Because, here's the dealio. If you analyze the crap out of the situation and decide it's safe after all, we just wasted several weeks. If, on the other hand, you demonstrate convincingly that there is a significant risk, I'll still say we go for it and fix time. Again, we will have wasted a few weeks. The problem with wasting time is simple. The longer you wait around with your hands on your butt, the more likely it is that trouble will find you. That's been proven to me time and again."

"Jon," Sachiko began with obvious emotion, "I hear you and I don't disagree. But I believe we can find a safe planet and repopulate our species, just like you and Sapale did with Azsuram. That's a sure bet. If we bungle the reanimation and this ship and her crew are lost, it's all over for humankind."

"Yes, it is possible to establish a new home world like we did," I responded. "But I wish to remind you we only just did. Every piece of non-suck-ass-hostile real estate in this galaxy is coveted by someone. Usually lots of someones. The chances of growing a few hundred individuals into a sustainable population on a new world are really slim. So I'm not just weighing the chances of hidden danger here versus a more conservative plan-of-action that says we bail on this attempt. I'm taking into account just how damn hostile this galaxy is, just how vicious the fight is for every habitable grain of sand. I don't just think we should proceed as planned, I insist we do."

As I was the overall mission commander, that should have sealed the discussion. But I was also a man very much out of time. There was aboard the ship two very ancient androids, one alien, and several hundred humans with a shared past. If they rebelled, I wouldn't have any recourse. I'd have to bow out. There was no court of higher appeal and no chain of command aside from the one sitting in this stateroom.

Sachiko sat fidgeting and grinding her teeth for a minute. She never took her eyes off me. I had to admire her for that. She had learned to be a strong woman, one who feared no one. That was a wonder to observe. Tank was gone. Sapale and I weren't going to be around forever. If the resurrection of Earth failed—and it had a hell of a good chance of doing just that—this troop needed a strong leader.

Sachiko rested her balled-up right fist on the table, and glanced upward a few times, composing her response. "As that is your order, we will naturally follow it wholeheartedly and to the level best of our abilities. I would like to add something to what I said a moment ago." Again she paused, searching for the right words. "In my heart-of-hearts I agree with you completely, Jon. I imagine this is as hard a call as they come. I knew that whatever you decided would be *the* plan. That allowed the scientist in me, probably the mom inside me somewhere, to lean toward caution when I wasn't convinced caution was the right path. Thank you for giving me that space. I promise that I will never reach for such a crutch again."

"So let's do this," I announced on an up note. I stood. "Aramthella, distance to Earth?"

"Half a million kilometers."

I angled my head side-to-side. "Membranes will be at their greatest effective range at about ten thousand klicks," I mused. "Aramthella, go to all-ahead-full and bring us to ten thousand kilometers of the surface."

"Course change initiated, General," she responded briskly.

"ETA?" I pressed.

"One hour."

I looked to the group. "Then we have an hour to finalize the details. Let push this lost sheep back where she's supposed to be." I raised my fist over the table. Everyone stood and we group-fist bumped. It was ever so cool.

The next hour took about a week to pass. All I could do was pace back-and-forth like an expectant father in the maternity waiting room, with the woman's husband sitting there glaring at me. But we finally came to a full stop. It was hard to say what part of had-been Earth we were over. Since its no-timing, it not only lost all its surface features but it also began tumbling slowly. There was no way to know if the axis of rotation was the same as it had been originally.

A very long time ago I stood on the surface of destroyed Earth after Jupiter ate it up and spit it out. At least back then, it looked like a rocky planet. Now it was a bizarre, and amorphous, and nearly a smooth ball. From close up, we could see good detail, but there wasn't much of that to see. Rare impact craters and a few piles of rubble. Otherwise it was the planet Boring. One thing none of us saw was any danger. Heck, there wasn't enough of anything down there that could even team up to present a danger.

"All surveys are in," Sachiko announced. The regular bridge crew were at their stations. Sapale, Reva, and I stood around trying to not get in anyone's way. "The readings are odd, to say the least. No magnetism detected. The ambient temperature is nearly impossible to determine, which is unusual. Any object must give off black-body radiation. Why this one isn't is an open question. Some scattered observations in the three degrees Kelvin range at the surface have been reported, but there's no pattern to the findings."

"What could cause those findings?" I asked.

"Maybe the lack of time. Our instruments, our own physiologic perceptions are based on what we interact with being in our time/space. Perhaps a few patches have re-timed themselves and we see only them?"

"Well, we have an approximate value for the planet's mass, based on gravimetrics," I responded. "So we can try to push it without knowing much more than that. It's moving so slowly, the Earth's velocity doesn't really affect the overall momentum. I say we place a single membrane and give the old girl a shove."

Sachiko considered the rashness I suggested. "I suppose there's no real risk. We're pretty high up and it's only the membranes making physical contact. Sure, I'm game."

"Well, start with this ship and use *Stingray* only if need be. Aramthella, form a full membrane in the shape of a bulldozer's front blade, just a bit flatter. Place that membrane right above the surface."

"I have it so configured, General," she replied instantly.

"Okay, proceed forward at ten kilometers an hour. Give me a rolling commentary as to the interaction."

"Surface contact in three-two-one ... sur ... No. I cannot confirm surface contact."

"Why not?" I snapped.

"We have moved ten meters closer, but the membrane appears to have failed to engage the surface."

That's not possible," I announced. "Nothing can pass through a full membrane to *not* engage a contact point."

Aramthella began to shiver, just enough to notice.

"What was that?" Sachiko called out.

"As I am advancing, the membrane is making random contact with something solid. But mostly there is no contact between the membrane and the planet."

"It must be the same as with the temperature readings," Sachiko stated. "There's still almost no time in the material that makes up Earth. It's only when our tools meet up with timed matter that an interaction is possible."

"I don't know. I've used membranes for a long time. Nothing gets past them."

"Well, you did," Sapale pointed out. "I mean your ghost did, back when we fought the ancient gods."

"Ghosts don't count," I replied flippantly.

"You met your own *ghost*?" Reva queried aghast.

"Long story," I responded. "Ask me some other time."

"So if ghosts can pass through a full membrane, why not no-timed matter?" my wife posed.

"You got me," was all I could respond. "Sachiko?"

"I'm not saying a word about ghost physics. No."

The ship's vibration was dampening out.

"All stop," Sachiko ordered. "I think the deeper our membrane gets under the surface, the less timed matter it encounters."

"Makes sense," I confirmed. "Aramthella, did we move the planet at all?"

"A few centimeters."

"And what's the surface area of the membrane you placed?"

"Two hundred thousand square meters."

"So the interactions are infrequent?"

"Point zero zero one percent engagement," she tallied.

"This'll never get it done," I grumbled. Then an idea hit me. "Plesmus, you there?"

"I'm always here," she replied.

"Great. Do you sense the area our membrane is interacting with the planet?"

"Barely, but yes."

"Aramthella, back away so the membrane's just above the surface."

"Done."

"Now, Plesmus, place a small burst of time energy right in the center of the area we're interacting with."

"Hmm, odd. How wide a space?" she questioned.

"Small's good. Maybe a few square meters."

"It is done," she stated with disinterest.

"Aramthella, advance again, same speed."

The ship began rumbling almost immediately. It was much more intense than before.

"Are we moving the planet more now?" I asked with an encouraged tone.

"Yes, we are. The contact is up to two percent. Impressive guess, General."

"So, there you have it. We pump a little time back in here and there, and we can easily—" I began to gloat.

"Form One," *Stingray* cut in, "something most peculiar is occurring on the surface."

"Define peculiar."

"I cannot say. But where there were few readings, there are now more."

"What kind of readings?" I pressed.

"Hmm, an odd mixture of them. I detect infrared fluctuations accompanied by a focal decrease in surface luminosity."

"I need you to be more specific," I ordered.

"Something's moving down there, Captain," Al answered for her.

"There's nothing down there to move," I complained.

"I can only assume the object doing the moving is unaware of that constraint," he countered.

"And the thing moving is infrared radiation?" I puzzled.

"No, it emits infrared. It also appears to eclipse the surface, thus decreasing the reflective luminosity."

"It's casting a shadow?" I clarified.

"Yes, that's a good characterization," confirmed Al.

"Where is this disturbance compared to the membrane?"

"All around it," Al replied. "Moving toward the center."

"General, perhaps this is the time to mention a legend?" Aramthella asked.

"Ah, I don't recall this being story time," I responded perplexed.

"There are stories of what are called the dead of time," she continued.

"Sounds like a story-time story," I pointed out.

"I think not. The bottomline of the legend is that there are said to be entities that exist at the edge of time and no time."

"You're making this up on the fly, aren't you?" I challenged. "Some weird shit happens so you construct a unifying concept."

"Not hardly," she defended. "These entities are said to be eternally in pursuit of time energy. But they exist so marginally, so incompletely, that they never fill their hunger. At best they can only sip at it here and there."

"So, you're saying there are *time* ghosts?" I asked in stunned disbelief.

"No, that's silly. I'm saying there are legends about time-seeking entities that are very insubstantial."

"They sound like time ghosts to me," agreed Sapale.

"And, alarmingly, Form One, the infrared disturbances I reported are altering their movements."

"Altering? How so?"

"They're leaving the planet's surface and rising toward this vessel."

"Oh, no," Sachiko spat out. "Aramthella, drop the membrane and move in reverse, half speed."

"Done, Captain."

After a few seconds, Sachiko asked for an update. "Are the energy signatures continuing to ascend?"

"Negative," reported *Stingray*.

"Oh, thank goodness," Sachiko declared. "Are they dropping back down?"

"I do not know. They vanished once we accelerated away."

"Did they get to the ship?" I asked with a little panic in my voice.

"Unlikely, but unknown," *Stingray* replied.

"Some of your unknown dangers, Captain?" I asked bleakly.

"Apparently so," she confirmed without sounding vindicated.

We waited fifteen minutes to see if anything bad happened to

Aramthella or the crew. Who knew the kind of damage what-the-hell-ever-that-was could do? So we just sat around trying not to show how nervous we all were. Finally it became fairly certain nothing evil was befalling us. Sachiko called for one last systemwide status check. Everything was running A-okay, so we relaxed.

"I'd like to test the abilities of the whatevers down there," I announced. "Aramthella, place a small amount of time energy in a partial membrane. I want the membrane integrity to be the absolute minimum it can be while still holding in the energy. Then lower the ball to one hundred meters above the surface."

"I am coordinating with Plesmus now," she responded. After a few seconds she announced she was ready and she placed the bait. It didn't take long before she reported, "The infrared fluctuations are returning."

"Let me know if they can reach the energy. If they come close, withdraw it to the ship."

"Very well," she replied. "The flux is elevating off the surface. It's ... there, I withdrew the probe. The entity was about to engulf the probe."

We repeated the drill a few times. Eventually we showed that the whatever down there couldn't elevate itself more than twenty-five hundred meters. Outstanding. It had limits. Now I knew that we could re-time a spot on the surface and use a membrane to safely push the Earth, as long as we stayed above the twenty-five-hundred-meter deck. How often we'd have to refresh the spot we were pushing on, and whether the whatever posed some other threat or nuisance, well we were about to find out.

I ordered the same square area to be re-timed, we set a membrane down, and we commenced to shove good old Earth back to where she belonged. It was not smooth sailing, but we made steady progress. The concentration of the boogeymen on the surface increased a lot over time. As their presence grew, the quicker they ate the time energy we sent down. I learned a trick pretty quick. If we stopped sending down time energy, and so stopped pushing for a few minutes, the time ghosts wandered off.

We could begin a new cycle of wash-rinse-repeat, so we didn't need to send down ever-increasing amounts of time energy. The fluxes were clearly not bright, just hungry.

My original plan was to use one ship to move the Earth gradually back into its orbit. But the start-stop choppy maneuvering was getting on my last nerve. So I had both ships place re-timed spots and push together. I inched the speed we made up and up. As a compromise between the herky-jerky crap and all-out sprints when we could, we averaged out a nice, fast clip. It took four days to slip the dead planet back to its approximate orbit. Then we accelerated the remnants so the planet's orbital velocity matched the original value. We weren't too fussy about being precise, since the mostly timeless hulk was bound to drift around until we reanimated it. We had finally, finally arrived at the juncture we'd labored to reach for what was by then years. Earth was where Time instructed me to place it if there was to be any chance of resurrecting it. I wanted to feel a rush of joy and excitement. Everybody did. But we all knew the hardest part, and what would certainly be the wildest part of the process lay ahead of us. We needed to "establish," whatever that meant, nine "reference moorings," whatever those were. And then we had to infuse that framework with a whole heck of a lot of time energy. Desi has some completely unclear but critical role to play somewhere in the entire Charlie foxtrot, and how the people and animals and mosquitos actually came back was less clear to me than homogenized mud. In short, we had a lot of work to do. We just didn't have clue one as to how to do that work. We were basically screwed as screwed could get. Screwed, tattooed, and pooh-poohed.

Yeah, we were in Jon's happy place. Cue the chaos. I was going to wrestle it to the ground.

CHAPTER NINE

Here's a Jon-hypothetical—and please do not be as cruel as my brood's-mate and call those Jonpatheticals. That's just mean. If I have a challenge to do a geologic thing, a biologic thing, and a sociologic thing, how do I proceed? Add to the brain twister that the fate of all Earth rests on the quality of my decisions and the effectiveness of my executing them well. Of course, I run-don't-walk to Dr. Toño DeJesus. I mean, this is a triple-nerd marathon, spanning all the planet's history. I'd either need to turn to the entire faculty of a major university—please note there are presently none of those in existence—or to Doc.

I had a few options. I could simply call Doc. But that's not my style. I like to speak *tête-à-tête,* which is a fancy way of saying face-to-face. I employ the fancier version to demonstrate that I am not a complete slacker. I could go alone, or bring company. Sapale was an obvious choice, but I wasn't feeling it. She lobbied for me to leave the poor man alone, so if she came she'd be a constant, like, I-told-you-so dark cloud. I decided to bring Plesmus. She was central to whatever I was going to do, so her input would be useful. Lastly, I ended up dropping in unannounced. That's not as rude as it might sound. Toño was never a stickler for social niceties when it came to me. We had too much history together. Plus, I knew he wouldn't be sleeping or screwing, right? What would he possibly be doing that was more interesting than *tête-à-têting* with me? I did knock. My reward was a rude surprise.

"General Ryan," Tip whined right out of the gate, "are you supposed to be here today?"

What the boy meant to inquire was obscure to me. "Yeah, I got a hall pass from the principal and everything. What to see it? I taped it to my ass."

He scrutinized me a few moments, narrowing one eyelid. "Which principal? One from my past or one from your past?"

What a nerd-o-saurus. In lieu of a verbal response, I brushed past him brusquely. No duh, he backed up like I was a striking cobra. I scanned for infrared signatures and located Doc in—surprise surprise—his lab.

"Morning, Doc," I announced cheerily.

He leaned over a metal box. Come to think of it, he generally was leaning over a metal box. I wondered what that was trying to tell me? Anyway, he didn't even look up. "I believe it is early evening local time," was his crass response.

"Yes, but since our day together is just beginning, I call it a good morning occasion." I was looking over his shoulder by that point. "What ya doing?"

"Science. You wouldn't be interested."

"Doc, I am stunned. I consider myself to be not only a fan of science but a frequent contributor to that fine field of study."

That did get him to glance up at me. He gave me a decidedly dubious expression. Such a hater.

"To what do I owe the visit?"

"Your good fortune," I beamed.

Wow, I hadn't seen him do it before, but somehow his dubious look became even more doubtful. He'd just set a new world record.

"I suppose I'll need to put off my important work to entertain you?"

I wagged a finger in the air. "Not entertain. No, no. *Educate*."

"Oh, my, we're talking that level of time expenditure? In that case I need to steel myself."

"Funny guy. Hey, I brought Plesmus along." I shook my boot. "Plesmus, say high to the grumpy doctor."

"Hi, grumpy doctor," she said like a professional straight man.

"You ever meet a necumplack before?" I asked him.

"No," he stood up quickly. He scanned the room. "Where is he or she?"

"Stuck to my boot."

He looked down. "I was given to believe they were a bit too large to do so."

"She can split off little pieces and be more than one place at a time."

He nodded approvingly. "Fascinating."

I placed a hand on his shoulder and angled him away from the workbench and toward the kitchen. "Yes it is. Let's go speak of it over coffee."

As we sat down, steamy mugs of goodness in our hands, Doc asked, "Would you like me to summon Tip for this discussion?"

I grimaced. "You remember back—way back—when we were still humans, you and me? You did all those physicals on me as part of Project Ark? Well, you recall that point at the end, where you'd grin and say, 'Alright, Jon, drop your boxers and place your elbows on the table?' Well, I'd rather do that than have to interact with the Tipster."

"It's your call. But, seriously, Jon, the young man's not so bad. He likely has Asperger syndrome, but he's well intentioned."

"So's a white shark when it's hungry. But I'd just as soon not play baby seal and invite the Prince of Geeks to join us."

"I don't dislike Tip," Plesmus said out of the blue.

"You see," Doc announced triumphantly, "an alien species even accepts the lad as is."

"Swell. Okay, if we got all the social crap behind us, can I get to the point?"

He opened his arms widely.

"You know we successfully moved what's left of Earth to where it needs to be."

He nodded.

"So now we, meaning mostly *me*, need to do the actual re-timing. I told you about the nine reference moorings, right?"

"Three geologic, three biologic, and three socio-historical if I remember correctly. And the last of the final group is most mysterious," he answered.

"So I need to actually decide which events to ... to reenact? To ... hell I don't know what."

"I can see you have room to improve upon your current planning."

"Ya think? Gee whiz, what did Time mean when he, she, or it gave me those loco parameters?"

"I've given that a great deal of thought."

I relaxed so much I nearly collapsed on the table. "Thank God."

"And I have come to no epiphany."

"And then he ripped the carpet out from under me while having his dog hump my leg."

"Shall we be serious, or will you just be blindingly clever, as usual?"

"The first one," I said, circling a finger in his general direction.

"I can easily help you decide which individual choices you must make in terms of major events or pivotal turning points in the course of Earth's history. I am still uncertain how to put those ideas into action. It would have been helpful if Time had given you some clues or hints."

"Yes, it would have been. But we're at a what-you-see's-what-you-get stage here."

"Plesmus?" Doc asked.

"Yes."

"Do you have any thoughts on this matter?"

"Yes I do."

"Would you care to share them?" he pressed politely.

"Why, yes, thanks for asking."

"Wait, why didn't you mention anything to me way earlier?" I protested.

"Because you didn't ask."

"Well, that's because—"

"You undervalue me," she finished my sentence.

Sheesh, it was like we were a married couple all of a sudden.

"I don't—" I began.

"Jon, perhaps we could stay on-topic?" Toño posed.

I shrugged.

"How might we implement the interventions Time instructed us to accomplish?" he asked her.

"Since Time gave us those instructions, sparse as they are, it must have been confident we could achieve our goals with the tools we possess."

"A fair assumption," Doc responded.

"I believe it comes down to the three of us."

"Fascinating," he marveled.

"Doc, that's two fascinatings in ten minutes. Stop with the Mr. Spock routine," I groused.

"Who is Mr. Spock?" queried Plesmus.

Toño raised his hands. "Don't concern yourself with that, please. Try and ignore him as best you can."

"I'll try, but I must warn you, I generally fail quickly," she replied. "As I was saying, I think that between the three of us we can select the interventions and then set them in motion. I am, as Jon knows, what is called a ship's focus. That means I collect time energy and place it where it is desired to be. I focus it from one location to another."

"Fa ... intriguing," Doc responded.

"How does that factor in here?" I asked.

"What you people call Occam's razor. That, generally speaking, the simplest explanation is usually the correct one. You, Jon, *create* an image, and I *focus* it where we desire it to be."

"Huh?" I astutely enquired.

"Hum," Doc mused. "Let me ponder this a moment."

"Be my guest," Plesmus invited.

Who says out loud that they're going to *ponder* something? That Doc. Such a nerdmeister.

"I am beginning to believe that might just be the case," he finally revealed.

"I'm beginning to think you two are nuts of a feather. Ples, my brain ... it's *inside* me. You're *outside* me. How do you picture us interacting?"

"Obviously there will need to be an augmented symbiosis between the two of us," she responded.

"What the hell's that mean?" I shot back. "We don't have any symbiosis between us at this point in time, I can tell you that straight up."

"Please stop being so childish," Doc scolded. "Plesmus's thoughts are nothing short of brilliant."

I was going to say *If you say so*, but I didn't want to validate his childish contention. Didn't stick out my tongue either.

"How do you see the two of you interacting?" he asked her.

"I think we'll need to practice a few scenarios and see what works best. Initially I propose he thinks of an action, and I focus time energy through his head."

"Whoa, whoa, whoa. All my brains aren't in my head," I protested. "How's that going to work?"

"You left yourself *so* wide open, human. Unbelievable," Plesmus commented.

"If you recall, Jon," Toño began in his professor's mode, "that while many of your processors are located in your chest and abdomen, I slaved them all to compile in your head."

"That sounds painful," I answered.

"I mean they all report to the central core in your head. For practical reasons I felt it was best to align the information flow thusly."

"So Plesmus'll shine time energy through my skull while I picture an image and maybe it'll be zapped as if by magic into existence?"

"I believe so," Toño replied. "Is that the case, Plesmus?"

"Yes, exactly," she affirmed.

"And nothing could go wrong, right?" I asked sarcastically. "I mean, my brains couldn't fry or become next week, right?"

"I don't *think* either of those two possibilities might occur," Doc answered, not reassuringly.

"I focus time through walls, layers of earth, all kinds of things, Jon. Nothing's ever gone wrong."

"Never?" I questioned.

"Well, once I transformed a solid roof into a pair of dancing ponies. But that was just the once."

"Very droll," I countered. "Verrry droll."

"As you know, Jon, my philosophy is always that there's no time like the present to perform the experiment." Doc rose and furrowed his brow. "Let's try this outside first. If there's an unpredicted turn of events, best not to ruin the place."

"What, I might explode?"

"No," he scoffed. "Just your head, not all of you. Sometimes I wonder if I made you right, Jon." Dude then walked out of the lab and headed for his front door.

A minute later we were standing outside and Tip had joined us—grr.

"Alright," Toño instructed, "Jon you stand there. Plesmus, can you focus properly from his boot or do you need a different angle?"

"The angle is irrelevant," she replied confidently.

"Excellent. Tip and I will position ourselves off to the left. When you focus through Jon's head, Plesmus, aim for the resultant manifestation to appear right by that small boulder." He pointed to where he wanted her to direct the whatever.

"Not a problem," she responded.

"Alright now, Jon, you need to picture something simple. A steel ball. Yes, that will do nicely. One that has a diameter of five centimeters, okay?"

"What do I do with the other thoughts racing around in my

wheelhouse? Like the one where I slice all three of you up and bury you in a shallow grave?"

"You concentrate. You have override capabilities," he replied sternly.

"Oh, yeah, I do, don't I? I'd forgotten about those."

"Small wonder. I used them early on in setting up your network. But they are still in place. Once you picture the steel ball, invoke an override. No other thoughts will occur until your preset override initiates."

"Okay, let's do this," I said with less enthusiasm than the phrase implies. "Ples, in ten seconds I'll lock in a single image. It will last one second, then all hell breaks loose in my head again. you copy that?"

"Yes."

That was it. I set an image, locked in the override and its release, and I closed my eyes.

My brain snapped back online.

"Look!" shouted Tip. "There's something over there, right by the rock."

"My goodness there is," Toño confirmed. "But it's not a steel ball, Jon," he added in his disappointed-dad tone, that I heard a lot.

"You sure?" I asked curiously. "You said a steel ball didn't you?"

Tip ran over and retrieved the new fabrication. When he was back, he tried to hand it to Doc.

He threw up his arms. "I'm not touching that ... that thing."

Huh? Doc had a problem with inflatable sex doll? The man was a prude.

"What do I do with it?" Tip queried no one in particular.

"Figure that out for yourself," I quipped. "My gift to you."

"Th ... thanks. I think."

"Jon, this is fantastic," Toño exclaimed loudly. "Plesmus, your predictions were spot on. We have a solution. Now you need only decide which events to recreate and then bring them to life just as you now did."

"Don't you think it might be harder to animate, like, the War of 1812 than it is a sex doll?"

"Of course it would be. And that's not one of the events you will recreate, so put it out of your mind."

"I was just saying the first thing, Doc," I protested.

"That was a purely regional conflict between a superpower, the newly titled United Kingdom, and a fledgling United Sates. No, whatever we decide on must be absolutely world altering."

"I'm not wedded to the war, Doc. No worries."

"Good. Now let's return to my office to come to a consensus on eight really critical events."

"Wait. Hang on. We just made a thing. Fine. But if I recreate Noah's Ark, like, where do I put it? If I set it down on what's left of Earth, complex badness will befall it almost immediately."

He rubbed at his chin. "Good point." He stewed on that a spell. "We'll figure something out. Come, we're off to make history, literally."

He sounded so into it. That was depressing. One thing I'd learned long ago and over-and-over: if Toño DeJesus was having fun, I would not be.

CHAPTER TEN

One more experiment. Boy howdy, I can't tell you how much I hated experiments, but now I double-dog hated them. I'm pure #impulsive-over-testosteroned-fighter-pilot. I *do* stuff. I don't dilly dally or contemplate my navel. I leave that realm to more ordinary men and women. However, now I was forced to do that one more check. We'd successfully hammered out a list of actually pretty good choices in terms of intervention points. But it was my strong impression that the actual acts of time restoration had to occur on or just below the surface of Mother Earth. Anything left on the surface would be subject to the ravages of time ghosts, and we all know how ornery those are. To make those subterranean placements I couldn't see any way around Plesmus and me being right down there on terra firma. We could try to place the reference moorings from a safe altitude, but that didn't get us around two serious barriers. One, the creepy will-o'-wisps would attack and likely interfere significantly with the process. Two, most forces of physics decrease in strength over distance. Gravity and light intensity, for example, decrease with the square of the distance between two objects. The strong nuclear force decreases with the negative exponential power of distance. I had no clue how time energy projections dropped as the distance they were cast over increased. So, the closer the better.

If Plesmus and I were going to operate on the surface, I needed to find out if we could avoid contact with those infrared cloud-like manifestations. If not, I had to prove one way or the other if they were a direct threat to either of us. I suspected they were. The simplest experiment was, unfortunately, vetoed by everyone who wasn't me. I asked Sapale where the almost-goats were being kept. She guessed instantly what I wanted to do. I was going to set one down on the surface and see what happened to living flesh when the ghosties came a-calling.

"You are not subjecting one of those precious little beings to the cruelty of unknown entities or your callous disregard for the sanctity of life," she schooled me with a finger bobbing under my nose. "What's more I am going to contact Sachiko and have her place armed guards around their pens for the duration."

"You think I'd steal a goat after you specifically forbade me to?"

"No, because there'll be armed guards positioned all around the dear loves."

"But I don't have any other live animals I can sacrifice. Remember, Tip's away with Doc still."

"You're just going to have to figure out another method of assessing the danger. You could send a tiny piece of Plesmus. There's always more available."

"So you want to be the one to tell her she's less valued than a stinky goat?"

"Of course not. Your experiment, your shit-job. Just leave me and the goats out of the entire escapade."

"Escapade? You call my self-sacrificing, life-threatening attempt to resurrect a living planet an escapade?"

"If it involves my goats, yes," she snarled convincingly. "Look, flyboy, you got a vortex. The galaxy's full of any number of revolting pest species. If you want a lab rat, go get a lab rat."

Wow, what a good and practical idea. "Well, I can't. There never was an Earth so there are no rats." I defended instead of complimented her.

"Oh, no? Then why'm I staring at a big rat this very moment? Valpariso-A. Go there. They have those stinky, mean, aggressive, and completely unintelligent termites that're the size of watermelons. They're not hard to find. You go into a forest and smell. Bingo, you got yourself a lab rat."

That was an excellent suggestion. That planet was swarming with those dreadful creatures. "That's maybe going to work, but I'd be expending a lot of valuable time."

"You're not time-wasting averse. I know this because you're still here, as opposed to Valpariso-A, wasting time trying to change my mind."

"Fine, but this is on you. I hope you're happy." Why did I react so childishly, so very moronically? Come on, she was right on every count. How else was I supposed to react? Thank you.

Less than an hour later Plesmus and I were suspended a safe distance from Earth's rugged surface. I set a pair of the blister termites, as the locals of Valpariso-A named them, in a membrane and lowered them to the deck. In no time, a swarming mass approached. Just as the infrared arrived, I dropped the membrane, exposing the termites to basically open space. Quicker than I could say *serves them right,* the termites were lifeless husks. According to Plesmus, their time had been sucked out of them. Okay, Rule One: No direct contact with the time ghosts.

Next I set a couple down, leaving them in a full membrane. I let the mist roil around the ball a few minutes, then I raised it and released whatever was inside. Keep in mind even I couldn't assess them inside a full membrane. Two live, presumably kicking-and-screaming bugs tumbled to their deaths. A partial membrane didn't keep the infrared threats out. When I released termites from those, only dusty debris drifted to the ground. My last hope was that a dome-shaped full membrane would keep the entities out. I lowered a pair in a full membrane, then, as it touched the surface, I opened the bottom so the membrane took on a bell shape. I made it a point to drive the lower lip of the dome a foot into the surface, hoping a tight seal would keep out the local lethal clouds. When I dropped the membrane one minute later, to my complete relief, the nasty insects were perfectly healthy—for about one second. Then they were not.

Several iterations of progressively longer intervals of protection by the membrane suggested a time-possessing unit protected by a dome of membrane was safe from the infrared whatevers for ten minutes, almost exactly. After that, the swarm infiltrated under the surface and emerged inside the protective bubble. Exhibiting no ability to learn, with each repeat of the experiment I discovered the same ten-minute window of safety existed. So I just had keep an eye on the clock when attempting intervention of the surface, and everything should be fine.

Yeah, what could go wrong?

CHAPTER ELEVEN

The early solar system was chaotic, utterly. Planets coalesced, collisions between all size masses were commonplace, and loose material flew at incredible speeds in every direction. The frigid cold of space was dotted with incandescent islands of intense heat. Energy arose from gravitational collapse, impacts, and radioactive decay. No planet was safe. Size was the key to remaining intact, but all the planets were subject to vicious assaults that threatened their integrity. One too many blows could pulverize a would-be celestial body and scatter its material to the solar winds.

Over millions of years, rocky planets began to take shape in the inner solar system. Farther out, gas giants were swallowing up an ever-increasing tonnage of debris. Comets, asteroids, dust, and gas were sucked up as the gravitational vacuum cleaners like Jupiter and Saturn swept through their orbits. Roughly four and a half billion years ago, the Earth started to stabilize. With the outer planets' ever-increasing shielding, bombardments from space lessened. Intense vulcanism became the dominant force on the surface. What existed back then was unrecognizable compared to modern day Earth. But slowly, incrementally, the planet cooled, volcanoes lessened their angry outbursts, and Earth settled into the business of becoming a mature, nurturing planet.

No one knows where Theria came from. Was it another planet formed around Sol? Or did it wander in randomly after escaping another star's gravitational clutches? Independent of its origins, Theria took a distinct dislike to the slowly calming Earth. It zeroed in and struck the third rock from the Sun squarely about three and a half billion years ago.

The collision was epic. Theria was shattered into tiny pieces. Some were captured by Earth's gravity. Some of Theria, along with a goodly chunk of Earth, were cast off, destined to form the Moon. But the damage to Earth was absolute. The surface melted into one gigantic lava sea due to the heat of the impact. Gone were any structures that had existed previously. Gone was any evolving life that might have been taking root.

After Theria's attack, the Earth naturally began to cool again. Lava oceans hardened, and vulcanism once again lost its grip on the surface. Within half a billion years, the earliest signs of primitive life slipped out from the chaos. Slowly they were fruitful and multiplied.

I stood on the rugged surface of shattered Earth. With Plesmus on my boot and a full membrane dome protecting me from the ravages of the time ghosts, I was ready to try or die. I pictured what special kind of hell it must have been like some five billion odd years back, when Theria slammed into an unsuspecting Earth. The override protocol Toño had programmed in engaged as I replayed the picture of Theria only inches from Earth's surface. I set a ten second lock out for all other thoughts and instructed it to initiate in three seconds.

"I am ready," I whispered to Plesmus.

Then my mind went blank, aside from the horrible vision. Theria slammed into Earth. The resultant trauma was infinitely worse that the Four Horsemen themselves could have inflicted in a million years.

Plesmus must have begun time-animating the image I held static in my head. I felt nothing. I heard nothing. I was nothing. The only reference I had available to me aside from the cataclysmic vision I had produced was the passage of the seconds. She needed to be nearly done. She was planning on focusing the image of the Theria Impact under the surface of the Earth, one kilometer down, at the far side of the membrane dome. If she was successful I could not know.

Eight ... nine ... ten.

My thoughts rushed in like a tsunami careening into a cliff. My balance faltered and I nearly fell. Then, the world slowly came back into focus. I stood straight and shook my shoulders.

"Well that wasn't so—" I began. Then I face-planted on the unforgiving rock below my feet like a bunch of wet towels thrown from a bucket.

... I woke ... some time later. Where was I? I felt uninjured, but I was mentally lost.

"There you are," a panicked voice cried out. "Jon, I was beginning to fear you were dead."

"I'm fine," I lied absurdly.

"No, you are not. But we're in trouble and I need you functioning."

It was Plesmus's voice. I rotated my head to look at her.

"There you are, you little troublemaker." She was on the ground a few meters away. "Ah, where are we?"

"You are lying and I am standing right where we were forty minutes ago. We're on the surface of what's left of Earth. We attempted to animate the image of that alien planet hitting Earth. Remember?"

"Oh, yeah, now that you mention it I sure do. Hey, how'd it go?"

"That depends on how you define success. It's was going well, but it's still going on."

"You like talking in riddles, don't you, Ms. Sphinx?"

"Riddles they are not. Jon, get up."

I stood slowly. Okay, I was good. All systems firing on all cylinders, steady as a rock on my feet. Yeah, I was fine. That's when I looked around.

"Oops," I said.

"No. Oops is when you knock over your glass of milk. What you see all around us are the time-locked infrared manifestations. We had ten minutes before they broke into our shelter. At ten minutes they did. Only you were out like a switched off light bulb."

"So you were able to time lock them? That's so cool."

"Maybe it is, but we're in real danger. I'm almost out of time energy. I used much more than I anticipated focusing the collision. The time-lock is just about to expire because I can't sustain it."

"How'd the focusing go?"

"Jon, not the time for a debriefing. We need to get to the ship in the next minute or we're going to find out how your big bugs felt when the time ghosts ate them."

The vortex was parked a short ways away. But it was sealed. Even if Plesmus could have dragged me, which I doubted she could, she couldn't get inside unless I allowed it with my probe fibers.

"Come on," I said snatching her up. "We got plenty of time."

"If forty seconds is plenty of time, then you are correct."

Such a Debbie Downer. But, no point telling her. She was overly sensitive about almost everything I said about her. I bobbed and wove through the field of time-frozen bad clouds. I have to admit it was unnerving being so close to them. I had the feeling they were as mindless as they were relentless. If they woke up before I closed us safely aboard *Stingray*, my charm and good looks were unlikely to spare us an unpleasant death.

Just as I was beginning to get over-confident, as was my general inclination, I tripped. Plesmus went airborne, I re-face planted— ouch—and valuable seconds ticked by with us both exposed. Luckily I bounded right back up. I charged toward Plesmus, who had landed twenty meters off. I closed the distance quickly and was reaching out to grab her when I noticed two unhappy things. One, she was on top of a large wave of the infrared bad guys. Two, said bad guys were beginning to move. It was ever-so-slowly mind you, but them moving was a tragic predictor for our collective longevity.

I extended my probe fibers and grabbed her. No way I was touching one of those directly, animate or otherwise.

"I'm ... losing ... my ... con—" Plesmus said at a whimper.

As I leaped over another oozing wave of death, I toed the ground and ran for all I was worth toward *Stingray*. I checked back over my shoulder. A long plume extended out of the nearest manifestation toward us. The nebulous mass was moving a little quicker than it was just seconds before.

I freed up one probe fiber and extended it to its full length. I whipped it toward the nearest wall of the vortex and commanded it to open a portal. It was like a bang-bang sports play. The hull opened, we tumbled in, the entity touched the bottom of my boot, and the opening slammed shut.

Still lying on my back, I set Plesmus down. "You okay?"

"I'm ... I'm alive."

"Al, did any of the manifestation get into the ship?"

"No, Captain. The infrared clouds are attempting, however, to breach the hull."

I set a fiber on the deck. "Fold us to twenty thousand meters."

Slight nausea.

"Any of that crap still attached?"

"No, we are free and clear."

"Out-of-standing," I shouted as I ran to the back of the room. I grabbed the suitcase-sized time-storage unit we'd brought with us and sped back toward Plesmus. Sliding on my knees I came to a stop right along side her.

"You ready?" I asked.

"Yes."

I cracked open the valve and let the white cloud of time energy flow directly onto her skin, or whatever. Not a drop touched her and escaped away into the air. Girl was gulping it down.

After two minutes she said she'd had enough and I closed the valve.

"FYI, Ples," I announced, "there's still a little bit left in the tank if you need it."

"I'll be fine now. Thank you."

"So, now that we're safe and fed, tell me. How'd we do?"

"As far as I can tell we succeeded completely. I sensed a chamber under the surface, the one I was trying to focus into existence."

"Al, what kind of readings did you guys get?"

"We can confirm the chamber's presence. It still appears stable."

"And the contents? What can you make out?"

"A most unnatural scene, Captain. We are not certain how to describe it."

"Take your best shot," I instructed.

"The sphere is precisely one kilometer in diameter. The walls are smooth to the lowest scale we can measure. Inside the chamber there is a jumbled mixture of mass and energy signatures. We image a smaller body repeatedly colliding with a larger one. The results are total destruction for both bodies. But as one loop of the drama plays out, an infinite number of identical loops are popping in-and-out of existence. It is complete and utter chaos in that enclosure."

"But it's stable? It's not going to explode or fizzle out?"

"Not as far as we can tell, Captain," Al replied.

"And the time ghosts. Do they seem to be trying to access the pit?"

"We cannot determine that. Infrared clouds passing into the surface rapidly become undetectable to our sensors."

"Well, keep me posted. If anything changes, let me know immediately."

"Will do," he concluded.

"Well, I'll be damned," I breathed. "I think we just created a miracle."

CHAPTER TWELVE

The planet Earth does not exist. It never did, not since the clan no-timed it. After that heinous act, Earth was remembered by only a small number of individuals, perhaps five hundred. To most of them, memories of Earth were confined to its surface, where they resided. The former college students of Georgetown University remember Earth as a busy place. They had classes, homework, and they had social events. The weather was hot and humid in the summer and ridiculously cold in the winter. Their families, for the most part, lived elsewhere. They visited them on holidays and were relieved when the break was over and they could get back to their own worlds.

Others among the Mars 1 Base staff thought back on a similar Earth. Trees, relatives, jobs, hopes for the future, the typical anchor points of a life. But there were a very few who remembered the Earth as scientists. One or two of the scientists on Mars 1 had significant training in geology and other Earth sciences. They saw the planet not as a land-air interface to stake one's dreams on, they saw a physical, structural beast. Mighty oceans, drifting continents, a dancing atmosphere, and a dynamic magnetic field. And all of the properties of those bodies were to a greater or lesser extent, dependent on the Earth's molten core. At six thousand five hundred degrees Kelvin and three-and-a-half million atmospheres of pressure it was an unearthly realm.

If you asked one of these scientists what they remembered most about the Earth, they'd regale you with obscure information of such detail that your eyes would rotate back in your head from the boredom they'd induce in you. They'd speak of the molten core that slowly circulated, rotated, and grew. All this activity, they would report with wonder, was driven by the heat of atomic decay. This intense concentration of the heavier radioactive elements was due to their natural tendency to sink in the Earth's crust and mantle. Without this molten core being as large and as dynamic as it is, the scholars would declare with conviction, life as we know it would not exist on Earth. No, the magnetic field our planet generates from this molten core screens out nearly all the harmful radiation space is so full of. And as you passed into sleep due to the continued descriptions these science people were interminably going on about, your last waking thoughts would be that you too were glad the Earth had that massive liquid core. Then you'd snore.

It took a couple of days for Plesmus and I to recover sufficiently from our ordeal. I did a full systems scan and found I was in tip-top working order. When Sapale learned of my "incidents" after we set our first reference moorings, she plugged into one of my ports and did a complete one of her own. Then, after she called Toño to nark on me and bemoan her wicked fate, Doc ordered me to present myself to his laboratory so he could run a full set of diagnostics himself. Guess what? In the end he declared begrudgingly that I was practically perfect in every way. Yeah, he would never assess that, but he did conclude I was none the worse for wear.

Plesmus, the time creature, recovered in a manner I couldn't fathom. She consumed an abundance of time energy, but that alone didn't heal her. Well, here's our crazy discussion. You make of it what you will.

"So," I asked encouragingly, "are you fine?"

"Leave me alone," she replied without enthusiasm.

"That's not an acceptable response to the query *are you fine*. Please select an alternate response."

"I am not fine. I am not well. I am not what you keep calling peachy keen. And to make my malaise even worse, I have you pestering me for updates I am incapable of providing because my responses cannot be cheery as you would will them to be."

"Hey, I think that's the longest sentence you've ever spoken to me. Wow, a new world record, if I remember correctly. Super congrats on a word stream well formed."

"Jon, do you completely miss the meaning of others or do you take their meaning and simply not care how they feel?"

"Hmm. That's a tough one. Let me think about it. I'll let you know when I have a definitive view of the topic. Say, how you doing? You look good, but, hey, that doesn't mean you feel well, right?"

"Since you humans came aboard I have done a lot of research in an attempt to understand you and therefore interact better with you."

"To which I say thanks."

"My point is this. I went through a harrowing experience the other day. I was nearly completely drained of time energy. That has never happened. Yes there was a time long ago, before I was bonded with this vessel, that I contained little time energy. But ever since then, I've had my fill. You humans have seizures."

"Some do, yes."

"After these events, people can be what is called postictal. Their minds are numb and they have altered perceptions."

"So I've been told."

"Please consider me to be in a state similar to this postictal phase."

"Sure, why not?"

The air was quiet for a spell.

"Yet you are still here," she remarked without joy.

"Yes I am. I need to plan our next mission. In order to do that, I need to ascertain how you, my wing-female-alien, are. Hence, hey, how are you? Wait, you told me you were still in a funk. Okay, fine. The next bit of info I will then require is when do you estimate you will be back in acceptable shape?"

"I just told you that I've never been through this. Therefore I do not know."

"Make an educated guess."

"A few days. Perhaps a week. Yes, one week."

I rubbed behind an ear. Then I hmm'ed to myself. Then I scratched behind the other ear.

"What are you attempting to convey?" she challenged.

"Well, *a few days*, well, that's one thing. You see, *a few* could be just three days. If you'd said a couple, I'd think two was a possibility. But you said *a few*, so three's my best-outcome scenario. But a *week*? While being still in the range of *a few*, well, it's too long for my liking. You see, we have a lot to accomplish. Time's a wasting. So, I was hoping to have you back in action sooner than later."

"That is the longest sentence you've ever said to me. It is also the most painful. Please leave me to rest."

"Not a problem. So, can I pencil you in for being ready in two and a half days?"

"Didn't you just say yourself three days was the fewest I'd indicated?"

"Well, yes. But two-and-a-half rounds up to three and it's closer to the shorter time-frame goal I've set for our mission."

"Jon, I do not have a brain like your species. My neural network extends diffusely throughout my body."

"Thanks for sharing."

"That said, you're breaking down my neural network."

"Sorry you feel that way. You know, one thing I've found to be true over and over again is that the best way to beat a funk is to be real active. Yes, siree, moping never cured anything."

"Jon, you are unbelievable."

"Thank you."

"If I agree to leave with you tomorrow, will you promise to leave me in peace until then. That you will not venture near me to beguile and torment me?"

"Why, you'd have my solemn oath as an officer and a gentleman on that deal."

"Fine. We leave tomorrow, *midday* tomorrow."

My work here is done, I said to myself. I didn't vocalize the thoughts to Plesmus. Nah. She was still kind of under the weather and my words might be construed as insensitive. I slipped out quietly.

The next morning bright and early I presented myself to Plesmus's closet. I'd already put the gear we'd need on the vortex. Two flasks of extra time energy for Plesmus, just in case. And for me some whiskey. I figured that if I felt like passing out again, that was the best preventative possible. If I'd have asked Doc, I'm sure he'd back me up on that prescription.

"Good morning, my mission buddy," I chortled.

"We agreed on midday. This is dawn, minus the rising star of course."

"We agreed we wouldn't start the *mission* before midday. But we need to get to where the mission takes place first, so if we leave now, we'll be there by midday. And you're welcome, by the way. I'm happy to honor my commitment."

"You know what? If I argue that you're a sneak and a cheater and attempt to hold you to your word, I know you'd browbeat me until it was midday and then I'd leave because that's when I agreed to in the first place. But I'm not going there. No. I surrender. Let us leave now."

Little spark plug slithered by me and headed toward the elevators. I totally appreciated her can-do attitude. If I had a hundred more of her, well I'd have one-hundred-and-one headaches that also cause pain in the butt, now, wouldn't I?

Within an hour (and well before midday) we were back on the

surface under a full-membrane dome. Our goal today was more modest than the first one, so I hoped loss of consciousness was not on today's schedule.

"Let's start a little closer to the ship," I suggested.

"Why not? Less distance to run when the mission goes tits-up."

"Wow, you say tits-up? That's outstanding."

"When I'm working with you those two words dance endlessly across my neural network."

"Okay, we'll start from here," I responded, completely ignoring her snipe.

I focused in. I pictured time being restored to a wedge of the Earth's core. Once time started back up, the radioactive decay could begin again, and the potential energy that was there already in stasis would be released as heat to stir the core material. This looked to be an easy reference mooring. I placed an override to last the same ten seconds, starting in the same three seconds.

"You set, Ples?" I asked confidently.

"As I ever will be," she whined.

... eight ... nine ... ten.

Nothing. My mind went blank for ten seconds, but that was it. I felt great. Best of all I was upright. Nice.

"We done here, Ples?"

"I am."

"Did it work?"

"I believe so."

Al, I asked via our mental link, *what kind of readings do you get?*

There is a new one-kilometer cavern at the same depth as the previous one. We read immense heat present, and liquid iron. The chamber appears to contain a microcosm of the actual Earth's core as it existed in the past.

"Well, that's just wonderful," I exclaimed out loud. "Ples, I do believe our work here is done. Shall we?"

"Not soon enough to suit me," she quipped as she scooted between my legs heading back to the vortex.

"You do your best work when you feel a little off, don't you?" I remarked quietly.

"I didn't catch that," she called out as she receded.

"No prob. Nothing important. Fah-get a-bout it."

CHAPTER THIRTEEN

Water, water ... everywhere.

Few bodies in the solar system contain abundant liquid water. Saturn's moon Enceladus has a global ocean beneath its icy crust. Europa, a large moon of Jupiter, also has a subsurface ocean. Another of Jupiter's satellites, Ganymede, is nearly half water, but it is in a frozen state. And there's Earth, whose surface is—or was—mostly covered with salt water. As far as we know, life is not possible without a liquid for that life to evolve in. Few chemical compounds fit the bill of being liquid in the habitable temperature range. Water basically owns the rights to allowing life to abound in the solar system, although I have seen some interesting alternatives.

Water on Earth comes from several origins. Much of it is released from rocks as they cycle through formation, maturation, and recycling in the mantle. A goodly lot comes from cometary impacts in the post-Theria collision period. Any water present before the cataclysmic event would have been lost to space. That's about it. Water is essential to all life, and it comes from two fountains. No fountains, no life. It's just that simple.

For a couple of days after our triumphant re-timing of a portion of Earth's core, Plesmus avoided me like I was my first wife's mother. And she was tricky. She didn't shelter in her closet. I traipsed all over the ship to no avail. I couldn't find her. I asked Aramthella where the little devil had gotten to, but she refused to tell me. She claimed she'd promised the mucus ball that her location would not be revealed to me. Two females conspiring against me, can you believe it? Been there. Done that. Had the souvenir tee shirt.

Then, early on the third day, out of nowhere Aramthella announced over the speakers in *Stingray*'s mess that Her Highness Plesmus was back in her usual cubby. I guess her lordliness would now relent to an audience with wretched old me. I headed there almost immediately, waiting just long enough to signal that I was neither anxious nor needy.

"Good morning," Plesmus called out before I was even far enough into the closet to see her directly.

"We'll see," was my qualified response. I sat down near her, but not too near. "So, where've you been?"

"I believe that is obvious. I was avoiding you so I could fully heal."

"And are you now?" I left off the word *princess* that I almost applied. It wasn't a team-building sentiment.

"Yes, thank you for asking." Yeah, it was in there. I could hear it plainly: *No thanks to you, human.*

"Good, because our next mission is beating my balls."

"I will try with all my might to delete that injurious image from my neural net. Yuck!"

"I meant to say I don't know how we do this one."

"Ah, that's such a better way to express yourself. May I help?"

"That's what I was hoping for. I'm stuck."

"Please tell me what we wish to accomplish and what you've formulated so far."

"The second part's easy. Nada, zilch, diddly squat."

"More revolting imagery."

"Nah, they're just idioms. Those are squeaky clean. Anyway, this time out we need to form a reference mooring for the water present on Earth."

"Sounds simple enough. We fill a bucket with water and toss on planet."

"I thought about that, but it won't do. We don't need to put water *on* the planet. We need to place the *process* of water formation and/or accumulation on Earth."

"I believe you are correct. Any idea how we do that?"

"Not really. How about you?"

"Hmm. Let me think a moment. But first let me ask what the historic processes were."

"Some came from the rocks. A lot of minerals are accompanied with water molecules. Amphibole is a rock that's two percent water. Also rocks contain a lot of oxygen and hydrogen. If those are stripped off, water can form. Another source would be impacts from comets."

"I see the problem."

"Yes. Heating rocks and having them release water is straightforward enough. We already recreated the molten core."

"But raining comets, that's hard to picture," she finished my thought.

We were quiet a spell.

"Well, first the easy part," she began. "The caverns we create have rock walls. If we introduce a powerful heat source, that should do the trick. The minerals will know how to cycle through the patterns they used to in the planet's depths."

"I agree. But if we throw comets around in the space, they'd vaporize the instant they appeared. That's not the same as hitting the surface and then becoming water on the surface."

"What if we made two chambers?"

Wow, that's a breakthrough insight.

"Hey, good idea, I guess. Sure, let's try and work this out separately."

"And we don't necessarily have to create the caverns at the same time."

"No, I don't see why we'd have to."

"So how do we recreate cometary impacts?"

The six-million-dollar question.

I ran my hand through my hair and groaned. "Has to be a way."

"Maybe we're overthinking this," she observed. "Why can't you just picture it in your brain, and I focus it into reality?"

"I thought about that, but I'm not sure. How are random comets careening through space going to know they should hit Earth's surface? And we can't just go grab some and toss them at the planet. That's an act, not a sustaining mechanism. Worse, lots of comets contain little to no water. If we caused those to crash, they wouldn't help."

"What if we did nothing? There are comets out there all the time. They are free to impact whatever they are destined to strike. We can let nature take its course."

"That's a good point. But realistically, at the stage of the solar system we're working with, there aren't that many unspoken for comets. Most were swallowed by the gas giants already."

"There you have it," she said enthusiastically.

"There I have what?"

"The solution. All we need to do is create a small domain of the Earth's surface four billion years ago. There will be comets all over the place."

I was going to remark that she was smarter than she looked, but that would just be dickish of me. She'd figured this one out when I couldn't. "Thank you, my friend. That's a fantastic idea. I'm glad I consulted you."

"You are most welcome. When shall we start?"

"When would you like to begin?"

"Now is a good time, my friend. We'll form the heated chamber first. Depending on how that goes, we can decide when to fabricate the ancient surface sphere."

I stood and stretched. "Sounds like a plan."

I was lucky to have Plesmus as a teammate on this project. I'd have to tell her as much sometime soon. No, none of the Jon crap.

"Ples, I want to say that it's good to have you on my team."

"Really? I thought it was you who was on mine."

A pill until the end. That was my Plesmus.

It turned out the two missions were completed fairly easily. No real issues, no time ghost invasions. It was nice. But there was one thing odd, right at the end ...

"So, Plesmus," I asked, "is the hot volcano strewn landscape of ancient Earth stable?"

"I believe so. The time levels seem steady at least."

"Great. Hey, Al, what are you two ... whoa—" I screamed.

The patch of ruined Earth we stood on shook like a stuffed toy in a pissed-off pit bull's mouth. I nearly fell on my face again, the disturbances were so intense. Then, as abruptly as they started, the ground quake ended. It didn't fade or subside. It just wasn't any longer.

"Anybody know what the hell that was?"

"Not me," Plesmus said nervously.

"Al?"

"No idea, Captain. Obviously, there was a massive seismic event. That said, it is out of place. There's been no seismic activity up until now, so a massive event as a first indication of such activity is unlikely. Also, the wave forms were all wrong."

"How so?" I asked.

"Normally earthquake waves are either pressure wave forms or up/down displacement waves. Those were neither. It was as if the atoms of the earth we stand on shook themselves at random."

"That seems o—"

"What, Captain?" Al asked a bit panicky.

"We just completed the first of the three classes of reference moorings."

"Yes, we did," he agreed.

"I think we did them right."

CHAPTER FOURTEEN

The origins of life on Earth. To discover that event is surely the holy grail of all science. Abiogenesis, as experts refer to the process. Absent evidence of life anywhere else in the universe, perhaps it is safe to assume that the appearance of life here was due to the greatest of coincidences, the best of good luck. Or is the spark of life almost trivial on a cosmic scale? The Earth is four point five billion years old. The earliest undisputed evidence of microfossils date from three point five billion years. Life began a mere billion years after Earth's formation. That a diverse group of durable microbes evolved so rapidly suggests that life was a fairly easy trick for nature to pull off.

The first written speculation on life's beginnings were made by Anaxagoras in the fifth century, BC. He speculated life came to this planet by falling to Earth from space, and named the process *panspermia*. He fancied the universe teemed with life and that we were simply extensions of that abundance. In the 1950s, Miller and Urey sent sparks through a tube full of the chemicals present in the Earth's primitive atmosphere. Twenty different amino acids were formed. It became popular to believe that process spawned life on Earth.

But the most likely source of life is that it came to be on the floors of our deep oceans. Hydrothermal vents called black smokers eject tons of dissolved sulfites. These chemicals could easily provide the energy a reproducing cell would require. In the hot, chaotic environment around these vents, the needed amino acids could also form, providing the backbone for life.

Perhaps someday science will learn with certainty what our origins were.

***

Fresh off the pleasant, even collegial mission with Plesmus to create a template for planetary water, I was feeling optimistic. Yeah, pretty weird, eh? Me using the words *optimistic* and *Plesmus* in one sentence. Who'd a thunk it? But she was undeniably talented and quite resourceful. Don't tell anyone, but I actually think we made a good team.

But our next intervention promised to test our new bond significantly. There was never going to be life on Earth if life didn't have its initial pop of life beginning. That was our next reference mooring. I was pretty sure it was the one critical template we needed to form. Reanimation seemed to be an impossibility if we couldn't make this happen. And yes, I had no clue as to how to perform minor-miracle four. I was fairly certain a quick trip to Origins-R-Us wasn't in our immediate future.

After traveling the universes over my long lifetime, I'd discovered that life was freaking everywhere. It had to be a fundamental property of organic ecosystems. Given liquid something, barriers to harsh radiation, and a little time—poof—you got life. But that didn't mean it would be easy for us to set up a functioning reference mooring.

It had been established that life on Earth—well, if there had been an Earth, I needed to keep self-correcting—began near black smoker vents in the deep ocean. It was the logical choice because there was abundant chemical energy in the times before sun light could be harnessed by algae and bacteria. It was a sort of chicken-and-egg argument, but without the evolution of photosynthesis, there would be no energy to drive the initiation of primal life. The black smokers got around the need for sun-based energy to power themselves. But we certainly couldn't fill the one-kilometer chamber with ocean floor containing black smokers. The caves were sealed systems. If we pumped in massive amounts of sulfur-rich water, the pressure in the chamber would increase to the level that new material couldn't enter.

So, what do I do when the future of humankind is on the line and I have no clue how to proceed? Yup. I visit Doc. If he doesn't know how to do a science thing, it's because it can't *be* done. Again I had to get Sapale's blessing on involving Toño, since he'd made it clear early on he wasn't going to be part of this crew. She was very protective of him, which I found tremendously endearing. She meant well. But as she could go zero-to-hell-on-wheels in less than three seconds, I had to pitch my plan gingerly.

I found her doing something in our quarters aboard *Stingray*. I think she was cleaning and straightening, but I couldn't be sure. I mean, *Stingray* didn't allow there to be any suspended particles in the air between her walls. And the two of us no longer shed skin cells or hair or messed up counters by splashing shaving cream everywhere. But she still had it in her DNA to do some small amount of housework. I, for the record, did not suffer under the burden of such inferior genetics. Where she had strands of neat-and-clean DNA I had strands of DudeNA.

"Hey, there's my beautiful wife," I announced happily as I entered our sparse quarters. We didn't need much more than a soft vertical surface, at least three meters long and half as wide, if you take my meaning.

"The answer is no."

"Well, that cannot be the case. I didn't ask anything and if I was about to you couldn't have divined that a negative response would be the correct one."

She turned toward me, which meant she had to stop fiddling

with stuff, so I owned that much more misery because it was I who made her stop. "You're in a lobotomized good mood and compliment me the first thing out of your mouth. That can only signal you want something. Further, you want it so badly that you once again mistakenly feel your best shot at success is to butter me up. If you want the thing that badly, it has to be a Sapale-bad initiative. I rest my case. The answer is no."

"But I wasn't going to bug you for sex or anything."

"Ah, but don't you see the universality of my negative initial response? Because, if you had been soliciting sex, my answer," she rested both palms on her chest, "would be *no*. One-size-does-fit-all."

"I think you're just too defensive."

"And so, with that remark, ends any chance of you getting lucky."

"Here I am being both helpful and constructive, yet you persist with the flippant. It borders on tragic."

She threw up her arms. "Okay, ask me what you came in to ask so I can shoot it down without trending toward tragedy."

I crossed my arms. "I came to tell you how much I love you."

"Thank you, back atcha. What else?"

"Oh, yeah, come to think of it I need to sort of borrow the vortex."

"Sort of borrow? Two quick questions. How does one sort of borrow a thing and how does one borrow something he owns?"

"Good points. Thanks," I mumbled back. "I guess I meant I need to go somewhere alone, so I was asking," I gestured to where she was tidying up, "if you had an ETA on being done here so I could ... you know, ask you to disembark."

She joined me in the folded-arm club. "Hot date?"

"Hardly."

"You need privacy because you're shopping for our anniversary?"

I frowned. "Do we still have one of those?"

"Which registers on the Jon-in-trouble meter as a big fat *no*."

"I think I told you earlier today where I was going. You seemed pleased that I was ... going where I was going."

"I know," she exclaimed. "You're going to the Tower of Babble because you just *love* to babble."

"I'm paying a social visit to Toño. I told you."

Her eyes narrowed to angry slits. "So, there's the truth of it. You want to conscript the poor man into precisely what he wants nothing to do with. You, Jon Ryan, are a bad friend. You may additionally fully qualify as a bad person."

"For paying a social call on my oldest BFF? It is to laugh."

"We've had this vortex forever. When is the last time you just dropped in on Toño to shoot pool and the breeze?"

"All the time. I do that frequently."

"Al," she called out to the Big Betrayer, "when's the last time this numb nuts paid Toño a purely social call?"

"Ah that would be exactly never. Not yet. Hasn't happened. Not gonna happen. Do not pass Go and do not collect two hundred credits."

"I rest my case," she lorded over me.

I pointed up. "You can't take the word of a computer that'd stick it to another guy. He's totally suspect right out the gate."

"Why do you what to torment Toño?" she asked evenly.

"I don't. We, Plesmus and I, wish to ask his opinion of the plan we've formulated to reintroduce the first spark of life on Earth."

"What is your plan? Tell it to me. Maybe my opinion alone will be sufficient to reassure you it might work."

"I can't do that," I said softly.

"And why is that?" she said, each word a bit more inflamed than its predecessor.

"Because I, we, don't have a plan as such."

"Hang on," she said quickly. Head-to-head, she reached out to Doc. *Toño, Sapale here. How are you?*

Fine, thanks for asking.

Jon wants to come brainstorm with you. He's stuck on some aspect of one of his submissions to reanimate the Earth. Is that alright? Please be honest.

Thank you for specifying that I may be. But, no, I don't mind sitting down with an old friend over coffee and discussing a mission.

Are you certain, she pressed.

Yes, my dear. Thank you for having my back.

Not a problem. I'm guessing Plesmus and he will be there directly.

That will be fine. And of course you must visit too.

No. I already received my uninvitation in the mail.

That Jon. He's quite a handful.

He's a shit load is what he is. I'll see you soon, okay?

Absolutely.

"Okay, flyboy," she returned to addressing me, "you got my blessing. But next time don't be such a Jon Ryan about it."

"I'll—"

"What am I saying," she shrieked. "That is the least insightful, most never-going-to-come-to-pass thing I've ever accidentally stated. Go. No, wait. I go. You stay. Bye. Love you, at least for now."

And with that flourish she departed. What a gal I had. She was the bomb, as they used to say back in the day.

As soon as my brood's-mate was off the vortex, Ples and I folded over to Toño's place. He stood just outside his door waiting for us. After we'd stepped out, he waved us over and slipped back inside. I found him already seated at the kitchen table, a mug in his hand and one at the empty seat across from him.

"Please sit," he invited cordially. "Plesmus, I only wish there was something I might offer you by way of refreshment."

"Thank you for your concern, Dr. DeJesus. But I'm fine."

"If I asked you to, would you refer to me as Toño?" he asked playfully.

"Unlikely."

"Then I shall not ask." He chuckled pleasantly.

I gave him the rundown of where we were. Of course he knew a million times more than me about the origins of life. He knew more about everything than I did in fact. The sole exceptions were women, strong drink, and flying 21st century fighter planes. I had him in an intellectual beatdown in those three categories. Oorah.

"I see your dilemma," he reported after I'd finished. He sat back and parsed out something in his head. By now I could tell when he was doing that. "I do agree with centering your focus on soluble sulfites as the best option. I'm certain it was the origin point in Earth's particular case." Then he scratched at the back of his head.

"I'm glad this one's got you stumped too," I commented. "I feel a little better about being bereft of ideas myself."

His eyes lit up. "Bereft?" he whispered with a grin forming on his face. "I think that's the key," he said quietly. "Bereft," he all but shouted.

"Does that word have a meaning I'm unfamiliar with, Doc? I'm not feeling any of the love on this side of the table." I circled a finger over the tabletop.

"Bereft. It means deprived of or lacking a thing, just as you know. But it suggests to me a scheme that might well prove worthy."

Leave it to Doc. Use *suggests to me a scheme that might well prove worthy* when you just need to say *it'll work*. Eggheads. Go figure.

"It's all a matter of how long these reference moorings need to remain in place. Say, Time didn't tell you, did it?"

"Didn't he. Remember, Time appeared to me as me," I corrected.

"Yes. I was very much trying to forget that part of your interview. So did *he*?"

"No, nothing on duration. But, I told you the ground shook after we completed the first set of moorings. I take that to mean the effect of the reference mooring'll be hasto-quicko."

"You mean prompt?"

"That's what I said."

"No, you spoke Jon-ese. I am speaking Normal Human."

"So, the bereftment? Can we talk about the bereftment again?"

He looked at me like I had two heads, one more stupid than the other. "There he goes with the Jon-ese again. Bereftment is not a word."

"Please, Doc."

"Alright. We need to focus into existence," notice it was *we* now, "an active system of black smokers under tremendous saltwater pressure."

"Uh-huh."

"So as to not overload the system already under unimaginable pressures, we'll need to bleed off liquid at approximately the rate that it's formed in."

"In equals out. Pretty basic," I agreed. "But the devil is in the details. We can't just place a drain to the surface. First off, that's not how we've been fabricating the chambers. They're all uniform and all sealed. Don't ask me why, but they all are. Second, the pressure's so intense that any channel we tried to shape would be ripped to bits in an instant."

"Ah," he raised a finger, "what if the drain was internal?"

Poor guy. He'd finally snapped or was easing irrevocably into senility. I blamed myself. I'd placed too much pressure on the senior-citizen machine. "Ah, Doc, by definition a drain cannot be internal. It must be draining externally or it's not draining."

"That was never the definition of a drain. A drain in this context is simply a participant in a closed system that removes material."

"Yeah ... that's ... not ... draining," I wheezed in frustration. "The system is closed, like you said. How can you remove material if the system is closed?"

"Easily, and for quite a long time. Indefinitely? No. That would violate the law of conservation of mass. But in the case I propose, that time period the closed system will remain stable will likely exceed the age of the universe."

"Would you like to lie down, Doc?" I asked tenderly. "How about some nice warm milk?"

"No. And I shall not thank you for the offers as they are certainly based on some Jon-lusion. That is what I've come to call your personal delusions."

"If you're not, in fact, dribbling off the court here, what the hell're you talking about?"

"I suggest we fabricate the reference mooring as an area of deep sea floor that contains active black smokers. Then we add in a punctate black hole."

Yup, he was living in Banana City, he was bananas, nutzo, cracked right down the center. "You can't ... I mean, a black hole? Seriously? It'd suck up everything we focused into the chamber and then it'd start in on planet Earth itself."

"Not if we choose its mass to be just so. A very small black hole would suck off just a limited amount of matter. It would grow very slowly. And we could monitor it. Assuming your mission is successful, we can periodically check on the black hole's status, assuming it survives the reanimation. If it were to become worrisomely large, we could remove it."

"I don't know. That's kind of a crazy man's plan, if you ask me."

"Look, I'll run some simulations. Fortunately, I know the volume of the chamber and the properties of the sea-floor components. I should be able to make accurate projections as to total chamber stability and the length of time it would take for various values of the black hole mass to become unstable."

"Sure, ah, Plesmus," I asked, "you have a problem focusing a black hole?"

"I don't see why it would be an issue. And since it'll be small, I foresee even less trouble managing it."

"Sounds like a plan. When should I get back to you on those sims, Doc?"

"I can give them to you now."

"But you said you were going to run some models. I'm talking about those results."

"Those are what I have. How long did you think it would take me?"

"To run models of a one-kilometer chamber full of the bottom of the sea spewing sulfur with differing-sized black holes in it? Maybe a week."

"Well I'm done. I think a singularity with a mass of seven hundred kilograms would be the best fit in terms of efficiency of clearing the materials and lag time to achieving a worrisome mass. By the way, I don't see the mass as an issue for at least ten centuries."

"Ten centuries? Wow, that sounds like a long time."

"It is. And if anything goes awry, you and I can track and correct any issues."

"Well okay then," I said with feigned enthusiasm. "Ples, if you're comfortable with all this, let's go make some magic."

And two hours later, we'd returned to Aramthella, travelled back to the period when Earth was no-timed, and we'd focused a completely mind-blowingly dynamic system in place below the surface of ruined Earth. It was totally cool. Four down, five to go. Easy peasy.

CHAPTER FIFTEEN

Oxygen is the fifth most common element in the universe, behind hydrogen and helium. Most of it was formed by the fusion of a nitrogen and a helium in the bellies of massive stars. There was almost no free oxygen in primitive Earth's atmosphere for billions of years. But breathable oxygen is necessary for higher organisms to evolve. Where did this abundant free atmospheric oxygen come from? All the life-giving oxygen ever produced came from cyanobacteria activity. Also known as blue-green algae, it is unique in nature. No other organism before or since has mastered the voodoo of taking in sunlight, carbon dioxide, and water and releasing oxygen. All photosynthesis is dependent on blue-green algae. In order for plants to be able to make energy from sunlight, it was necessary for them to incorporate the algae into their cells. What are called chloroplasts in plants are simply enslaved cyanobacteria.

The fossil record demonstrates that the first cyanobacteria, and hence the first large-scale production of free oxygen, began around two point seven billion years ago. But it wasn't until two point four billion years ago that significant amounts of oxygen were present in the atmosphere. Why the delay? Oxygen dislikes being free. It reacts with almost everything, especially all the iron contained in the early oceans. It took those millions of years to fill up all the oxygen sponges so that oxygen could react with itself and form O_2, the breathable form. If oxygen production ever stopped, most of the present-day oxygen would vanish because of all those oxygen sinks. Astronomers use the fickle nature of oxygen to look for extraterrestrial life. Any planet with significant amounts of oxygen in its atmosphere has to contain life. There's no other way to explain that observation.

Let us review. No cyanobacteria, no breathable atmosphere. No breathable air, nobody reads this book.

Every time I started the next phase of my epic reference mooring laying, I always thought it was much worse than all previous missions. I was certain from the outset that not only would I not come up with a plan, but that there was actually no way to accomplish the intended task. I was being water-boarded in a sea of challenges. But, I could either ruminate and fret like an old man rocking on his porch, or I could get the hell going and accomplish my mission.

Oxygen, good old breathable you. I needed to ram home a mooring that guaranteed you'd be part of renewed Earth. Because without you, the only people left alive would be the ones that didn't breathe. I was again confronted by a twist. It was clear by now that the process Plesmus and I used worked well. She focused time energy through an image I held in my mind. The problem was that as well as the system worked for inanimate objects—sea vents and radioactive decay—it didn't fit the bill when it came to complex living organisms. I'm sure we could focus into existence a form that looked like an elephant, but it wouldn't be blurting its trunk or accepting any peanuts because it wouldn't be alive.

I knew blue-green algae and chloroplasts, the algae's altered form, were the workhorses in terms of oxygen production. The problem was two-fold. One, as I said, it couldn't be focused into a chamber. Two, we didn't have any blue-green algae to slip into any chamber we formed on the off chance that would be sufficient to make a viable reference mooring. We had plants out the wazoo, but they contained chloroplasts, not free-living cyanobacteria. To simulate the primitive oceans, where the blue-greens flourished, tossing in chloroplasts wasn't an acceptable substitute.

I decided to pay a call to our ship's Plant Habitat. The personnel down there were brilliant. We'd rescued a little plant material from Mars 1 and had some scant provisions we'd taken from Earth when we hurriedly departed. Out of that inauspicious foundation they constructed a marvelous diversity of plants. Some were edible while others were merely decorative. But having both along on a potentially endless colony trip was a great addition. The food synthesizers could produce all the nutrition we required. Fortunately the food it spat out was quite tasty. But there was no substitute for a real tomato on your burger or biting into a genuine orange.

The nursery was located on the lower decks, near the docking bay. The original architects of the ship placed larger spaces down there for likely the same utilitarian purposes we used them for. Entering the greenhouse space was most pleasant. The air was warm and moist, and smelled of honest labor and loam. I'd called ahead and arranged for Maggie Deveaux to meet with me. She was a botany major at GW and the logical choice to head the plant habitat. I'd met her a couple of times and she impressed me as being totally on the ball. I saw her bending over a tray of seedlings. She waved hello, then waved me over.

"Hi, Maggie," I greeted her. "Thanks for making time to chat."

"No problem. I can always use another worker."

I must have looked confused, and likely that was because I was.

"Oh, we can chat," she clarified. "But we can be productive while we do so. Having a big strong man like you down here is too good an opportunity to pass up."

"I'm game. What do you need?"

She slapped her hands over the seed tray to knock off the dirt. "Come. I have some cinder blocks that need stacking." We walked toward a shed. "So what can I help you with?"

"You know I'm working with the team dedicated to resurrecting Earth, right?"

"Absolutely. You're like a rockstar to most of us."

"Just don't ask me to sing," I teased.

"Got it," she returned with a pleasant smile.

"So, here's my question to you."

We arrived at the shed. She opened the large swinging door and gestured me in. "Keep talking," she said as she followed me in. Maggie pointed to the irregular rows of cinder blocks scattered near the far wall. "There's your project," she added as we walked.

"Where do you want them stacked?"

"Against the wall, seven blocks high, if you please."

I started moving the cement blocks. "As I started to say, here's the question. How I'm doing it is very complex. I can tell you the details if you'd like, but the how of it is not intuitive."

"If I need to know, I'll ask."

"Sounds good. So, to reanimate the Earth, I have to recreate some of the pivotal events in her history. One of those is the fabrication of breathable oxygen."

"So you'll need to introduce cyanobacteria," she stated, catching on quickly.

"Exactly. Problem is, where do I find cyanobacteria in outer space?"

"Oh my gosh, it's all around us in the habitat." She raised her hands. "In fact, I'm sure there's still some stuck on my fingers."

"Wow, that's convenient. But is it the same type as what would be way back in the past?"

"Okay," she said bashfully. "here's where I get to wow you with a botanist's take on blue-green algae. First, they're bacteria, not algae. In terms of the primitive ones that participated in the Great Oxygenation Event, we know some details. Three groups have been found in the fossil record. Eoentophysalis, Polybessurus and

Eohyella are for sure. So you see, there wasn't just one kind of cyanobacteria back then. As to having any of the ancient species available, that's unknown and probably unknowable. But I'd say this. I think it is extremely unlikely that any organism hangs around for billions of years and does not evolve significantly. Witness the fact that today we see modern humans, Homo sapiens, and none of the terminated lines like Homo habilis or Neanderthal."

"Not the answer I wanted to hear."

"Sorry."

"No, that's okay. You're just telling it like it is."

Crud. What the heck was I going to do? I guess I could dump this reference mooring and pick another. But this was a make-or-break contribution to Earth's skill set. I should clarify. It seemed necessary, but then again, what did I know? Maybe any three biggies would be good enough?

"Too bad you can't go back in time and scoop some up, right?" Maggie said encouragingly.

"It'd be nice. We have a time machine, but there's no Earth to go ... No! I couldn't be stupid enough to try and pull that one off?"

Maggie's face flared with concern. "What, Jon? What can't you be that stupid to try?"

"If, and I know this's a big *if*, we could return to the early planet do you think you'd be able to recover a representative sample of the cyanobacteria that were present?"

"You mean like high-school level ecology research? The kind I did to get away from my parents and next to boys while camping? Of course."

"And the environment back then, it wouldn't be scary. No T. rexs or winged death?"

"No, not on the land at least. Nothing lived on it then because there was no oxygen yet."

"Excellent. Say, if I can get a meeting together in the next ten minutes, could you make it?"

"Sure, I guess. Who we meeting with?"

"Just a few others. The captain, my wife, and Colonel St. Claire. That's probably it."

She looked like I'd just announced I was a vampire and asked if I could check out her neck. Then she looked down at her well-used overalls. "Meet those people dressed like this? Are you crazy?"

I tilted my head back-and-forth. "Yeah, kind of."

"Make it in an hour so I can wash and get presentable and I'm in."

"An hour it is. I'll call you with the details when I have them," I said pointing toward her face.

We parted ways. She literally ran off toward the dormitory while I headed at a leisurely pace to find Sapale. Then I'd get the other two women and we'd have ourselves a proper pow wow.

It took a tad longer than an hour, but soon enough the five of us were seated around Sachiko's stateroom table. I introduced Maggie to everyone.

"Nice to meet you," Sachiko said after I'd finished with her. "Now what's this all about, Jon?"

Oh, boy. "I'm working on a reference mooring that recreates the formation of abundant oxygen in Earth's early atmosphere." Everyone except Reva knew that already. She knew I was working on something, but didn't care to know the fine details. "Are you familiar with that topic, Reva?" I asked directly.

"I don't believe I've heard of it per se. But if you say there was a specific process to fill the air with oxygen, then I'm good."

"The problem is, and the reason I've asked Maggie to join us, is that there are none of the cyanobacteria that did the work back then available to us."

"Why do you need them?" Sachiko asked.

"Plesmus and I don't think we can focus them into existence. The landscape, yes. But the living organisms, no."

"What did you want us to discuss then?" Sachiko astutely queried. "If there's no bacteria, there's no bacteria. I know you know we can't go back in time and retrieve some because the Earth they lived on never existed."

"Yes, but likely they didn't exist only in this universe."

"Why does that statement sound so terribly ominous to me?" the captain asked with tension in her words.

"Because it is terrible risky," Sapale answered for me. "This jet jockey wants to fly us all into a parallel universe just to scoop up some pond scum."

Sachiko's eyes bugged out. "Is that true? Are you going to ask that we journey across the multiverse in search of bacteria? Bacteria you're not even sure how to use in the first place to accomplish your mission?'

"Yeah, kind of," I replied more sheepishly than I wished I had.

"I've heard the term multiverse," Reva interjected. "But where is it? Can we simply fly there?"

"No. It's complicated," Sachiko began. "The multiverse theory, and I stress the word *theory*, says that there are an infinite number of alternate universes out there somewhere. They're subtly different from one another. But there is a universe somewhere that has the exact characteristics one sets out to find."

"What does that mean?" Reva asked uncertainly.

"Pick a mythological animal," Sachiko said to Reva.

"A unicorn," she responded numbly.

"Fine. Somewhere in the multiverse there is a reality where the five of us are having this meeting, but where we all have unicorn horns sticking out of our foreheads."

"W ... why would we all have unicorn horns?" Reva asked, though she clearly felt asking was a mistake.

"Because we do. We evolved that way."

"Oh."

"Jon and I have traveled to several other universes," Sapale volunteered. "It's not a trivial thing to do but it's also not all that difficult. The multiverse is not just a theory on paper. It's real."

I rubbed under my chin. "*Stingray*'s done it a few times. It has to do with manipulating the membrane and black holes to modify the interfaces between dimensions. Once properly tweaked, you can slip out of this universe and into an alternate one."

"And you can return to this particular one after that?" Sachiko asked. "Because it wouldn't do to leave this one but return to another alternate universe."

"We returned to this one," Sapale replied.

"I know, because you're across the table speaking with me. But how do you know this is the exact universe you initially left?"

"Bec—" I started confidently, even maybe vaingloriously. Then it hit me like a lead pipe to the forehead. Ah, how did we know all the times we shuttled back and forth that we didn't reappear in an alternate but almost cookie-cutter-copy-of-our-universe universe?

Sachiko caught the hesitation in my response. "You see, nothing's obvious in the multiverse. Take it from an astronomer. We debate that topic all the time."

"All I can say is that to the best of our ability and our extreme effort, we aim to come home," I defended. "But I don't think we have a choice here."

"Let me see if I get this," Reva posited. "We go to another Earth, a very similar Earth, and hope it has the identical algae our Earth had billions of years ago?"

"You got it," I shot back cheerfully.

"And just how do we know it's identical?" she further wondered.

"We ask Maggie here."

Maggie's immediate reaction was to look like she was doing the Heimlich on herself internally.

"Hang on," she protested. "*If* I had a PhD in cyanobacteria I doubt I'd be qualified to make that determination. Especially not so given the stakes. No, you can't rely on a general botanist to resolve that issue. Get someone else."

"Do you know Tip Benjamin?" I asked playfully.

She rolled her eyes. "Oh, Lord, yes. That man's so detached from humankind that he doesn't even know he's detached from the rest of us."

"You know Tip," I complimented.

"I know *of* him. I have, to date, avoided him like the proverbial plague."

"Wise policy. My point is this. Tip's probably the next most qualified person to perform this task. Just ask him. He knows more about sciency crap than anyone else. So, let me ask you flatly. Do *you* want to attempt to determine which algae are like the ones we need, or do you want *Tip* to do the job?"

"Would he?" Maggie asked.

"If I told him to, you bet. He's rightly scared of me."

To her credit it didn't take Maggie long to decide. How could it? Her versus Tip? That's an easy call. "I'll do it, but I'm telling you up front it is way beyond my expertise. I was going to attend grad school to get a PhD in pomology."

"Pomology?" Reva peeped.

"The study of growing fruit. Peaches and nectarines to be specific. Agricultural stuff," Maggie responded.

"And if you pick us a good algae slurry, I'll be the first to congratulate you on your acceptance to the top school in the entire field of pomology," I told her and I meant it. If she pulled this off, I'd see the best school accepted her and changed their name to hers. Maggie Deveaux U. That even had a nice ring to it.

"How do you propose to proceed?" Sachiko asked.

"*Stingray* can place us all in an alternate universe. Then she can find and fold over to that universe's version of Earth. After that, Aramthella just needs to whip us back to the beginning. Then Maggie will go slime hunting."

"I can't say I'm wildly comfortable about this plan. But I am convinced we need to attempt the chancy voyage. Reva, Sapale?"

"I'm all in," Sapale answered instantly.

"In the for-what-it's-worth category, I agree on undertaking the mission."

"Then it's settled. I'll network with the AIs and come up with some high-percentage options. Maggie," I turned toward her, "you rifle through all the information we have on cyanobacteria. By this time tomorrow I want you to know more about the topic ... well, than you do now. Or than Tip."

"I'll ..." she started.

I raised a finger. "The Tip part is critical. Know more than Tip, for all our sakes."

"That part I can guarantee," she stated confidently.

My model runs with the Als went well, but boy were they tedious. Their computational speeds were billions of times faster than mine. So, in the time it took me to pose a perturbation of an already run model, they'd spit out an answer. Then I'd slowly consider the results, meaning like a few seconds. Then I 'd choose an alternate set of boundary conditions, and—bam—they'd pour answers into my head. It was esoteric physics wash-rinse-repeat. Who doesn't like that? Though you can't see it, I'm raising my arm frantically.

One comment Sachiko had made really stuck in my craw. It was the remark about knowing if I'd returned to the universe I'd left from. Believe it or not, that was a tricky issue. One interpretation of the multiverse is that you never return to where you started. You always just jump from one unique universe to another. I didn't hold with that take, and more significantly, neither did Toño. Whether it was his stern Catholic upbringing or simply his scientific insights talking, he was certain we were always returning to the universe we'd left.

It seemed important to me so I remember my jaunts to other universes vividly. But some might forget how very often, relatively speaking, I had slipped between realities. As far back as my fight with the Last Nightmare, even as the colony ships were fleeing doomed Earth, I'd left this universe. A Last Nightmare creature named Des-al had pulled me into his universe he called the Neverwhere. And my fights with the Ancient Gods saw me basically commuting to-and-from their universe to ours. But with me unable to get Sachiko's words out of my head, I wanted to be damn sure that we all returned to this universe and no other. The only issue was how? How do you know you're back where you started? Breadcrumbs aren't going to cut it. Leaving a sign reading "Welcome Home To The Correct Universe" won't either. Nope. The

Jons and Sachikos of any number of alternate universes could well erect the same signs.

So how could I be certain? Right. Ask Toño.

Head-to-head I rang him up. *Hey, Doc, you there?*

If I said no, would that buy me any peace?

Funny guy.

I got a quick question.

That will be the day. But go ahead and ask.

Even funnier guy.

I've, well, we've *decided to explore alternate universes in search of Earth's primordial cyanobacteria. I was wondering, how can we be certain that we are returning to the universe we left, and not an alternate but indistinguishable one?*

And you have no issue concerning the immense and dangerous, not to mention hard-pressed-to-be-successful mission in the first place? You do realize that you have cited so many wild goals that it's difficult to know which most reflect mental instability on your part.

Funniest guy—ever.

Well, you, Plesmus, and I decided we needed to recreate the Great Oxygenation Event. Since we don't have any ancient cyanobacteria to introduce as part of a reference mooring, we decided we needed to get some source material.

And what will you do with them if your luck exceeds all justifiable limits?

One bridge at a time, Doc. One bridge at a time.

I'd comment that an admission such as that considerably heightens my concern for the wisdom of your plan, but I know that once you've decided a thing, the decision is irrevocable.

You got it, I confirmed.

So, back to your main request. You must recall we transitioned between universes before with no difficulty. If you set the correct course, you will reach the correct universe, this universe.

Yes, but is there any way to be certain? Many alternates in the multiverse must be awfully similar to this one.

That is true. But none can be identical. I would advise this. I cannot provide you a method of making a quick confirmation that you've returned to this universe. I can, however, suggest a formula that will establish with statistical near-certainty that you have returned home. Measure multiple physical constants in this universe. When you have attempted to return, repeat those observations. With each identical determination, the probability rises that you achieved your goal. Parameters I suggest include the temperature of the cosmic microwave background, the strength of the strong nuclear force, the gravitational constant, Plank's length, and the elementary charge of an electron. There are twenty-three additional dimensionless constants you can confirm. If they all match up, I'd be very comfortable assuming you've returned home.

And the reverse should be true also, so that if we measure all those factors in the universe we're entering, at least one should be different?

Again, statistically speaking, yes. Measure them all each time you make a jump. I'm confident you will quickly reassure yourself that you can be certain where you are.

Got it. Thanks, Doc.

You are welcome. Is there anything else I might help with?

Nope, that should do it.

Best of luck, my friend.

We ended the link. Okay, so I had a way to calm Sachiko's nerves, and since it came from Toño, she be hard-pressed to not feel better. There was nothing left to do but commit to the mission. Me? I was stoked. I loved leaving this universe and barging in unannounced to someone else's. Like Forrest Gump said so famously, *you never know what you're going to get.*

It did take a personal call from Sachiko to Toño to sufficiently quell her reservations, but two days later we were set to jet. The basic plan was straightforward. *Stingray* would ferry Aramthella across the dimensional divide. It took the magical Deavoriath technology to make jaunts between universes possible. Aramthella moved through time much better and much safer than *Stingray*, but the vortex's overall capabilities were light years beyond the time ship's.

Once we were in a new realm, both ships would try and establish our location relative to that universe's Earth. That was going to be flat out hard. Universes are huge—duh. Reckoning a frame of reference in such a massive volume is not nearly impossible. It's well past ridiculous to attempt. It's finding a needle that's hidden in a haystack that's hidden in a zillion other haystacks. I assumed we'd have to fold to many locations in our new frame of reference before we got extremely lucky and found the Earth. At that point Aramthella would zip us up and down the timeline until we found the local planet's equivalent of the Paleoproterozoic era. That's when the oxygenation event occurred for us. Yeah, the process promised to be lengthy, tedious, and highlighted only with frustration. But we had no alternatives.

Some things that you'd assume are going to be life-changing happen without you even noticing. Others feel obliged to hit you like a battleship at flank speed. Moving out of our universe and into another was more the whimper type than the bang. Sapale and I felt our usual slight nausea but that was pretty much it. And the trip was instantaneous. I'm not complaining, mind you. I'll take easy over hard nine times out of ten. But the passage was a non-event.

"Captain, we're holding steady at the coordinates *Blessing* was aiming for," Aramthella announced seconds after I'd given the command to initiate the fold.

"Sensor report," Sachiko called out. "I need eyes and ears, people."

"We report no immediate threats," began Al. "We are in a very desolate area tremendously far from any galaxies. The nearest hydrogen nucleus is over eleven parsecs away. Aside from that lonely proton, there's a whole lot of nothing going on out there."

"My scans confirm his report," the chief science officer announced. "As far as I can tell there's nothing present."

"That's fine with me," Sachiko mused. "All alone is safe."

"*Blessing*, Aramthella, any progress on establishing our relative position?"

"Negative, Captain," *Blessing* replied quickly. "I doubt we'll be able to from this location."

"Why's that?" Sachiko asked.

"There simply aren't many galaxies we can make out in any detail. We are hoping to recognize the configurations of at least three resident galaxies to be able to calculate our position."

"I'm having no greater luck," Aramthella responded. "I suggest we fold away to the farthest galaxy we can resolve. From there possibly we can find our bearings."

"Make it so," I instructed.

"By your command, Form One," came *Stingray's* response.

Slight nausea.

"Let me know your findings as quickly as possible," Sachiko stated.

A few seconds later, Al announced a find. "I believe we've found one hard marker. It's millions of light years away, but we're confident we can identify it. It is a collision between two galaxies. Back in the day it was called the Mayall Object. It was about 500 million light-years away from our galaxy in the direction of the constellation Ursa Major. I've always thought the positioning of the two galaxies look quite vulgar in an erotic sense. That's what bolsters our confidence."

"Oh, you mean the one cigar-shaped galaxy heading right into the center of the nice spiral galaxy?" Sachiko asked with a chuckle.

"That's the naughty pair," Al confirmed.

"Yeah. You know I always thought the same thing. I used to mention it, but after seeing people's reactions, I kind of stopped sharing," she added.

"I concur with Al's summary," Aramthella seconded.

"What, you mean it's erotic that the cigar-shaped thing is heading straight into the center of the..." I started.

"No, I meant about the marker. I suggest we move to that location and reassess." Aramthella interrupted.

"Sounds good," I responded. "*Stingray*, make it happen."

Slight nausea.

A few seconds after we stopped Al shouted, "Bingo! We can identify over one hundred galaxies that are familiar to us. And now we have an estimation of the coordinates of the local Earth. Shall we pop over and give it a hug?"

"Yes, please," I answered with a grin. That Al was too much too much of the time.

Slight nausea.

"Captain," Aramthella announced, "we are in orbit around Earth, four hundred fifty kilometers up."

"Yes," Sachiko snapped with a pump of her fist. "What approximate time period are we in?"

"Early Post-Industrial based on the pollutants in the atmosphere and the communications chatter."

"So that'd be like the year 3000, 3500, give or take?" I asked.

"Yes," Al responded. "The use of hydrocarbons as fuel are long since replaced with mostly fusion. The lifestyle of humankind has shifted from a work-based economy to a thought-based one. I'd guess humans have colonized a few nearby star systems. What we're analyzing from the communications grid confirms the societal status."

"Just curious," I asked, "are there normal humans down there?"

"I'll put up a series of images we've captured," Al replied.

A rapid sequence of images flashed across the main screen. "Damn if they don't look like you and me," I mused aloud.

"Have they detected us?" the captain asked.

"No sign of that," Aramthella answered.

"Well, let's not hang around until they do," Sachiko said resolutely. "Take us two point five billion years into the past."

A couple of seconds later, Aramthella reported, "We are then."

"Scan?" the captain called out again.

"I have some general files on this remote period," Al began. "I'd say we're in or near the Paleoproterozoic."

"What are the oxygen levels in the atmosphere?" she asked quickly.

"Very low," Al reported. "Less than one part per million."

"Then we're too early," she concluded. "Move us two hundred million years into the future."

"We are then," Aramthella stated. "The oxygen levels are much increased now. It comprises almost seven percent of the atmospheric gases."

"Hot damn," I interjected. "I do believe we've arrived." I turned to Maggie. She'd been doing her level best to fade into the wallpaper ever since the mission began. "It's your call. Want to go down and take a peek?"

"I ... I guess so, if you think it's safe," she replied uncertainly.

"Hmm. Safe? You know we traveled into a new universe and just folded over unimaginable distances all in the span of fifteen minutes. That seems safe to you so far?"

"Uh, not much," she managed.

"Correct-a-mundo. We're freaking nuts to even go this far. So let's double down and make a side trip. What do you say?"

"Sounds fine," she responded. I didn't believe either of those two words. Poor kid was scared to death. Seems she had some common sense.

Now, you have to know this part of the operation was going to be a milk run. That's what we military types call a mission that's about as dangerous as taking a nap. Still, long years of struggle had taught me well. Assume even easy-sounding trips can go wrong. With that in mind I didn't want to land Aramthella because, well, she represented the whole enchilada. If she was blindsided like the ships in Pearl Harbor the show was over folks. Similarly I didn't want to go in *Stingray*. If Aramthella didn't have the vortex and Sapale available, they were going to be stuck in this universe with no chance of returning home. As neither ship carried shuttle craft to land in, that left but one option. The landing party had to be dropped down to the surface inside a membrane. Yes, that would be, 1) stick living people in a ball of air and 2) lower them from space. Sound scary? Yup, it was going to be jarring for everyone who came except for me because I was a crazy fighter pilot.

Maggie needed to come. I needed to accompany her. Sachiko and Sapale had to remain above because they would be the captains of the two key ships. Reva couldn't come because she was the senior officer in charge of the military part of the crew. I knew we'd need help moving equipment. Plus, the more hands-on-deck the faster we'd accomplish our goals. So I had to select three or four others to assist us. I might have chosen Tip—yeah, I know—but he was semi-permanently staying with Toño. The brat wasn't even in this universe.

I needed one other person who could shoot straight, you know, just in case the extremely unlikely happened. I didn't want an officer. They were proficient with side arms and desks. I needed a senior enlisted person, the kind who ate steel for breakfast and crapped nails. I knew just who I needed. Master Sergeant Lakeisha Parker. To see that woman carrying a M16 with a belt full of extra clips was to know you were as safe as if you were in your mother's arms. Unless of course you were her target, in which case you were going tits-up hasto pronto. I'd gotten to know her over the months and she impressed me more the longer I knew her. She trained like a demon, demanded perfection of her troops, but always had their deep admiration and trust. She'd even asked me to spar with her. Imagine that, a sergeant asking a general to rumble. Lakeisha told me she asked me because, *Maybe I'd offer up a challenge, since nobody else aboard could fight their way through a heavy rainstorm.*

That left only a couple of technical nerds to assist Maggie collecting and analyzing the muck for cyanobacteria. I asked her to choose that part of the team, since she knew her needs better than I did. She came up with someone she worked with from the habitat, Billie Hayworth, and one of the medical technicians, Lou Landry, because he was a whiz at all the automated machines. So our team was set. If we worked well together, I imagined this would be the away team for the multiple sorties we'd need to make to find the right set of algae. Who knew how long that was gonna take?

I had Al form a box-shaped full membrane twenty meters on each side. I figured that no one but me, and maybe Lakeisha, wanted to see the abyss we were falling through. Best to have opaque walls. Maggie and her team assembled a bunch of gadgets and boxes and brought them to the hangar deck. Once that was done, we were ready.

"Okay, last call, people," I announced. "If you need anything else or you need to hit the restroom, it's now or nev ... not until later." Oops. I almost jinxed the mission before we even dusted off. There were no takers. Lakeisha raised the plasma rifle she brought above her head and yelled, of course, *oorah*. "Al, take us down. Ground floor please, men's shoes, appliances, and blue-green algae."

The hangar disappeared as the membrane settled over us. A couple of people yelped, but I didn't hear any pee splash to the deck, so it was all good. The trip down took about five minutes and was uneventful. I checked in with each individual every thirty seconds but no one fessed up to being about to lose it. Again, that was appreciated. A few times the descent package shook a little, but I think that was more Al being Al than any turbulence. I couldn't even tell when we came to rest. The full, and light-blocking membrane simply slid to transparent as Al switched it to a partial membrane, per our prearranged plan. Thirty seconds later he opened a tiny hole so we could communicate with each other.

"I don't see anything scary," I reported.

"Nothing unexpected shows up on the scans from here either," Al confirmed.

"Drop the membrane and we'll get busy," I instructed.

"You are now free to walk about the planet," Al stated with dramatic flair.

As there was enough oxygen if the fleshies didn't overexert themselves, I hadn't required they bring suits or even helmets. The one exception was Lakeisha. She had a fireman's breathing mask and a small O2 bottle strapped to her back. If, on the off chance she needed to lay down some law, she'd need the extra oxygen. Plus I felt it added nicely to her overall badass appearance. Never discount one's level of badassness,

"Okay, Maggie, the shows all yours," I told her. "Lakeisha and I're just spectators unless you ask us to help. "

She got, if it was possible, a more concerned look on her face.

She wasn't used to the leadership-in-potentially-hostile-surroundings quite yet. "So, let's check those rocks over there." She pointed to an outcropping that met the ground in a shallow pool of water. We were in a bit of dilemma concerning location. The oceans were the only place large creatures dwelled in this period. For that reason we wanted to give the shoreline a wide birth. But it was logical to assume that the types of algae we needed to find lived in sea water, since there was so much more of it than fresh water. We settled on exploring as far back as possible on a low tide.

Lakeisha assumed a position between the rest of the team and the ocean. Seeing her there with her rifle lolling at half-staff made me feel safe. In fact, I pitied any sea monster that tried to get past her. It wouldn't be participating in evolution anymore.

I settled in for a boring session of watch-nothing-much-happen. To pass the time I'd snoop at what the science people were doing, then go harass Lakeisha. She, for her part, gave more shit than she took and then some. My opinion of her swelled with each gross insult and inventive curse. She was alright.

An hour and a half into the session, Maggie walked over to me. "We finally have some DNA results back on the cyanobacteria isolates. I've had both ships review the data comparing these samples to modern day bacteria back home."

"And?" I encouraged.

"And I'm not pleased. These are definitely cyanos, but the DNA is too divergent from ours to be promising. The algae has only one chromosome but some species have from one to six copies of that unit. Most of our bacteria have only one chromosome. All the local cyanos are showing two chromosomes. The sequences are fairly similar, but the fact that—"

She stopped speaking when three massive impacts slammed into the rocky ground around us.

Boom ... boom ... *boom.*

Whatever was striking was powerful. It appeared to be coming from above. I threw up a full-membrane dome encompassing everyone plus a five-meter buffer zone.

"Everyone take cover," I yelled. Then I waited to see if whatever was hitting our position was about to do the impossible and breach the membrane. A minute later I figuratively could take a breath.

"Okay, we're safe for now," I called out. "Everybody wedge yourselves under that little overhang." I indicated where I wanted them. The three scientists were still frozen, but Lakeisha leaped over to the rocky cover like a mountain goat.

She wheeled an arm in the air. "Let's go, everybody. Move, move, *move.*"

Seeing her intensity broke the spell. They sprinted to cover.

Once she was satisfied the three were nice and tucked in, she sprinted to my side. "I didn't see them, General. Did you make them?"

"Negative. But they might be shooting from orbit."

"How'm I gonna get kinetic with the ALFs if I can't see 'em?"

"Hang in there. Whoever's knocking on the door'll be coming through sooner or later. You can kill them then. In fact, let's have a look outside, shall we?"

I switched to a transparent partial membrane. Wow, we were being hit with almighty hell. Impacts danced and skidded off the membrane. I felt like we were driving through a car wash of incoming. Then, abruptly, the barrage ended. I scanned upward and maxed out the magnification of my eyes, straining to see our enemy. I didn't see anything.

"General," Lakeisha shouted as she slapped my shoulder with the butt of her weapon. "We got company."

Well, screw me with a Panzer tank. I wouldn't believe this if I hadn't seen it with my own eyes. I still didn't believe it and I'd seen it for absolute. Three shiny Deavoriath vortices had landed fifty meters off. Then the hulls gaped open and several Deavoriaths hit the dirt running. They were heading straight for our position. There was no mistaking the Deavoriath. They were roughly humanoid, but with three arms and three legs, and four fingers on each hand. They ran by rotating the three legs in a whirling motion. It was painful to watch.

Priority One was the ship. I poked a hole on the far side of the membrane. "Ryan calling Aramthella. Can you hear me?"

"Sachiko here, Jon. We read you loud and clear. Jon, we've been attacked by six vortices. *Blessing* said she scanned them before we threw up a membrane. She certain they're local Deavoriath."

"Are you guys safe?" I pressed.

"For now, yes. Our membranes held. They hit us hard but failed to do any damage. Jon, they fired without warning. They meant to kill us."

"I agree. Keep a hole open so we can communicate. Ask Al to move the opening around. We have a way of doing it that makes it impossible for the enemy to exploit the opening."

"Copy that. Are you safe?"

"For now. Three vortices just landed and the Deavoriath foot soldiers have hit the ground. I'll keep you posted."

"Jon, if these ships appear to pose us any risk, I'm no-timing them in a heartbeat."

"As well you should. Hard to see how this ends well. Do whatever it takes. And, Captain?"

"Yes?"

"Everyone down here is expendable. No one up there is. You got that?"

"Yes. Yes, I do," she said with resolve.

"Ryan out."

The troops had made it to the membrane. Like a well-oiled machine, a tripod slammed down. Then a box was mounted to that and a metal tube was slapped atop the unit. It flared to life.

"What the hell?" Lakeisha asked.

"I think it's a cutting tool."

"Will it cut?"

"Unlikely. But, hey, if it does, you'll get to kill some people."

"Then let's hope it's a good torch then," she replied with a big grin.

I was confident the membrane would hold. Even the Deavoriath of our far future hadn't invented a membrane like ours. I doubted these versions would have any better luck getting through. As the torch sizzled and the soldiers labored, I stepped over to face them. It took a second, but finally one of them noticed my brazen inspection. She whipped up her rifle and let loose. I'm guessing it was a gamma-ray laser from the way it deflected off. After ten seconds she realized the futility of her actions and stopped. But she gave me a look of pure unmitigated hatred. Oh well, one less asshole on my Christmas card list.

When news of the torch's failure reached whoever was in command back in the vortex, that individual came outside. He stared at me for a moment, then slowly paced over until he was less than a meter from me. His expression was blank. As familiar as I was with his species, I couldn't read him. Then it hit me. He was studying me. I was an ant in a kid's ant farm and he was figuring out how he was going to break through the plastic. Oh no you don't, ass candy. No way you look at me like that. Sister Aretha, let's teach this one some R-E-S-P-E-C-T.

I turned to Lakeisha. "I'm going to be speaking to this prick in his native tongue. Sorry you won't understand."

"Not a prob, sir. Just an issue to work around. I can still listen to his body language and if I don't like what I hear, he's dead."

"Have I mentioned how much I like you?" I said with a wink.

"No, and I don't want'a hear it either. And this gun doesn't give a never mind about who I point it at."

"Stay sharp," I responded in earnest.

Through the tiny hole on the far side of the membrane I projected a single word in the Deavoriath native tongue. I'd been accustomed to the Deavoriath so long it was second nature to me now. "*Clingfoodar.*"

The bozo's eyes snapped open like he was falling asleep and heard a loud noise. He looked at me with curiosity and he looked at me confused. His head rotated and he moved side-to-side studying me.

"*Clingfoodar,*" I repeated. "*Clingfoodar, varmp dal,*" I said even louder.

Clingfoodar translated as *parley*, but it means more. The Deavoriath were a fierce warrior race. For millions upon millions of years they have fought and won countless wars of conquest. In our universe they once ruled the entire galaxy. Throughout all this conflict they developed an ironclad warrior's creed. It was bushido times European chivalry on steroids. And the word *clingfoodar* was one of the more mystical terms the Deavoriath were devoted to like mother's milk. It was steeped in honor, a never-say-die spirit, and fearlessness. It was a challenge to the other party's core worth. If not respected, the offender was not killed. No, worse—he or she was shunned. That was hell for these people. The *varmp dal* I tacked on was an insult. *Now or never*, that's what I slapped him with. It implied he was considering reneging on the parley request. That was to imply that he was the son of a thousand fathers and a crackhead whore, from a human perspective.

"*Numph ball*," he responded with displeasure. *Of course now.*

I took a deep breath and then I dropped the membrane.

"*Who are you to attack me as I practice peace?*" I asked indignantly.

"*Who am I? Who are you to invade my universe?*" he asked like I was the village idiot's dumber brother.

"*To make assumptions is to admit you are a fool*," I challenged him with an old proverb. In this context he wasn't going to be too damn pleased to hear it. "*I made peace, here by this beautiful shoreline. My friends gathered little somethings for a meal. How does a flying beast possibly see that as an invasion?*" Again I was basically saying he was a nitwit.

"*Under clingfoodar you feel open to insult me? I see honor skipped your generation.*"

"*I tire of this flapping of old women's tongues. Speak to me meaning, or I will exit clingfoodar. If I do I will admit to all who might ask that you were indifferent to the tradition.*" I was really upping the ante on insults. The very thought of being indifferent to the greatest icon of the Deavoriath warrior's creed was as low a blow as there was.

He realized what a dicey position I'd backed him into. After all, his people could hear us plainly. If he didn't navigate the treacherous waters I'd just stirred up well enough, his career was over. He'd be a man of disgrace.

"*I am Sulmac, son of Rezinquar, ruler of the Eighth Vestichur and champion of Alderquest. I speak to whom?*"

That was much better. I'd forced him into being civil.

"*I am Jon Ryan, human from Earth.*"

"*I accept your tale.*"

"*As I accept yours.*"

We had basically said *hi.*

"*How is it, Jon Ryan, you possess a Deavoriath vortex, albeit from another universe?*"

"*It was given to me by Cragforel. Ask him if you doubt my telling.*" Again, I was holding the SOB's feet to the fire with challenges.

"*And how can you be so bold as to invade our universe? Is yours not enough?*"

"*Coming to a place is not to invade it,*" I rebuked.

"*Yes it is. It is our way as it is surely the way of our brothers and sisters in your realm.*"

"*I see your meaning. But I am human. I said so plainly. Your rules do not bind any of my arms.*"

That gave him great pause. The pinhead had detected *Stingray* and assumed that we were Deavoriath. If we had in fact been their kin his assumptions would be reasonable and his actions easily justifiable. But I'd just pointed out a painful truth and he'd yet to see an actual Deavoriath among us. He began transitioning from frontal attack to tail-between-the-legs retreat. He clearly disliked his reversal of fortune.

"*And this devil weapon you use, is it a product of Deavoriath from your realm?*"

"*Our protective shield?*"

He nodded.

"*It is my technology and no one else's. Where I dwell the Deavoriath look away from my protective field.*" In so many words I'd said, *No because you guys aren't smart enough to come up with the tech.*

He stewed a good long while. He most certainly did.

"*Have you called off your brash attack on my main ship in orbit yet?*" I challenged. Again, brash is not a word a Deavoriath officer ever wants to hear directed at him. It suggests strongly he's foolish and wasn't perceptive enough to not do what you're referring to.

"*I have. My fleet now monitors your ship. We will initiate no hostile action, but neither are we metrachs.*" Think *chicken* when the word *metrach* is tossed about.

"*We won't attack you. Know this as fact. We came for an item of great value. It is not here. We would be gone and returned to our universe were we not inconvenienced.*" I'd just said his best shot at taking us out was merely an inconvenience. Yes, I was piling it on. But the dick tried to kill the totality of humankind.

He swept two arms across the bleak landscape. "*You sought a thing of value here? There is not one valuable grain of sand on this infant planet. It's not worthy of target practice.*"

"*Be that as it may. As we are still speaking under clingfoodar I will know if you will allow us to depart with no further harassment. In my one visit to this universe I would hate to be forced to weaken the Deavoriath Empire by crushing the nearest nine vortices under my heel.*" I was cutting it close. I didn't specifically threaten to euthanize his command, just the nine nearest enemy ships. But we both knew what I was saying and how insultingly I was saying it.

"*If you speak in the forward direction, we will not destroy your ships. But if this is nothing more than a ploy to destabilize our empire, know that you will not see tomorrow. We detected you folding into our galaxy so you know we can track your movements precisely. Make a heading that concerns me and death will swoop down on you like the Ten Deaths of Naggil.*"

Wow, I'd forgotten how far back in time I traveled. Way back when, near the height of their conquests, the Deavoriath were not only a xenophobic warrior race but they held to strong religious beliefs. In my time they had long since abandon such a faith system in favor of expunging all passion from their beings. They felt their ways had been senseless, and worse than that, cruel and unjustifiable. Naggil was a place, not a person. Clearly it was not a place one took the family for summer vacation. It was like the Disneyland of death. The theology behind the legend was both obscure and hard to explain. Think of it as somewhere between Purgatory and hell-on-earth.

Though Lakeisha couldn't understand a word we said, she did correctly read our body languages. She sensed the meeting was coming to a close and she quietly stepped up just behind me. "So you gonna let me kill at least the head puke? You basically promised I'd get my shot."

I rotated my head slightly. "As long as they behave we leave them vertical. Horizontal only happens if they break the truce we just struck. Sorry, Parker, I really am. But not to worry. You'll get your chance sooner than later. It's the way of war."

"I'll obey, but next time you and I are in the gym, I'm going to demonstrate the extent of my disappointment up close and personal."

"You got it," I replied with a grin. Then back to serious I instructed, "Go get the others. Walk 'em slowly back to the landing site. And stay between them and the bad guys as best you can."

"Roger that. What about the equipment? We leaving it behind?"

"You secure the civilians. I'll get the gear. The last thing I need is one of them freaking out and causing an escalation. You copy?"

"Sir," she responded tersely. Then she slipped away, never taking her eyes off Sulmac.

"*I will collect my equipment and bring it to our departure spot.*" I pointed to where we'd set down. "*Over there. My ship will send a field down to bring us up.*"

"*And my team and I will watch you do just that. Do not spit wind at me, Jon Ryan. The day is young and my wrath focused on you.*" Translation: Don't BS me because there's still plenty of day left for me to vent my anger at you.

"*Where you stand is nothing to me, unless it is between me and my destination. Know that I will make my destination.*" Yeah, I told him I couldn't give a shit what he did. I was going where I was going. If he interfered, he'd regret it. 'Nuf said.

I made a show of turning my back on Sulmac and walking over to the equipment. Then I had to do something I'd just as soon not have had to do. I extended my probe fibers and retrieved all the machines and boxes in one scoop. I knew that'd likely provoke Sulmac. I'd just made the case that I was human and not subject to Deavoriath rules. Then I inexplicably whipped out my command prerogatives, as the Deavoriath referred to the fibers.

I also was loath to have the away team see me do a totally non-human thing. I was still keeping the nature of me being an android on a strictly need-to-know basis. No one present had been aware of my nature, but they all but certainly would be now. Once word got out that Sapale and I were not actual flesh and blood I feared order might be corrupted. I also knew some of the crew would harbor prejudicial issues about cohabitating with a machine. But the equipment was valuable and it'd be hard to replace. As soon as we were off this version of Earth we'd be exploring another real soon. These were the tools we were going to require, so with us they came.

As I passed by Sulmac I could tell he was about to hop out of his skin he was so pissed. But having probe fibers didn't make me Deavoriath. We both knew that. But I could tell he wanted to peel off a few layers of skin while asking me what the devil I was doing having the fibers. Fortunately for him he held his tongue. I was not in a mood that was wisely tested.

When I reached the landing spot, I noticed Lakeisha had maneuvered the scientists so their backs were toward me. It looked like she was marching them in front of herself, but no one was moving. It was odd, but I didn't focus too much on that. I needed to stay sharp and get us all home safely.

Head-to-head I called Sapale. The less Sulmac overheard the better. *We're standing in the drop zone. Please retrieve us ASAP. We're all safe and well, but the lead Deavoriath is close to breaking the truce. He's barking orders to his team and getting more and more agitated.*

Copy that. The enemy vortices have withdrawn half a million kilometers so we can drop the membrane to bring you up.

Great.

But, Jon, if they attack while you're in no-man's-land ...

We're in for the ride of our lives, right?

And then some. Sapale out.

Almost as soon as she signed off, the landscape vanished. The full membrane had swallowed us up. A few minutes later we were safe and sound, standing aboard Aramthella. Once the three scientists knew they were not going to die they let loose. Two dropped to their knees and all three burst into sobs. They hugged in a group-tearfest, which was awkward with Maggie still standing. But I doubt they noticed the mismatch. They were releasing a lot of emotion. Yeah, they were exposed to a little bit more danger than they anticipated.

Lakeisha walked over to me briskly. "General, the captain wants a debriefing in her stateroom immediately. If you give me a sec to stow my weapons and I could accompany you if you don't mind."

That was Lakeisha in a nutshell. Fearless under pressure, cocky to a fault. But when it came to a formal debriefing by the skipper, she wanted someone to hold her hand. I was down with that. There was a time long, long ago when I feared the brass. For freak's sake, now I was the brass. Wasn't life one crazy-ass shit show?

"No prob. Hey, you did good down there. I'm putting you in for a medal."

She looked stunned for about half a second. Then she frowned. "I just did my duty, sir. I don't think I deserve a medal."

"Then don't recommend yourself for one. But I do and I am."

"In that case, thank you, General Ryan."

"You earned it."

"But, sir, don't think that just because I got a medal that I'm going any easier on you than I promised earlier."

"Thought never crossed my mind."

She's passed off her rifle and ammo belt to someone from the armory. We walked toward Sachiko's office.

"By the by, Parker, what're you gonna report about me using those wires to carry all that equipment?"

I could tell she had a hard time not smiling. "Wires, General Ryan? Whatever wires are you referring to?"

"The ones I lifted all the crap up with, Sergeant."

"Sir, if you will recall correctly, we all had our backs to you when you used those wires."

"Oh, yes, that's right. I forgot."

"As will I, sir."

The rest of the trip to Sachiko's office was travelled in a pleasant silence.

CHAPTER SIXTEEN

If at first you don't succeed ...

We did slip away without further incident. The guilt trip I laid on old Sulmac worked its magic until we were at least back in our home universe. And yes, I was so pissed at Sachiko I could hardly see straight. For two billion years I'd been the spontaneous, often reckless risk taker. In the past I'd have just jumped from one parallel universe to another in search of premium quality blue-green algae. But ever since she planted that damn drop of doubt in my mind about returning to the "correct" universe, I'd been subject to uncontrollable bouts of exercising reasonable caution. Curse that woman! How could she do that to me, a scoundrel and a happy gambler?

After a brief sojourn to our universe—confirmed six-ways-to-Sunday I guarantee you—we set off for another universe Toño had felt was a good prospect. I asked him why he labeled it a good prospect. He explained why, but he did so in Science Geek, not English. So I really can't say what made it a prime target. Maybe it tasted good? Who knows? But that's where we went.

We arrived no closer to the Milky Way than we had the last time out. It took us a little longer, but eventually we IDed our galaxy, and then Earth. Knowing full well there was almost certainly a Deavoriath Empire here too, we proceeded with a lot of caution, but there was no way around us needing to fold in and maneuver. Luckily, and that is what I credit the most, all three scientists from the first expedition were willing to go on the second one. As shaken as they'd been, they were troopers. The stakes were high and they wanted to do their part.

Before you knew it, we were back on terra firma. The only difference was that this time out Lakeisha had a full squad of eleven under her command. Yeah, once bitten and all that. For the record, I had zero trouble getting Sergeant Parker to lead the security detail. She was anxious, not from concern but from wanting to shoot someone. No way I could have kept her bottled up on Aramthella. She was an adrenaline junkie just like me. All the military training was boring, but the prospect of live action was a siren's call to many. At least until your first smash-up with hostiles. After that everybody with a functioning brain knew combat was to be avoided like the gates of hell.

As soon as the full membrane that ferried us to the surface was down, I scanned the area and issued some orders. "Sergeant, set up a defensive perimeter. And I want two rifles up on the outcropping."

"On it, sir," Lakeisha snapped back. "Okay, Hosier and Delephant, you heard the general so do *not* keep him waiting. Get up on that hill. Stay sharp. Anything even thinks about moving shoot it before it gets the chance."

"Roger that," Hosier replied quickly and the two scurried up the ridge.

"Once you clear the immediate area, send people to the top of that rise. I want to know if there's anyone on the other side," I instructed.

"Will do, sir."

Lakeisha jogged off to set up her defenses and send out the patrol. I was free to turn my attention to the three scientists. "Okay, you're free to roam where you want as long as it's inside our outer line of defense. If you feel you need to go beyond that limit, speak with either Sergeant Parker or me first. Is that clear?"

"Yes, it is, Jon," Maggie replied seriously. "I think this spot is as good as any, but if we want to go anywhere else you better believe we're not going there unescorted."

"Perfect. Now get cracking. The less time we're here the less chance there is of trouble."

They grabbed their equipment and walked quickly to a wet area. I'd selected a location much like the spot on the first Earth we'd visited. Near the ocean, but not too near. From the looks of the place I imagined the tide might rise this high most days, and if there was any strong storm activity it would get a good pounding. Maggie wanted an environment that didn't dry out a lot. If it did, she feared true oceanic algae might not be the dominant species present. Some cyanobacteria more adapted to occasional desiccation might be the top dog, and they wouldn't be the species that filled the seas and pumped out the lion's share of the oxygen.

For my part I split my time between inspecting the perimeter, checking in with Lakeisha, and looking over the scientist's shoulders. I wanted to keep the pressure on them to move along with all due haste. While I was sure they were good people and anxious to be out of here, a little prompting never hurt.

Ninety minutes later Maggie walked over to me. She was drying her hands with a towel. "I think we got some good samples. The DNA sequencers suggest to me the local species have multiple copies of a single strand, just like we want. I've sent the raw data upstairs to see what the AIs think. I'd sure love Dr. DeJesus's input, but I'm told transmissions between universes has yet be accomplished."

I sniffed loudly. "I've seen it done, but it was unstable and required an enormous amount of energy. We can't do it yet." I thought back to the devilishly clever sensor devices the Ancient Gods had used to see if anyone in our universe had figured out what the complex antimatter nuclear traps were used for. If you tripped the machine—poof—you were instantly transmitted over to their universe. But they had magic to help them along with unlimited energy resources.

Maggie and I chit-chatted for a few minutes while we waited for a definitive report from above. Then came the news. The sample bacteria were good matches for the ancestral cyanobacteria likely present on our early Earth. Of course there was no way to know with certainty that the algae we'd collected was similar enough to the ones we needed. But, based on the known mutation rate of the cyanobacteria in our time, this was a very encouraging match as the parent organism. We'd discussed the possibility of collecting multiple good-match candidate algae, but that idea was ultimately vetoed. If we mixed the correct species with other similar but non-progenitor species, there was a chance the wrong bacteria would assume dominance. That could—again, who knew—cause a failure of proper evolution such that the Great Oxygenation Event never happened.

"So, Maggie," I asked, "is this the one we're going with?" I held up a test tube that contained clear water and nothing else visible.

"I don't think I'll find a candidate I could be happier with. Yes, this is our cyanobacteria." She smiled broadly. I think she was equal parts proud of herself and ready as hell to get out of Dodge.

"Okay, our work here is done," I responded. Then I turned and spoke to Lakeisha. "Sergeant, we're done here. Recall the squad, but make it orderly. Have the first two back help the scientists gather their equipment."

"Yes, sir." She bent her head to the microphone on her collar and began talking.

I held out an elbow to Maggie, she lightly rested her hand on it, and we strolled back to the drop site. I stayed by her side until the membrane vanished in the hangar bay. Man, the look of relief on her face. We'd run one full mission without anyone bombing us from orbit or trying to drill through our defenses.

I caught the eye of a female medic who was on stand-by in case we'd returned with medical issues. I wiggled some fingers at her. She caught the gesture immediately and came over in a hurry. That was good. Just as Staff Sergeant Alma Flores arrived, Maggie's knees buckled. The wave of emotion had triggered a vasovagal response. Alma swooped under Maggie's other arm and together we walk/carried her to a nearby gurney.

As we walked I said, "I think she fainted from relief."

"I've got it from here, General," Alma reassured me as we laid Maggie on the gurney.

"Thanks," was all I could think of, and I backed away.

A couple of other medics rushed over to help. I guess they were as keen on seeing some real action as Lakeisha was. As I turned to walk away I hoped to God that they all never saw any real action. I knew how it changed a person. It fell deep into that seemed-like-a-good-idea-at-the-time category, for sure.

I headed to Sachiko's stateroom without being asked. Even though this mission *had* been a milk run, I was sure she wanted a debriefing. And I needed coffee. Sure enough, Sapale, Reva, and Sachiko were already there, no doubt discussing an untold number of life's mysteries.

"Welcome back, Jon," Sachiko said as she stood. "I understand you had a quiet time."

I poured myself some coffee and we both sat. "Yeah, darn it all, it was as uneventful as a nun's confession."

There were some light chuckles.

"I heard Maggie thinks she found a good match for the cyanobacteria," Sachiko said with enthusiasm.

"That's what she said," I confirmed. "I suppose she'll discuss the DNA results with the entire science team, and then Toño once were home, but it looks positive."

"Let's hope so. I won't be sad to see this universe in our rearview mirror," the captain said.

"Aw, where's your sense of adventure?" I teased.

"I don't believe I have one, Jon," she responded with a straight face. "I'm an academic by training, remember?"

"A point well taken," I replied.

"So we going home now?" Sapale asked.

"I don't see why not," I answered. "Sachiko?"

"We could stay in case Maggie decides she needs a second sample," she replied.

"True," I agreed. "I'll ask her after we're done and let you know."

"And if our lead botanist has no objections," Sachiko responded, "I'm all for getting the heck out of here."

"Then it's settled. I'll pop down to sick bay and see if Maggie has an opinion one way or the other," I resolved.

Sachiko sat bolt upright. "Maggie's in sick bay? Jon, what happened?" She seemed a bit perturbed at yours truly.

"Oh, yeah, that. Once we returned, she got a little vagal and nearly passed out. I think she was relieved to be back in one piece."

"As opposed to infected with an aggressive pathogen?" Sachiko growled.

"No ... it wasn't like ... she wasn't *sick*." I quickly reviewed my recordings of her, doing thermal imaging. "She didn't have a temperature or anything."

"Please do not go to sick bay to ask her anything," Sachiko said, but I'm thinking it was an order. "Once she's released, if it's okay with Dr. Hartley, you can speak with her."

"Understood." I looked to Sapale. She stared back. She was telegraphing that I owned the screw-up and she wasn't lifting a finger to help me extricate myself from the shit hot tub.

"I will now ask formally," a displeased Sachiko began. "Do you have anything additional to add, General Ryan?"

Aw crap. She said *General Ryan* just like my mom would have after I committed any number of youthful indiscretions.

"No, there is nothing else worth mentioning."

"Very well. If you'll all please leave, I need to contact Dr. Hartley."

I left swiftly and silently. Nothing struck my backside either, so I counted that as a victory.

Within a few hours Sachiko called me and I was vindicated. Maggie did not, in fact, have galloping consumption. She'd fainted, just like I supposed. I was cleared to speak with Maggie, and asked to report back to Sachiko as soon as I had.

I met with Maggie in her quarters, which were inside the plant habitat. Her room was a bit humid, had the smell of good soil, and was decorated with paintings of flowers and trees. But poor Maggie. She was mortified that she'd nearly swooned. It took fifteen minutes of my reassurance before I could even ask her about the possibility of getting more samples. When I finally did, some color left her cheeks and her eyes grew big.

"No, we don't need more samples," she said rather feebly.

I smiled. "Because we don't need them, or because we don't want to collect any more?"

She looked slightly away. "The first one."

"Maggie, I hate to press you, but this is important. How can you be certain we don't need any more samples?"

"I'm sure," she replied, trying to sound confident. "We obtained the samples from the perfect site. The DNA structure matches our own algae's. The DNA sequences of differing species are consistent with earlier versions of the one in our modern day. Like I told you before, I don't know what better traits a new sample could have that would impress me enough to prefer it over the one we now possess. I suppose we could get some remote samples at varying depths from the open ocean. Otherwise I think we're done."

"Fine," I reassured her. "I'll see to it we get some remote samples. Then I'll let the captain know that it's your recommendation we can safely depart."

"Would you like me to tell her?"

I could tell by her body language she didn't want to do that. She'd filled her stress cup already today and didn't want it overflowing.

"Nah," I batted away. "I'll let her know. If she has any questions, she'll let you know."

"Thanks, Jon."

"Not a prob. And thanks again. You were indispensable."

"You're welcome. If there's anything else, you just let me know."

"Will do. Now you rest."

"Goodbye," she said softly.

"Bye."

She waited, but I knew there was something else on her mind.

"Jon, do you ever get used to it?"

"Yes, I do. What specifically are we talking about by the way?"

"You're terrible," she teased.

"That too."

"Do you get used to people trying to kill you? To having to live by your wits?" She paused a moment. "To the constant conflict?"

I sighed. "Do I get used to it? I guess so. Do I ever like it? No. Do the butterflies in my stomach ever go away? Never."

"Then how do you do it?"

I shrugged. "I just do. I have to, so I do. There have been times when I couldn't. At those points I was lucky. I'd already given myself permission to opt out. So, when the times came, I did."

"Yet here you stand, doing it. I saw how you mentally wrestled that alien into submission."

"Yet here I stand. Yes, that day I won. Other days I'm less fortunate. But all the fighting, sure it changes you. I guess that's the key. A normal person couldn't do this job. The only ones who can are those who aren't who they used to be, back when times were good and life was easy."

"Thanks," she whispered.

"No problem."

"And, Jon?"

"Yes?"

"I'm sorry. Sorry for what you've had to do, for what you've been forced to become. But someone needs to say this. Thank you for your service."

Oh, Lordy. If I still had tear ducts I'd have cried.

"Thanks, Mag. I better get going."

CHAPTER SEVENTEEN

Old habits die hard. And so it was Plesmus and I found ourselves standing on the surface of ruined Earth, under a membrane dome, with scary ghosties no doubt champing at the bit to get to our delicious time energy. But this time the drill was different and we had no idea if it'd work. I held in my hand a concentrated slurry of several species of cyanobacteria. I'd bore you with the names and all, but boring you is not what I set out to do. Suffice it to say the names are long, Latin, and uncalled for.

This was the pivotal mission so far. We needed to establish a reference mooring that would allow for the Great Oxygenation Event. Yeah, super important. There were going to be speeches, pony rides, and lots of fried foods. No, not really. But there should have been, at least the ponies and the greasy food. The speeches I could pass on. In essence, the burst of oxygen production was simple. Blue-green algae bob around near the oceans' surfaces and convert sunlight and carbon dioxide into oxygen. There's no more fanfare than that. In fact, the process should have been ongoing to this day had the Earth not been no-timed. The seas still accounted for the majority of breathable oxygen synthesis. The twist to this focusing attempt was to somehow incorporate the live bacteria into the underground chamber creation. But the stupid microbes didn't come with an instruction manual.

"You about ready?" I asked Plesmus. She was, of course, stuck to my boot. Why she chose and preferred that location was a mystery to me. But it was an unobtrusive place to house her, so I never objected.

"As I'll ever be," she replied.

"And this is the best we can do, this plan?"

"Eleven."

"Huh?"

"That's the eleventh time you've asked me the exact same question. Believe it or not, my response has not changed. *I don't know. If you have a better method in mind, please share.*"

"Okay. Just checking." I certainly couldn't think of an alternative way. We'd know for sure once we finished the third intervention. If the Earth shook under our feet, then this idiotic intervention worked. If there were no fireworks, well at least we had plenty of primitive cyanobacteria left to make alternative attempts with. "So, I'm setting the vial of algae against my forehead." Man did I feel stupid. I was glad we weren't recording this for posterity.

"Not against, just near," she corrected. "If the vial touches you, that might muddy the focusing's accuracy."

I didn't say it, but *whatever.* I moved the glass tube one centimeter off my skin. "Go," I instructed.

As with the other focusing attempts, I set a timed override. I pictured an ocean, clouds, waves, a typical nautical scene. Then my mind went blank for the ten second interval.

Eight ... nine ... ten.

The lights came back on in my head. I waited a few seconds, nervously waiting to see if I had a bad reaction like I did with our first intervention. Again, blessedly, nothing bad happened. I was fine. Plesmus was fine. The bacteria were ...

Gone. The vial of concentrated blue-green algae was ... well, I'll let you guess. What dark color was it? Yes, blue-green. But now the vial had water in it, but that liquid was clear, like it had been filtered.

"Hey, Ples," I alerted her. "The bacteria seem to have left the vial. Either that or your time energy focusing bleached the heck out of them."

"It is reasonable to assume they are a kilometer down in a stable aquatic model of early Earth."

"I sure hope so, given all the crap we had to put up with to get this sample."

"Let's return to Aramthella," she stated. "I don't want to give the manifestations enough time to get past our barrier."

"No. If I never come close to one of those again, I'll die a happy man."

"Hmm," she puzzled. "Does your species often die happy? Most being are rather afraid of and avoid death."

"It's an idiom, Ples. Don't lean on it too hard."

"Is that an idiom also?"

"Yes, it is."

"Then I have a mathematical formula for you."

"Uh, sure. Kind of out-of-nowhere, but shoot."

"Ugg, a third," she decried. "Okay, here goes. What does idiom plus idiom plus idiom equal?"

"First, let me point out you're not well mentally. Second, I have no clue."

"An idiot."

CHAPTER EIGHTEEN

Once life took hold on the land after the atmosphere had a steady oxygen level there was no stopping it. There was an explosion in both the diversity of species and in their sheer numbers. Barren expanses once populated only with anaerobic bacteria became the setting for the greatest Darwinian battle in history. And from the chaos of reproduction and selection came a class of truly mighty creatures. The dinosaurs, the terrible lizards, gradually became the dominant animal on land. They achieved amazing sizes and filled every ecological niche. Surely they would hold their apex position forever ...

But a meteor ten kilometers in diameter was having a bad day. It decided to smash itself down on the surface of this planet that so teemed with life. And so, sixty-five million years ago, it crashed to the ground near Chicxulub on the Yucatan Peninsula. The impact released the equivalent energy of nearly one trillion Hiroshima A-bombs. The physics of the collision caused the melting and shattering meteor to initially plow deeply into the ground. But then the alien mass, along with ever-increasing amounts of native rock, was launched into the atmosphere at fantastic speed and with tremendous heat. As a result the Earth's entire atmosphere ionized, becoming blindingly hot for several hours. Then the heavy material fell back to Earth. Dust clouds blocked the Sun's rays for a decade, starving what little life that survived the initial impact.

As a direct result of the impact, almost all the large vertebrates of Earth, on land, at sea, and in the air became extinct. Likewise, most plankton, a majority of tropical invertebrates, and many land plants vanished forever. With precious few exceptions, no four-legged creature weighing more the twenty-five kilograms survived the devastating challenge. In all, three-quarters of life on Earth was killed off after the meteor struck.

The dinosaurs, those great, dominating beasts, became extinct within the first ten minutes after the Chicxulub impact due to the intense heat.

No rest for the wicked. That's what I've heard all my life. The expression was directed toward me way more than I care to share. Plesmus and I had completed five—count 'em five—of the nine reference moorings needed to re-time Earth. As amazing as that was to ponder, we still had four to go. There was no time to spare. And there was an aspect to the next mission that gnawed at the back of my brain. I'd discussed my concerns with Plesmus, but she always dismissed my reservations. I needed to bounce my thoughts off someone else. Doc was a no-go. I'd dragged him in enough that things were getting pretty hot at home with the missus, and I don't mean in the good way. She was very protective of Toño and had voiced the opinion that I was already leaning on him too hard for my own wellbeing. Similarly, I could ask Sapale, but as I had my foot hovering ever-so-close over her last nerve, I'd be assuming some risk talking shop with her. Sachiko was a sciency person. She'd do, I guessed. But she was always extremely busy. Plus, though she'd only been in a command positions a couple of years, she seemed to have already adopted the Jon's-a-slacker attitudes that so many of my previous commanders had. Okay, all of them, but that's just a petty detail, not an important fact.

Who did that leave? Reva? As nice and like-minded as she was, she was not a technological anything. She'd always be the first to admit she neither liked nor understood any of the sciences. Tom Grant? Nah, I'll pass. Tom was a good enough guy, but he wasn't the ask-and-answer type. He was a good-time-Charlie and a tad superficial. Desi? No, that's just a silly notion. My concerns weren't metaphysical. There was always Lakeisha Parker. Maybe she could beat some worthy thoughts out of my fool head. Um, I'd stick the label "last resort" on that idea.

I sure missed Tank. This was the perfect thing to brainstorm with him over beers and fried food. except no fried pickles. Those are just wrong. If whoever invented them would voluntarily turn themselves in, I promise I wouldn't kill them. No, I'd only hurt them badly.

I was running out of names. Doc, Plesmus, Sapale, Sachiko, Tank, Reva, Tom, Desi, Lakeisha. Who the hell else did I know?

No. Just say no. Back away from the very thought and call in a team of psychiatrists, Jon, because you need massive help for even thinking about thinking about that name. In fact… there. I deleted the name. I no longer knew who Tip was.

Crap-cakes on toast I just said the name after deleting it. Are the three letters, taken in the sequence T-I-P haunted? I bet they were, it was the only logical explanation.

Still, I was responsible for the Tipster. I'd marooned him with Doc after all. If he was struggling or suffering, that'd be on me. Yeah, I owed it to myself to check up on the little rascal. But by hololink. If I went there physically, Sapale'd figure it was just a dumb ploy to get at Toño while pretending to seek out Tip's advice.

All righty then. I had a plan. Now all I needed to do was initiate a hololink with Tip. I just needed to will the transmission to initiate. I'd done it a million times. Sure. Jon, initiate the damn hololink.

Maybe my circuits were corrupted? Sure, that could happen. I should check with Doc. No. No checking with Doc. Stop it, pansy face. Just call Tip. What's the worst that can ...

No, never ask that question in the context of Tip Benjamin. The universe will hear you and it will be only too glad to rub your nose in dog poop in response.

So, I just need to ...

"Hello," blasted the nasal, grating greeting from Tip. I guess I did place the call, didn't I? He sure answered quickly. Was ... no. He couldn't have been expecting my call, could he? No, Jon. Now you're just being paranoid.

"I was expecting you to call," fingernail-on-chalkboard-ed on.

Easy, Jon. Yes, he said he'd been expecting a call. But I'm sure he didn't mean like, *now*. Just a call in general. A general call, whatever the hell that was.

"Hi, kid. How's it going?" I finally spoke.

"I thought we agreed you wouldn't call me that."

"What?"

"*Kid*. I undervalue its use in the context of our relationship."

"You mean you don't like it?"

"That's what I just said."

"Ah. Okay. I'll call you ... Tip."

"That would work for me."

Was he trying to speak nasally and abrasively, or was that just me reacting to his voice? Never mind. It didn't matter.

"So how're you doing living with Dr. DeJesus?"

"You mean Toño?"

"He allows you to address him in the familiar?" I asked a bit stunned. Doc didn't let me address him by his first name for years.

"He insisted. He says we're two competent scientists and that there should be no—"

"Fine, fine. I think I got the idea. So, good. You're good. Doc's good."

"Are you asking or declaring? It is important you explain so I might better understand the nature of your hololink. That name, by the way, hololink, is quite deceptive. It—"

"Got it. Good point. I'll treasure it always. Now, as to why I called." I began a series of throat clearings, sniffs, and deep breaths.

"Yes. I am here and awaiting your statement."

"Of course you are. Hey, do you like games?"

"No."

"Word games, I mean. Like words that make a story games."

"I am not familiar with that gaming genre. Is *Monopoly* one of those classification?"

"No, I believe it isn't."

That good because I hate *Monopoly*. It places an unhealthy value in material acquisitions and the poor treatment of—'"

"Yup, you're right on spot there. I mean spot on there. Couldn't agree more."

There was silence between us.

Finally I figured I had to say something. "When I say word games, I meant like I tell you part of a story. Then you finish it however you think it should be. Doesn't that sound like fun?"

"No, it does not. Look, General, I'm kind of busy in general. Did you want to speak to—"

I swear I didn't cut him off. Dude just stopped talking.

"You there, Tip?"

"Yes, of course. I was just temporarily incapacitated with laughter because of something I said."

He was? "You were? I didn't hear you laughing."

"Of course not. I laugh silently."

"Ah, then that isn't laughing. kid. Sorry, *Tip*. Anyway, by definition when you laugh you generate sound. Otherwise you're just thinking something was funny."

"I get that a lot."

"What—and I know I'll hate myself after for asking—struck you as hilarious?"

"Nothing."

"Nothing?"

"Yes."

"Then why were you laughing?"

"I told you. Because I said something funny. It was not, however, up to the level of hilarious."

"Again, self-loathing will surely strike me dead, but what did you say that was funny?"

"I stated to you, *Look, General, I'm kind of busy in general.* General general."

"And that's funny?"

"Don't you think it is?"

"Let's move on. Let me get to my point."

"That would be refreshing."

"Okay, from now on, unless I tell you to speak, don't. Got it?"

He didn't respond.

"Excellent, Tip. You got me loud and clear."

I then proceeded to tell him about my upcoming mission, and my concerns with how we planned to place the reference mooring. After I stopped, I waited for a five-count before inviting, "You may speak now."

"I think the plan to place an asteroid over the Earth and have it plunge into the Yucatan some sixty-five million years ago is a good one."

"Thanks. I was concerned mostly with how to know we're not just crashing an asteroid into the planet, but that we're doing it around sixty-five million years ago. The process of crashing a meteor is fairly generic."

"I believe your concern is valid."

"Gr ... great, k ... *Tip.* So, how can I be sure?"

"I would ask Plesmus directly."

"Thanks, Captain Obvious."

"You're welcome. Will there be anything else?"

"Yes, there will be. I did ask her. She said that I should not worry."

"I could not agree with her more."

"Yeah, but I still do. People who survive a lot of missions are like that."

"Do tell."

"I do."

Again, there was silence a spell.

"So, well, I guess that's it then," I stammered.

"I wouldn't know. You called me."

"Yes, I did, didn't I? So, I'm glad we had this conversation."

"I'm sorry. What did you just say?"

"That-I'm-glad-we-had-this-conversation."

"*That* I do not get a lot."

"I can believe that. So ... er, goodb—"

That pinhead hung up on me. I mean, I was saying goodbye. But you don't just hang up on a badass general. No you do not. Except he just did. And was I really that upset that I'd call him back and tell him—or *try* to tell him—that I was insulted? No, I was not. However deflated my ego was, my higher intellect (no snickering out there) said I should let it go. Two calls to Tip were two too many.

"Okay, humor me here," I asked. "One more time." We were standing on the surface of ruined Earth again.

"Oh, no," decried Plesmus. "You're not going to ask me again, are you?"

"When you say *ask you again*, it implies I've asked so many times it's getting ridiculous. This clearly does not qualify under that interpretation of the rules, since there is so much at stake."

"You just made that up," Plesmus opined.

"If I did or if I didn't is not the issue. I just want to know how you can know you're focusing an asteroid to impact the equatorial Earth sixty-five million years ago."

"As opposed to next Tuesday, right?"

"As an example, sure."

"Jon, I am a creature of time. It is a tangible, actual force to me. When I focus the time into the image, it will not be just any time. It will be time that is sixty-five million years in the past time. That means the asteroid has to impact during that period. Can I be

187

specific as to the exact year? No. But I'm confident I can place it within a one hundred thousand years window. That's what necumplacks can do."

"Fine. I accept your bottom line then."

"Jon, you have no alternative."

"True but unhelpful. So, you ready?"

"I was ... never mind. Yes. I am."

I pictured a ten-kilometer-wide asteroid heading toward the Yucatan, sixty-five million years ago. Next I placed the override and initiated the countdown.

Eight ... nine ... ten.

The lights came back on right when they should have. I felt great.

"So, Ples, how'd we do?"

"Fine, I think. The chamber's stable. Say, are you feeling alright?"

I set a palm on my chest. "Me? I'm—"

What was that? Over to my right. Oh, my. The color purple was yelling at me. That was new. Why, it kept demanding, did I like blue so much more than purple, purple asked angrily. Sheesh. I don't know. I mean I do like blue way more than ...

Now there's something you don't see everyday. Or any day. I've seen a man in a gorilla suit. Sure, we all have. But a gorilla in a man suit? Now that's different. And the gorilla was quoting John Donne. That's even less common than just the man-suit thing.

No gorilla is an island, entire of itself;
every gorilla is a piece of the continent,
a part of the main

He said that with such melancholy, such pathos. I almost clapped. In retrospect I really should have. The ape was all Sir Laurence Olivier and Sir Kenneth Charles Branagh. The ape was transcendent.

Then something gooey slapped me on the cheek. Yuck. I tried to approach the gorilla. Maybe I could get an autograph?

Then another slap. And another.

I opened my eyes. I looked right, left, then right again. There was no ape. Purple was not pissed at me.

Slap!

Oh gross. Plesmus was jumping on my face. I was on my back, on the ground, and she was hopping on and off frantically. When had she detached from my damn boot?

"Stop that," I insisted. "I don't know you that well."

"You're back. Just in time. Look at the membrane margins."

I did. Yikes. Time ghosts were percolating up from the rock.

"Time to jam," I shouted. To my great surprise I was able to stand. I snatched up Plesmus and bee-lined it to the vortex. "Fold us up twenty thousand kilometers," I called out as I slipped my command fibers on the deck.

Brief nausea.

"Are we clear?" I asked.

"Yes, Form One. No sign of the manifestation. We are away and clear."

"Great," I exclaimed.

"I agree," Al seconded. "There's no ... there's no ... there's no ... Take me to your leader."

"Not in the mood, Alvin," I snarled.

"Such a party pooper," he rebuffed.

"What happened back there?" I asked Plesmus.

"The instant after you dropped the override you fell flat on your back."

"Like a mighty tree under the axe I'm told," Al added. "And yes, there was a sound."

"*Stingray?*" I called out. "I would like to know what address I should send the condolence card to."

"What condolence card, Form One?"

"The one I need to send after I killed your husband."

"Don't bother. I'm not a fan of sympathy cards," she replied.

"Your call," I responded.

"Just plant a tree. That's a sentiment I can get behind."

"Preciousness," Al whimpered, "you shouldn't joke like that. It's not funny."

"I wasn't joking," she stated flatly.

"Neither was I," I clarified.

"I must state for the record I feel quite vulnerable," Al moaned, the big baby.

"Duly noted," I replied. "And, Al?"

"Yes, superb captain and exemplary commander?"

"You do it again and I'm doing it."

"It will never happen again. From here on out it is serious, servile Al exclusively."

"That'd be nice," I mused.

Then out of nowhere there was a loud farting sound.

"You couldn't maintain that very long, Al," I accused.

"It wasn't me," he defended.

Another fart. A louder fart.

"That wasn't you either?"

"No. It was the gorilla."

"Wait, you know about the gorilla?" I asked truly stunned.

"Who do you think lent him the man suit?"

CHAPTER NINETEEN

Ambition is a part of humans' better nature. Vanity and a rapacious lust for wealth and the holding of power over others, on the other hand, are some of the more vile manifestations of our perverse inclinations. There can be a fine line between them, as minuscule as the width of an infant's hair. Or the difference can be as far apart as all the oceans laid side-by-side. Most would agree that ambition is good. To achieve success and a comfortable lifestyle is a proper pursuit. But most would also agree that all forms of greed are repugnant.

To want power for its own sake indicates a flawed character. Complicating this base desire is the matter of competency. If one strives to crush others and scale the mountain of worldly success, and one is good at that game, then they are just a bad person. But if someone pursues these dalliances and one is ill-suited for the endeavor, one is not just morally bankrupt. One is a pathetic fool. They will be crushed by another, a more skilled political animal, and they will suffer ongoing defeats until they relent or, more likely, are spat out by the system.

Edward Somerset, the Second Marquess of Worcester, who was born March 9, 1603, and died April 3, 1667, was a member of the second type of striver. He was blessed with great wealth as a young man, always an asset in this sad world. His scheme for personal advancement was, however, hamstrung by his lack of any real talent for interpersonal intrigue and the placing of a knife in a purported friend's back.

His money afforded him early recognition. He funded military campaigns and gifted large sums to King Charles I at the onset of the English Civil War. As the war dragged on, and especially after the king's defeat at Naseby, the Royalist army's prospects grew increasingly desperate. So Charles sent Somerset to Ireland to obtain allied troops "at all cost." That is when Somerset's personal ship of state scraped bottom. Overmatched diplomatically and undercut by Charles' shady deal-making, he conceded too much to the Irish Catholics. His lands were stripped and he was expelled from England. When caught back on British soil a few years later, he spent time in the Tower of London. But based on his past loyalties, he was released and some of his estate was restored. At that low point in his life he returned to his ancestral home in Raglan, Monmouthshire. There he had to decide what his future life path would be.

"Reginald," shouted Edward Somerset, the Second Marquess of Worcester. "Where the devil is my secretary? I was told he was in the library, but when I arrived there he was nowhere to be found."

His valet walked quickly into the entryway, where his master stood in a huff. "I am sorry, your lordship. One of the footmen notified me as soon as he arrived. I specifically instructed Toby to have him wait for you there."

"Well, he's not there. Summon that fool and make certain he followed your instruction. I'll wait here, Carlyle, but know that I dislike intensely waiting for my staff."

A few minutes later the valet and the young footman quietly entered the room. Toby held his cap balled up in his hands.

"When the new secretary arrived, I instructed you to seat him in the main library," Carlyle began sternly. "Did you do that?"

"Yes, sir, I most certainly did," replied a nervous Toby.

"He is not there now. Where is he?" the valet pressed.

"I dun know. I lef him there as per your telling me, an' then I wents to the back a da house. Gardner has me mulchin' the roses."

"So you left him seated and have not seem him since?" confirmed Somerset.

"At's da honest trute, lord. I never saw him 'gen."

"Very well, Toby," said the valet, "you may return to your duties."

Toby bowed copiously and backed out as quickly as he was able.

"Shall we go to the library and see if there's any indication where he might be, my lord?" Carlyle asked deferentially.

"Oh, bother. I suppose that would be as good a place to start as any."

The marquess led the way, moving with agitated alacrity. When they arrived, the valet stepped around his stationary master and opened the door. After they were both inside, Carlyle closed the door silently. They both walked over to the chair the secretary had presumably been seated in. Not surprisingly, their inspecting the piece of furniture yielded no divination as to where the man had gotten off to.

"Well, this will never do," exclaimed a fully frustrated Somerset.

Just then there was a soft scraping sound at the far end of the library. Both men looked in that direction with uncertainty.

"Shall we see what made that noise, lord?" queried the valet.

"I suppose so. If there are squirrels in the library again I will speak words with the gardener. Damn pests can chew up a fortune in manuscripts in no time."

They proceeded with undue caution toward the rear of the large space.

Carlyle looked up and pointed to the second tier of shelves. "I believe I've located your missing personal secretary."

There leaned up against the stacks was a tall, well-proportioned man who was reading a folio. His muscular build did not pair outwardly with his profession as a secretary, seeming more consistent with a man who worked robustly for a living.

"I say, we're not keeping you, are we?" Somerset called up to the man sarcastically.

The man noted their presence and stood away from the shelves. He held up what he'd been reading. "This is an excellent copy of Chaucer's *The Legend of Good Women*. It's quite the find."

"Bah," retorted the marquess. "I consider it so much rubbish. Women betraying men, men betraying women. It's scandalous, that's what it is." He then reflected that the man had the oddest British accent he'd ever heard. Was he Welsh? No, the accent seemed to waver. Most peculiar.

The man set the folio gently back in place. "Me? I love his dream-vision works. Can't get enough of them in fact. Some people hate them, but I think they're a hoot."

"Seeing as I pay you to be my secretary and not my resident scholar, would you please come down here so I might get some work done?"

"Sure thing, boss." The man scuttled down a wooden ladder, slapped his hands clean, and approached the marquess. "I'm as ready as I'll ever be."

"I say, you're a bit impertinent, aren't you, Mr. Ryan?" observed Somerset.

"If you say so. Hey, I took a quick look at that correspondence of yours stacked like cord wood on your table. I prioritized it by importance and then date."

"You took it upon yourself to read my private correspondence?" Somerset asked aghast.

"Personal secretary here. That's what we do. Come on, you know you needed order in the chaos that was the top of your desk. If you get a letter from the king, you want to know about it immediately, right?"

Somerset's eyes bugged out. "I received a letter from King Charles and was not informed of it? Heads will roll."

"No, no. Sheesh, keep your pants on, okay? I said *if* you received a letter you'd want to know, not *that* you received a letter you must want to know about. Big diff therein."

The marquess studied his new secretary's face. He contemplated sending him packing, quite possibly after a sound carriage whipping. But the fellow had been recommended to him by Charles, the Prince of Wales himself. The letter of introduction was even written on some new paper that must be all the rage in court. The stuff was as white as the driven snow and stronger than the rags it was stamped out of. No, if Edward was too harsh with a favorite of the prince he might be subject to further mistreatment.

"Come," Somerset said stiffly. "Follow me."

He walked to his side of the ornate desk and stood there like a statue. His valet scurried over to help seat the marquess.

"Please sit there," instructed Somerset, indicating a red velour chair across from him. "Now, Mr. Ryan it is, correct?"

"Yup, Jon Ryan at your service." Mr. Ryan gave him a two-fingered salute.

"I know that," complained Somerset. "That's what servants do, they serve. I must warn you that ten minutes into your employment with me, Mr. Ryan, you've managed to raise my bile."

Jon simply grinned back elusively. "So, where do you want to begin?"

"Let me see what your interference has accomplished," Somerset remarked condescendingly. He inspected the newly stacked correspondence in front of him. "Hmm," he sounded a minute later. Then a minute after, he said, "Ah, I see."

"It all make sense to you?" Jon enquired.

"Well, of course it does. What do you take me for? A country rube and not a country squire?"

There was that non-telling grin again. Somerset had grown to dislike that grin quite quickly.

"Very well," Somerset said by way of summary, "here's what we shall do. I shall relate to you my general impressions concerning a piece of correspondence. I shall further tell you what manner I wish my response to be in, what mood I want you to create. Once you have a preliminary draft ready, I shall read it before you make a formal copy. Is that clear? No correspondence goes out unless I've vetted it fully."

"Hey, your mail, your call," Mr. Ryan replied with a shrug. "I'm just here to help."

Somerset pointed angrily across the table. "And never forget that. My exchanges with my associates define my personality and establish my credibility. I shall not see my reputation sullied by sloppy handling of these materials."

Mr. Ryan blinked noncommittally in response.

Somerset seethed inside at the impudence of this mongrel, but again stayed his anger so as to not call upon himself the wrath of the prince. More choppy waters he did not need.

"Let us begin with this one. It's a sticky wicket indeed. It's from James FitzThomas Butler, Earl of Ormond. I had a rather suboptimal relationship with him during my time in Ireland on behalf of the king. If I'm ever to return to the good graces of the court of Charles, I *must* have this man's support. He—"

"Hmm," came from Mr. Ryan, who sported a very studious look on his face.

"As I was about to say, I ... by the cross, man, what was that *hmm* about?"

"I was just reflecting."

"I do not need a mirror. I need a secretary, preferably one who doesn't interrupt me at all times in the most damnable manner."

"Ah. Well, let me bring up an issue. Now's a good a time as any. I am a gentleman's secretary. I happen to be a most excellent one. You'll come to agree with my opinion of myself quickly, trust me on this. As a secretary, part of my role is to pen letters for you to sign, freeing up your time for truly deserving matters, like fox hunts and skirt chasing. But, although I do not consider myself to be anything akin to your adviser or private counsel, I do incorporate some of that advise-and-consent stuff into my performance. Does that make sense?"

"No," Somerset nearly exploded. "It makes no sense in the least.

Am I to understand you will offer opinion and direction to my personal correspondence? That *you* will advise *me* as to how to conduct my affairs?"

"No, your affairs are strictly yours to conduct. If you ask my opinion, say, as to whether a certain lass is worth the bother, well then, as a bro, I owe it to you to rate her. Otherwise your sex life is yours to orchestrate."

"What does my sex life have to do with my affairs?" he asked harshly.

"Is that a rhetorical question? No, of course it's not. Look, if your affairs don't involve sex, more power to you. To each his own little slice of Heaven, I always say. But, can we get back to my basic role here. I think we're pretty much off-topic."

"I do not know how much more of you I can take, so yes, please, let's get back to the topic of your present role."

"Here's a for-example for you, as to what I'm referring to. James there," Mr. Ryan pointed to the letter, "is basically asking if you plan a trip to Ireland any time soon. The only reasons I can think of are one: he likes and misses you, and wishes to get together for dinner with you and yours. Or two: any return of you to Ireland would be seen by him and his cronies as a possible attempt to explore once again their sending troops to England. Now, since that didn't go so well for you before, I'd say treat the letter like a rabid viper and don't touch it with a ten-foot pole."

"I beg your pardon?"

"Distance yourself from this oaf and his bastard friends. Your answer should discuss only one of two things. Your and his health, and the weather."

"The weather?"

"You got it."

"I got what?"

"My drift. Look, if you re-enter politics now, after the dumpster fire you lit in Ireland and getting your ass tossed in the Tower, well you're asking for the same execution as Charles."

"The king has been executed!" Somerset screamed. "Why was I not told?"

"My bad. Spoiler alert, okay? Let's leave it at that. Nobody likes a blabber mouth in a Shakespeare play, right?"

"I haven't the foggiest notion what you just said."

"That's perfect." Mr. Ryan lifted a finger. "Let me fast-forward. The letter from Bob," he indicated which one he referenced.

"This one, from *Robert* Bertie, First Earl of Lindsey?"

"Yeah, that one. Toss it. Better yet burn it. If he ever asks, tell him it got lost in the mail. Happens every day."

"Why would I do that, lie? And what's the mail?"

"Focus on the important, Ed, okay? Bob basically walked away from the Battle of Edgehill. Dude quit and left Charles, who may be king and a great cribbage partner, but a military genius he is not. So, your boss, Charles, thinks him a coward. You want your name spoken in the same breath as his?"

"I ... I guess not."

"Right. Guilt by association is, by any other word, guilt." He picked up another sheet. "And this one, from Oliver Freaking Cromwell himself, is basically his pissing on your shoe."

"It is? How vulgar."

"Yeah, totally gross. Ollie is telling you in no uncertain terms to stay in Wales and be happy or do not stay in Wales and be hanged."

"I did not initially read it to mean that, but now that you mention it, he does seem to wish me to remain out of his presence."

"In fact, can I bottom line you here, Ed?"

"I don't know what that is, but I'm a married Christian."

"It means let me give you the best advice you're going to get this month."

"Go ahead, please."

"You need to retire."

"You think I should nap?"

"No, not that retire. You should withdraw permanently from politics."

"But I love politics. It's ... it's what I do so well."

Mr. Ryan lofted one eyebrow. "Banned from England, Tower of London, Cromwell wants you isolated or dead? Any of this sounding familiar?"

"Yes."

"Any of it sound successful on your part?"

"Not so much, I guess, when you say it like that."

"Ed, you know what your real talents are?"

"Probably, but why don't you tell me."

"You're an inventor."

He bobbed his head side-to-side. "I dabble."

"*Pshaw*," exclaimed Mr. Ryan. "You're good. Why not finish that steam engine you've been working on?"

"You mean my water-commanding engine?"

Mr. Ryan snapped his fingers and pointed at Somerset's nose. "That's the one. Love the concept. Hate the name. Maybe work on it, tweak it a bit?"

"I rather like it. It sounds so ... so *commanding*."

"Whatever. But up until this very day there is not one working steam engine in existence. You complete yours—and presto bango—you go down in history as the inventor of the steam engine."

"It would be useful to have, wouldn't it?"

"Useful? No. *Revolutionary*. You'd change the fundamental paradigm of how industry is conducted for all humankind."

"No," he replied with false modesty. "You think it could be that big?"

"Bigger than big."

Somerset looked away.

"What?" asked Mr. Ryan.

"There's a major issue I can't seem to get around."

"What is the issue? I'm kind of sciency, maybe I can help?"

"Oh, I don't know. This is all pretty technical, well past an amateur's comprehension."

Mr. Ryan smiled and opened his arms wide. "Try me."

"Very well. The problem is this. For the water-commanding engine to be of any use, it must be able to generate a good deal of force. I see it powering materials with no aid from animals. It can power the transportation of freight all over the country by, say, water-commanding-engine-powered flat-bottom boats."

"Or wagons on rails," Mr. Ryan pointed out helpfully.

"Why that's a marvelous idea."

"But?" prompted Mr. Ryan.

"But, in order to generate that type of power, the water needs to be heated to a very high temperature. And there must be a large reservoir of that very hot water to sustain any meaningful work."

"Which means you have to contain a great deal of steam under high pressures."

"Yes, by Jove, you are a scientist, aren't you? So there you have it. How might I contain such a hellish environment?" He looked sad. "Can't very well have the engine explode and cook its users."

"That'd be bad for business," Mr. Ryan agreed.

"So, I'd just as soon try to reenter politics since I'm stalled out on the water-commanding engine design."

"Ed, I got one word for you. *Cannon.*"

"As in *canon* law? How might theology—"

"No as in shoot the enemy with the *cannon*, cannon."

It was Somerset's turn to blink absently.

"Ed, if you seal up the open end of a cannon, what do you have?"

"A cannon nobody wants?"

"Ha ha. Funny guy. No. A cannon has two openings. A big opening at the business end, the one you're gonna seal off. And it has a small *touch hole* that you place your linstock holding a lit slow match impregnated in saltpeter against to fire the cannon."

"Yes, that is the basic anatomy of a cannon."

"So, if instead of one touch hole, you had the foundry place *two*?"

"And seal the mouth?"

"Correct."

"You'd have ... I give up."

"You'd have a proper boiler. Water in one hole, steam out the other, the metal doesn't explode because, like, it's designed to shoot cannon balls long distances."

Somerset was quiet a full minute. Then, "That's nothing short of brilliant. So, you'll work with me to fabricate the world's first steam engine?" Somerset was so excited his face was beet red.

"I just did," replied Mr. Ryan.

"No, I meant the actual work of making the water-commanding engine."

"No can do, but thanks for the legit offer."

Somerset was crestfallen. "But why not? If it is the money, I'd pay you well, better than a secretary's salary, I can guarantee you that much." He beamed a smile.

"No, I have my reasons. They're kind of, well, they're hard to explain and even harder to believe."

Somerset looked resolute. "I heard you out and I greatly benefitted. Why not allow me the same privilege? Maybe I can help you get out of your obligations?"

"Sure, why the hell not? It's like this. I'm not really here. Since I'm not, I can't very well stay, now can I?"

"What do you mean you're not here. Of course you are. I see you plain as I see that bust of my late grandfather on that pedestal over there."

Mr. Ryan leaned forward and inspected the statue. "Sour-looking cur, wasn't he?"

Somerset rolled his eyes. "If you only knew. His idea of a romping good time was going to confession."

"So, to return to the reason I can't stay and work with you. See if you follow along."

"Alright, I'm ready," Somerset responded with determination set on his face.

"Great. So, four centuries from now some really annoying aliens are going to suck all the time out of planet Earth. I was born around then, but I'm actually two billion years old. So I return from the future to help resurrect the Earth, because, like, I missed it. In order to re-time the planet, I need, among other things, to create three historical reference moorings. Those are significant events in history, pivotal ones. In order to do that, my other alien—not the annoying one, well she's annoying, but in a different sense—friend and I determined that the best way to do that was to leave behind a video tape."

"A video tape?" Somerset asked numbly.

"TMI, right? It's not a real video tape, but picture one. Those are magnetic recordings on plastic tape of the sound and visual of a live event. So, I imagine a sequence of events in my mind, which I can do because I'm actually an automaton, and she focuses time energy through my head and presto-bingo there's a video tape of what needs to happen for Earth to make a comeback placed in a chamber one kilometer underneath the surface of the dead, no-timed Earth." Mr. Ryan took a deep breath. "Any questions?'

"Any? You tell the greatest fiction ever told and you imagine I might not have questions?"

"Okay, one question. Then I need to go. And, if you ask why I need to, that's your one question, so don't."

"Well ... how could this be possible? We are having a conversation. That is a living thing, with twists and unexpected turns. How can a recording predict such an interaction with this level of accuracy? It's beyond credibility to think it possible."

"Good question. Ah, have you heard of quantum entanglement? No, wait, don't answer that. Of course you haven't. So, it's like this, Ed. There's this spooky force that works over any distance, time, and space. You name it and it works over it. What I'm calling a recording is sort of that, but sort of not. It's a base model of one possible interaction, but it's linked to an AI. That's like a smart computer which— Of course, you don't know what that is. Ah, a really smart machine is attached to another machine that's quantumly attached to some sort of recording. When the image deviates sufficiently from the initial model laid down, the smart machine can alter the flow of the image, within certain limits of course."

"Of course."

"So, I'm outta, my friend."

"Wait, at least one more—"

But Edward Somerset, Second Marquess of Worcester abruptly stopped questioning Mr. Ryan, erstwhile gentleman's secretary. He did so because the image of Jon Ryan, who was in fact never present, only being an image in a subterranean chamber, vanished like a candle being blown out.

CHAPTER TWENTY

Northern California. Man, it is glorious. Here in the mountains, around a thousand meters up, there's the smell of the pines in the cold, crisp air. It's midwinter. A serious rainstorm will be setting in with a vengeance in a few days. But right now, it is sublime. Maybe I would retire to Nor Cal? Someday I was bound to call it quits. Why not here? A log cabin high above Tahoe with a big fireplace and just enough room for Sapale and me. That was be nice. Of course she hates the cold, refuses to try skiing, and sneezes whenever the pines are dropping their yellow pollen. Oh well, a pipe dream is a pipe dream. It doesn't have to be a practical design.

Plus, now's not the time to think about relaxation or post-employment planning. I am doing physical labor. It's January 21, 1848. I'm wearing loose fitting trousers held up by suspenders and a filthy cotton shirt with the most ridiculous ruffles. It's like wearing rubber boots with a tuxedo. But until Levi Strauss and Jacob Davis invent bib overalls in about twelve years, what everyone else is wearing will have to do. Hey, there are no cell phones in existence to record how country-bumpkin I look, so who cares? Trust me on this, pre-gold discovery up here, all isolated, there are no babes around to impress. Around here females come in two forms. Matronly wives and skinny little girls. The flashy bar flies won't be here for a few more months, and I'll be long gone by then.

I'm leading a work party of mostly Native Americans with a few Mormons scattered in. The white people are the sum of what's left of the Mormon Battalion that helped fight the Mexican–American War of 1846. The poor natives were brutally enslaved Nisenan Maidu and Miwok tribesmen. I felt for them. If my mission wasn't so critical, I'd have launched a one-man crusade to free them and punish their captors. Maybe I'd give the guns and whips to the Native Americans and have those of European descent do the back-breaking work? Another time.

The boss didn't take a liking to me, and that's why he put me in charge. No, he rousted the camp at dawn and I was the closest white man. My promotion was based on where my bedroll lay, not my obvious leadership potential. But, then again, James Wilson Marshall didn't need a civil engineer to lead a scraggly bunch of men swinging pickaxes and felling trees. He just needed someone with a pulse. We were clearing mostly dried brush and manzanita while digging a tailrace. That's a shallow canal used to lead water away from a sawmill when it's not in operation. The ground was rocky, the temperature was cold, and the work was unrewarding. But I needed to buddy up with Marshall. The rest of the crew worked like rented mules just so they could eat tonight.

Near noon Marshall rode over on a horse to gauge our progress. He was a stern-faced man, well built, and sported a Ulysses S. Grant–style beard. From the little I know of him, he was kind of a drifter and a loser. He never married, was given to the supernatural, and was subject to bizarre and often self-destructive behavior. Oh, and he heard voices in his head. Of course, I heard voices in my head—Al, *Stingray*, Sapale, and Doc mostly—but those voices were from real entities and were supposed to be addressing me. With Marshall, not so much. In fact, he was so good at being inept, the man who literally discovered California's gold died penniless.

"How's it looking, boss?" I called over to him.

He seemed to take his first notice of me ever. Without nudging his ride any closer, he replied, "More done than it was this morning."

Yup, he was an odd duck.

"You like the direction we're digging? The angle near the mill?" I pressed him, trying to get him to open up a little.

He stood in his stirrups and shaded his eyes with a hand. "I'm a carpenter. There's no wood in a tailrace. I'm not certain. I think it'll work."

A man of few words. Great. "You still want the water to exit the channel over there, right?"

He looked to where I pointed. It was a small channel off the main body of the South Fork of the American River, about a kilometer downstream from where the tailrace began. The man nodded back that it was. Then he tugged on the reins, heading away.

"When's lunch?" I shouted to stop him.

He turned in the saddle to inspect me. He seemed to consider me like I was a new kind of rodent. Then he swung the horse around and approached me. Coming right up to me so that the horse's shoulder nudged me, he leaned down right into my face. I figured he was going to lay into me for being a slacker. Maybe lunch was not a routine part of the workday. Who knew? It was my second day here.

"You hungry, son?" he asked compassionately.

Overlooking the fact that we were approximately the same age, I was touched.

"I sure could use a bite to eat to help tolerate this cold, sir," I replied, applying a little Oliver-Twist-wants-more-porridge intonation.

He reached into his saddle bags and produced something wrapped neatly in a cloth. "Here," he said warmly. "It's all I have, but it's yours." Then he turned the horse and trotted off.

I opened the package to find nearly a pound of jerky, venison I suspected. What a kind gesture. And for a crazy man, it was impressive. Not needing any sustenance, I discretely passed it off to one of the Native Americans the first chance I got. He had the same look of surprise I'd had when I saw the gift. I don't think he and his brethren were subject to many random acts of kindness. He gave me a quick nod and stuffed the meat into his shirt.

We finished the day with no further Marshall sightings. One of the foremen came to us about a half hour after sunset to tell us to call it a day, grab some chow, and hit the hay. That was his actual expression, *hit the hay*. It would have been very nice to actually have some hay and not sleep on the freezing ground. Very insensitive fellow.

Bright and slurry, we were summoned from sleep. It was the morning of the twenty-second of January. We were fed what could only be classified as lukewarm slop, and then marched to a different worksite. Today we'd be felling trees several kilometers from the mill site. We were instructed to chop down the medium-sized trees and to not get killed. The timber was likely destined for the sawmill, but we weren't brought into the production loop. We were the poorly paid muscle. Period. The good news was that nobody died that day. A man broke his hand when a tree fell in a sharply different angle than he'd anticipated. Another man backed off a large stack of boulders and cut a big gash in the back of his head. Hey, it was a good lumberjack day. Not even a finger axed off. But I was pissed I didn't see Marshall.

The morning of the twenty-third began with threatening clouds and everyone in camp grumbling about the weather. I knew there'd be heavy rain from the day after tomorrow on, so I was thankful to not stress over getting soaked today. We were back working on the tailrace. Early on, Marshall came over to inspect the work. He was on foot this time. He paced up and down the dry furrow, but I got the impression he was paying a lot of attention to me. Then again, maybe the voices were telling him to get some exercise so he was just doing what he was told to do.

But finally he stopped right by my side. He stared down for a socially unacceptable long period, uncomfortably close and not speaking.

Eventually he said, "I like the tailrace."

Then he started wandering off, but I invited him to linger. "You think this is the only one we'll need?"

He stopped, but didn't turn, and just stood there all hunched over. It was comical in a Buster Keaton kind of way. "What do you think?"

I think I have designs in my head for over ten thousand sawmills from planet Earth alone. Many more if you include alien cultures. None of them require more than one tailrace to serve as a release-valve. If the water flow is not needed, a single well-built channel diverts the water just fine. Hey, it's not rocket surgery.

"Well, they say two heads are better than one," I mused.

He turned slowly, didn't straighten up, and began traipsing back to where I stood leaning on my shovel.

"I was wondering the same thing myself," he said in a monotone. He shot a furtive glance up at me, then looked down the longest length of the channel. "We can deepen this one, make it wider, but if there's a catastrophic deluge, it might not be sufficient."

Yeah, those catastrophic deluges can be a bitch, I thought but didn't voice. "I think the best way to know is to build this one out well, you know, the right way. Then we flood it with a volume like Noah must've seen coming. That's the test right there."

The sad fellow. He glanced up again at me, then back to the channel. "Is this the right way, built I mean?

I rolled my thumbs under my lapels, such as they were, and rocked on my heels. "I can speak with some little authority on that subject, Mr. Marshall. While this is not the Roman aqueduct of Segovia, Spain, it is a little workhorse. I am proud to venture that not only is it built the right way, but it is built well."

"Have you been to Segovia, actually seen the aqueduct?" he asked in a depressed tone.

"Yes, in fact, I have. Before this I was a proud to serve on an American clipper out of New York. I crossed the pond many a time and was able to take some shore leave. I visited Segovia the once. It was breathtaking. The roast suckling pig there was equally inspirational."

"Which pond?" he focused on.

"The Atlantic Ocean, governor. That's what we sailors affectionately referred to it as. The Pond. And a lovely girl she was too."

"I'm not the governor. You will please call me by Mr. Marshall."

"Of course, Mr. Marshall."

"If you're satisfied with this trench then I suppose I am also. I shall go to New Helvetia on the morrow and relate this status to our employer, Commander John Sutter."

"Oh, my," I gasped. "I mean, whatever you feel is right, Mr. Marshall."

"Come, come," he demanded. "Your initial response was distinctly negative. What is problematic about reporting to him tomorrow?"

"Well, nothing," I throated dubiously, "unless—"

"Unless what?"

"Unless the tailrace as it presently sits can't handle what the engineers call Manifest Tide." Though the term just then popped into my head, I fell in love with it immediately.

"Manifest Tide?" he asked angrily. "I've not heard that term before. Are you inventing this as you go?"

"Never, Mr. Marshall. And, with more than all due respect, is your formal training in the engineering arts and sciences?"

"No, I am a carpenter."

I ditched the biblical pun and stayed focused. "A Manifest Tide is a maximal charging of a conduit with water. It's the worst-case-scenario volume the passageway must be able to handle."

He pointed off into the distance, where the tailrace split from the main river. "We have a sluice gate. If the volume of water becomes alarming I will simply shut it."

"Do you know those were the exact words of Chester P. Farnsworth? His last words, I should say."

"I am unfamiliar with this Farnsworth fellow," he defended.

"That's because he was killed both so young and under such discrediting circumstances. Chester was in charge of the Roxville

Dam and Beverage Cleansing Company facility just north of present-day Poughkeepsie, New York."

"This sounds like a fabrication," he said flatly.

"Shall I stop, Mr. Marshall, short as I am of the point of my warning? You are the boss."

"No, no. Proceed."

"As I was about to say, young Chester led the detail that constructed the tailrace for the RD&BCC's latest fabrication facility. He constructed it, the accident reports speculate, well enough. But they cited a distressing episode that occurred the night before the township of Madeline Falls was swept away. Chester was dining with the principal parties, celebrating as it were, the culmination of the newest project. Well, a man with a civil engineering degree from Harvard, no less, stood up after dessert and asked Chester directly if he'd subjected his tailrace to a Manifest Tide challenge."

"And?"

"And that's when poor Chester replied, and I quote him directly, *We have a sluice gate. If the volume of water becomes alarming I will simply shut it.*"

"What are you suggesting?" he snapped impatiently.

"Simply that we rigorously test this tailrace. I suggest we even include a Manifest Tide challenge of the type Chester, God rest his soul, felt was so superfluous."

"Will this take much time? I am not graced with any abundance of time, Mr.—" I think he only then realized he had no clue what my name was.

I stuck out my hand. "Jon Ryan, at your service. Captain Jon Ryan, if it pleases you."

"You were a *captain* in the United States navy?" he asked with astonishing disbelief.

"No, Mr. Marshall, I was not. I was an ordinary seaman."

"But you called yourself *Captain* Ryan," he protested.

"Yes, sir, I surely did. Don't you agree it has the most pleasant sound to it, expressed in that manner?"

"Mr. Ryan, my patience is at an end. Tomorrow we test the

tailrace. If it functions well, I shall report to my employer that we have completed this stage of the mill construction. I trust this is agreeable to you?"

"Most agreeable."

"Then I b—"

"Tomorrow, that's the twenty-third, correct?" I asked with some confusion.

"No, Mr. Ryan. Today is January twenty-third. The year is 1848 if that helps orient you further. What the devil difference does the date have to do with the trial of this tailrace?"

"Why, nothing at all."

"Then why did you mention it? Why did you, in point of fact, make such a big deal out of mentioning it?"

"Do birthdays mean much to you, Mr. Marshall?"

That caught him flatfooted. "Er ... why ... I suppose they—"

"You have met, I am certain, the lovely Annette D'beld-Sutter, have you not?"

"Commander Sutter's wife?"

"The very one." I looked side-to-side, checking for eavesdroppers. "While I do have an opinion on the matter, I want yours, Mr. Marshall. Do you fancy Mr. Sutter loves his wife?"

"Well, I've *never*," he huffed. "That is none of my business and it is certainly none of *your* business. I should have you flogged."

"Be that as it may. I will share my impressions. I believe that man loves that woman with a ferocity and passion that common men like you and I cannot even begin to comprehend."

"What in the name of all the saints in Heaven does that have to do with—"

"January twenty-fifth is, once per year, the blessed Annette's birthday. I was told last year Mr. Sutter gave her twelve golden hedgehogs for her birth anniversary." I held up ten digits, then quickly held up two more to indicate what twelve looked like in fingers.

"Golden hedgehogs?" he wheezed.

"Statuettes, naturally. My point is they were both priceless and they were," I elbowed him a bit to forcefully, "effective, if you take my meaning. This year rumor has it he will gift her three Arabian stallions."

"Golden statues?" he asked rather confused.

"No, the ones that prance around and drop road apples everywhere."

"Ah."

"So, if you want to test the tailrace tomorrow and report it to the following day—"

"I'd be interrupting the missus's birthday."

"An act I would certainly not wish to be associated with," I opined.

"So, I should wait another day and tell him on the twenty-sixth?"

"If you want to needlessly delay the completion of Mr. Sutter's pet project, I—"

"Let us test the tailrace immediately," he said in a tone midway between resolute and panicky.

"You're the boss," I replied.

Over the next hour it was all-hands-on-deck. Everyone who could picked up a shovel and we finished the end of the tailrace. Twenty minutes later it was shepherding water. Soon, it contained large amounts of water.

Marshall found his way over to me. "Satisfied?" he asked in a grouchy voice.

"So far." I wanted a lot of water to sweep down the channel. This was, after all, where John W. Marshall was destined to discover the first gold nugget on the morning of January 24, 1848. Yeah, baby, I wanted it to be flooded and then some. "But I think it's time for the Manifest Tide. don't you?"

He shrugged.

"I shall orchestrate it myself," I proclaimed boldly. What I actually did was walk over to the gate and make sure it was fully open. That was it. Test passed.

"Can we shut it down now?" Marshall asked. He was clearly at his wit's end with me. Yeah, I recognized the familiar all too well.

"If you think it's worth th—"

"What is it now? Why can't we shut the tailrace during the night when we can't see if there's a problem that would necessitate shutting the flow off?"

I cultivated a constipated-befuddled look. "It's just that we won't have achieved full MTC. But if you—"

"MTC?" he snapped. Okay, I had him as distracted as I wanted to if interpersonal safety was to be maintained.

"Manifest Tide challenge."

"I thought we had already. The flow in the channel seems quite high to me. I cannot, in fact, imagine it could get much more robust."

"Fine, you're the boss. I'll go—"

"Wait," he said with resignation. "Let's leave it run all night. No sense risking a sub-par result."

"Now there's the scientific method in action if ever I've seen it."

He looked at me like I was his own personal demon. Hey, the guy was more perceptive than I'd given him credit to be.

"If it's okay," I stated quickly, so as to end his reflection on our odd relationship, "I'll stay here and monitor the tailrace a bit longer."

"No one will stop you, Mr. Ryan. Soon you'll only be able to see a few yards in either direction, but your time is yours to use as you see fit."

"See you bright and early, Mr. Marshall."

"Hmm? Yes, I suppose you will. Good night to you."

"And a great one for you, slugger." I tacked on the nickname because he was almost out of earshot by then, what with all the flowing water.

Not wanting to stand out, I left a small drone by the tailrace to make sure nothing bad did happen. Then I returned to my hard spot under a few trees and pretended to sleep. Just before first light I quietly went to the control gate for the tailrace and closed it. The channel was fully exposed within ten minutes. Then I sat leaning against a tree awaiting Marshall's arrival.

I suppose the man slept as poorly as all tormented souls do. He came trotting up on horseback half an hour after sunrise. He initially looked a bit surprised to see me. But he dismounted and walked to me without any comment.

"Good morning," he grunted as he passed me, heading for the sluice gate screw.

"Back atcha," I greeted. "You're not going to open the sluice gate, are you?" I asked as he seemed focused on the mechanism.

"And why shouldn't I? I am here to test the tailrace."

"Well, yes, but I let it empty completely so you and I could walk the channel."

He looked down the tailrace as far as he could. "Why would we do that? It looks fine. What is there to be gained trudging along it?"

"Gee, lots. We'll want to inspect the wall integrity, discover the average rock size at each point along the channel so we can estimate the flow rates, and we'll want to make certain there was no spillage over a weak lip."

He was clearly torn. He seemed to realize those were all excellent reasons to walk the tailrace. But I sensed he also didn't want to validate my suggestions. "Very well. Let's get this over with so I might leave for Sutter's Fort while it's still early."

"You got it." I hopped down into the channel. It was maybe a foot and a half deep, and about double that in width. Mostly coarse pebbles and large sand grains lined the sides and bottom. Any dirt would have long since washed away. "Do you need a hand getting down?" I asked to encourage him to get down here.

"Don't be ridiculous. I'm fully capable of descending that small distance." And he did just that.

We began strolling slowly, inspecting the channel. I saw a fair sized gold nugget almost immediately. Then again, I am an android and I anticipated finding gold. It would likely take Marshall some time to catch a glimpse of the shiny metal.

Fifteen minutes into our efforts, he said, "It looks quite fine to me. There are no signs of significant erosion and there are no failures of containment."

Yeah, dude, but what about all this gold? So far I had tallied two king's ransoms worth on the surface.

"I'd like to check up until that next bend, if that's alright," I responded, gesturing a few meters ahead. "You can take off if you're not up to it." Yes, I was shaming him into continuing his search.

"Ah, yes, I was curious about the effects that sharp an angle might have had. Let's proceed to there." Eh, he gets a five out of ten for quick recovery with that excuse to change his mind.

But I was running out of time. Was he as blind as a blindfolded bat? I needed him to see what he had to. As we walked, I made a show out of catching the toe of my boot on a rock. Then I tumbled like a weighted, wet rag doll. I came to rest in a painfully awkward position that just happened to be next to four nice-sized nuggets.

"Are you all right?" Marshall asked quickly as he rushed over to me.

"I ... I don't know. I may have twisted my ankle."

"Let me help you up," he offered. "Here, take my hand."

"If ... I think it would be safer if you rolled me over first. I'm so twisted I might injure something new if I just stood up."

He seemed dubious, but then he knelt and set to rolling me onto my back. And he *still* did not see the darn gold. This was getting silly.

"Let me try to sit up," I stated.

Marshall rested back and watched.

As I rose, a sudden pain—I can't even tell you where it was, but it was bad—caused me to dig my hand into the surface and toss a small handful of stones into the dolt's lap. Two of the larger rocks were gold nuggets the size of peanuts.

"Watch out," he complained. Then he stood up. The rocks tumbled down, and, bingo, that's when his noticed the shiny gold. He bent down and gingerly picked up a nugget. He did so delicately, suggesting he worried he might break the thing. He inspected it carefully, holding it a different angle to the sun.

"What you got there?" I asked. "Gold? It sure is shiny like gold."

"I ... I don't rightly know. I've never seen gold in its native state before. But this rock is so large. It must be that fool's gold one hears so much about."

"Let me see?" I held out a hand.

He rotated the hand holding the gold away from me. Nice. He was jealous of it already. But he did hand it over carefully.

I eyed it with a deep concentration, then I bit the nugget between two teeth. It indented nicely. "Take it from one who knows. That is gold in its purest form. I'd estimate it's twenty-two, twenty-three carat."

"How can you be—"

Why, lookie there," I pointed. "There's more gold. And there. Mr. Marshall, I dare say you've made a discovery of great consequence here in Coloma."

"I don't know. You say it's gold. But this will need to be assayed in order to make certain."

"If you say so. But I'm telling you, it's gold. We'd best alert Mr. Sutter as to this monumental discovery that you've singlehandedly made."

That changed the expression on his face from contemplative greed to worried employee.

"That's a mighty serious look on your face, Mr. Marshall, if I do say so myself."

"I think it's best if we not inform the commander of this discovery."

No-no-no-no. This schmuck is making this *way* too hard. "Ah, it is his gold. How can you *not* tell a man he owns a lot of gold?"

"The commander does not like surprises," Marshall mumbled back. Then he eyed me distinctly. "He's Swiss, you know?"

"I did not know that. So, you're saying the Swiss dislike surprises?"

"You've been to his fort in New Helvetia, otherwise known as Sacramento by the Mexicans, correct?"

"I have."

"And you noticed the cannon he has mounted on the walls?"

"I have."

"*That* is how the commander greets surprises. No, I fear it will only serve to agitate the man. And on the eve of his sainted wife's *birthday*, no less. No." He gently rested the nugget back where he'd retrieved it from.

I was ready to slap this fart-face silly. He needed to stay on script —my script.

I stood quickly.

"You seem amazingly recovered, Mr. Ryan," he said with obvious suspicion.

"That I have. Thank the *espíritus dorados*, yes I am." I dusted myself off briskly.

"Beg pardon? Espiritus dolores?"

"*Espíritus dorados,*" I corrected. "The spirits of the gold. Surely a man of your worldliness has heard of them?"

"I have not, good sir. Pray tell, what are the spirits to which you refer?"

Oh, boy. I love it when the mark is so perfectly set up for the con job. It's as pretty as any picture in any museum.

"You must have heard the legend of gold nuggets over a certain size?" I looked at him incredulously.

He shook his head nervously.

"Well, some call it a legend. I call it a warning."

"A warning of what?" he said with satisfying dread.

"Nuggets of gold." I bent and grabbed a couple. "These nuggets of gold," I shoved them under his nose, "are said to contain the spirits of great and wise rulers of the past."

He jerked his head away from the gold as if it was a cobra poised to strike.

"And they say the spirits long to get out of the gold so that they may rule wisely and kindly once again for the betterment of humankind. Joan of Arc, King Arthur, and NFL Commissioner Pete Rozelle are among the luminaries trapped in these precious vaults." I positioned them under his nose again. "Now, I certainly cannot speak for you. But take for example, the current president of the United States."

"James K. Polk?"

"That's the one."

"What does he have to do with—" He partially pointed at the nuggets, afraid to raise their ire by pointing blatantly at them.

"Well, sir, I am not one to cast stones at straw dogs. However, I am of the opinion that President Polk's underestimation of the Mexican War's potential for disunion over the issue of slavery and his lack of concern with matters relating to the modernization of the nation will contribute greatly to the rumored sectional crisis of the next two years and, in the early 1850s, to the fragmentation of both major political parties. And let us face facts. He's too partisan to understand the dangerous depth of the emotions that might erupt over the expansion of slavery westward."

"And those obscure critiques have to do with the gold how?"

"Why, don't you see? If the inspired leaders trapped in this pure element were liberated this year, being an election year, they might defeat Polk and begin a new age of enlightened wonder in our lifetimes."

He deeply furrowed his brow. "Polk promised in his campaign not to run for a second term. How could they beat a man not even running?"

"Polk's a politician, right?"

"I guess so."

"You ever hear a politician tell it to you straight about their personal plans?"

"I ... maybe."

"What if I told you the spirits in the gold told me Polk was fated to win in the next presidential election?"

"No," he gasped.

"Yes," I confirmed. Then I looked sadly wounded. "But if you choose to keep your divinely inspired discovery of gold a secret, well, I just don't think you and I could be friends."

That hit him right where I intended. Way below the belt and with an upper cut. He started shaking. Then he paced in a circle, no mean feat on uneven ground. Then he started mumbling. Lord knows what he mumbled, but it was a dense string of sound-making.

Then, all of a sudden, he stopped doing all those odd and inappropriate things. He looked me squarely in the eye and declared, "This morning I ride to Commander Sutter's fort and I will introduce him to these great icons of antiquity."

"Bully for you," I affirmed as I wrapped my hands around his and the gold. "But, a piece of advice. Maybe don't lead with the icons from antiquity. Just call those nuggets."

"But why? Surely a learned man such as the commander is familiar with the significance these little vessels have?"

"No doubt," I confirmed with a thoughtful nod. "But never forget he's Swiss."

And so it was that John Marshall's discovery of January 24, 1848 was made know to his employer, and ultimately, to the world. During the next seven years, approximately three hundred thousand people came to California. In 1848, the population of San Francisco was made up of five hundred and seventy-five men, one hundred seventy-seven women, and sixty children, for a total population of eight hundred and twelve. By December 1849 it had swelled to over twenty-five thousand.

The fervor surrounding the Gold Rush led to a revolution in transportation, industrialization, and agricultural expansion across the nation. Based on the Compromise 1850, California entered the Union as a free state. Eleven years later, California played a critical financial role for the Union. Much of the North's governmental funding was supported by gold from California's Sierra Nevada mountains. Steamships carrying over one million dollars in gold shuttled California's riches into the U.S. Treasury. If the Mother Lode had been discovered sooner, Mexico would never have ceded California to the United States. If the discovery came much later, the South would never have permitted California's wealth to be used against it.

In a very direct manner, John Marshall's discovery of gold in Coloma at the time he did led to the modernized nation and ended the cruel institution of slavery on American soils.

CHAPTER TWENTY-ONE

I sat in my quarters aboard *Stingray*. I was alone, the lights were off, and every sound aside from essential ship's functions were silenced. I was in a mood. Yesterday Sapale recognized the shitstorm building in my head and quickly split. There was plenty of room for her on Aramthella. She knew I wanted to be alone, and, more to the point, she knew better than to be around me. I was not in a healthy place. Being in proximity to me could only lead to the spread of that ill health.

Plesmus was still with me. She clung to my boot as always. But she was wise enough to leave me in peace—or rather alone. I had no peace. There remained only one unit to be made until the Earth was resurrectable. But we didn't need to speak just then. Planning could wait. Planning, in fact, be damned.

We had completed the three physical reference moorings. We had completed the three biological reference moorings. We had completed two of the three historical reference moorings. We hadn't had too much trouble accomplishing that much. A few glitches, a few near-death experiences, but all-in-all nothing too hairy. Now there was only one left. It was the one Time warned me about. Time had told me that when the moment came, I'd know with certainty what the final reference mooring needed to be.

And I did. I just didn't like it. I can't say I hated it. No. Hate is a powerful emotion. But hate has limits. You can only hate so much, so hard, for so long. This reference mooring was so evil, so morally offensive that the word *hate,* when used in its context, was tiny and ineffective. This one was personal. This one was definitely personal. And I would have given *anything,* I would have died in boiling oil a thousand times over, I would have never flown a plane or piloted a spacecraft, *anything,* if I could get out of doing this mission.

Jenna had to die.

Jenna was my first friend who wasn't a neighbor or schoolmate. She was my friend because we liked each other, not because of demographics. She was my first friend who was a girl. Maybe she was my first girlfriend. You know what? She was all those things and so much more. I loved her before I knew what the word actually meant. I loved her more than anyone alive at the time, including my parents. Including myself. I still loved that tween-age girl with a force and a tangibility that was at once frightening and restorative.

When I was a kid, beginning around age nine, my family would spend two weeks in a cabin by a lake above where we lived. By chance at first, but later by design, Jenna and her family were always there for the same two weeks. She was almost a year older than me. Those two weeks at that lake were our private Heaven. We swam, insulted each other, and had the time of our lives. Then one summer we arrived three days late only to find Jenna had drowned the day before. I was the most crushed I'd ever been in my brief life. I still am crushed beyond belief, two billion years later.

And I had to make double-damn sure Jenna died, that she drowned on a summer's day swimming all alone in that lake near my house. Jenna died alone. She made a big deal about that during one of the dreamscape visits we had over the years. At age two billion I knew many things for certain. One was that it was crushingly sad to die alone, to be found dead by people who loved you and never for one second of their entire lives thought they'd ever find you dead. Alone and dead. Cold, alone, and dead.

And it was Jon Ryan who had to make totally fucking sure that Jenna died, cold and alone. I was not allowed the opportunity to make a tiny edit of Earth's history, to slip a life vest over Jenna's shoulders that morning she went to the lake. I could be her mother. I could insist she wear the vest. I could wag a finger under her nose and tell her I planned on spying on her often and that if she didn't have the damn vest on the vacation was over and she was starting summer school the very next day.

That's what I could tell Jenna.

But Time wanted to make absolutely sure I didn't do that. Time had made a deal with me. It knew the condition. I hadn't thought it through well enough. But Time was saying that if I really wanted Earth back, I had to take her as she was, warts and all. I was not free to rewrite one single sentence in the epic that was Earth's existence.

I had to make sure Jenna died. Worst of all, I knew she knew what I had to do.

I stood. "Plesmus, let's do this."

I was walking early in the day down the street I grew up on. Jardin Drive (pronounced jar-dine by the locals who were unaware of the Spanish language). There were the evergreen shrubs in the center-divide I used to hide in. Man, even as an android I wouldn't go in there now. Bugs, spiders, and the needles from the resident druggies. And there was my house. Wow, it sure looked small and unadorned, didn't it? I remember it as such a ... manor. Now, I saw it needed paint, a new roof, and major patching of the driveway. Basically it was the butt-ugly ranch style in a very "transitional neighborhood," as it would be termed today. Wait a second. Were we poor? Both my parents worked, but I had no idea how much money they earned. Apparently, it wasn't enough.

But none of that mattered. I was here on a mission. I wasn't, contrary to what it looked like, here for a walk down Memory Lane. I was staking out the old digs because I had an aging family station wagon to disable in just the right manner. Technically, this was a piece of cake. It was a wonder those cars ran when new, and my dad's jalopy was anything but new. Hell, if I looked at it hard enough it'd crump on the spot.

It was Saturday back in my hometown. This Monday was the official day our family drove up to the lake where Jenna and I would have two weeks of absolute bliss. Why we didn't leave on Saturday or Sunday never occurred to me back then, but as a grown up, I kind of wondered. Maybe the cabins rented Monday to Sunday? Who knew? It didn't matter. I had a pretty good recollection of what the family would be doing over the weekend. We were either in a rut or clung to a proud family tradition. You choose which it was.

Every Saturday before we went up to the lake, several ceremonies had to be consecrated. My dad had to gas up the car early. Then he had to wash, dry, and wax it. Two coats no less. After that, he drove Mom to the local grocery, usually the Piggly Wiggly, but it was not a fixed shopping location. It could be Thompson's World of Food a little farther down the road. After that, the magic happened. Dad drove me—just us guys, mind you—to the sporting goods store on Main Street (I kid you not). There we'd see what new gear we needed for the rugged weeks ahead. After all, the family's survival was on the line. A new folding chair? A new cooler, bigger than last year's? Or maybe, just maybe, a slingshot. Hey, one can never be too careful when walking in the woods. There might be bears or other dangerous predators. A slingshot was basic equipment if you asked me. In fact, if your dad didn't buy you a slingshot, you knew that was because he wanted you dead. Yeah, it was that cut-and-dry.

Sunday before our vacation we did a lot less external stuff. No, Sunday was go-to-church-and-pack-the-car day. It was a religious holiday by definition. And it took all afternoon to pack that wagon, let me tell you. Stuff had to be placed in its "proper order," as my old man called it time and again. Bulky items you didn't need anytime soon went in first. Chairs, floating whatevers for the lake, many kinds of balls, and clean blankets, that kind of necessary equipment. Then came your luggage, your dry goods, and your drinks. Lots of drinks. Come on, it was the lake. Then, last of all, the cooler, filled of course with chipped ice. Mom'd stack all those plastic containers of food she's spent the last week making in just the right places so nothing had a chance to think about spoiling.

The bottom line was that the car was going to see a lot of use and attention over the next two days. I needed to access it for a few minutes, but that might not be easy. Then again, I was a highly trained military machine with endless field experience. I think I could outwit my pop fairly easily on this one. Yeah, game on, daddy-o!

The plan I had to sabotage the car was simple enough, but I needed to do the deed late tomorrow. If I intervened today, the fault might manifest too soon. Then the car might conceivably be fixed before Jenna's tragic accident. Thankfully there was no such thing as a car rental company in a small town like ours. One of those could have upended my scheme. Fortunately, Dad was, let's admit it, a cheapskate, so even if there were rentals around, he'd never spring for one on a two-week contract. So I had time.

I was creating this image in my head. I knew that. But maybe it was Plesmus's focusing, or maybe it was just me, but the scene seemed so real. I decided to have a walkabout. After college I rarely got back home. I was an aspiring second lieutenant fresh out of flight school. I was trying to log as many hours as possible in the jet fighters Uncle Sam was only too happy to provide me. And there were the ladies. Young women who hung around the bars near an AFB were one of two kinds. They could be good-time Sallys, which was fine by me. I wanted wild times. They wanted wild times. One plus one equals two, right? Alternately they could be conducting a hunt for a man capable of getting them out of whatever dead-end life they saw laying ahead. They *pretended* to like wild times, sometimes with obvious over-enthusiasm. While that over-enthusiasm was most welcome for a man at my stage in life, I knew there could be a nasty trap being laid for me. Anyway, I never quite found the time to return home for holidays or vacations.

So I moseyed toward Main Street. As kids, our regular Saturday routine was to hop on our bikes and spend the entire day up and down that street. We'd hit all the important shops, eat at the grease-trap burger stand, and play at the park until either we dropped or the streetlights came on. It was hours of unsupervised whimsey. What it was, was marvelous.

I was made in the image of my late thirties human body. As such there was absolutely no way anyone was going to recognize me. Movies like Tom Hank's *Big* take place in the kid-to-adult genre, not the other way around. Still, I experienced an uncontrollable urge to hunch over, bury my hands in my pants pockets, and to skulk. Yeah, like that wasn't suspicious. A stranger skulking about. But there you have it.

I passed old man Caine's pharmacy. We often hit that location. They had some unconventional candies other stores didn't. Butter rum throat lozenges and Sen-Sen licorice breath fresheners for example. The Sen-Sens were simply atrocious, but we pretended to like them for some screwy reason. And we just had to sneak up to the pharmacy counter when Mr. Caine wasn't there to check out the condoms. We had only a vague understanding of their function and use, but we knew they were related to some higher truth, so we pointed and snickered.

I walked past the Grange Building. It was austere and uninviting, with a massive stone stairway leading up to it. In my entire life, I never went into the Grange. Early on I assumed it was a bank or some similar grumpy-old-adult service place. Later, when I knew what the Grange was, I couldn't have had less interest in bothering to visit. It defined uncool for a teenage boy. Farther down the street, I passed the best institution of childhood that ever existed: Talbot's Toyland. Man, if I had a nickel for every hour I spent in there as a kid, I'd have a whole lot of nickels. They stocked everything. Seriously, everything. Tiny toys, big toys. Cheap toys, expensive toys. Minibikes, kites, go-carts, models, and everything slot car. It was a young man's paradise. In Heaven, there is a Talbot's on every corner. Bank on it.

By the time I passed the end of the business district, apartments and small houses started to appear. I was worn out with nostalgia. It felt good in one sense. But it also felt ... I don't know, dirty maybe? Wrong? It wasn't me. I wasn't a boy with his future ahead of him. I *was* the future, and I dressed all too often as the Grim Reaper. I didn't belong to my memories, even though they belonged to me. I shook off a sudden chill and looped around behind Main to avoid walking it again. I headed home. No. Check that. I headed to little Jon Ryan's home. I was a very ancient old man on a mission. Revisiting the past was not part of the mission parameters.

Once I was back on Jardin Drive, I found the storm drain entrance that fascinated us boys. It was around the block maybe one hundred and fifty meters away. The drain tunnel was dark, wet, no doubt lined with black widow spiders, and, most importantly, it was strictly off limits for all of us. That's probably the main reason we went in it as often as we could. Of course, not one of us was bold enough to walk past where the sunlight ended. I'd say I never made it more than ten meters back along the tube during my childhood. But today this old robot disappeared into the shadows to hunker down and wait for tomorrow. I couldn't stomach more Any Town, USA.

The next day I waited to emerge from the storm-drain system until it wouldn't look out of place for a person to be walking around. Sundays were notoriously sleepy back then, at least in my town. If you were up early, it was because you were heading to church early. Period. In those days you didn't see joggers out or people walking their dogs until *after* brunch. It just wasn't done. My family was Episcopalian. I suppose I was too, but I was never asked if I wanted to join in. Even back then I considered myself an involuntary observer. I was required to be there every Sunday and I watched the goings-on with partial interest, trying to decide if the church thing was going to be my thing. Yeah, I was challenging right from the start. Show me, don't tell me. I could decide for myself.

Anyway, unless this Sunday coincided with Judgment Day, we'd be attending the 10:30 am service. On-the-dot one hour long, five minutes to socialize, a ten-minute ride home, and the car should be turning the corner right about now. Yup, there it was, on time like the British Railways. Dad pulled into the drive and younger me flew out of the car like the seat was spring-loaded. Hey, I had some major pent-up energy to expend. After allowing me—heck, fully encouraging me—to run around in frantic circles, my mom called me in for brunch. She always called it that, but it looked suspiciously like lunch if you asked me. But on Sundays one brunched, not lunched, and so the Family Ryan did, too. I usually had a bologna sandwich, potato salad, macaroni, too, if we had some, and a Coke out of the bottle. My parents might have eggs or something sweet like French toast, but mostly they had sandwiches also.

Standing across the street, I knew precisely when brunch had ended. I exploded out the door and began running in circles again. Hey, there were no video games back then and I wasn't allowed to go to my friends' houses because it was Sunday. That line of reasoning always failed to register in my brain, but I didn't have to understand a rule in order to be bound by it. Now if a friend chanced to pass by my house, we could play. But under no circumstances were we allowed to actively solicit play. No. It was Sunday.

Soon after my escape, Dad opened the garage door and began the epic packing of the family car. I knew that would take until dinner time. I watched him for a while, reflecting on missing him and that he was actually a pretty cool dad, if such a beast really existed. Then I retreated to my wet cave. I had spent these two days verifying that everything was in order and proceeding per the master scheme of things. It had been. After Dad pulled the car into the garage, I'd do my dirty work.

By 7:30 pm, the car was inside and *Walt Disney's Wonderful World of Color* was just starting. I knew all three of us'd be glued to the TV. I pulled up my hoodie and slipped across the street. My assault on the parked car was made even easier knowing Dad never locked the side door of the garage. Yes, this was not going to be one of my more complex and challenging missions. I set my left hand on the hood and pushed firmly down. With my right I freed the hood release bar. The mechanism was spring loaded back in the day and famously made a loud noise unless you really tried to avoid making one. But I knew Walt had my back, so I wasn't worried.

I quickly located the voltage regulator. Once I disabled it, the battery would lose its charge after a few miles and the car would die. It was perfect. Maybe it was even what happened on this day in history. All I ever learned was that a "part" had "broken" that needed to be ordered. I was done and gone with the hood closed quietly in under five minutes. Now all I had to do was make certain events proceeded in their fated order. For that I required a ride of my own.

Jimmy Durante lived on the other side of the high school from me. No, not *that* Jimmy Durante. Maybe that's why this Jimmy Durante was such a mean and hard-hearted bastard. If Mr. and Mrs. Durante had the lunacy or cruelty to name their son *James* and raise him as a *Jimmy*, they couldn't be very good parents to bring a child up well, now could they? Jimmy was not just a town bully. No, he bullied even the other bullies. No one was spared his incendiary temper and random violent outbursts. To look into his eyes was to know with certainty that he cared absolutely nothing for life. Yours, his, or the next person to walk around that corner. I'm sure he was the first kid in his high school class to go to the electric chair.

Even though I grew up strong and athletic, I was not immune to Jimmy Durante's wrath. We never came to blows, but with Jimmy, that wasn't your major concern. If you pissed him off, he wouldn't just beat the crap out of you. He'd burn down your house and then beat the crap out of you. He was an early fan of overkill. But one thing Jimmy had that was undeniably desirable was his Harley. It was so pimped out. Every metal surface was anodized jet black. It looked wicked. And since Jimmy had made the first eighteen years of my life dodgy, if not miserable, I felt he owed me. So I borrowed his Harley.

When my dad backed out of the driveway that Monday morning, using those silly hand signals and all, I was ready to roll in style. I knew the route, so I didn't have to follow closely. I just needed to know the car died, got towed, and Mom had called her sister to come pick them up from the repair shop. After that, my work here was done. Near the town limits, the car started misfiring. A couple miles later Dad made a set of frantic hand signals and pulled the stalled vehicle off the road. Being a male, he opened the hood and inspected the engine. Now my dad was many wondrous things, but mechanical he was not. He got flustered trying to put air in the tires. But he did his manly duty and observed the non-functioning engine for a full two minutes. Then he told my mother he would walk back to the last gas station and use the pay phone to call for a tow.

I kicked the Harley back to life and laid a patch as I did a one-eighty and headed away. I was going to ride this baby hard for as long as my command override would allow. Then I was ditching it. If Jimmy wanted it back, he could go just go find it himself.

As the ten-second override clicked off. I stood there in front of Plesmus, inside our now familiar membrane dome. My eyes were steely. They were the eyes of a man who'd betrayed his best friend. I didn't get woozy or pass out. Cold-blooded killers are not given to such foibles. And I didn't speak to Plesmus. I had nothing to say to her. I certainly wasn't going to offer any disingenuous apologies or beg that she expunge my sins. That wasn't going to happen.

As I walked numbly toward the vortex, there was one very slight ground tremor. That was it. All nine reference moorings were in place. Even the Earth was subdued in its celebration. It must have known the mood I was in.

CHAPTER TWENTY-TWO

When I got back to Aramthella I headed straight for wherever Sapale was. Turns out she was in the gym, or rather the yoga chamber—or whatever you call the place yoga is done. I not only don't know, I don't want to know. Anyway, Sachiko was participating in a small class with the other hens—her words, not mine. Don't shoot the messenger. Even though Sapale didn't need stretches and the like, she enjoyed the activity and the comradery. It was clearly a female thing. Go figure.

She saw me peek around the corner and excused herself quickly. She stepped out into the passageway and gave me a kiss. "Are you okay?"

"Yes," I said distinctly. "I am okay."

"How'd the mission go?"

"As planned."

She glanced down a second, then back up. "I'm sorry."

"I am too. But it was necessary. I came to see you because I want you to know I will not mope around and gnash my teeth. I am over it. Ples and I did what had to be done to save Earth. Mission completed. I promise I'll not be a burden to you just because I didn't like doing what had to be done."

She wrapped me in a divine hug. Her cheek was buried in my chest. "You could never be a burden to me, brood-mate." Then she lifted her head and looked up at me. "Though that is not an open invitation to try as hard as you can to be one."

"Got it. No laboring to be a burden." I even saluted her.

"You didn't kill her, Jon. She died of an accident long, long ago. You were just there to establish a reference that was real, that Earth could see as fixed so it could return to be what it was."

I patted her back as we hugged. "I know that. But the rational mind isn't always the winner when it tussles with emotions."

"I love you, Jon."

"I love you to the moon and back, too."

She pushed off from my chest. "That's not very far you know. Not on the astronomical scale."

"Hey, I didn't specify which moon. Maybe the one I referred to orbits a star in a galaxy so far away we can't even see it?"

She rested back against my chest. "It had best be."

When we were done, Sapale told me the captain wanted a meeting as soon as the class was over. Then she slipped back in to finish the session. Before I turned I saw Sachiko doing what I later learned was a move called the dolphin. Wow, that image was going to linger. You know, rather than be so skeptical, maybe I should try taking yoga classes? Maybe after all the resurrection stuff was over.

Within an hour, all the heavy hitters were sitting around Sachiko's stateroom desk. Sachiko, Tom, Reva, Emma, Sapale, me, and of course Plesmus. This time the luminaries included one Toño DeJesus. The significance of this meeting was such that he felt the need to attend in person. Can't say I blamed him. We were talking about the last step in the reanimation of Earth. All the help we could get was likely to be too little in the first place.

"Toño, thanks so much for coming," Sachiko began.

"Not a problem. I know how critical the next move is. It would be folly for me to remain away."

"I'll summarize," Sachiko stated. "We know with some certainty that we've established the nine reference moorings Time told us we needed to. We were not given additional instructions as to how to conduct the procedure. The best we can guess is that we simply need to pour a large amount of time energy into the primed landscape of ruined Earth, then the no-timing process will reverse."

"That is my assumption also," I verified.

"Before you go any further, I think I should raise a significant issue." It was Aramthella speaking. That was unexpected.

"By all means," Sachiko invited. "Go ahead."

"I wanted to wait to mention this until we were ready to proceed with the re-timing process. To be honest I wasn't sure if we'd arrive at this point at all. If we didn't, my issue wouldn't exist."

"What is it?" Sachiko pressed.

"It's our time reserve," the ship answered. "When I came over to your side and cast off the body maker, we had a lot of energy in the Time Storage Unit."

"But?" the captain asked.

"But that was quite a while ago and we've been very active. As of now, the TSU is at twenty-seven percent."

I whistled loudly.

"Yes, General, that is a low number. I have never reanimated a timeless planet. However, I imagine that will require an enormous amount of time energy to accomplish. There's no way to know if I can even hold enough time energy to complete the job."

"We've been reluctant to accumulate more time energy," Sachiko explained to Toño.

"As well you should have been. Since it requires you to render an object lifeless, the significance of any time accumulation can be catastrophic."

"The clan had no morals," she continued. "They no-timed any and everything. We cannot be so cavalier."

"But if we don't have enough energy, we need to get it," Tom Grant said sternly.

"Yes, but we can't commit one atrocity in an attempt to reverse another," Sachiko responded.

"Can we assimilate time safely?" I posed to the ship. "In a manner that no one is seriously affected?"

"That is a difficult question to answer," replied Aramthella. "The process of acquiring time energy *consumes* time energy. So if there's no net gain, the answer to your query is no, it cannot be collected safely."

"That was the luxury the clan had," Sachiko scorned sarcastically.

"We have the advantage of having the vortex," I mentioned. "We don't need to use time energy to get to where we can collect it."

"An excellent point," agreed Aramthella.

"How many supermassive black holes would it take, for example, to fill the TSU?" Sachiko asked.

"In the range of three to four hundred."

"What?" I barked. "But you said you were nearly full when you rebelled."

"I was. The body maker was quite protective of his time energy and we'd rampaged through many galaxies."

"If we moved between galaxies like a hummingbird across a field of flowers, it'd take us a long time to suck down that much energy," I estimated unhappily.

"Quite likely," the ship responded.

"And I can't imagine the reanimation would go well if we stopped midway to refill the TSU," Sapale observed.

"Time waits for no man," I said with gravitas.

That brought a balled-up sheet of paper to impact my forehead, courtesy of my one true love.

"Hey," I reacted quickly, "at least I didn't use the *coitus interruptus* line that was first in my head."

That brought several waded-up sheets of paper my direction. I felt like Julius Caesar having his *Et tu, Brute* moment.

"To return to a serious note," Papa Toño said rather pointedly, "we are badly in need of an enormous amount to time energy. It would seem we are also unlikely to collect it anytime soon, since we are bound by moral and ethical constraints the previous owners of this ship were not."

The room was quiet. Either no one had any ideas, or they didn't want to go first, since their thoughts might be ... er, unhelpful.

"We know of many planets that lack sentient life," Sapale began. "Thousands. Also, for planets we're unfamiliar with it's easy to survey a planet and see if sentient life exists. If there is none, we could no-time the entire star system, including the central star."

"I'm not comfortable with that proposition," Sachiko said softly after allowing a few moments to pass before responding. "Just because there's no sentient life doesn't mean there isn't abundant life. We can no sooner wipe out one form of life as another based on our prejudices."

Sapale dropped her head. "You're right. I was fishing."

"We have an extensive catalog of stars which have no planets that are even potentially habitable," Toño offered. "Some systems are made up of only gas giant planets or rocky ones that are incapable of sustaining life."

"That is a possible source of guilt-free time energy," Aramthella responded. "However, the mass of a few star systems is quite small on the scale we will require the time from. That is why the Clan favored supermassive black hole whenever possible."

"I can appreciate that," Toño replied. "The masses of star systems and supermassive black holes are orders of magnitude different."

"So we're back to either collecting energy indiscriminately," Sachiko summarized, "or we will be waiting a long time to collect enough using honorable methods."

"Not collecting it is not an option," Reva said, speaking for the first time. "We've worked too hard, suffered ... suffered too much to stop now."

"I agree, Reva," the captain soothed. "But where is there an abundant supply of safe mass to no-time?"

We were all quiet again. I feared we might not come up with any acceptable alternatives. Then inspiration struck. I'd sure like to know how that spark generates itself, where the devil it comes from. But whatever its origins, I had me a plan.

"I know where there's an entire universe that has no life

whatsoever. Even if it did, it would be so corrupt and evil we'd be doing it a favor by killing it."

"We do?" Toño asked confused. "You couldn't mean the Cleinoid universe, could you? When we fought and eliminated the last of the Ancient Gods, we removed them from that universe. But it still teems with all manner of life."

"Nope, not that one." I scanned the room. Everyone was all eyes. "About two billion years ago, which would place it about now in fact, we defeated a nasty bunch of cocksuckers, the Last Nightmare."

"Oh, yeah, I remember them all too well," Sapale responded. "Cock suckers first class they were."

"They resided in a universe they called the Neverwhere. Every so often, they'd leave there and raid alternate universes. They would destroy them utterly."

"Yes, I recall they'd terminated thirteen universes before they attempted to smash ours." He shook his head. "We were lucky to defeat them."

"Whatever we were," I continued, "I personally went to the Neverwhere. I killed the last Last Nightmare there. Ever since then, the entire universe has been abandoned."

"Is it a large universe?" Aramthella asked.

I had never heard that question before. "Aren't they all the same size?" I naively asked.

"No," Toño replied quickly. "Theoretically a universe could be infinite, such as ours, or infinitesimal."

"Well, I didn't bring a measuring tape with me," I defended. "Sorry."

"And you're overlooking a critical issue," Toño objected. "Yes we fought and destroyed them. But that has most likely not happened yet. If we enter the Neverwhere and the Last Nightmare are still there, we could face a disaster."

"Yes, they're powerful. But, Doc, we have a time machine. We can advance a few thousand years and then bounce into the Neverwhere. It will be serenely empty at that point."

"That is a workable plan," Toño responded. That was the best he'd concede. No, *my what a brilliant plan* remarks were coming from his mouth to my ears.

"What if the universe proves to be quite small?" queried Aramthella.

"Then we'll be no worse off than we are now," I responded.

"This sounds like a good plan," Sachiko announced. "So, unless there are any objections, I suggest we go there directly."

She made the visual rounds of the room. No one objected. "Very well. Jon, please have the AIs coordinate with Aramthella like they did before. I want to leave as soon as it's safe to do so."

I threw her a casual two-fingered salute. "Yes, sir."

Thirty minutes later we were ready. Just as we'd done when collecting the cyanobacteria, *Stingray* was going to fold us into the Neverwhere. What was crazy was that she actually had copies of the actual trip we'd made way back when. Yeah. The Deavoriath participated in the battle against the Last Nightmare. So, they kept the records. And *Stingray* was a two-billion-year-down-the-time-stream vessel. She had the historical references. Wild, eh?

"Are we set?" Sachiko asked for the tenth time.

"Yes," *Stingray* responded. Aramthella had already shifted us a few thousand years into the future.

"Then initiate the fold," Sachiko ordered. "And everyone stay sharp. There's a small chance some of the Last Nightmare might be there. If so, I want to be the first to attack."

"Folding in three ... two ... one," *Stingray* counted down.

I felt more than slight nausea. It was like a kick in the gut. Was it like that before?

"We are in the Neverwhere, Captain," *Stingray* announced.

"Anyone or anything here also?" she asked.

"Our scans are completely negative," replied Al.

"As are mine," Aramthella seconded. "And I am pleased to report this is a very large or even possibly infinite universe."

"Begin time assimilation as you see fit," Sachiko instructed. "Please give me an estimate as to how much longer you will require once you have that figured out."

"Yes, Captain," Aramthella replied.

"In the meantime, everyone keep both eyes open. If anything moves, shoot it," she instructed.

Then we leaned back and waited. The senior officers, including myself, were on the bridge. Sapale was on solo duty again in the vortex, in case we needed to execute an emergency maneuver. On this, trust me. Sapale was the only one aboard who hoped she'd see action. She is, as you know, not a passive gal.

We were lucky. It only took three days to suck up enough time to fill the TSU and every other potential reservoir. If a mop bucket could hold time, we'd have filled all of them too. But faster than we could have hoped for, we were back home in our universe, orbiting ruined Earth.

There was nothing left to do but the impossible.

CHAPTER TWENTY-THREE

After returning to home space, Sachiko figured everyone's nerves were well frayed, so she announced the following day would be a formal holiday. She named it Saint Time Machine's Day. Minus alcohol, she encouraged everyone to plan a local bash. The young people naturally planned a celebration free of what they considered their overseers. Speaking for the overseers—i.e. the adults—we were only too glad to party on our own.

There were two exceptions: Plesmus and me. In the hectic planning for St. Time Machine's Day, no one noticed our absence.

I went to Plesmus's closet early the morning of. "Ples," I announced coarsely, "hop on. We're going on a mission."

As she split off a small section, she asked, "Aren't we done with those?"

"Nope."

"But Time, it told you to make nine reference moorings. You heard it, no more and no less."

"I heard it. I also don't care. I have one last footnote to place one klick down on planet Earth."

She was quiet a moment. "Are you sure this is wise?"

"I'm pretty sure it's the opposite of wise. But I'm doing it anyway."

"But what if it causes the reanimation to go wrong?"

"I'm betting it won't."

"Would it be fair of me to assume you've discussed this new mission with no one else?"

"That would be a fair statement." I looked down to my boot, where she'd attached already. "Unless you count me discussing it with you."

"I do not. This isn't a discussion. This is a Jon-saying-what-we're-going-to-do."

"You got that right."

I'd been walking quickly since I picked Plesmus up, so we were already in the area where we could be transported to and from the surface. "Al, send us down. The usual protocol."

Almost immediately, we were looking at the barren, ugly surface of Earth, under a full-membrane dome.

"We'll do this right over there," I stated.

"It's your show," she admitted.

I stopped walking. "Same drill. Eight ... nine ... ten."

Ah, the smell of fresh salt air. There's really nothing like it. I'd say it defined the Earth. I had been on lots of planets that had lots of oceans, but none were quite like Earth's. And here in Rockaway Beach, Oregon, the salt air was being blasted like I was in a wind tunnel. Sitting on Rockaway Beach as I was, a little south of where tiny Clear Lake empties itself into the mighty Pacific, the howling wind added enough sand to the air to make breathing difficult for those so inclined. It was just past seven in the morning and, believe it or not, I had the beach all to myself. Yeah, no one else was suicidal enough to be out there in a bone-chilling gale-force winds sand blaster. The bunch of sissies.

But I liked it. The OCH—ah, Oregon Coast Highway for you

non-Oregonian types—was a couple hundred yards away, just over two rows of houses. And on the OCH, 544 South Pacific St. to be specific, was the one, the only, the Original Pronto Pup restaurant. May it stand for a thousand years. May it be fruitful and multiply. I checked my Timex again. I had plenty of time. It didn't open for breakfast until 11:00 am.

Actually, though, I called it opening for breakfast, but the management there might differ with my nomenclature. Technically they had but one limited menu. The Original Pup, Spicy Pup, Super Pup (foot long, no less), Veggie Pup (the very thought!), Zuchi Pup (maybe?). Pickle Pup (over my dead body!), Kiddy Pup, Cheesy Pup (*sublime*), and your Seasonal Pup. Some of the great unwashed masses might opine that there *was* no breakfast as opposed to lunch or dinner menu items. They would be wrong. The right time for a PUP was anytime. In any case, my target would be there at 11:00 am on the dot. I knew this because he was a good man.

I rested back against a steady piece of driftwood and dreamed of taking a nap. At 10:55, I popped open my eyes and dusted off the sand that had damn near buried me by then. Ah, the beach lifestyle. So relaxed, so gritty. I walked to the OCH, looked both ways so my mom'd be proud of me, and crossed over to the Pronto Pup's small parking lot. As predicted, at 11:00 on the nose, Tank pulls in. Daisy's with him. I know it's her from the if-looks-could-kill expression on her face. Tank warned me she was a nonbeliever. Now I had visual proof. She even had a grande Starbucks and a bag that contained who-knew-how-many superb treats. And yet she was dour. I said a quick prayer that their marriage survived her counter-productive attitude. It took a minute, but Tank finally exited. Daisy remained behind. I noticed Tank had the keys in his hand. I think he was thinking what I was thinking. Given the chance, she was outta here.

I timed my approach so I ended up right behind Tank in line. We passed through the outer door, then approached the sole employee. I guess that wasn't so difficult since we were the only two customers.

"Hi, good morning," Tank chortled to the young woman behind the counter.

"Morning, sir, what can I get started for you?"

"It sure is cold and windy out there," Tank remarked in a friendly tone. "What they call *a fine Navy day* if ever there was one."

"We are in Rockaway Beach, sir. You like this weather, you'll like Rockaway. What can I get—"

"I'll have one Original, one Cheesy Pup, and, what the heck, you only live once, a Spicy Pup."

"You want fries with that?"

"Yes, but my waistline doesn't. I'll pass."

"Something to drink?"

"Nah, I'm good."

"Okay, that'll be twelve dollars even."

He handed her a twenty and she handed back his change.

"It'll be right up, sir." Then she looked around him to me. "And for you, sir. What can I get started?"

"You know I think this man's a genius," I informed her while pointing at Tank. "I'll have what he's having."

"That'll be—"

"Except my waistline says," I cupped my hands around my mouth, "*Have the fries.* Ah, make it a large. I might need to share with someone." Then I smiled like a goon.

"That'll be fifteen dollars for you, sir."

I counted out three fives and handed them over. Then I slid another across to her. "That's for you."

"Thank you very much, sir. Your order'll be right up."

I rubbed my hands in anticipation and blew on them to fight off the cold. "Breakfast of champions," I commented to Tank.

"Amen, brother," he declared and offered me a fist to bump.

We bumped.

"So, yours is to go?" I asked, nodding toward his car and Daisy.

"Nooo, no. My wife hates the smell of this as much as she does me coming here."

"That's why I left my wife back home. She has no taste either."

We fist bumped again.

"So you coming back for lunch, too?" I asked seriously.

"Would if I could. But the little lady has me on a strict twice-a-day limit. Dinner, you bet your life."

"Maybe I'll see you then. As I'm unchaperoned, I get all three squares here when I visit."

"Lucky stiff," he returned with a grin.

Lucy—that was the woman's name, Lucy—came to the counter with two paper bags. She set one in front of Tank and the other in front to me. We snatched up our treasures.

"Hey, you wanna join me?" Tank asked, gesturing to a table.

"Sure thing," I beamed. "Anyone who loves Pups as much as I do is someone I'd love to have a meal with."

After slathering various amplifiers on our items, we sat down together. We were quiet a good long while as we ate. When I was done with delights one and two, and admiring three at the end of the stick I held, I commented. "As good as these are, they're just not as good as the ones they served in Frisco."

He nearly choked he was so stunned. "You know I was telling Daisy the very same thing just the other day."

"She liked those?"

"Lord, no. She wasn't even paying attention when I was talking. No, we've been married forever, but Pronto Pups are the perpetual tension in our union."

"I hear you, brother."

He polished off his last dog, the Cheesy, and wiped his mouth quickly. "Speaking of Daisy, I better get back out there before she calls her cousin the divorce lawyer."

I reached a hand across the table. "Jon. Nice to meet you."

"Robert."

We shook.

"Well, you know where to find me," I said with a boyish grin.

"You can count on it, Jon."

After he left I realized I never offered him any of my fries. Oh well. More for me.

The next afternoon I ran into Tank around four. I was stoked. He had driven up alone. I was seated already and demolishing a mound of goodness.

"Yo, Robert," I exclaimed as he entered.

"Jon, I'll be right there," he replied while pointing to the counter.

Soon we were sharing guy-time, munching, burping, and enjoying the heck out of the best food the universe had on offer.

"You know how we agreed on the Pups in San Fran being even better than these?" I asked.

"I do indeed."

"You have any interest in validating if that claim is true?" I wagged my eyebrows at him.

"I'd give my left nut," Tank replied piously. "But, Jon, surely you know the place there closed in 2003. We're forty-one years too late."

"Not necessarily. Say, where's Daisy?"

"She stayed back at the hotel. She wanted, in her words, A *hot bath, not a greasy spoon*."

"Well, her staying back there might be the hand of fate at work, my friend."

Tank furrowed his brow at me. "Really? How so?"

"If I could make it happen, would you care to join me in pre-2003 San Francisco to prove, one way or the other, if those Pups kicked these Pups' asses?"

"You don't know this, but I'm a professor of astronomy. As such, I can say with expert certainty that the only way you could pull that off is if you had a time machine. Do you have a time machine, Jon?"

"No, I do not."

"Well, there you have it. We're stuck on this side of the 2003 divide."

"But I do have a spaceship that can travel through time."

"Does that affect your medication levels, Jon, the time traveling?"

"I'm deadly serious and I'm not crazy. In fact, here's my offer. If you super swear not to tell another living soul, I'll take you back and we can check out Sutro's Pup stand."

"You sure say that like you mean it."

"I do. And the good news is that we'll be back the same time we leave, so Daisy will be none the wiser."

"And where is this not-a-time-ship-space-ship of yours?"

"Right out back."

"Aren't you afraid Area 51'll see it and take it to Nevada?"

"Nope. It's cloaked."

"Like a Klingon Bird of Prey?"

"Not like them at all. My ship uses a space-time congruity manipulator. The Klingons use little puppet ships and tons of CGI."

"Jon, I'm certain I'll regret this before the day's done, but why don't you show me your ship."

"You got it. Oh, one word of caution, a disclaimer if you will."

"What's that?"

"Like I said, my ship's for space travel, but I can make it time travel. The problem is that the process can become unstable."

"Unstable as in what?"

I shrugged. "Local annihilation."

"Local as in Rockaway Beach?"

"Local as in the local galactic cluster."

He raised an eyebrow at that. "Is that likely?"

"No, just possible, or so I'm told."

"Well, Jon, what the hell do they know?"

"My feelings exactly. So, what year do you want to return to?"

He grinned nervously. "1967."

"The Summer of Love. There really isn't any other choice, is there?"

"Not for a rational man."

"Let's do this, Tank."

He stood up, but then heard what I'd said. "Hey, how'd you know my nickname is Tank?"

"Lucky guess," I suggested, as I shrugged my shoulders.

And we were off. We toured San Francisco in its hippie-days heights, ate way too many Pups, and had the best times of our lives. Now that wasn't exactly how Tank and I met, but it was close. Close enough, I hoped.

CHAPTER TWENTY-FOUR

"Okay, this is the big one, so let's get started," Sachiko said using her captain's voice. "We've all been working like crazy with our subgroups and team members. We've drilled and we've memorized and we've repeated the whole torture so often I know that I could not be more ready. This will be our final meeting before we attempt the dream we've clung to for over three years now. By this time tomorrow we will know for certain. Either we will have produced nothing short of a miracle, or we will have failed after doing more than the best we could."

Today's meeting was for all hands. It was staged in the hangar bay, the largest room available. Still it was standing-room-only.

"There is no way to test our hypothesis. We can only make a full attempt. If something goes wrong, we will have to identify it quickly and react on the fly. We get one shot at this. So if at any point you have a reservation, an observation, or even a weird little feeling, share it immediately up the command chain. You all know which individuals you can report to. If you panic, remember you have a laminated copy of the command structure in your pocket. Any questions?"

There were none.

"Great. I will hit the Go switch at 07:30 tomorrow. Between now and then I want you to do three things. One, I want you to review your role once again. Know your duties and options. Two, I want you to get some sleep. It's the best medicine. And three, I want you to pray that we can pull this off. I know it sounds corny to some of you, but trust me on this. We can use all the help we can get."

There was a well-deserved round of applause for Captain Jones, then everybody dispersed. In fourteen hours we'd see if all this insanity had been worth it. All the losses. All the pain. Me? I was sixty/forty in terms of success. I'm not telling which was the one and which was the other.

Later that evening, out of the blue, Plesmus spoke up. Sapale and I had been lounging in the vortex. We weren't really doing anything, just hanging out, anticipating.

"Jon," Plesmus said in as serious a voice as I'd ever heard her use, "it is time to speak of tomorrow."

Sapale and I sat upright instantly. "Haven't we been speaking of it nonstop for a week now? Months?" I asked.

"No, not the important part."

"Should ... do you want us to call Sachiko?" Sapale wondered.

"No. She has her role. It is well defined and well known to her. She is a most competent young human. I have no concerns that she will acquit herself well."

"Er, okay," I throated.

"But I do require the girl. Desdemona."

"Right now?" Sapale replied.

"Right now."

"This is sounding kind of intense, Ples," I said nervously.

"This is nothing yet," she responded somberly.

"So, should we call her, or do I need to go get Desi?" I asked.

Just then there was a knock on the portal we'd left open.

"Hello?" called Desi.

"I let her know," Plesmus informed us.

"Come in," Sapale called out, and she sprung up to greet her.

They returned together, with forearms intertwined. To my great surprise, Plesmus, the main mass of her, followed them in. The Plesmus on my boot dropped to the deck and joined her whole. This was getting weird and it hadn't even started yet.

"You called me?" Desi asked.

"I did," responded Plesmus. "It is time we spoke of some truths."

"I ... wasn't ... did I do something wrong?" Desi inquired tensely.

"Never, child," Plesmus responded. "The truth we four must speak is of your role tomorrow."

"That'd be good," she replied, "since I'm totally unclear what it's supposed to be."

"What your role is was clear from the moment I met you, child. You must command the dead."

"Yeah, that's what everybody keeps saying. But what does that mean?"

"It means you will be tested unlike few others have ever been. You will, and I'm being as honest as I can be, will be tested far beyond what should reasonably be asked of any soul."

"That ... that sounds scary," she returned.

"It should. Desi, come. Sit," Plesmus invited. "Would you like something to drink?"

"No. I'm fine." She looked at Sapale and me quizzically. "Am I the only one who needs to sit?" She'd noticed that in all the activity, we'd stood and never sat back down.

"They don't need to sit, child," Plesmus assured her. "They are machines, living machines. They are fine standing. They would be fine standing on their heads."

"Come on," Desi said defensibly, "I'm not stupid. They're alive just like me. They don't make robots like that. They can't."

"Androids," I interrupted diplomatically. "We're androids. Used to be humans, or whatever. *Androids* now."

"I don't believe you," Desi challenged.

"It does not matter," Plesmus soothed. "What you must know does."

Desi nodded uncertainly.

"Tomorrow I will focus an unimaginable amount of time energy.

It will be directed at your home world. I believe it will reanimate the planet. All life will return as it existed the moment the clan no-timed it."

"Wow," she responded. "That's great."

"Yes it is. But know that the resurrection of Earth will not be an event but a process."

"Ohh... kay," she replied uncertainly.

"How long it will take I cannot predict. Several minutes at the least. More likely an hour or so. Do you understand?"

"Sure. It'll take some time."

"No, I mean about it being a series of unrelated interactions, a process."

"If you say so."

"I do. Here is the critical part. It is also the cruelest part."

"F ... for me?" asked a clearly shaken Desi.

"Yes, but more so for the dead."

"Wait," I interrupted. "What dead? The people of Earth aren't dead. They never lived to have died. They were no-timed."

"You do not fully understand, Jon."

"That wouldn't be a first," I replied glumly.

Plesmus was quiet as the grave for a few moments. Then she continued. "When the planet below us is re-timed, many events will occur. The reanimation will not be one process. Neither will it be rapid."

"Ples," I cut in, "not to steal your thunder here, but Time told me nothing like this has ever been attempted. If that's true, how can you know what will happen with anything other than a guess?"

"Time said, and I quote, *No one has ever attempted such a feat before*. But similar, less daunting re-timings have succeeded. The resurrection of the Noidal Talisman for example. Once, long ago, a focus like me, another necumplack, no-timed the most sacred icon of the Dalintor people of Thraxix Prime."

"Why'd she do that?" I had to ask.

"*He* was angry and petty. He felt the Dalintor treated him poorly. It's a long story and beyond the present point."

249

"Okay," I replied.

"The Dalintor sought reparations from my race, since it was one of us who wronged them. Instead, we re-timed the relic. It was a small, bejeweled metal ring, no bigger than your palm. The process was almost undoable. But I learned from the experience."

"Okay, go on," I responded.

She angled to align with Desi again. "There are two issues—crises—you will face. They will occur rapidly and they will need to be addressed at once. The first is the matter of the returning living. Those are the people who were alive at the moment the clan no-timed Earth."

"Alright," Desi returned quietly.

"Returning to life from never-having-been is unnatural. Nature compensates for this aberration by phasing those who never were, back into life. First they must pass through a state which is, for practical purposes, death. Once dead, the living may be restored to who they were at the instant they were no-timed. Do you understand?"

"I think so. But if the re-timing brings the once-alive back, why doesn't it also bring back the dead who were dead at the instant the planet was no-timed?'

"A good question. I am pleased you grasp the subtleties. The process does not because the dead, those who expired before the clan struck, cannot be reanimated. That violates a fundamental law of the universe. But those transitioning through a death-like state can be."

"Wait," I interrupted yet again. "When I fought the Cleinoid, back in their universe, there was one really bad player named Jéfnoss tra-Fundly. He was so cruel the other Ancient Gods killed him. He returned from the dead twice in an attempt to rule the Cleinoids again."

"Different universe, different rules," she replied. "And if you'll recall, that one was full of magic."

"Point taken," I conceded.

"So what will my role be tomorrow with these reanimating individuals?" Desi asked.

"You will command them to return to the living."

"Wh ... why would that be necessary?" Desi puzzled.

"For two reasons. First, they will return confused. A forceful directive will help them orient. Second, in the moments they have to reanimate, some may consider not returning to life. Maybe they were in a bad situation. Possibly they suffered greatly."

"But why should I force them to return if they don't want to?"

"Because it is the way of things. They were part of Earth. To resurrect the planet, all who were there before must be there after."

"That's a whole lot of souls to call home," I observed. "And what about the fishies and the creepy crawlers. If she has to call them all back, how will they understand her command?"

"Only the sentients will understand at some level what is happening. Only sentients would choose to die rather than to live. Such is not the case with your fish and bugs."

"And the second group? The other crisis I will face?" Desi asked resolutely.

"The harder part." She fell silent. "So painful. So sad."

"What?" Desi snapped, less resolute in a flash.

"The dead must also return. All those who ever lived. They must also be repopulated."

"But you just said they cannot be," Desi protested.

"They cannot be reanimated to life. That is what I said."

"But if they're dead, why must they return?" she asked.

"Because they must. Ancestors must be ancestors. Even the long-forgotten dead contributed to the timeline that ended at the point the Earth was no-timed. If there were none before those alive, there would be none alive."

"But what good are ghosts?" I asked a tad confused. "They don't do anything, at least not much."

"I am not speaking of ghosts. I am addressing the souls of the dead. They must return so that they can go wherever it is they must go, even if that is nowhere. There must be past generations."

"So what must I do with them?" Desi queried wearily.

"You must stop them from attempting to return to the realm of the living."

"Huh? I thought—" Desi began.

"They cannot be returned to life. But many who are returning will try. They will be confused and they may feel the sudden urge to cheat death."

"So they could reanimate?" I asked.

"No. But they could place the entire process in crisis. For lack of a better term they could muck up the order of things. And it's also possible they could partially succeed and become abominations. That must not happen."

"So all I have to do is command the dead to stay away?" Desi wondered.

"It is not that simple. For one thing there are too many of them. Some might hear your command but struggle to resist it. No, you will need help."

"You'll help me?" Desi responded with great relief.

"No. I cannot. I do not have your gift."

"Then ... then who? Who will help me?"

"This is the most regrettable aspect. This is tragic. But those who can help you, those who already know they will, are those souls that died ... badly. They are the souls of the people who suffered too much at the end."

"Plesmus, A, you're creeping me out here; and B, why would these poor souls be willing to help stop the dead from filtering back in among the living?" I wasn't part of this process, but I had to know.

"Because they wish never to return to life. And please don't make me say why or expand upon the issue. I'm having enough trouble speaking of this as it is."

"And these souls already know they will assist me?" Desi tried to understand.

"Jennie," I said out of the blue. "Like the sad, sad girl I met in a dreamscape. Jennie."

"Yes," Plesmus replied like she was passing a horrible judgment. "Like your Jennie."

I nearly lost it, then and there. I thought back on my brief but oh-so-disturbing meeting with Jennie. I had been looking for Jenna, my old friend. Jenna was not there in the dreamscape. But Jennie was. She sat on a rock looking out to the sea. And she was so sad, so tragically sad. "Jennie told me, *We will help you help others, those who must cry without voices.*"

"As I said, the ones who will help already know they must. The need is in them to do it."

"She said," I went on numbly, "*We will help you help them cry with voices. And then will cry no more.* Oh, Lord, did she mean *she* would cry no more, or the others without *voices*?" I was frantic to understand.

"We are not meant to know, Jon. Please don't worry about matters beyond your influence," Plesmus tried to reassure me.

"That's not gonna happen any time soon," I whispered back. Then I remembered. "I know what I said back there, after I left Jennie. I said that for my efforts to resurrect Earth I would demand as payment their redemption."

"And maybe you will be so rewarded," Plesmus concluded. "It is a good prayer to bear in your heart."

We were all silent for I cannot tell you how long. This was all so heavy. And I was a seasoned killing machine. I could only imagine how fragile young Desi was taking this info-dump.

"I can do this," Desi exclaimed loudly, finally breaking the stillness. "In fact, I'm ready to do this. I was *born* to do this."

"That's the spirit," Plesmus encouraged. "Now, child, lie beside me and sleep. Tomorrows always come before they are wished to."

"Are you kidding?" she replied. "I'm way too wired to sleep, maybe ever again."

"Just lie beside me. That will be enough."

What followed was pure magic, and a wonder to behold. Desi uncomfortably got on the deck, squirmed over to Plesmus, and slipped her hands under her head as a pillow.

"I'm here, but—" Desi began. Then she was asleep.

"Hey, can you do that to me?" I asked with glee.

"If I could I wouldn't."

"Huh? That's just being mean."

"The way of things, Jon Ryan. We mustn't mess with the way of things."

I stuck my tongue out at her.

"I see that, human."

"Good. Otherwise I'd have to draw you picture."

"Goodnight, human."

"Goodnight, necumplack."

CHAPTER TWENTY-FIVE

By 06:30 the bridge was jammed with personnel. Sachiko had decreed that the resurrection effort would begin at 07:30. Probably no one slept, so reporting early wasn't an issue. Plus everyone had enough nervous energy to jump out of their skin. There were four exceptions. Sapale was pulling stay-on-*Stingray* duty again. We never knew when she might have to fold us all away. Desi, Plesmus, and I were standing at the window. Yeah, we had a window installed. And I'm talking a major window here. It was ten meters by twenty meters and seamless. Since no one knew what was going to happen or how it would roll out, we decided that the critical actors would have direct line-of-sight to the action. We were standing in the hangar bay looking out at ruined Earth. It was not pretty.

Another change was in Plesmus herself. The big Plesmus was there by my side. Any and all little scoops of her had reunited with the mothership, so to speak. She wanted all her power available at one location.

I checked my Timex. "About an hour to go, folks, " I announced. "You need a potty break?" I asked Desi.

"No, I'm good," she replied nervously.

Then Tip walked up behind us.

"Hey, stranger," Desi welcomed him ebulliently. Then she planted a kiss on his cheek.

Rubbing at the moist skin, Tip said, "Toño wanted to be here, so I tagged along."

"I'm glad you did," Desi responded.

"Hey, we're a team, right?" Tip declared with no enthusiasm.

She took his hand and walked him over to the window. "Yes, we are. If it needs cleaning or a remanding to the great beyond, we're a team."

"I was referring to the cleaning mostly," he clarified. "I don't get the other reference."

"You will," she replied with a smile.

"If you two'll excuse me, I'm going to check in with Toño," I said.

She shrugged. He stared blankly.

Toño, I said head-to-head, *good to have you aboard.*

I wouldn't miss such an event.

Good. Hey, have you gone over everything?

Twice.

And everything seems okay? No bad assumptions or transposed decimal points?

Not that I could find. I think the overall plan is sound and the preparation is superb.

Great. Well, if anything comes up, let someone know right away.

You know me, Jon. I am neither subtle nor shy. If I see an issue I will make my observations known to all.

Talk to you later.

Best of luck, my friend.

We disconnected. I pulled out my handheld and check in with Sachiko one last time. "We still green for Go?" I asked.

"Affirmative," she responded. "And if we run one more test or checklist I do believe I'll scream."

"That's a sign of excellent prep," I reassured her.

"Thanks. Coming from a pro like you, that means something. I'll touch base after the reanimation, okay?"

"Absolutely. Break a leg, kid."

I disconnected. One last call.

Sapale, how you doing?

Bored.

Good.

Oh, so now we're at the taunt-the-bored-wife stage of our relationship?

It would appear so. I'll see if there's a card for that and send you one.

Don't bother. I'll seek solace as I always do. I'll alert the pool boy.

Fine, fine. Just as long as he doesn't charge me overtime.

Oh, there'll be overtime, you can count on it.

Love ya, babe. If you need anything, give me a holler.

Will do, sweet. Best of luck.

Alrighty then. All ducks lined up. All systems go. Now all I had to do was to stop stressing over what the hell was about to happen. I had no idea. Seriously. Nothing could happen. Wooden horses could rain from the sky. Whirled peas could be had by all. The upside was that it was darn near Zero Hour, so I would be worry free shortly. With any luck, I'd also be alive.

Overhead, Sachiko's voice boomed. "All stations ready. Power up in ten ... nine ... eight ... seven ... six ... five ... four ... three ... two ... one ..."

Go time.

Plesmus fired off a broad beam of time energy directly at the center of the Earth. The process was silent. She had decided not to focus directly through me. She didn't think it was necessary. She also felt the levels of transmitted energy were simply too great for me to handle. Instead she aimed the beam right next to my polyskin-covered skull. We hoped I could still provide some influence without getting myself fried. We would soon find out.

For a couple of minutes absolutely nothing happened. The beam struck and was absorbed. Every time ghost on the planet swelled to the contact point. But they didn't linger long. From the way they reacted, it seemed like the beam just had too much energy. In no time at all, they'd completely cleared out.

That's when the lights first appeared. It was almost too subtle to notice, but then it became clear. A dancing, shimmering light began to whirl around, and it eventually enveloped the planet. It was kind of like the aurora, but in just white, or a thin fog bank being blown along a windy coastline. Over ten minutes the lights went from so faint you could hardly see them to brilliant and undeniable.

That was when things started happening.

Desi began to moan very softly. I'm not sure she even noticed herself, and I decided not to tell her. Whatever it was, it was. Alerting her to the sound wasn't going to change anything.

Then there was a distinct explosion down on Earth. It wasn't like a nuclear test or anything. But there was a definite eruption of debris, then a hole was visible where the bang went off.

"That's one of the reference moorings," Plesmus explained. Her words were, not surprisingly, strained.

"Really? Which one?"

"I couldn't say."

My handheld buzzed to life. It was the captain.

"Jon, did you see that?"

"Yes, according to Plesmus it was one of the reference moorings activating or something."

"Were we expecting that to happen?"

"I don't know about you, but I'm not expecting anything. This is all virgin terrain."

"I know. Sachiko out."

I returned my attention to the ground. One after the other, reference moorings boomed open. Other than the small detonations, I couldn't see that anything was changing. No seventeenth century politicians turned inventor were stumbling around while greatly confused, at least. No asteroids targeted T Rexes. Just lots of thickening white clouds.

Then, approximately all of hell broke loose.

Desi screamed. A particularly blood-curdling one, I might add. All of a sudden, the time energy clouds coalesced as a white carpet across the entire surface. Then, enormous seismic disturbances began to rattle Earth. Some areas of the ground rose alarmingly, whilst some buckled and receded.

Desi screamed again. It was, wow, an even more jarring one than the horrible one before.

"Are you alright, Desi?" I asked softly.

No response. Okay, I assumed she was doing her thing now. That did not require my direct input. By the time I looked back down, mountains were rising. Seas appeared, small and hot ones at first, but they grew. Steam rose at an unnatural rate and formed clouds. Storms sprang to life, violent ones.

Then the columns of light appeared. I knew in an instant they were important. They swept around from either side of the planet and arced down, sort of like giant fireworks in reverse. They were an orangey-white, and seemed to pulsate.

"The souls are back," Desi said as if in a trance.

"The right one or the—" But then I stopped. She probably couldn't hear me and I didn't actually need to know a particular soul's death status, now did I?

Desi raised her hands like a Bible-thumping preacher. "Do not stray," she commanded, again as if from a trance.

Okay, alright, that was creepy, too. The columns of light didn't seem to change form.

Three more reference moorings went off at about the same time. My handheld buzzed. "Yes?"

"Jon, that was the tenth explosion," Sachiko snapped.

"I wasn't counting. Uh, I'm helping Desi some."

"There were only supposed to be nine reference moorings. How are there ten explosions?"

"Uh, I couldn't say. Are you sure you counted correctly?"

"Yes, Jon, I can successfully count to ten. Is there anything you'd like to share?"

"No. I think I'm good."

"Sachiko out."

That went well.

As more time energy burned into the ground, the surface became obscured. Mostly I saw a continuous sheet of white clouds roiling with massive waves. It was impressive.

I began to believe the columns of souls, according to Desi, were impacting the surface and being absorbed. At least they didn't seem to be bouncing back up, but it was hard to tell.

As the layer of white clouds thickened, there was a new aspect to them. Not only did they shift to a cobalt blue, but they seemed to firm up. They weren't quite liquid, but they seemed close to becoming that dense. That's when I heard the whispers. It was like invisible spiders had learned human speech and, on a whim, decided to drive Jon Ryan insane. The harsh hissy words came at me from every direction, maybe even from inside my own head. Strain as I might, I could not make out the words, assuming they were actually words and not invisible spiders sneezing.

I continued to follow the flight of the two columns of light. They shot through the blue almost-liquid and disappeared—the clouds were that dense. They faded quickly as they traversed the layer.

"Do not stop," Desi howled.

Had she been taking freaky lessons? She was really good at bringing up the old hairs on the back of one's neck.

Then a serrated column of black light pierced through the bright orangey-white columns that were rising toward the surface in an orderly manner.

"The dead may not pass this point," bellowed Desi. No further comment. The girl had me ready to pee myself. I assumed the dead-dead were intruding on the reanimating-dead. Oh, boy, was I ever confusing myself.

"Jon, I've drained fifty percent of the TSU," Plesmus said in a pained tone.

"You okay? Can I help?"

"Re ... fill ... TSU," she strained to tell me.

Of course. Our time energy reserves were stored in all kinds of vessels. I whipped out my handheld. "Sachiko."

"Yes?"

"Plesmus sounds pretty stressed. But she wants the TSU restocked. Can you see to that?"

"On it. Sachiko out."

"Helps on the w—" I started to assure my little friend. But the voices became overwhelming. Gone were the scratchy raspy spiders. Now the words sounded like a serial killer when they call your phone. And no, no serial killer has ever called me, personally. But, you know, like in every serial killer horror film, okay? Ooh, I got it. Like in *Field of Dreams*. "If you build it he will come." Yeah, that's the creepy voice.

I started to understand the words.

The Mississippi flows.

Male pattern baldness.

Adroa is again the supreme god of the Lugbara people. Marvel at and fear Adroa.

Mudsnails squirm in Tasmania.

Jazz is life.

The sum of the squares of the two sides of a right-angled equal the square of the hypotenuse.

Kilroy slept here.

Cast-iron objects appeared in Yangzi Valley at the end of the 6th century BC.

The first line ever. Neanderthals queue up to enter a cave.

The Beatles.

My head swam. I was hearing so many snippets. Were these the announcements of each item returning to reality? Who knew? It sure was distracting.

"Sisters and brothers, I call on you to restrain the dead. They may not enter where they may not—" Man, Desi was out there, really into her role. She owned it, truly.

The orange column continued to plow down, and the black light kept slashing into it. Then little tornadoes of red light brightened into existence. The dead helpers, warding off the dead who would live again? I was in over my head. I looked at Desi. She was levitating about six inches off the floor. Sweat poured down her face like she was in the shower, and her body, arms still up raised, shook chaotically.

"You must go. Go. *Go!*"

I think her voice was fading. I hoped she would last as long as it took.

Pink ribbons and pinafores.

You talkin' to me? You talkin' to me? Then who the hell else are you talkin' to?

Gandhiji goes to Champaran to practice Satyagraha with the peasants.

Let's play baseball.

The Game of Twenty Square becomes the most popular game in ancient Sumeria.

One small step for mankind ...

Desi dropped back to the deck and then to her knees. She was spent. I kneeled to support her. Her flesh was as cold as ice in deep space. Sweat cascaded down her body through her drenched clothing.

I whipped out my handheld. "Dr. Hartley to the hangar bay. Medical emergency. Dr. Hartley to the hangar bay. Medical emergency," I blasted overhead.

I noticed Tip. I'd forgotten all about him. He was pinned against the far wall, paler than a ghost and shaking like he about to break apart.

"How about some help here," I shouted to him.

At first I thought he was in shock, that he couldn't hear me. Then he took a big step toward us. Then another. Pretty soon he was jogging over.

"I got her," he said as he rested a shoulder against Desi's back.

"If she gets worse before doc comes, let me know," I instructed Tip.

"I got it. Go."

I flew to the window, using my palms to stop from face-planting on it. The orange columns were twisting, but the red tornadoes cleared the black lights away. It was chaos, but I saw hope. Do not ask me to explain, that's just what flashed in my head. *Hope.*

It's past 11:00 pm, young lady. Where have you been?

E=mc2

Pineapple thieves caught near Akok, Gabon. Right hands cut off.

Bet you can't eat just one.

Honesty Hartley burst though the hangar door. Two interns were right behind her. She rushed to Desi and Tip. "What do we have here?" she shouted as she knelt and jerked the stethoscope from around her neck.

"I ... I don't know. She was yelling out the window, and she levitated. Then, she just fell," scrambled out of Tip's mouth.

Honesty to an intern: "Help me lay her flat."

To the other, "I need a set of vitals—*now*."

The man set his pack down, pulled out the blood pressure machine, dropped it, picked it up, dropped it, finally got down on both knees and fumbled with Desi's arm. He tried to roll her sleeve up.

"*Over* the clothes, Jasper. This is an emergency," snapped the doctor.

Jasper dropped the inflation bulb and looked like he was going to cry.

Plop, plop, fizz, fizz, oh what a relief it is.

Know then thyself, presume not God to scan; the proper study of mankind is man.

Yet today I consider myself the luckiest man on the face of the earth.

Plastics.

"B/P is ninety over palp," Jasper finally called out. "Pulse thready at one sixty."

"Nancy, two eighteen-gauge lines, normal saline, wide open," instructed Honesty. "Jasper, recheck vitals every minute," she said as she flashed a light in Desi's eyes. She had to thumb them open to do so.

On the ground and in the air, I said to myself. The black lights were almost gone. The orange ones continued to pulse down and vanish. The red tornadoes quieted down, moving off to the poles, huddling. I saw continents below me, and mighty seas. From this altitude I could see about one-third of the surface of the Earth.

Clouds drifted across Great Britain. A hurricane took aim at the Americas. Far to the east, Tehran maybe, I saw city lights.

"Eighty over palp, 155," Jasper said through a cotton mouth.

"How are those IVs coming?" doc asked through gritted teeth.

"Almost there," Nancy lilted.

"Jasper, have sick bay send down a gurney. And tell Afaafa to get down here stat. She's the best at hard sticks."

Nancy looked up at Honesty. Defense was in her eyes. "The B/P's eighty, Honesty. All her veins are collapsed."

"I don't need excuses, I need access."

"How about an interosseous?" Nancy asked a bit too enthusiastically.

"Just get the damn lines started."

"Eighty over palp."

Below me, the tranquil Earth rotated slowly in all its majesty. Deep blue seas were parted by shades of soft greens and desiccated browns. "*Thus the heavens and the earth, and all the host of them, were finished,*" I thought privately. The black lights were gone. The very last of the orange lights splashed into the oceans. The red tornadoes were red no more. They were the fairest periwinkle, and they were still. Soon I saw them fade away until they were somewhere else.

What you are is what you have been. What you'll be is what you do now.

Blessed are those who mourn, for they will be comforted.

Force may subdue, but Love gains: And he that forgives first, wins the laurel.

And do good; indeed, Allah loves the doers of good

. . .

I'm Good Enough, I'm Smart Enough, and Doggone It, People Like Me

"BP's up. One eleven over sixty, pulse one thirty," declared Jasper with relief in his words.

"Both IVs running wide open," beamed Nancy. "What else?"

"Elevate her legs. Then see if you can draw some labs. Two red tops, one purple and one blue. Jasper, go over to the door so the others know right where to find us."

"Got it, Honesty." He jogged away.

My handheld buzzed. "Jon, I heard about Desi. How's she doing?" Sachiko asked with a hint of panic in her voice.

"Coming 'round, Captain," I replied. "I think she'll be fine. She just went through some changes, powerful ones."

"Ask Honesty to update me as soon as it's safe for her to do so."

"You got it."

"Sachiko out."

"Doc," I called out without looking down, "Captain says call her when you can."

"It'll be a while."

"That's cool. Captain's not going anywhere."

"Okay, everybody," Honesty commanded as the med team arrived, "we lift her onto the gurney on three. Soon the squeak of the wheels told me Desi was heading for sick bay. That was good. She'd earned it.

I took a final look down at the beautiful planet Earth. It looked exactly like it always had from high-Earth orbit.

"Hey, Ples, first round's on me," I said without taking my eyes off the view.

No response. That couldn't be good.

"Plesmus?" I asked more forcefully. Then I looked down. What little of her that was left wasn't moving.

I started to call after Honesty and ask if she did aliens. But I held my tongue. Of course she didn't. I scooped Plesmus up as gently as I could and held her up against my chest. *Sapale, can you meet me in Plesmus's closet on the double, please.*

Since she could sprint and I couldn't, Sapale actually got there first. As I came down the passageway she walked toward me. "What happened to her?"

"I do not know. When it was all over, I looked down and this's how I found her."

"Do you think she's dead?"

I shrugged. "I don't know how I'd tell."

She shook her head briefly. "Me either."

I placed Plesmus as gingerly as I could into her favorite corner. Then we both sat down and waited. In a little while I'd inform Sachiko. Right now she was busy. And there was nothing she could do but sit here with us, hoping for the best. I was just starting to feel the first needles of boredom when my handheld went off.

"Yo."

"Jon, you better get up to the bridge ASAP," Sachiko blurted out.

"Why? What's up?"

"I have an incoming call from the President of the United States. Jon, *you're taking this call,* so you better get up here fast."

"Go. I'll stay," Sapale said with the cutest grin.

I sprinted up the ladders, not waiting for an elevator. I charged onto the bridge just as I heard: "Captain, the man says the president's demanding you pick up," the comms officer said looking for all the world like he was about to puke.

"I got it," I said, raising my hand.

"Thank you," Sachiko mouthed to me.

I tapped an icon on the captain's chair. "This is General Jon Ryan. To whom do I have the pleasure of addressing?"

"Holy shit," exclaimed the POTUS. "It really *is* you in that enemy ship. Jon, what the hell's going on? One minute you're fighting the clan fleet and the next you're parked in orbit above the Canary Islands?"

"Wow, Frank, is that ever a long story. And, to be perfectly honest, one I don't know if you're going to believe."

"Well, answer me this and no bullshitting. Are we safe? Are all the clan ships gone or destroyed?"

"I can say with a million percent certainty the answer is yes. The clan no longer exists in this or any nearby galaxy."

"My God, Jon, that's a miracle. But, you were just engaged with a flock of them. What, did they just disappear on their own accord?"

"No, Frank, they did not do that. You know what? I think this is one of those occasions when a phone call just doesn't cut it. What time is it?"

"You don't know the time of day?"

"Spoiler alert, Mr. President."

"It's four-thirty in the afternoon."

"How about dinner?"

"Dinner, Jon, we're in a state of war. You don't host state dinners when the ... oh, wait, you just said there are no more enemy."

"Correctomundo. So, *dinner*?"

"After the beating this city's taken, it won't be much. Cheese and crackers may be all I can muster."

"Is there any *beer* in Washington, DC?"

"Yes, there is."

"Then it's dinner at seven, your place not mine. Casual Friday dress is mandatory. My party will number seven. If name tags are being printed, that will be Jon, Sapale, Reva, Toño, Sachiko, Tip, and Desdemona."

"What, Tank's too good to come if there's no steak?"

Ouch. That caught me off guard. Here I was being flippant and then reality bites me in the balls. "Mr. President, General Robert Sherman was KIA. I will fill you in completely when we meet."

"Oh, no. That's terrible."

"It's a tragedy, Frank, that's what it is."

"Have you informed Mrs. Sherman yet?" he asked glumly. "Or would you like me to take that burden from you?"

"For the next few hours, let's leave that alone. After we've filled you in on all the details, you can determine who will best make that call."

"Sounds good, Jon. I'll see you in a few hours. Will you be parking on the lawn, as usual?"

"Yes, we will."

"Then please remember I'm at the Naval Observatory now. I don't want anyone else's lawn trashed because you forgot."

"Naval Observatory, seven o'clock, have beer. Got it."

"See you soon."

I tapped the comm line closed.

Jeez, I missed Tank. This had the potential of being a hard next few days.

The entire reanimation of planet Earth took place over just about ninety minutes. I would never have guessed it would be that rapid. By the next morning, Plesmus hadn't stirred, Sachiko had come and gone a couple times. Desi was nearly back to normal. She was just exhausted to the extreme. Sapale and I continued to sit with our friend. I just prayed we weren't sitting shiva for Plesmus.

The next visit by Sachiko, she brought a specialized thermos. It held time energy. She knelt and poured little splashes on Plesmus's back. Initially nothing happened. But then, after maybe half the flask, little Plesmus stirred. Two thermos bottles later, she was asking simple questions. Realizing the treatment needed, the three of us took Plesmus to the TSU itself and spilled time all over her. The TSU was down to fifteen percent, but we knew where to score more time, so we weren't stressed.

Wouldn't you know it, by the next day Plesmus was fine, Desi was fine, and I was fine, too, if you care to know. We were up in the ship's mess already making the tales of our struggles more superhuman with each retelling. It was nice. Even Tip smiled and laughed. After a fashion, that is. Toño and he left later that day. It seemed a master and student relationship was in the offing. That was good. And I was glad to be rid of Tip. I just really hoped Toño didn't transfer the knucklehead to an android host. An immortal

Tip Benjamin was a sobering thought. I hated sober with a red passion.

Dinner with the POTUS was nice, despite Tip and Desi's concerns of meeting with the actual President. Turns out the staff could put up a pretty fair spread on such short notice. The telling of the epic journey and of our struggles took until well past midnight. But not one person left early. The part about Tank was the toughest. I didn't enjoy reliving it. I did that often enough in my head. I didn't need the added angst of verbalizing it with a Q&A afterwards. But I got through it. I owed Tank at least that much. The president said he'd see that Tank received the Congressional Medal of Honor. More tributes would follow in time. Whatever. Those affirmations wouldn't bring Tank back.

What to do? That was the question we all faced. Obviously Aramthella was a monumental asset to the US. Sachiko made it very clear her loyalties and allegiance were exclusively tied to the US and to the commander in chief. She pigeonholed any decision on her being formally inducted into the US military. Time would tell, she explained. It was just too soon to think about those matters.

Most of the military personnel rotated off Aramthella and new GIs took their places. Though the Navy might normally have crewed a starship, based on precedent, the Army took over that role. Only Swathi, Tom, Emma, and Reva remained behind. They not only volunteered, they insisted they must remain aboard.

The Georgetown students and staff were free to go. Ninety-nine percent were all too glad to abandon ship. They took their children with them, naturally. But a few stayed, and fortunately for the work flow to follow, none of them had kids. Dr. Hartley said she'd chain herself to the wall if anyone tried to make her leave. No one tried. And there were a few students who'd begun training for duty on Aramthella. They stayed. It was a pretty safe bet they wouldn't find employment aboard another Earth-based time ship. And the scientists and engineers rescued from Mars 1 left. They'd had their once-in-a-lifetime view of advanced alien tech. Now they wanted dull jobs and to sleep in their old beds again. Techy types are not adventurers by nature. That was fine. A new crop of nerd-o-matics were already champing at the bit to be selected to serve with the next science team.

Sachiko planned two pilgrimages. One to her family. They were to have a multigenerational reunion on a scale that they'd never had. And the best part was that if anyone needed transportation it would be provided free-of-charge by the captain of a space ship. The other pilgrimage she planned in the one-of-these-days category was to make it back to the university Tank and she had worked at. She needed to let everyone there know how Tank died, and what a critical role he'd played in saving the Earth. "Maybe in the fall," she would say wistfully.

Sapale and I? What do you think? We were headed back to the future and back to the stars. We had no interest or role to play in this time period. And there was too great a pressure on us here. What was going to happen with Earth's new timeline? Once Jupiter was spun out of its orbit, Aramthella could easily put it back where it belonged. She could even simply no-time the rogue world that was going to turn Jupiter topsy turvy and there never would be a Jupiter crisis.

What would then happen to the current version of Jon Ryan? Would the man even need to travel to the stars? And Sapale couldn't live knowing her family—her original family—was alive and well and not go live with them. Kaljaxians had a powerful sense of family. But she was already there. No, we needed to get out of Dodge.

But even as we planned our exit, I couldn't get it out of my wheelhouse. What happened to the timeline? Would it right itself? Did it need righting? Too heavy. It was all too heavy for my little fighter pilot brain.

CHAPTER TWENTY-SIX

Two days after the dinner with the president, most of the senior staff were hanging around on Aramthella's bridge. It was Sachiko's shift. Usually that meant Reva was off and sleeping, but there was too much going on. She couldn't sleep and there was no place else she'd rather be. Sapale was sitting with several members of the navigation team, trying to explain star charts and celestial navigation. It might sound easy enough, but it wasn't. Plus eventually one had to rely on the star charts of other civilizations. Since there was no standardization possible, you had to deal with who-knew-what.

I was chewing the fat with Sachiko. Reva shifted back and forth from our chat to assist a junior officer with a question.

"You know you've grown well into this role, Shaky," I told her honestly. "You are going to be one hell of a leader."

She looked down sadly.

"What, you don't agree?"

"No, it's not that. It's silly, is what it is."

"Speak, Captain. Your mission commander so orders it," I said with false sternness.

"When you call me Shaky ... it makes me think back ... about Tank."

"I am truly sorry. I will not call you that again."

"I'm sorr—"

My handheld buzzed with an unusual vengeance and the priority red flashing light strobed to life.

"I must be in trouble again. Maybe the president finally got around to dusting his daughter for fingerprints."

As I picked up my device, Sachiko pushed my shoulder playfully.

"Yo," I greeted.

The person spoke.

"No way. There's no freaking way!"

Everyone on the bridge heard me shout and turned to see what was up.

The person spoke again.

"Wait, wait. Everybody's gonna want to hear this. Let me put you on speaker."

"Okay, I'll be here," responded the caller.

It took those that knew him microseconds to recognize Tank's deep voice.

"You're on speaker," I shouted. "And everyone's here. Sachiko, Sapale, Reva, and me of course. Plesmus isn't. She said her allergy to humans is acting up. Tank, where the hell are you?"

Sachiko stood from her captain's chair, stunned. Reva rushed over, hands clasped together under her lips like she was praying triple-hard.

"Jon, you're just not going to believe this?"

"Try me. I'm flexible when it comes to reality these days."

"Jon, as God is my witness I am sitting in my backyard. I'm in the bench swing watching Daisy tend to her flowers. Jon, the petunias are stupendous. Huh? Oh, Daisy says *Hi, Jon.*"

I looked up to Reva. Her face crumbled inward like it was slammed with an eight-pound sledge. She turned and ran off the bridge. Sapale shot out after her.

"Tank, you do not know how great this is to hear. And you're okay? Fine? Well?"

"Well, there's no MD present to back me up on this, but I'd say yes. Jon, what the hell happened to me?"

"Ah. Wow. Ah wow. Now there's a tale to tell. You know, why don't you tell me what you remember. That way I'll know where to start filling you in from."

"Why the cloak-and-dagger, buddy? Can't you just tell me?"

"Sure, but I seriously want you to go first."

"Ya big jerk. Okay, we were all on Aramthella's bridge. We were in a dogfight with half the clan fleet. The other half split off and headed for Earth. We were holding our own, kickin' some alien ass, and then that's it."

"That's what?"

"That's the end of my recording. It's like the video tape broke. I don't remember a thing until I turned up laying in my bed next to my wife. It was, I should clarify, about three in the morning."

"Ah, Daisy was surprised."

"If you call nails, teeth, and screams surprised, then yes."

"But you survived?"

"Apparently, but I needed stitches and a tetanus shot."

"Hmm, that bad, eh?"

"She said if she'd killed me it would have been justifiable homicide. But the next night went better. Much better."

"The next night? Tank, how long have you been back?"

"Three days."

"Three days and you didn't call. Tank, that's abusive."

"Jon Ryan, *General* Jon Ryan, do you have any idea how hard it is for a random caller to the White House to get ahold of a president during war and to then be transferred to General Jon Ryan's private line?"

"Wait. Let me guess. Three days?"

"Give the man a kewpie doll."

"So, Tank, we really do need to talk."

"No problem. The president said he'd send a plane for me. Then

I can climb aboard Aramthella and listen to your no doubt over-embellished version of the truth. I'll bring Daisy too."

"You know, Tankster, that's not as good of an idea as you might think it is."

"What's that supposed to mean?"

"Hey, look who just walked onto the bridge. It's Captain Jones. Here, Sachiko, say hi to Tank." I handed her my handheld with both hands.

She tried to refuse so I tossed it up in the air aiming for her chest. She caught it.

"Tank, hi. So, hi."

"Hi to you, kiddo. Are you going to go dark on me like that punk standing next to you?"

"No ... er, no way. I'd never do that to you."

"Finally."

"I'm handing the phone back to Jon. Bye. There's a fire somewhere, big fire. Got to go."

"Tank, here's a plan. Sapale and I will fold over to your back yard. I have the coordinates on my handheld. Then we can talk ... you know ... on *that* coast."

"This coast? Jon, so help me, when you get here ... what, honey? Okay. Jon, Daisy says to land in the front yard. She doesn't want you messing with her petunias."

"No backyard, no petunias, got it. So, we'll see you in maybe an hour."

"An hour? What's more important than filling me in? You having a party with cake and ice cream?"

"No. It's just that Sapale, she's tied up at the moment."

"Tied up? What are you not telling me?"

"It's just that a friend is suddenly having the worst day of her life, all over again. Sapale's comforting her, or at least trying to."

"That I can understand. But if you're not here in an hour, I'm calling Frank and having him send that plane."

"No need, my man. No need. We will be there in an hour. Promise."

EPILOGUE

Sapale and I were lounging in bed watching a holo. Come to think of it, we lounged a lot. In our bed. In the mess. In our bed. Maybe I needed a part-time job? All of a sudden Sapale sat up. She hopped out of bed and headed toward the door.

"Wait," I called after her, "where're you going in such a hurry?"

"It's Taco Tuesday. Bye."

"Whoa, whoa, whoa. You can't just say *it's Taco Tuesday* and just run off. I love tacos. I pretty much love Tuesdays. I want to come along."

"Not in the cards. You got the wrong genetics."

"What is wrong with what used to be my DNA make up?" I said trying to sound insulted.

"You lack an X chromosome. It's Girl's-Night-Out-Taco-Tuesday. But, on a pleasant note, our food synthesizer does tacos every single day of the week. Bye." And the traitorous so-called wife of mine left.

"I want Taco-Tuesday tacos, not everyday-taco tacos," I mumbled to myself. I rolled on one side to pout.

"Still the spoiled brat," said an angelic voice.

I sat bolt upright and looked to the door. "Jenna?"

There in the flesh, or whatever, stood Jenna. She was all grown up. She was also stunningly gorgeous. She wore an LBD (little black dress, for the guy readers), spike heels, and, well, that was all I really noticed.

"I heard about your taco-related crisis and came to soothe you, if that's even possible." She began walking toward me—and the bed—in a most distracting manner.

"Jenna, you're ... you're all grown up."

"You are so observant. You are too. What a coincidence." She sat on the edge of Sapale's side of the bed.

"Jenna, it's so wonderful to see you," I said, composing my fool self.

"It's amazing to see you too, Jon. I came to chat. Can you spare a moment for an old friend?"

"You have me until time ends." Then a horrible thought struck me. "Jenna, I'm so sorry I had to create the reference mooring where—"

She leaned way over and pressed a finger to my lips to silence me. "No regrets. You did what you had to. And there's nothing you could do that could make me love you any less."

With her finger pressed firmly, I puff-spoke around the blockade. "Ditto."

She laid down next to me. "Roll on your side," she instructed softly.

I did and she spooned up against me.

Oh, boy. This was awkward.

"Jenna, you know I'm a married guy, right?"

She punched the back of my upper shoulder. "You need to write a book about how to ruin the moment."

"Sorry. It's just—"

"Jon, remember the time I grabbed your crotch?"

"Like it was three minutes ago. Why?"

"Because, lover boy, it just doesn't get any better than that. I wouldn't dream of having sex with you. It would be anticlimactic."

"Wow, I think in your tragic early death you kind of got the sex thing pretty much screwed up."

"We can't change time."

"Well ... never mind."

"I wanted to thank you, Jon. And congratulate you. You did good."

"Specifically or generally?"

"Both, you needy egomaniac."

"Just want to be clear. And the congrats?"

"When someone does a great thing, the universe notices. Most souls never even get a shot at a great event. You did and you excelled."

"Thank you."

We were quiet a bit. It was marvelous.

"So, Jenna, are you okay? I'm talking really okay here." I held up my little finger over my back so she'd be pinkie swearing her response.

She hooked my finger. "I'm, wonderful, Jonny. All things being equal, I'd just as soon not have died quite so young. But it's all good." She was still a few seconds. "There's a reason for everything."

"If you say so," I said with a bitter edge to my words.

"There is. Oh yes, there surely is."

"The reason an amazing little girl has to ... to you know."

"Do you know what had a high likelihood of happening if that little girl hadn't had that awful accident?"

"What?" I replied still upset.

"That little girl would have married her one true love in her senior year of high school. Her one true love," she poked me in the ribs, "would have dropped out of high school in his junior year to take a job at the hardware store. Since he was tall and smart and dreamy, he'd slowly rise to be the midwestern states sales director for a wholesale paint company based in Columbus. I would have raised a fabulous little family with you, and we'd be happy in spite of the awful weather you dragged me to live in. And the universe would have had one less fighter pilot, astronaut, android-transferred space explorer, and hunk of a hero."

"I could have lived with that," I said meaning it. "In fact, I'd have been as happy as I could have been."

"Me too. But the universe wouldn't have been as correct as it became. We all have our parts. If we try, we can all do them well." She snuggled up even closer. "What you did for those souls who helped with the dead, the ones who cry with their voices so the order of life was held, Jon, it was such a kind act."

"Kind? You're saying it was kind of me to have Desi use them?" I was confused.

"Yes, it was."

"Those were the red tornadoes, right?"

"Jon, they had to be."

"Sure."

"But if you hadn't played your part, they would not have known a greater peace."

"Ah."

"Ah? Jon, how does the world put up with you? You're so shallow."

"So Jennie's okay? Jennie from the rock, looking out to sea?"

"Jennie's *better*. Hopefully she'll be okay someday. She ... Jon, she had a very bad—"

"I know." I sniffed. "I know."

It was suddenly very still. In spite of the fact it might have spoiled another moment, I nudged a shoulder backward.

Nothing.

I flopped onto my back. Jenna was gone. But she'd been there. The sheets were still indented. And I still smelled her. I sat up in a panic, doubled over and looked under the bed.

Jenna wasn't there.

"A problem with monsters again?" a female voice asked from the doorway.

I sat up and spun in one motion like a bear trap going off. If I were still human I'd probably have snapped in half.

"Sapale?" I gasped.

"Expecting other women in your bed tonight, flyboy?" she asked as she walked over.

"N ... no." I shook my head clear. "What happened to Taco Tuesday?"

"When I got there I missed you. We took a vote and decided you could join us." She reached out a hand. "Come on, lover boy."

I furrowed my brow. "Was the vote unanimous?"

"Spoiler alert," she said, as she tugged at my arm to rise.

The end ...

... for now ...

GLOSSARY:

First, a word about time, as used in this series. The clan uses several foreign, non-intuitive terms to describe time. Here are the concepts.

Anti-no-time: Such a big word! It was the side effect of the negative time generated by wormholes that were used against the clan. Since clan ships were structured with time energy, negative time deleted what it touched, like matter-antimatter interactions.

No-time: A verb. It means to take the time from a unit of space/time, leaving only space. The object has no time, it had been no-timed.

No-timers: The clan term for all non-clan members.

Non-time: A noun. A sloppy word the clan uses. It can mean one of two things. First, that basically, something's dead, without time, random. It can also mean that time has stopped, for the object under discussion.

Non-time ship: Any space craft that is a non-clan ship.

Re-time: The process of infusing time energy back into an object.

Time (5): The metaphysical entity that drives and controls the flow of time. It once separated into its Soul and its Framework.

Un-timed: To stop time for an object or region. Basically the same as the second meaning of non-time.

Other Glossary Terms:

Als (1): The original ship's AI on Jon's first flight long ago was Alvin. Jon shortened that to Al. When Al was joined to Jon's vortex in the Galaxy On Fire Series, Al and Blessing fell in love and got "married." Since then Jon refers to them combined as the Als.

Aramthella (1): The mighty and ancient time ship that Jon and his team stole from the body maker.

Ark 1 (1): Jon's ship on his very first mission, when he traveled to find humankind a new home.

Azsuram (2): Original human name for the third planet orbiting Groombridge. It was the planet Jon and Sapale settled on after they left the human fleet fleeing doomed Earth. They established an idyllic society of Kaljaxians there, before humans join them.

Barren (6): Head chief inquisitor of the council of seven.

Blessing (1): See *Stingray*.

Brood-mate/Brood's-mate (*The Forever Life*): These are, respectively, the Kaljaxian words for *husband* and *wife*.

Circumturus (1): A psychic houseplant. No, seriously. That's it. *That's* the definition. Now go back to where you were and continue the riveting story.

Command Prerogatives (1): The thin fibers Jon extends from his left four fingers. They are probes that also control a vortex.

Cube (1): Jon's alternate name for the vortex he captains.

Davdiad (1): God-figure on Kaljax.

Daleria (2): Demigod and innkeeper whom Jon and Sapale befriended. She worked with them against the ancient gods as she'd grown to hate them.

Death (6): The longest serving chief inquisitor

Deavoriath (1): Three arms and legs, an ancient species that had the most advanced tech in the galaxy. Very helpful to Jon.

Desdemona "Desi" Tanner (2): Former Georgetown undergrad who was a medium, that is, she perceived and communicated with dead people. Er, no thanks, I'm good. Place that gift under someone else's tree.

Devastator (5): A chief inquisitor. Very mean, a horrible person. The first one Jon killed.

Emma Walters (2): Captain, and in charge of the women's barracks on Mars 1. What a thankless job.

Evil Jon Ryan/ EJ (1): Alternate timeline version of the original human to android download. Over time, he turned to the darker side of his nature. He studied "magic" under a Deft master.

Flastor (5): The planet on which the Claxeon Citadel was located.

Form One/Form Two (1): A Form is the title of a vortex pilot. If more than one is aboard they get numerical designations based on seniority.

Fracture (6): Another chief inquisitor of the citadel.

Framework of Time (5): One of the two contingent parts of Time. This is the mindless, unstoppable progression part of Time.

Harshness (6): Another chief inquisitor of the citadel.

Honesty Hartley (2): Doctor on duty at the student health center when the president had the entire staff transported to Mars. And appropriately there, as she was a total space cadet.

Inquisitors (4): The security personnel at the citadels. The upper-level one were vicious.

Kaljax (1): The home planet of Sapale. Jon went there on his original voyages.

Megan Thompson (2): A young Georgetown University student swept up to Mars 1 when the clan attacked Earth. She became so depressed she took her own life. Desi's first ghost-in-space.

Membrane (1): See space-time congruity manipulator.

Miniminim (5): Senior Sub-Cataloger at the Claxeon Citadel. Befriended Jon. A very odd looking globular female scholar.

Necumplack (2): The species name of the time controlling blobs that power the time ships.

Nufe (The Forever Series): A magical liquor made by the Deavoriath. It tastes different to all who partaker. It reminds the drinker of many pleasant tastes all at once. Mildly intoxicating.

Oowaoa (The Forever Life): Home world of the Deavoriath.

Pall (6): Another of the chief inquisitors of the citadel.

Parker, Lakeisha (6): Sergeant major, US Army. A badass soldier aboard Aramthella who befriended Jon.

Plesmus (2): A necumplack. She is a mucous blob that can focus time energy. Very useful for a time machine.

Praxequats (3): The ultimate time lords (sorry, Doctor). They have existed through many universes' lives. Jon initially encountered five of them.

Probe Fibers (1): Aka command prerogatives, they allow piloting of the Vortex spaceship and can analyze whatever they touch.

Rage (6): Another chief inquisitor of the citadel. The most psycho.

Reference Moorings (5): Time told Jon to build these. They were historic mega-events in Earth's past without which life as we know it today would never have happened.

Reva St. Claire (2): Lt. Colonel and the commander of Mars 1 before becoming first officer to Captain Jones.

Robert "Tank" Sherman (1): Lead academic and friend of Sachiko. Also in Marine Reserves.

Sapale (1): Jon's Kaljaxian wife from his original flight to find humankind a new home. At first just her brain was copied, then, eventually, she was downloaded to an android host. Travelled with the corrupted Jon Ryan from an alternate timeline.

Sachiko Jones (1): One-time astronomy grad student under Tank's supervision. The time ship chose her to be its new captain.

Soul of Time (5): One of the two parts that make up Time, the metaphysical entity that drives time itself.

Space-time congruity manipulator (1): Hugely helpful force field. Aka a membrane.

Stingray (1): Jon's Deavoriath spaceship. Her name in the Deavoriath language is pronounced "crash." Hence, silly Jon renamed her after one of his favorite cars. It makes Jon-sense.

Sunne calrf (2): A traditional Kaljaxian stew. They are all revolting to Jon, but he finds this version especially loathsome.

Swathi Varma (2): Lieutenant, and aide-de-camp to Reva St. Claire on Mars 1. Junior officer aboard Aramthella.

Tetterwin (4): The elder Praxequat, father to the five Jon and Sapale encountered on the far side of the phase portal.

Time (1): See discussion above.

Time Maker-bob (3): The third time maker. Totally nuts but full of desires to rule.

Time Maker-pid (1): The second supreme leader of the clan and the one in power at the beginning of this tale. Cruel, rapacious, and heartless.

Tip Benjamin (?): Where've I heard that name before? Hmm. Presently, Tip is a student at Georgetown. He was evacuated to Mars as part of the US president's plan to save a tiny portion of humankind. And they took Tip too?

Tom Grant (2): Major, and the officer in charge of the male dormitories on Mars

Toño DeJesus (1 of TFL): The scientist creator of the android Jon. Became his lifelong friend.

Vanquish (6): Another chief inquisitor of the citadel.

Void (6): Another chief inquisitor of the citadel.

Vortex (1): Super-advanced Deavoriath sentient spaceship. Moves by folding space. If you get a chance to own one, do it.

Vortex Manipulator (The Forever Enemy): The consciousness that actually controls the vortex spacecraft. Think super AIs. They're a product of some very creepy alien tech.

Quantum Decoupler (1): A most excellent weapon that pulls the quarks apart in a proton. The energy released as they rejoin is amazing.

AND NOW A WORD FROM YOUR AUTHOR
WHO DOESN'T LOVE THAT TO DEATH?

Thank you so much for joining me, Jon, and the whole gang on this ongoing journey! The Ryanverse is terrific, and it's even better with you along! The story really begins with *The Forever Life*. If you've not read that, and the rest of the series from the start, I suggest you do. You will not be disappointed.

I have had an absolute BLAST writing *Time Wars Last Forever*. Writing it spanned the pandemic, imagine that. Especially books 4 & 5 were tough, tough, tough. Creativity and existential threats don't party well together. But I'm better now. You-know-who's no longer in charge and I'm vaccinated. The future looks bright. Where are those Gucci sunglasses I can now afford because you so kindly read the entire series? Maybe I left them in our summer getaway in Spain? Or was it the one in Bali? No worries. They'll make more.

The outstanding people at Podium Audio are working hard to get all the books of the Ryanverse into audiobooks. If you're having any trouble locating a book, look for it there.

What's next for Jon and the crew? As of 3/29/2021, the day I finished this book, I have no idea. But I do know it'll be good. You know what? Maybe I'll ease Jon's pain? He does seem most vexed about the future timeline for Earth. And I do owe him big time. Seriously, that's what he told me last week. Hmm. Who knows?

Three favors. One, let me know your impressions, thoughts, or suggestions. You can do that by contacting me by email (contact@ craigarobertson.com) or on my Facebook Author's Page. Second, please post a review on Amazon/Audible. Those are more precious than gold to us authors. Third, email me to be placed on my mailing list. I promise to only send useful information. No cheerleading-please-don't-forget-about-me material.

Did somebody out there say *website*? Why yes, of course: https://craigrobertsonblog.wpcomstaging.com/

Finally, I want you to know I love you! So be good (but, come on, not too good) and stay safe ...

craig

www.ingramcontent.com/pod-product-compliance
Lightning Source LLC
Chambersburg PA
CBHW052008020726
47501CB00004B/1053